PASSION HOTTER THAN
THE TEXAS SUN!

When Nichole was within his reach, Fowler pulled her against his bare chest and pressed his lips to hers.

With only the thin coverlet between them, their bodies seemed to ignite.

His hand moved down her back to cup gently and then caress her soft behind. He held her tight against his hardness as he kissed her deeply. His tongue slipped into the sweet recess of her mouth to mate gently with hers.

She moaned, heedless of the cover slipping to the floor, and wrapped her arms around his neck. Pressing her hot body hungrily against his, she ardently returned his kiss.

A groan of agony rose from deep within him as he tore his lips away from hers, trying desperately to retain some control while he still could. He was on fire with desire as he pushed her away only to pull her hard against him again. "God, you feel so good. Nichole, Nichole," he groaned, covering her mouth once more.

Texas Woman

Connie Harwell

LEISURE BOOKS   NEW YORK CITY

For my husband, James,
who always believed in me
and encouraged me to
reach for my dreams.

A LEISURE BOOK®

October 1991

Published by

Dorchester Publishing Co., Inc.
276 Fifth Avenue
New York, NY 10001

Printed in the United States of America.

Chapter One

March, 1869

Nichole wondered if she would have any teeth left by the time the stage finally bounced and careened its way into Waco. She was certain that if the driver had missed any holes in the road it was only because they hadn't been formed yet!

Her first impulse had been to complete the last leg of her journey by horseback when the railroad line had ended in Calvert. Now she sorely regretted her decision to take the stagecoach instead.

Even though she knew without a doubt that she was going to be in disfavor with her parents for leaving Cousin Emmalee's so abruptly, she was so glad to be back in Texas and almost home, she didn't care what the consequences were.

Besides, trouble seemed to be her constant companion no matter what she did. It wasn't her fault that trouble trailed behind her like a puppy dog! She *tried* to control her temper. Well, most of the time, anyway.

She chuckled to herself as she remembered the look on the French diplomat's face when she had dumped her bowl of ice cream, accidentally of course, in his lap in order to "chill" his overheated libido.

Her stay in Washington, D.C. hadn't been as bad as she had dreaded. Mostly because Cousin Emmalee was something of a temerarious old dowager herself, bless her madcap heart. Nichole had felt a close kinship with her from the first.

She didn't know how she would have survived that frigid February day when she received the letter from her mother telling her that Grandpa Westerfield had died from pneumonia in January if it hadn't been for Cousin Emmalee's comforting strength.

It had taken more than three weeks for the letter to reach her, ironically arriving on her seventeenth birthday. She had wanted to go home then, but Cousin Emmalee had talked her into staying and completing the finishing school, reasoning that, after all, she had already completed more than a year and only had ten months left to go.

So Nichole had agreed to stay and finish school. However, the desire to go home grew stronger as March blew in. She began to have vague feelings of unease and apprehension. She had tried to explain them away as cabin fever from being housebound for days on end due to the bad weather. But then she began to have horrible nightmares.

She'd wake up in the middle of the night, drenched

in a cold sweat, her heart pounding from fear. She could only remember bits and pieces of the distorted dreams which were always about Nick.

Nichole had tried to make Cousin Emmalee understand about her apprehensions but, in the end, she had packed her bags and stated flatly that she was going home. That very day if a steamer was leaving for Galveston.

She was so relieved when she caught the first glimpse of Waco Village on the horizon that she almost shouted.

She had already decided to rent a horse at the stables and ride the rest of the way to the ranch. Someone could return the horse and pick up her trunks tomorrow. Since no one had met her at the docks or at the end of the rail line, she figured that her letter had not yet reached her family.

John was playing in the yard when he saw a rider come racing down the road to their house. He shaded his eyes from the sun's glare to be sure he was seeing his sister before running into the house shouting at the top of his lungs.

"Mama! Mama! It's Nolie! Nolie's coming down the road. I see her!" He raced back out the door.

Cassie and Maria almost collided with Mark and Cody as they all ran toward the front of the house.

By that time, Nichole had reached them and dismounted, running into the arms of her mother and father, tears of happiness streaming down her face.

"Please don't be mad at me, Daddy," she cried. "I *had* to come home. I couldn't stand being away from my family and having those awful nightmares."

By this time Amy and Kathleen had joined the rest

of the family, hugging her and crying at the same time. Nichole looked around quickly for Nick, needing to assure herself that he was okay.

"Where's Nicky?" she asked when she didn't see him anywhere.

Nichole caught the look that passed between her parents at the mention of her twin.

A chill ran down her body. "Where is Nicky?" she repeated almost breathlessly.

"Let's all go in the house. I'm sure Maria has some cool lemonade. You're probably thirsty, maybe hungry, after your long trip." Mark sounded nervous even to his own ears.

Nichole was on the verge of panic. She could tell by her family's downcast faces that something had happened to Nick. She dug her heels in.

"Tell me what's happened to my brother? I know you're trying to keep something from me. I want to know what it is," she stated firmly.

Cassie prodded the family toward the door. "Let's go inside and we'll . . . talk."

Nichole waited, just barely, until her father had shut the study door behind them before she turned her questions loose.

"What is it you're not telling me? I knew something was wrong with Nicky. I could feel it. That's why I've been having those dreams, isn't it? Is he hurt? Is he—" She suddenly paled, unable to voice the rest of her question.

Mark cleared his throat, not sure how much to tell his daughter. One look at her face, however, and he decided she had the right to know the whole truth.

"Nichole, I . . . we . . . Oh, damn!" He raked his

10

hands through his hair as he tried to find the right words.

"What your father is trying to say, Nichole, is that we're not sure where Nick is. Come and sit down. Dear, why don't you start at the beginning and tell her the whole story," Cassie said to her pacing husband.

Mark poured himself a whiskey as he paced by the bar. With drink in hand, he organized his thoughts. "Shortly after you left for Washington, Nick decided that he wanted to be a Texas Ranger. He felt that he would be more 'useful' is the way he put it, helping to put a stop to some of the lawlessness taking place in the state at that time. And still is, for that matter.

"Almost from the beginning, he has been working undercover with the Rangers. Several months ago he infiltrated a gang who is suspected of being the source of much of the trouble in central Texas. The Rangers knew that this band of . . . of no-goods was taking orders from someone higher up because the leader didn't have sense enough to pour pi . . . water out of a boot." Mark took a sip of his drink.

Her father seemed to be aging before her eyes. She didn't remember him having any gray hair when she'd seen him last, and his face looked tired and drawn from worry.

Mark continued, "Nick would never tell us, both for the family's safety and his own, what he was working on, but, every month or so, we'd get a note by way of the Ranger station from him, letting us know he was okay." A great sadness seemed to overwhelm him.

He threw back the remainder of his drink. "Three

weeks ago he failed to meet his contact. No one has heard from him since. If his identity was discovered, he could be dead someplace and we'll never find his bo . . . him."

Nichole gasped as the full impact of her father's words hit her, stealing her breath as surely as if a hand was tightening around her heart and squeezing the life from it.

Cassie sought the comfort of her husband's arms, no longer able to hold back her sobbing.

Nichole jumped to her feet and started walking back and forth. Now she understood why she had had the nightmares. "Nick is not dead," she stated firmly and emphatically. "I'd 'feel' it if he were. He may be in trouble or hurt but he's not dead. So what we have to do is find him. What do the Rangers tell you?"

"They don't have any answers either. When I talked to the captain yesterday, he assured me that every Ranger in the unit is looking for him. They have to move carefully because they don't want to reveal his identity if he hasn't been found out. All we can do is wait until they learn something," Mark concluded despondently.

That answer did not sit well with Nichole at all. She'd be damned if she'd sit around twiddling her thumbs when her brother was in serious trouble. But she knew better than to let her parents know that she was already speculating on a way to help.

"I see," she responded aloud. "Well, I guess they know what they're doing." *In a pig's eye*, she thought to herself.

That night, she paced her room until a plan started forming in her overactive mind. If Nick had last been with that gang, then that's where she had to start to look for him. The only problem was she didn't know the name of the gang. But that was a minor problem. After all, if you wanted to know something, all you had to do was ask. First thing in the morning, she was going to the Ranger station and talk to the captain.

"Oh my God!" Amy's hand trembled as she read the note her sister had left on her pillow. "Mama! Daddy!" she yelled as she raced out of Nichole's room and down the stairway, taking the steps two at a time. "Nolie's gone!" She waved the piece of paper in her hand as she ran into the kitchen. "Nolie's gone to find Nick!"

Mark grabbed the paper from Amy and read it out loud.

Dear Mom and Dad,

    I've gone to find Nicky. Please try to understand that this is not a thing I decided on an impulse. You know how it is with Nicky and me. I have no choice. I must try to find him. Don't worry, you know I can take care of myself. Love, Nichole

"Don't worry!" he shouted. "Don't worry! My son is missing and now my hardheaded daughter takes off to find him and says *don't worry?* My God! What the hell does she think I'm going to do?" he roared.

Cassie shook her head contritely. "I should have known she was up to something last night when she meekly accepted the fact that there wasn't anything we could do to help. Why should I have thought sending her away to school would have changed her? She's still the same headstrong, willful girl as when she left here."

The slim figure, clad in faded denim breeches, a long-sleeved plaid shirt, and black leather vest, was fit to be tied. She stood by her horse with a scowl on her face.

"Damn that man!" she muttered to her big chestnut gelding, Cocoa. "He refused to tell me anything. The arrogant buffoon told me to 'go home and tend my knitting and let the *men* chase the bad guys,'" she mimicked sarcastically.

The brown-eyed animal snorted and bobbed his head as if he understood and agreed with every word she said.

As she stood there contemplating her next move, she noticed the big, rough-looking man who entered the captain's office.

Something pricked her memory. She was certain she knew him from somewhere but she couldn't quite remember where. She wracked her brain trying to place him.

Suddenly she had her answer, both as to where she knew him from and what her next move would be. She quickly twisted her long hair and stuffed it under her hat. She patted the gun she wore on her hip before walking over to lean casually against the building, resting one booted foot on the wall behind her. And waited.

It wasn't long before the tall, broad-shouldered man walked out the door.

Fowler Barclay's golden-blond hair was longer than

she remembered. It, along with the beard, which was also not there before, leant him a mean, unkempt appearance. If she had any doubts about his identity, they were dispelled when he glanced in her direction with those piercing blue eyes.

She ducked her head, not wanting him to know she was watching him but she was positive it was him. There couldn't be two men with the same deeply tanned and ruggedly handsome features who might have a reason to be at a Texas Ranger's post.

Fowler glanced at the skinny kid leaning against the building before rolling a smoke. The hairs on the back of his neck were bristling. He knew from long years of guarding his back that someone was watching him. As he lit his smoke, he casually glanced around the area.

Not seeing anyone but the kid, he shrugged his shoulders, tossed the match to the ground, and snuffed it with his boot. *Must be the long weeks of tension catching up with me,* he thought. His report displeased him just as much as it had the captain.

It had been two weeks since they had asked for his help in locating the missing Ranger and he didn't feel he was any closer to an answer today than then.

He rubbed his whiskered face and frowned. He hated having a beard. It was a necessary part of his disguise but, damned, the thing itched! Besides that, he grinned, the ladies complained that it scratched their tender skin. And he certainly didn't want to cause them any pain, only pleasure.

Which is exactly where I'm heading now, he thought, *after I stop by the hotel in Waco and take a bath.* He was sure he smelled as bad as he looked.

"Don't make any sudden moves, Mister. Don't even think about going for your gun unless you want a window in your back."

He felt the cold end of the gun in his back at the same instant he heard the low voice behind him. His instinct had been right. Someone had been watching him.

"What do you want?"

"You are going to take the reins of your horse and then you and I are going to mosey out of here real casual-like," came the muffled voice.

"You won't get away with this you know."

"Shut up! If you like your anatomy the way it is, you better make sure you don't do anything to alert the guard at the gate, *Mr. United States Marshal*," the voice threatened.

Fowler's blood ran cold. There was only one person, other than the captain, in the state who knew his real identity.

As they walked out the fort's gate, Fowler growled, "You can't kidnap a United States Marshal!"

"I just did, buster, now you mount up real slow and easy-like and we're going to ride down the road a piece. And, just in case you get any notions about trying something, I can shoot a gnat's eye out at forty paces."

Nichole kept her gun aimed at him as she mounted and rode slightly behind him. She wasn't about to give him a chance to catch her off guard. Her hunch had been right. She didn't know why he was in Texas, but he didn't want anyone to know he was a U.S. Marshal. And that suited her just fine.

If need be, she'd blackmail him into helping her

16

find Nick. Whatever it took, she needed a man of his caliber and experience, because, come hell or high water, she was going to find her brother and he was just the man to help her.

Fowler patiently rode beside the kid, waiting for just the right moment to make his move. Even though the kid seemed to have more than his share of guts, sooner or later, he'd let his guard slip.

Fowler's curiosity was piqued. How did this kid know who he was and why was he trying to kidnap him? He glanced over at the boy. He was certain he had never seen him before.

Nichole motioned toward a clump of trees off the road. "Ride over there and get off your horse."

"How do you know who I am?"

"Shut up. I'll do the talking and you'll do the listening."

When they reached the seclusion of the trees, she motioned for him to stop and dismount.

Fowler had learned in his twenty-eight years of living that you could glean more information by being patient and observing than by asking direct questions. He decided to let the kid expose his hand before he jumped him.

Fowler leaned against a tree, casually rolling a smoke. "So talk, I'm listening," he said insolently.

"Nick is missing and you are going to help me find him," she said without preamble.

Fowler took a draw off his cigarette. "Just like that?"

"Just like that. I know I can't do it alone, so you're going to help me. Those idiot Rangers haven't found out anything in three weeks. So I'm . . . *we* are going to do it ourselves. Daddy will pay you whatever you ask when we find him."

Fowler was careful not to show that the name "Nick" meant anything to him. "Just out of curiosity, how do you know who I am? And, what is this 'Nick' person to you?" He watched the kid closely.

He had long since learned to watch his opponent's eyes. They were a sure giveaway when he was fixing to make his move. The emerald-green eyes that locked with his were not the eyes of a killer, but he didn't like anyone pulling a gun on him. Whether they intended to use it or not, it made his hackles rise.

Being careful not to take his eyes off the kid, he carelessly thumped his cigarette butt to the side. Just as he had expected, the kid's eyes followed his hand movement. That little trick worked almost every time.

Fowler pounced on Nichole like a panther on a rabbit. He easily toppled her to the ground on her back with him on top, wresting the gun from her hand in the process.

"Now, you little brat, tell me who the hell you are and who told you about me!" he spat angrily.

"Get off me, you big ape!" She kicked at him with all her strength. "You're crushing me." She gave a final buck, trying to throw him off her before he broke every bone in her body. Her struggle to unseat him, sent her hat flying and her long black hair cascading around her.

If Fowler hadn't been so intent on getting the "kid's" gun and pinning "him" to the ground, he would have noticed that the kid's low, tough-sounding voice had suddenly turned high and feminine.

18

When her hat went flying, exposing the kid for the girl she was, Fowler couldn't believe his eyes.

"Holy hell!" he exclaimed as he rose to his feet, pulling the struggling girl with him. "You're a girl!" He swung her around to face him, grabbing her by the shoulders with both hands as he stared at her.

"Of course I'm a girl, you idiot!" she shouted at him as she struggled to free herself from his viselike grip. "Let go of me. You're hurting me." She kicked at him, her booted foot making contact with his shin.

"Ouch!" He whirled her around and grabbed her to his chest, spoon fashion, as she struggled to get free.

"Not until you tell me who you are, you little hellion!"

He had her arms pinned securely to her sides. She ceased her struggling, and trying to catch her breath, she let her head fall back against his chest.

Her head came just under his chin. Her hair smelled so good, he couldn't resist the urge to bury his face in it, taking a deep sniff as he held her tightly to him. She smelled just like the yellow roses that grew around his grandmother's front porch.

Nichole felt his grip loosen and took the opportunity to ram her elbow in his midsection in a desperate action to free herself. But she couldn't break his hold.

"Dammit! Who the hell are you?" he growled when he got his breath back.

"Let go of me and I'll tell you."

"Oh, no, lady, and I use the term loosely, not until you start doing some fast talking. Otherwise, I'm going to truss you up and haul you back to the Ranger post. Now start talking!" he demanded menacingly.

"I'm Nichole Westerfield and Nick is my brother.

19

He's a Texas Ranger and he disappeared about three weeks ago and the captain won't tell me anything about where he might be or who the gang is he was watching. And I'm afraid he's hurt and I'm going to find him with or without any help from any of you," she replied rebelliously.

Everything rushed out at the same time, all the tension and frustration and worry suddenly overwhelming her. She didn't realize she was crying or that Fowler had released her and turned her to face him when he heard her name.

She was talking so fast and sobbing so hard that he was only making out about every third word.

"Whoa. Whoa. Slow down." He pulled her to him and held her close until her sobs melted into sniffles. He handed her his handkerchief as he led her over to sit beneath a tree, and pulled her onto his lap, liking very much the feel of her in his arms.

"Okay, now let's see if I can make some sense out of all this. You're Nick Westerfield's sister, right?"

She nodded as she wiped the tears from her face.

"And you are going to find him even though all the Rangers haven't been able to locate him in three weeks, right?"

Again, she nodded. She hated to cry because her eyes always turned red and her nose always ran. Some women cried so gracefully; unfortunately, she wasn't one of them, she thought as she blew her runny nose.

He looked at her in a patronizing way. "And I'll just bet that you already have a plan as to how you're going to accomplish this feat, right?"

Nichole heard the patronizing tone in his voice and

her temper jumped over her tongue. "Of course I have a plan, you nincompoop! Do you think I don't have *any* sense?" she challenged.

She has guts, I'll give her that, he thought to himself. "And is it safe for me to assume that I am a part of this scheme of yours since you kidnapped me at gun point?"

"Since I don't make a habit of collecting U.S. Marshals, of course you're part of my plan. What other reason would I have need of you, pray tell?" she asked haughtily.

"Oh, I don't know. My good looks and vibrant personality, maybe?" he quipped, a smirk tilting one corner of his mouth.

"You *must* be kidding! You look like you just crawled out from under a rock." She sniffed disdainfully. "And you smell like it, too. Why are you dressed like a . . . a desperado?"

"You ask too many questions. How do you know who I am? I don't remember meeting you before today."

"I'm sure you don't," she said disgustedly. "You were too busy panting after that . . . that overly endowed redhead to barely acknowledge me when we were introduced at the president's party last spring." She was miffed that he hadn't remembered her, even after learning her name. She had thought he was absolutely the most gorgeous man she had ever laid eyes on, and he had acted like she was just a child when Cousin Emmalee had introduced them.

He remembered the party and he certainly remembered the redhead. Boy, did he ever remember the redhead! It was the first time he'd ever had to exit a lady's bedroom via the window—a second-story window, at that! But the lady's husband had come home unexpectedly and. . . .

Wham! She hit him up side the head. Nichole had watched the emotions chase each other across his handsome face and she could just about guess what his thoughts were.

"Why did you do that?" he questioned, surprised.

She tried to give him her most intimidating glare. "You can reminisce about that strumpet some other time. Right now, we have to find my brother."

"Since I'm to be a part of your plan, would you mind telling *me* what it is? Or shall I simply assume that you are going to offer me in exchange for him?" he asked sarcastically, rubbing the side of his head.

"Don't be ridiculous. We are going to find the gang who Nick was with, follow them to their hide-out, and rescue Nick, of course!" Honestly, she thought, how dense could one be, for heaven's sake?

"Just like that?" he asked incredulously.

"Of course, just like that. How could it be any simpler?"

"That is the *stupidest* idea I've ever heard!" he roared, dumping her to the ground as he stood up. "Did it ever cross that addlepated brain of yours that you might get yourself killed chasing after robbers and cutthroats, for Christ's sakes, woman!" he shouted loud enough to be heard in the next state.

"Well, no, but—"

He grabbed her hat off the ground and slammed it back on her head. "Well, you could, and probably would, get yourself killed or worse, before you got within a mile of Linc Travis's gang." He hauled her to her feet and pushed her in the direction of her horse. "Now, go home and let the rest of us do our job without any interference from a kid sister!" he stormed.

"I am not a 'kid sister.' I'm the same age as Nick and I am going to find my brother, and you are going to help me and that's that!" she stormed in return.

She stood with her hands on her hips, her green eyes flashing like emerald-colored lightning, her hat skewed on her head, and dirt on her face, just daring him to refuse to help her.

"And if I refuse to go along with your harebrained idea, just what do you propose to do about it?" he challenged.

She smiled a too-sweet smile before stating, "Simple. You wouldn't be looking like a . . . a . . . *that*, unless you didn't want somebody to know who you are. So, unless you agree to help me, I'll just tell everybody I know who the *real* Fowler Barclay is," she said smugly.

"Why, you you—" he sputtered. "That's blackmail!"

"Exactly."

"You won't get away with this," he insisted.

She picked up her gun, holstered it, and mounted her horse before acknowledging him. "Yes, I will. Now let's get going, too much time has already been wasted."

Chapter Two

"Come back here, you mule-headed brat!" Fowler jumped on his horse and took off after Nichole.

He grabbed the reins of her horse and pulled it to a halt. The gelding, not used to such rough handling, began to roll its eyes back and lay its ears down.

Fowler saw the horse's intent and managed to snatch his hand back just seconds before it tried to remove a couple of his fingers with its big teeth.

"Good boy, Cocoa," she praised him.

Fowler glared at Nichole as she lovingly patted the horse's sleek brown neck. "If you can control that man-eating horse of yours, I have a few things I'd like to make very clear to you, young lady."

"Well, make it fast. We need to stop for supplies and I want to make a few miles before we have to stop for the night," she stated matter-of-factly.

Fowler was fast losing his temper with this sassy termagant. "In the first place, 'we' are not going anywhere. I was already working on this case *before* you came bouncing along. That is why I 'look like this,' as you so kindly put it. In the second place, this gang is a murderous group of outlaws who wouldn't blink an eye at killing a woman, *after* they, *all of them*, were through ravishing her. In the third place, even if I did take leave of my senses, which I won't, and let you come along, just what the hell do you think you could do that I haven't already done to locate this gang? And, finally, the last thing I need is a whining female to slow me down. You are not going and that's that! Do I make myself clear, Miss Westerfield?" By the time he had finished his very loud tirade, the horses were prancing and snorting at the disturbance.

Nichole's temper was every bit as volatile as his. She was not cowed one bit by his outburst. If anything, it only served to light her fuse. She shook her finger in his face as she countered his allegations. "Now you listen here, you arrogant jackass! For your information, I do not 'whine' and I am just as good with a gun and a horse as you. And, as to what *I* could do that *you* haven't done, that's even easier. Seeing as how you haven't done anything yet, I'm positive I can do better than that! In fact, now that I know who to look for, *you* would probably slow *me* down!"

Emerald-green eyes locked in combat with sapphire-blue ones, neither giving an inch.

"You are not going with me," Fowler snarled through clenched teeth.

Nichole smiled triumphantly. "You're right." She

whirled her horse around and headed in the opposite direction at a gallop. "I'm going *without* you."

Her action caught him completely by surprise.

"Dammit to hell! You come back here!" he shouted as he pulled back on his reins so hard that his stallion reared on its hind legs before changing direction to race after her.

Nichole knew exactly what she had to do. If she couldn't find the outlaws, then she'd make sure the outlaws found her.

She was in such deep thought about her plans that she didn't realize Fowler was following her until she was suddenly yanked off her horse and slung across his lap in a most unladylike manner.

"Put me down, you big lummox!" she screamed in outrageous indignation.

Fowler ignored her outburst. He gathered the reins of her horse and turned off the road, riding far into the woods where they would not be seen or heard should anyone happen along. He was determined to put an end to her foolhardy plans once and for all. And he knew from their recent shouting match that it was very unlikely that they could have a civil, quiet discussion.

When he reached a clearing, he let her slide down the side of his horse as he dismounted. He turned her to him, trapping her between the horse and his body.

He had decided that the only way he could convince her that there was no way she could hold her own against Linc's band of cutthroats was to give her a mild taste of what would happen to her if she fell into their hands.

Fowler had been so furious at having a gun stuck in

his back, that even after he had uncovered the female beneath the male attire, only his subconscious mind had registered her beauty.

Now, for the first time, he noticed the slight flush of her cheeks, the luscious cherry lips just begging to be kissed, the long, sooty black lashes that framed the purest green eyes he had ever seen. Emeralds. That's what they reminded him of, exquisite emeralds.

Her hat had come off again, and her long, curly black hair had been tousled by the wind, giving her a wild, almost abandoned look as it tumbled around her shoulders and down her back.

His eyes surveyed her body slowly, passing her creamy white throat, pausing briefly at the two buttons that had come undone to hint ever so slightly at the ripe fullness of the breasts heaving beneath her man's shirt, past the tiny waist, over her gently rounded hips, and down her long slender legs to her small booted feet.

Damn, he thought to himself as he licked his suddenly dry lips, how the hell had he ever mistaken this luscious beauty for a kid?

Nichole didn't like his slow appraisal of her. He looked like a cat fixing to devour a saucer of milk!

"Stop gawking at me like I'm some kind of—"

Fowler jerked her roughly to him. "What happened to the brave little girl who thought she could take on the whole Travis gang, huh?" He grabbed a handful of her hair as he forced her mouth to his. He had never been brutal with a woman but he knew he had to give a convincing performance, to really frighten her for her own good.

He ground his lips into hers, and when he raised

his head, he could tell that she really believed the worst of him. Good. Maybe it would save her life. "What's the matter, baby?" he snarled at her. "Did I forget to say 'please' and 'thank you?' Believe me, baby, those bastards will do a lot worse to you than I'm going to," he threatened as he sought her lips again.

Nichole tried to pull away from him, but his grip was so tight that she couldn't break his hold. His fingers were bruising her tender skin unmercifully. She struggled frantically as the significance of his words settled in on her mind. Surely he didn't mean to force himself on her!

"Stop it! Let go of me, you monster!" she screamed as she struggled even harder. She brought her knee up sharply, aiming for his groin, but, seeing her intent, he deftly side-stepped the intended blow.

Her strength surprised him as she fought him like a wildcat. He had expected her to succumb to tears of fright, not fight him tooth and nail. What the hell was he going to do now?

He silently berated himself as he tried to hold on to the fighting little spitfire. "Now why should I have expected you to act like a normal female and plead for leniency? You haven't done a damned thing normal for your sex since the first minute we met," he grumbled as he tried to figure out how to turn loose the tiger's tail without being clawed to pieces.

"Okay! Okay! Stop fighting me. I promise I won't hurt you. I was only trying to scare you by showing you what would happen if you fell into the clutches of those outlaws. I'm sorry. I should have known scare tactics wouldn't work on you," he confessed.

Nichole suddenly quit trying to do him bodily harm and glared at him. "Why, you son of a b—"

Fowler placed his finger across her mouth. "Naughty, naughty. Ladies don't use language like that," he scolded mildly.

Again, she opened her mouth, ready to give him the what for, but before she knew what was happening, he suddenly pulled her against him and covered her mouth with his once more.

At first, it was more of a demand than a kiss. He had only intended to stop her verbal assault, but this time when his lips touched hers a fire ignited in his veins. His blood ran hot, burning its way through his body.

No longer feeling endangered, her struggling ceased as his kiss gentled. His tongue plundered the sweetness of her mouth as his hands swept down her slender form. Pulling her against him, he gently kneaded her bottom. A muffled groan of pure sensual desire echoed through his body.

She wasn't aware at what point her struggles to get away from him turned into a struggle to get closer to him. She only knew that her body was on fire with feelings she had never before experienced. She had never known that such pleasurable pain existed until now.

Fowler's muffled groan penetrated her passion-clouded senses with a sharpness that made her tremble. She pushed against his chest, twisting her mouth from his.

"Stop. Let me go." Her voice sounded breathless and weak to her own ears. Again, she pushed against him, this time succeeding in breaking his hold.

She quickly stepped away, turning her back on him

as she waited for her pounding heart to slow to normal.

Fowler swore under his breath as he nervously began to roll a cigarette. "I'm sorry, I didn't mean to—"

"You did that deliberately!" she stormed at him, not giving him a chance to finish his apology. "But your little scheme won't work, you—you bounder."

"What?" he asked in surprise. His hand shook as he placed the cigarette to his lips and inhaled the calming smoke deep into his lungs. "What are you talking about?"

She looked at him accusingly. "You know exactly what I mean. You thought you could scare me and make me go home. But it won't work. I'm still going after my brother, and neither you nor anybody else is going to stop me."

At least he had the decency to look shamefaced. "I'm sorry. I was trying to scare you in the beginning, but then things just got out of hand and I lost control. I never meant to kiss you like that."

"Well, don't worry about it. At least, now I won't be afraid of what the outlaws might do to me. It couldn't possibly be worse than what you just did or tried to do!" She'd be damned if she'd let him know how much his attempt at lovemaking had affected her.

"Worse than what I did!" he shouted in disbelief.

"That's right, Mr. Barclay. Now, are you or are you not going with me to help me find my brother? Because with or without your help, I'm going!"

He couldn't believe his ears. Apparently what had happened between them had not made any impression on her at all. She could just dismiss it as if it were an everyday event. Boy, did she have a way of hurting a man's pride.

"Fine!" he roared. "You go after your brother, but don't holler for my help when you find yourself surrounded by vultures fighting over who gets you first, you hardheaded wench! I'm going to Waco and find me a hot bath, a hot meal, and a hot woman. Hopefully one who has enough sense to know when she is being made love to by a *gentleman!*" he shouted as he slammed his hat on his head and stomped off to get his horse.

"You can go to Kentucky for all I care, you conceited jackass! And, for your information, *if* I did get in any trouble, you're the last person on earth I'd call to help me!" she shouted back at him as she, too, slammed her hat on her head and stalked off to mount her horse.

They gave each other one final glare as they reined their horses around and headed in opposite directions.

"Gentleman, indeed," Nichole mumbled to herself. "He could practice till kingdom comes and not ever make the rank of gentleman. He's got to be the most infuriating male I've ever met!"

Fowler tried not to think about the woman riding away from him. In the short space of a couple of hours, she had kidnapped him at gun point; tried to blackmail him; assaulted his manhood; caused him to lose control and take liberties he hadn't intended to take; stomped all over his pride; and then had the audacity to expect him to drag her along with him while he did his best to find her brother.

"That mule-headed wench needs a keeper," he

31

grumbled to the only living thing within hearing distance, his horse, who didn't particularly care one way or the other.

"She has got to be, without a doubt, the most infuriating female I've ever had the displeasure of running into! Damn her hide, anyway! No telling what kind of a crazy plan she'll cook up in that fruitcake brain of hers."

It suddenly dawned on Fowler what he was doing. "That crazy woman has me talking to myself!" He turned in his saddle to look behind him at the figure that was growing smaller in the distance as he watched.

"She's going to get herself in trouble. I know it just as surely as I'm sitting here. No telling what mischief she'll cause." He pulled his horse to a standstill as he continued with his one-sided conversation.

"I know she's going to get into trouble. She couldn't keep from getting in trouble if she tried. She might even get herself . . . killed." A chill ran down his spine at that sobering thought.

He looked over his shoulder once again. Finally, he shook his head in disgust. "Who do you think you're trying to kid, Fowler? You *know* you can't let her go off by herself to rescue Nick. You said yourself that she needs a keeper. Well," he jeered disgustedly, "guess who just *volunteered* to do the job?"

He turned his horse around to follow in the direction that Nichole had taken.

As he rode to catch up with her, a thought suddenly occurred to him. He snapped his fingers as the plan fully developed in his mind. They had to go into Waco to get supplies, so he'd pretend to go along with her until they got there. But, once they were there, he'd just toss that pretty little butt of hers in jail and send word for her father to come and get her. That way, he'd get her off his hands, she'd be safe at home where she belonged, and he could get on with the business of finding her brother. The more he thought about it, the more he liked the idea.

Perfect! He smiled to himself, pleased that he'd found the solution to everyone's problem. But. . . .

"Why didn't I think of that in the first place? And how come I get a sneaky feeling that it sounds too easy?" he pondered out loud.

He turned his eyes skyward. "You're getting back at me for that redhead, aren't you? I knew it! I knew some woman would be the death of me."

His horse picked that particular time to snort. "Aw, shut up, what do you know about anything anyhow?" he grumbled.

Chapter Three

Nichole was so deep in thought that she didn't hear the rider gaining on her until he was almost even with her.

"Nichole! Nichole, wait up." Fowler reined in beside her.

She didn't slow her horse's gait as she looked over at the man riding alongside her. "What do you want, Fowler? If you're worried that I'll expose your identity, don't be. I'm only interested in finding my brother. I don't care who you're hiding from."

Fowler took a deep breath much like a man plunging into water above his head. "What I said before is true. I have spent the last two weeks trying to locate Nick. I was recently assigned to this territory by President Grant. He and Governor Pease have their own reasons for wanting to rid the state of people like

Linc Travis." He could tell by the look she gave him that she didn't know whether to believe him.

"Good grief! What is Nick mixed up in that the governor *and* the president would concern themselves with?" she asked incredulously.

"I'm sorry, Nichole, I can't tell you any more than that. You'll just have to trust me."

Nichole pulled her horse to a stop. "Does this mean you are going to help me?"

Fowler wiped his hand over his face in resignation. "Yes, I'm going to help you. I can't let you go off on your own and probably get yourself killed. But you have to promise me, and I mean this, Nichole," he warned. "You have to absolutely promise me that if I tell you to do something, you'll do it without asking questions and without hesitation. It could be the difference between living or dying. And, this time I'm serious, I'm not trying to frighten you. I can't afford to be distracted even for a second because it could mean death for either one or both of us."

Nichole could tell by his tone of voice that he was serious. She nodded her head in agreement. "I understand and I promise I'll do whatever you tell me."

She hesitated a minute before continuing, "Fowler, I really am as good with a gun and a horse as Nick is. I can take care of myself. Daddy regrets it now, that's why I was sent away to school, but I learned everything that he and Grandpa taught Cody and Nicky. I'm not a fainthearted female," she insisted.

Fowler laughed as he tweaked her nose. "Now why doesn't that surprise me? I mean, after all, sweetheart, look at the way you're dressed, and how often does a U.S. Marshal get kidnapped by a mere wisp of a girl? Gosh. That must happen at least two or three times a day," he teased, his blue eyes twinkling in amusement.

"Go ahead and tease me. But don't be surprised if you discover that I'm the one who has to save your hide one day. After all, God gave me a brain, too, you know, and, I insist on using it whether it ruffles your male pride or not," she teased back.

He couldn't help but admire her spunk. He had already discovered firsthand that she was different from any female he had ever known.

"Okay, I believe you. But do you mind humoring me just a little, and let me think I'm protecting you? If for no other reason than the fact that I'm bigger than you? Okay?" He chuckled.

She gave him a smile that made his heart cartwheel in his chest. "Well, I guess I'll have to give you credit for superior strength."

During their playful banter, Fowler hadn't been paying much attention to where they were headed. Now he got the distinct notion that Nichole had a particular destination in mind and it wasn't Waco.

"Since we agreed to let me be the boss, do you mind telling me where we're headed and exactly what you have in mind?" he asked.

"We're headed to Aerl Station. We're going to pick up supplies and start asking some questions. Unless you have a better plan?"

"Why go to Aerl Station instead of Waco? Waco's closer." *And there's a nice jail waiting for you in Waco.*

The look she gave him made him believe that he was about to lose his "boss" status.

She patiently explained her plan to him as if he were a child. "Since Nick is working undercover, he would avoid going to places where he would be recognized. That means he'd naturally stay as far away from Waco as possible. Also, since you or the Rangers haven't gotten anywhere trying to find the Travis gang, why not let them 'find' us?"

Okay, so I'll toss your butt in Aerl's jail instead.

Grudgingly, he had to admit that her plan did have a degree of merit. "Most of what you said is logical, except why would Linc want to find us?"

"Not 'us,' the Brazos Kid, silly." Again, she gave him that you-better-watch-out-before-you-get-demoted look.

"Wait a minute. Did I fall asleep somewhere in the middle of this conversation or what? *Who* is the Brazos Kid?"

Nichole laughed. She knew she was being a little minx, but she couldn't help herself.

"When Nicky and I were kids, we played a game we called 'bandits.' Nicky always called himself the Brazos Kid when he played the bandit and I was the sheriff. Since Nick couldn't very well use his real name, because of the fact that the Westerfield name is well known in Central Texas, I'm betting that he used the name of—"

Fowler interrupted her, "Let me guess, the Brazos Kid. Right?"

"Right. Makes perfect sense to me." She laughed at his pained I-should-have-known look.

"Lady, your logic is beginning to make sense to me and that frightens me," he quipped.

She chuckled as she gave him a mischievous glance. "I take it that this is your first encounter with a female who has brains instead of fluff between her ears."

Her laughter was a very pleasant sound to Fowler. It had a husky, almost sensual quality to it. And, he thought in retrospect, it was a sincere laugh, not at all like the fake and ofttimes patronizing giggles of the women out to catch his eye and his wedding ring.

He prided himself on being a good judge of character and he'd wager his last dollar that if Nichole had something to say, she'd say it plain out and not play coy games like a lot of women. Also, given his brief encounter with her so far, he'd stake his life on the fact that once she got it in her head to do something, she'd be as tenacious as a little bull dog until she did it.

He hated to admit it, even to himself and he'd *never* admit it in a hundred years to the little termagant riding beside him, but she was right in her appraisal of the type of women he had pursued over the years. Brains had definitely not been a prerequisite in his lovers.

Just before they reached Aerl Station, Nichole twisted her hair up and stuffed it under her hat.

Fowler gave her a puzzled look, waiting for her to explain herself. When she didn't volunteer an answer to his unasked question, he was certain she was up to something—again.

"Why did you do that?" he questioned.

She just smiled and replied cryptically, "You'll see in due time."

As they rode into town, Nichole asked Fowler if he would purchase the supplies they would need while she took Cocoa down to the blacksmith's shop.

"It feels like he has a loose shoe and I need to get it fixed before we head out," she explained.

"Sure." He looked down the row of buildings that lined the main street. *Oh, hell! There is no jail here!* "Let's meet over at that cafe when you're through," he replied absently. *Now what the hell am I going to do with her?*

"Okay," she readily agreed.

Fowler headed for the building that proudly proclaimed to be The Emporium in big red letters painted across the large front window, as he pondered this unexpected turn of events.

Well, he thought, he couldn't start a ruckus right in the middle of town, so he'd just have to wait until they left. But then, dammit, he was going to truss her up and haul her back to Waco!

Nichole slowly headed toward the stables. After making sure Fowler had had enough time to enter the store, she turned her horse around and pulled up in front of the only saloon in town.

The sounds of a twangy, off-key piano and men gambling reached her ears from behind the swinging doors. Even though it wasn't dark yet, the saloon seemed to be doing a brisk business.

After looping the reins around the hitching post, she pulled her hat down to shadow her face before swaggering into the smoke-filled room.

The barkeep wiped a greasy rag around the bar in front of her before asking, "What'll ya have, young man?"

She lowered the tone of her voice before answering, "Beer."

The bartender sat a mug of foamy yellow liquid in front of her and walked away.

39

Nichole picked up her drink and walked to the dimly lit back corner of the bar. She propped one booted foot on the brass rail, taking a nonchalant stance. Making sure to keep the brim of her hat shadowing her eyes, she sipped the foul-tasting liquid as her eyes slowly scanned the room.

Most of the men were just your average cowboy, blowing off a little steam and washing the dust from his throat at the end of a long work day. Her glance didn't linger on them.

A few of the men were obviously drifters, and she surveyed them a bit closer. Although no one seemed to be taking any notice of her, she let her eyes slowly drift around the room again.

After securing the saddlebags to his horse, Fowler looked up and down the street for Nichole. Not seeing her, he crossed the street and tied his horse to the railing in front of the cafe.

Fowler glanced in the window of the eatery. Not seeing her inside yet, he decided that he had time for a quick beer before meeting her for supper.

As he walked next door to the saloon, he couldn't help musing to himself that she had at least one thing in common with other females, tardiness.

Fowler stopped just inside the swinging doors to allow his eyes to adjust to the dimness before walking to the bar and ordering a beer.

Nichole, of course, saw him the instant he walked in and quickly turned her back to him, hoping against hope that he wouldn't spot her. No such luck.

After taking a long swig of his beer, he turned and leaned back against the bar on his left elbow, holding the mug in his right hand. He casually watched the table where a hot poker game was in process as he sipped his beer.

He briefly glanced around the room, more out of habit than expectation of seeing anyone he might know. At first, his glance slid past the slim figure at the far end of the bar only to screech to a halt and swiftly move back to it.

"What the hell!" he muttered. Maybe no one else had recognized her, but he'd know that figure anywhere! Now he knew why she had been so agreeable with his plans. Dammit! What was she up to now?

Nichole watched in the mirror as Fowler walked over to the table where the game was taking place, then turn back and saunter to the end of the bar where she was.

"Barkeep! Another beer." He tossed a coin on the bar as the man sat the mug in front of him, and waited until he walked away before asking in a barely controlled voice, "What the hell are you doing in here?"

"Keep your voice down," she cautioned. "See the two men at the table behind and to the left of the poker game?"

Fowler glanced in the mirror above the bar at the two men in question. "Yeah, I see them. What about them?"

"When they first spotted me, they acted as if they had seen a ghost. They've been arguing about something ever since." Nichole took another swig of the gold-colored liquid, trying not to grimace. "This stuff tastes awful. How can you stand to drink it?"

Fowler ignored her question. He had been watching the two men as they continued their debate. Nichole was right. It did seem to be about her. As he watched, one of the men rose to his feet and shot her a glance before leaving the saloon. The sound of hurried hoofbeats quickly echoed down the street.

"Never mind about the refreshments," he warned. "Right now I want you to walk out of here casually and get mounted. One of the men just rode off in a hell of a hurry and I don't like the way the other one is looking at you. I'll be right behind you, but don't stop for anything until you get on your horse. Understand?"

Nichole nodded her head as she turned and walked toward the swinging doors.

Fowler tensed as he saw the man move his hand under the table to rest on his pistol.

Just as Nichole stepped past the table where her back was to the man, he made his move.

"Hey, Brazos!" he shouted, standing and pulling his gun at the same time.

Nichole involuntarily looked in his direction at the sound of a chair toppling over. Her mind registered his intent at the same instant she heard the roar of a gun being fired.

She felt a hand at her back as she was unceremoniously shoved out the doors.

The drifter was dead before he hit the floor.

Fowler stood with the smoking gun in his hand, aimed at the startled players at the poker table. At the sound of the gunshot, some of the men had dived under the table out of the way. Others were frozen halfway between standing and sitting.

He waved the gun at them as he warned, "Everybody just stay where you are and nobody else will get hurt."

Keeping his gun aimed, he slowly backed his way

past the swinging doors. Quickly mounting his horse, he ordered Nichole to get going as he raced after her, keeping his gun aimed behind them.

They didn't slow down until they were well out of town.

"I guess that proves my hunch was right," Nichole proudly proclaimed. "Nick *is* known as the Brazos Kid. Damn, I wish we could have seen which direction that other man took off in. I'll bet he would have lead us to Linc's hide-out." She hit her saddle horn in disgust.

Fowler pulled off into the woods without uttering a word. He was so furious he didn't trust himself to speak until they were safely away from the road.

When he stopped, Nichole didn't have time to dismount before he had reached her and yanked her off her horse.

"What the hell did you think you were doing back there!" he bellowed. "Do you know you almost got yourself killed!" His rage was so great that he wanted to shake her until her teeth rattled, but instead he pulled her to him as if he would never let her go.

"You don't have to yell, for heaven's sake!" She pushed away from him. "I saw his gun. If you hadn't pushed me out the door, I would have shot him myself." She stood, feet apart, hands on her hips, glaring into Fowler's furious face. She refused to be intimidated and treated like an inept child.

"Why, you little brat! What you need is to have that butt of yours blistered until you can't sit down for a week!" He took a step toward her as if to enforce his words. "Let me tell you something, young lady. I have no intention of taking you with me to find your brother. I was only pretending to go along with you until we got to a town. Then I was going to put you in jail and send word for your father to come and get you. And I'm still going to do just that!" he declared emphatically.

Nichole didn't budge an inch, refusing to be bullied. "You'd just be wasting your time, because the minute my father turned his back, I'd just strike out on my own again. Fowler, why can't you understand? This is not something I decided to do on an impulse. I have no choice in the matter. I have to try to find my brother. How could I live the rest of my life knowing that I didn't even *try* to help him? I've already told you I can handle a gun as good as most men. The fact that you refuse to believe me is *your* problem, not *mine.*"

They stood glaring at each other, waiting for the other to capitulate. Fowler uttered an expletive before finally throwing his hands up in exasperation. He could tell by the defiant look on her face that she would do just exactly what she said she would. Then who would look after her? Nobody. What choice did that leave him? None.

"Dammit to hell, woman!" He was so furious he could spit nails. He shook his finger in her face as he warned her. "All right, I'll let you go with me. But I'm going to lay down some ground rules and you are going to swear by everything you consider holy, to obey them. And if you don't, so help me, I'll lock you in the first jail I come to and I won't tell anyone where you are until I've finished this job! Do I make myself perfectly clear?"

Nichole nodded her head and opened her mouth to assure him that she'd follow his rules explicitly when a rustling noise in the bushes caught their attention.

Before Nichole could turn around, Fowler held his finger to his lips in a hushed warning. "Don't make any sudden moves. Just walk slowly toward me as quietly as possible," he cautioned as he slowly backed up.

Nichole could still hear the rustling noise behind her. Without hesitation, she moved soundlessly toward Fowler, resisting the urge to turn around or to look over her shoulder. They moved a dozen or so feet deeper into the woods before Fowler stopped.

Nichole felt it must be safe to look behind her now, so she did. She watched as the black-and-white animal with its tail raised high in the air, ambled out of the bushes where they had been standing. The skunk nervously sniffed the air and looked all around, satisfying itself that it was not in any danger before slowly waddling back into the undergrowth.

"Looks like this spot is taken," Fowler joked. "Shall we find ourselves other accommodations for the night?"

"I do believe that would be the prudent thing to do under the circumstances," she agreed readily.

After finishing their supper of hardtack and a tin of beans, they sat by the fire, sipping the last of the coffee in companionable silence.

Fowler watched Nichole as she absently brushed her long, silky black hair. He could tell by the faraway look on her face that she was deep in thought. He almost feared to ask what she was cooking up in that pretty little head of hers.

Suddenly she turned toward him, gesturing with the brush as she talked. "You know, what we need to do is get a look at that dead man's saddlebags. We

45

might be able to find something in them that would give us a clue as to who he was and where he came from."

She didn't wait for his response as she turned back and continued brushing her hair. "Yes," she said absently. "That's what we have to do. Tomorrow we'll go through his things and see if they give us any answers."

Fowler shook his head in wonderment at her remark. "I almost fear to ask this question. But how do *we* plan to get his saddlebags?"

When she turned her sparkling green eyes on him, he was sure he didn't want to know the answer to his question.

"Simple. Tomorrow I'll just ride into town and claim them," she said matter-of-factly.

"Nichole, I hate to tell you this, but it's not exactly finders keepers when you shoot a man."

"I know that, silly. But, as his next of kin, I'd have a right to claim my 'brother's' belongings."

"But you're not his sister, you don't even know his name!"

"I know that and you know that, but *they* don't know that. Besides, they'll be so glad to have someone to pay for the burying, they won't ask too many questions. Trust me. I'll be back before you know it," she said confidently.

Fowler rolled his eyes skyward. "Trust her, she says. Lady, I'm beginning to think that you've been lacing your corsets too tight and it's addled your brain. Didn't it ever occur to you that they'll recognize you the minute you ride into town?"

"No, they won't. They haven't seen *me*. They saw

you and a young man. Don't worry. I know exactly what I'm doing, you'll see. Right now, it's late and I'm going to sleep. We have a lot to do tomorrow," she said as she wrapped herself up in her blanket.

"It's not going to work, I tell you," Fowler admonished as he, too, wrapped his blanket around him.

"Yes, it will."

When Nichole stepped out from behind the bushes, Fowler couldn't believe his eyes. Almost like magic, she had turned from a skinny young man into a beautiful woman.

She was wearing a blue calico dress that hugged her tiny waist and she'd left her hair loose to dance about her shoulders. She did, indeed, look like someone's sister. However, Fowler was glad she wasn't *his* sister because the thoughts he was having were definitely not brotherly.

"It's a bit wrinkled but it'll have to do," she said nervously. He was looking at her in that predatory manner again. "Will you stop looking at me like that? It makes me nervous," she scolded.

"What's wrong with the way I'm looking at you? You look . . . beautiful," he replied honestly.

"Thank you, I think. But you're still looking at me like a cat fixing to pounce on a saucer of milk."

"Meow. Meow," he teased as he stalked toward her.

"Now, cut that out," she warned as she backed into a tree.

He reached out and pulled her to him. He looked deep into her eyes before slanting his mouth over hers. He kissed her like a man starved for life-giving

47

nourishment, who had just stumbled upon a table set for Sunday dinner. He wanted to feast until his hunger was appeased.

Nichole felt the heat radiating from his body. When he kissed her and caressed her, it was almost more than she could stand. She felt as if her legs had turned to water. If he hadn't been holding her up, she was sure she would have melted into a puddle at his feet.

Fowler suddenly stepped back from her as he remembered why she was dressed as she was. He still didn't like this crazy idea of hers but he hadn't been able to talk her out of it.

"Promise me that you will be careful," he pleaded as he helped her mount her horse.

"I'll be careful. Will you quit worrying? Nothing is going to happen, I tell you," she insisted confidently.

"If you aren't back in two hours, I'm coming after you. And, if any one acts the least bit suspicious, you get on that horse and get the hell out of there, do you understand me?"

She nodded her head. "I promise, I won't take any more chances than I have to." She hurriedly reined Cocoa around and left before he had time to comprehend her words.

She smiled when she heard him holler at her but she didn't stop.

Have to? "Nichole, you little brat, you come back here!" he bellowed.

Nichole stopped in front of The Emporium. Since the town was too small to have a marshal, she wasn't sure where they would have taken the body. But she was betting on the fact that the storekeeper would know everything going on in town. After dismounting, she looped Cocoa's reins around the hitching post and entered the building.

She was relieved to see that she was the only person in the store. She put on her best little-girl-lost look and approached the balding little man behind the counter.

He glanced up at the young girl and smiled. "Yes ma'am. What can I get for you today?" he said politely.

She chewed on her bottom lip as if really worried about something. "Well, I'm not sure if you can help me. I think I may be lost." She paused to look around anxiously. "You see, I came to get my brother but I can't seem to find him any place."

He looked at her in puzzlement.

She hurried on before he could begin asking questions. "We camped not too far outside town here. We're on our way to Waco, to take our daddy to the clinic. My brother came in yesterday to get supplies but he didn't come back yet and Daddy is getting worse." She managed to make big tears run down her cheeks when she turned her big green eyes toward him.

"Now, now, little lady," the shopkeeper crooned as he walked around the counter to comfort the distraught young girl. "He probably just lost track of the time. I'll help you find him." The kindly man patted her on the back. "You just tell me what he looks like and we'll see if we can't find that rascal."

Nichole described the man Fowler had shot the day before, right down to the clothes he was wearing. Before she had finished, she could tell that the man had already begun to make the connection. When she finished, she turned her pitiful look on him again.

"Have you seen my brother? This is the only store in town, isn't it?" she questioned innocently.

He shook his head sadly, not wanting to be the one to break the bad news to the poor child. Sometimes life just wasn't fair. A sick daddy and now a dead brother.

"Ma'am, maybe you better sit down. I'm afraid I have some bad news for you."

"What . . . what do you mean? He's not hurt or . . . sick, too, is he?"

"Well, ah . . . ma'am. It's like this. He . . . ah . . . he's dead, ma'am. I'm sorry."

"Dead? Oh, no, that just can't be," she wailed. "What—what happened?"

"Well, you see, he, ah, got kind of drunk, I guess. And he pulled a gun on another man, but the other man was faster. And, when it was all over, your brother was dead. Everything happened kind of fast-like, but it was a fair fight," he hastened to add.

"Oh, no!" she wailed. After crying what she figured was a sufficient time, she dabbed at her eyes as she made a show of pulling herself together. "Where is he? He ought to have a decent burial."

The storekeeper looked apologetically at her before answering. "We thought he was just a drifter. Didn't expect no family to claim his body, ma'am. So Blacky done went ahead and buried him this morning."

"Blacky?"

"Oh, he's the blacksmith, ma'am. Everybody 'round here just calls him, Blacky."

She nodded as she dabbed at her eyes again and delicately blew her dripping nose. "I see. Where do I find Mr. Blacky? I need to pay him for taking care of things and . . ." She hesitated as if it pained her to continue. "And I guess I should take my brother's horse and . . . things back to Daddy."

Nichole hadn't counted on the storekeeper being so nice. She felt guilty when he insisted on personally going with her to collect her "brother's" stuff. While she was paying Blacky, the storekeeper saddled the horse and attached her "brother's" saddlebags to it.

He kindly offered to help her get back to their camp and take a look at her daddy.

She smiled gratefully at him but she was thinking to herself that she wished he'd stop being so nice. She already felt guilty for all the lies she'd had to tell him.

"Well, I do appreciate your offer, but Daddy's fever has been so high and then those spots showed up this morning . . ." She hesitated to let her words sink in before continuing. "You don't think it's anything contagious, do you?"

The two men visibly paled and took a step backward. Fever? Spots?

The shopkeeper was kind but he wasn't *that* kind. "Well, if you think you can manage, I really should get back to the store. I hate to leave it unattended too long, you know, people needing to buy stuff all the time," he stammered.

She thanked both men and assured them that she could handle everything before heading out of town, trying not to act as relieved as she felt.

Nichole met Fowler halfway between town and the place they had camped the night before. She had tried to hurry but she didn't want to appear too anxious and cause them to get suspicious.

Fowler's heart had been beating in double time

since she had ridden out of his sight. His relief upon seeing her gave way to a momentary flash of anger. "Damn high time you got back," he scolded mildly.

He looked at her admiringly. "I'll be damned!" he exclaimed. "You did it! You really pulled it off. I can hardly believe it." He shook his head in amazement. "You're something else, lady. You know that?"

She smiled at him, basking in his praise. "I didn't realize I was such a good actress. I surprised myself," she admitted.

"Well, tell me what happened, dammit. I've been in agony for two hours!"

"Let's find a place where I can change clothes and I'll tell you while you go through this stuff and see if there's anything that will help us."

After changing back into her breeches, she stepped from behind the bushes in time to see Fowler jump to his feet, holding a piece of paper in his hand. She could tell by the look on his face that it was important.

"What is it? What did you find?"

Fowler looked up at her.

"What? Let me see!"

He silently handed the paper to her.

She read it intently, before raising her eyes to meet his. The color drained from her face. "Oh my God!"

Chapter Four

"Is he still alive, *mi hija?*" A worried frown marred the countenance of the dignified woman.

"*Si, madre.* He is a very strong *hombre.*" The young girl looked at the man lying on the bed with a look of awe. "Is he not the most handsome man you have ever seen, Mother?" she questioned in an almost reverent tone.

The woman tried to look at the young man through her daughter's eyes. Even near death, his head and chest swathed in bandages, his features as white as the sheet on which he lay except for the blackish bruise on his forehead, she had to admit that, yes, he was indeed quite a handsome man.

"*Si, mi hija,* he is a very handsome man," she agreed. "I believe that you should go eat some lunch now. One of the servants can stay with him. It is not proper for a young, unmarried girl to be alone in a man's bedroom," she admonished, again. "I have told you this before. I do not approve and I'm certain that your father will most surely disapprove of your behavior, Carmencita.

"When he returns to the villa in three days time, he will tell us what we should do about this *hombre*. Until that time, we will do what we can to make him comfortable and pray for his recovery." Again, she looked at the young man and sadly shook her head.

She felt that it was hopeless to expect him to recover. When the *vaqueros* had brought him to the hacienda three days ago, he was unconscious. He had lost a lot of blood and had a high fever and infection from the two bullets in his back.

She and *Tia* Rosie had managed to dig the lead balls out and bring down his fever. They had cleaned and dressed a wound on the side of his head that looked as if he had been grazed by a bullet there, too. The bruise on his forehead was probably where he had hit his head when he fell from his horse. The swelling had gone down some, but it was still a nasty-looking bruise.

For three days and nights, she, *Tia* Rosie or one of the servants had forced broth between his lips every half-hour in the hopes of fighting off dehydration and helping him to survive. In all that time, even while *Tia* Rosie probed for the bullets, not a sound had escaped his lips.

The only sign that he was still alive was the rhythmic rise and fall of his chest.

She had tried to keep her impressionable daughter away from the man to no avail. A mother's instinct told her that her daughter's Spanish blood had begun to flow hot through her veins.

Consuela well remembered those first exciting emotions when the handsome young *vaqueros* began to look at a young girl with a different eye. Hadn't she fallen in love and married Miguel when she was no older than Carmencita? And, Ricardo, her son, was born just three days before her seventeenth birthday.

Could she expect less from a daughter born of her and Miguel's blood? Of course not. Now she understood why her *duenna's* hair had turned gray at such an early age!

At sixteen, Carmencita was a beauty in her mother's image. Her smooth olive complexion made her dark brown eyes look almost black. Even with her coal-black hair braided and coiled on top of her head, she still barely passed five foot, two inches tall. She was a petite bundle of curiosity and energy.

Carmencita had finally worn her mother's patience down. Consuela had reluctantly given her daughter permission to sit with the unconscious young man on this the fourth day. She knew that her optimistic daughter wanted to be a part of his recovery, but she had not counted on Carmencita becoming so enamored with the stranger. This caused her some alarm.

They knew nothing at all about him. Not even who he was. The *vaqueros* had found only him, no horse, no identification, nothing to give them the slightest clue as to who he was or where he came from. He could be a *bandido*, running from the law or a *caballero* set upon, robbed, shot, and left to die. Until he could tell them, he remained a mystery.

Consuela sighed as she picked up the cup to spoon a little liquid into his mouth. She would be very glad when Miguel returned to the hacienda.

* * *

Another night and day passed before the man began to moan and move about. For the first time since he was brought to the villa, they began to have some real hope that he would survive his injuries.

In the wee hours of the morning on the sixth day, Nick opened his eyes and looked about him.

His vision was blurry and his head hurt like hell! His body felt like someone had used it for a punching bag, and he was so weak he could barely lift his hand to rub his burning eyes.

This was the worst hang-over he'd ever had in his entire life! Strange, he didn't remember getting drunk.

He tried to lift his head to look around him, but the room immediately began to spin before his eyes. He closed his eyes tightly, waiting for the dizziness to pass. When he regained his equilibrium, he slowly moved his head to the side to look at his surroundings.

He didn't recognize anything in the room. Slowly, his eyes traveled the unfamiliar area. He saw a middle-aged woman nodding in a chair across the room. He didn't recognize her. Why was she in his room, anyway?

Then his vision fell upon the young woman sitting by his bed. Her head was resting against the side of the chair, and she seemed to be sound asleep.

His eyes traveled the length of her body. Lord, she was beautiful, but who was she? And, more important, why couldn't he remember where he was?

He raised his hand to rub at his eyes again, this time his hand coming into contact with what felt like a bandage. He tentatively felt his head. A moan escaped his lips when his fingers touched his wound.

Carmencita immediately came awake at the slight sound. "*Señor*, please you must not move. You have been badly hurt. What can I get for you?" she asked in her softly accented voice.

"Wa . . . ter," he managed to croak. His throat felt like sandpaper rubbing together. "Water, please."

"Don't try to drink too fast," she cautioned as she held the glass to his lips.

He slowly sipped the cool liquid, feeling it soothe his scratchy throat. When he lay back, he looked into the most beautiful brown eyes he had ever seen.

"Where am I?"

"Lupe, go get Mama, quickly!" she said to the other woman in the room before turning back to him.

"Shhh, *señor*, you must be still. You might cause your wounds to start bleeding again."

He followed her glance to his chest and left shoulder. Until that moment he had not realized that half his body was wrapped in bandages and throbbing painfully in time with his heartbeat. It was almost as if by acknowledging the wounds they had begun to pain him greatly.

"What happened? Where . . ."

An elegant-looking woman swept into the room, followed closely by an older woman carrying a glass of cloudy liquid.

Without preamble, the older woman raised his head for him to drink whatever was in the glass.

"This will ease your pain, *señor*," the regal-looking woman assured him.

Nick looked from her to the younger woman. It was obvious that he was seeing mother and daughter. But who the hell were these people?

As if reading his mind, the mother said, "You are at

57

Villa de Cardona. I am Consuela Maria de Cardona and this is my daughter, Carmencita, and this is my Aunt Rosie," she stated, motioning to the older woman who had given him the painkiller.

"Now, you must sleep, *señor*. We will talk when you are feeling better."

Except for the excruciating pain in the upper half of his body assuring him that he was still among the living, he would have thought he had died and gone to heaven with this roomful of beautiful women fluttering about him, trying to make him more comfortable.

The last thing his mind registered before slipping into oblivion was the sweet fragrance of the beautiful girl with the braided hair atop her head, bending over him as she straightened the sheet.

When Nick awoke later in the day, it was to see the aunt sitting by his bedside instead of the beautiful young girl with the braided hair of whom he had been dreaming.

"How do you feel now, *señor*? Do you think you could take some solid nourishment?"

"I feel like I haven't eaten in a week and my stomach is sticking to my backbone to be quite truthful, *señora*," he laughed. "How long have I been here?"

Aunt Rosie laughed. "You probably aren't far from the truth. One of the *vaqueros* found you half-dead and brought you here six days ago. He said it looked like you had been shot one, maybe two, days before. I will tell Cook to fix you some eggs and toast. After you have eaten, we will talk." She helped him to sit up and propped some pillows behind him.

Eight days! He had lost eight days of his life! He shook his head as if to recapture those lost days. How could that have happened? Who had shot him and—why? The harder he tried to remember, the more his head hurt. He clutched his head in his hands in an effort to ease the pain.

This was the way Carmencita found him when she peeked into his room.

"*Señor?* Do you need something for the pain? Should I go get Mama or *Tía* Rosie for you?" She was still standing at the door, almost as if she were shy about entering the room.

It was the beautiful girl with the braided hair. He had been half-afraid that he had only dreamed her, that she hadn't been real at all. But there she stood, even more beautiful than in his dreams.

"I was afraid I had only dreamed you," he admitted.

"Pardon?"

"Never mind. Please, come sit and talk with me. I can't remember your name," he apologized. "I'm sorry. There seems to be a lot that I don't remember. Maybe you can fill in some of the blank spots."

Carmencita looked around hesitantly before taking the chair by his bed. When he was unconscious, it had not bothered her to be in his room, but now she felt a funny kind of nervousness. Maybe it was because she knew her mother would not approve of her actions.

"Only for a few minutes, *señor*. It is not proper for me to be here. Mama and *Tía* Rosie will fuss at me if they find me here again," she admitted candidly.

"Why?"

She looked at him, her eyes wide in astonishment. "Well . . . because you are a stranger. And this is your bedroom, and I am an unmarried young girl, and . . ." She hesitated as she recited all the reasons she had been given for why it was not proper for her to be in his room.

He smiled at her frankness, even though it sounded like she was repeating her lessons. "And?" He arched one eyebrow in question.

She felt the heat travel up her neck and into her face. She knew that he was naked beneath the sheet covering his body. "You do not have any . . . I mean . . . you are not properly attired," she blurted in spite of her embarrassment.

He laughed out loud. "Well, I'm afraid I can't do anything about your marital status or my lack of proper attire. But we can remedy the stranger status if you will tell me your name again. And this time I promise not to forget it when I fall asleep," he teased.

The smile she turned on him sent his heart ricocheting around his rib cage.

"My name is Carmencita Maria Pilar de Cardona," she stated proudly.

"Good heavens! Your name is longer than you are tall," he exclaimed. "How about if I just call you Carmen for short?"

She grinned impishly. "That's what Daddy and Ricky call me, unless I'm in trouble."

Ricky? Who was Ricky? Her boyfriend, maybe? He didn't take the time to wonder why that thought bothered him.

"Who's Ricky?"

"Ricardo. He is my older brother. He hates it when

I call him Ricky in front of people. He says that is a little boy's name and he is *muy* big." She shrugged her shoulders carelessly. "But I still call him that anyway," she admitted mischievously. "Now, for us not to be strangers, you must tell me your name."

"Well, Carmen, my name is . . ."

She waited expectantly for him to finish his sentence. "Yes?"

"My name is . . ." He grabbed his head with both hands as the pain seemed to pierce his brain. "Ohhh," he moaned.

Carmen jumped to her feet in alarm. "Please, *señor!* What is it? What is the matter?"

Consuela entered the room with a tray of food just in time to hear his agonized confession.

He looked pleadingly from one to the other. "I can't remember my name. I don't *know* who I am!"

Miguel Reynaldo de Cardona swirled the remaining brandy in his glass as he thoughtfully digested what his wife had told him.

"And his memory still has not returned today?"

She shook her head. "No. I tried to assure him yesterday that when his head wound healed, he would regain his memory. I hope I have not given him false hope."

She snuggled closer to her husband. "He is so young and afraid. He seems to be an educated man. He has good manners, he's very polite and respectful. I believe that he comes from a good family." She sighed. "His people must be terribly worried about him. Yet how can we let them know that he is safe if we don't know who he is?"

Miguel threw back the last of his brandy before enfolding his lovely wife in his arms.

"I will speak with him tomorrow. Right now, *querida*, I want only to hold you in my arms and make passionate love to you. It has been a very long week away from you, *mi amora*."

"Yes, my husband, I too have missed you very much. I counted the days until your return," she answered breathlessly.

Carmen took a deep breath before entering Nick's room with a breakfast tray.

This *hombre* disturbed her greatly. When she was in his presence, her stomach fluttered like it was filled with butterflies. He had only to look at her with those magnificent green eyes for her heart to pound as if she had been riding with the wind. A secret part of her turned warm and moist and throbbed when he smiled at her.

Was this the way Mama felt when she looked at Papa? she wondered.

"Good morning," she said as she glided into the room. "Did you sleep well?"

Nick looked at her with yearning. She was so beautiful, her face so open and fresh it seemed to glow like the morning sun.

"Good morning, sunshine." He watched as her rosy glow seemed to deepen. "You look especially beautiful this morning. Is there any special reason for it?" he questioned as he helped her to settle the tray across his lap.

"Yes, my papa came home last night. Everyone misses him when he is away, especially Mama. They love each other so. Can you not feel the difference in the *casa* this morning?" She wasn't about to admit that *her* rosy glow was caused by him.

A strange look came over his face. He laid the fork back on the plate, leaving his food untouched.

Had she said something wrong? Why was he frowning? Was he in pain again?

"What is the matter? Do you not like the food? I can ask Cook to fix something different if you wish. Do you need *Tia* Rosie to give you something for pain?"

For just an instant it seemed as if something was trying to surface from deep within his memory. It was more a feeling than a solid thought. He sensed that his family was also a close and loving family.

Her question brought him back to the present. "No. The eggs are fine. I just thought for a second that I was remembering something. But it wouldn't surface," he said dejectedly as he picked up the fork and began to eat.

"When will I meet your father?" he asked to change the subject. He could tell by the look on her face that she was as disappointed as he that the memory had not surfaced. He wanted to see her twinkling eyes and happy glow again.

"Oh, it will be many hours before they leave their room. They have been separated for too many . . ." As her words suddenly trailed off, her face reddened in embarrassment.

She moaned silently. She had not meant to imply what she had. Her too-quick tongue had gotten her in a mess, as usual.

As the meaning of her words settled in, and the

becoming blush on her face left no doubt of their meaning, Nick couldn't control the laughter that bubbled up from deep within his chest.

"You're as bad as Nolie. I swear her tongue is forever getting ahead of her brain." He laughed.

His laughter suddenly died at the shocked look on her face. He had only been teasing her. He hadn't intended to insult her.

"*Señor*, you said 'Nolie,'" she said tremulously. "Who is Nolie? Is she perhaps your mother or sister or . . ." She watched his face intently as he tried to remember. She didn't want to but she had to finish her question. "Or your *novia?*" *Please don't let him answer yes to the last*, she silently prayed.

"Nolie? Nolie? She must be someone important to me, but who? Who is Nolie?" he agonized. "Why can't I remember?" Frustration wrinkled his forehead with a frown.

Nick was trying so hard to remember that he didn't notice Carman's crestfallen face. "Do not worry, *señor*. Mama says it will come back to you with time."

She tried not to sound as sad as she felt. She couldn't abide the thought that this woman might be his sweetheart, or maybe even his wife. She had fallen in love with him even before he had ever regained consciousness and that love had grown with each passing day. And now to think that he might already belong to someone else and could never belong to her made her heart ache painfully.

For the first time since he had discovered that his memory was gone, Nick felt a ray of hope. He had been afraid to believe *Dona* Consuela's reassurances. But, surely she must be right since he had remembered *something*, even if he couldn't remember why the name was important to him. At least it was a beginning.

"Carmen, do you think you could find my clothes for me? I would prefer to meet your father dressed rather than in bed." He even felt better. That small beginning gave his spirits a tremendous lift.

"Your boots, belt, and things that you had in your pockets are over there." She motioned toward a dresser. "But your clothing was beyond repair. My brother, Ricky, is about your size. I will have one of the servants bring you something of his to wear." She picked up the breakfast tray and left without looking back. She didn't want him to see the tears that she could no longer hold back.

Tia Rosie met her in the hallway that led to the kitchen.

"What is it, little one? Is the *hombre* worse?"

She shook her head negatively. "No, *Tia* Rosie. He seems to be getting better each day."

Her great-niece's attitude puzzled her. "Then why do you look so sad? Did he say or do something to insult you?" she questioned.

Carmencita had never been taught to be deceptive or coy, and she wasn't now.

"Oh, *Tia* Rosie. He remembered a name. A woman's name. But he cannot remember what she is to him. I am so afraid that she might be his fiancée or maybe even his wife. I could not stand that, if it should be true." She turned woeful brown eyes on her aunt. "I love him very much," she admitted honestly.

Carmencita's confession did not surprise her. She

had seen that same look on her niece's face when Consuela had first meet Miguel and his answering look. She had also seen it on the stranger's face when he looked at Carmencita. It was the look of love. True love.

"Now, *nina*, remember what I have always told you. Don't go looking for trouble. If your love is meant to be, it will be. If not, there is nothing you can do to change fate. Was it not fate that brought the stranger to our *casa?*"

"*Sí, Tia* Rosie."

"Then have a little faith, Carmencita. And do not be sad if the stranger remembers things that are unpleasant for you to know. He must fully regain his memory to continue his life in peace, little one."

"I know and I will try not to let him know that I am saddened," she promised.

Knowing her great-niece as she did, she doubted that would be possible.

Nick sat in a chair in front of the window that overlooked a garden. He was so exhausted from the simple task of dressing that he hardly noticed the beauty of the spring day or that some of the flowers were beginning to bloom.

He had lost some weight, but taking that into consideration, Ricardo's clothes fit him fairly well.

He had protested loudly but to no avail when Aunt Rosie had insisted on helping him dress. Helping him get into the shirt was one thing, but he had insisted that he could put his pants on without any help, thank you very much! And she had insisted right back that he would open his wounds if he tried.

It had turned into a battle of wits. However, Aunt Rosie held the trump card—the breeches. The old woman had declared that she had seen more bare bottoms in her days of healing than he could ever count. Either she helped or no breeches! She helped.

When *Don* Miguel walked into the young man's room, he motioned for him to stay in his chair. It was obvious from the man's pallor that he was both weak and in pain.

"Please, *señor*, keep your chair. There is no need to stand on formality when you have been so ill."

He walked over and shook hands with Nick. "I am Miguel Reynaldo de Cardona, at your service."

Nick quickly took in the features of the very dignified man. He was just under six feet tall and solidly built. The graying hair at his temples gave him a very distinguished appearance.

Nick gave him a rueful grin. "I'm sorry I can't properly introduce myself, sir. But I'm sure you've been told that I seem to have misplaced a part of me."

Even though the young man was trying to take it in stride, Miguel knew that he must be worried, as anyone would be in the same situation.

"I'm sure everything will come back to you as you heal. My daughter tells me that you have already remembered someone's name. That is a start, *señor*." He tried to reassure Nick.

Nick rubbed his hand over his eyes before replying, "Maybe so, sir. But, it's damned frustrating not knowing who you are or what you are."

"I can imagine it would be. But, if it would ease your mind any, I can tell you a few things about

yourself—from my own observations, you understand."

Nick looked at him skeptically. "What can you tell
me after such a brief meeting?"

Miguel settled himself on the window ledge, half
sitting with one leg crossed over the other. He
glanced out the window briefly before replying.

"I pride myself on being a good judge of character.
I can tell you come from a good background by the
way you conduct yourself. Your manners are flawless.
You carry yourself like a man sure of himself and his
abilities. You look me directly in the eyes when
talking; that indicates confidence and integrity.

"You either come from a wealthy family or you
have wealth of your own. This I can tell from the
expensive boots and gun belt you possess. And,
finally, you are obviously very well educated."

"How can you know that? About my education, I
mean?" he questioned.

Miguel laughed. "Because, *señor*, you are a *gringo*,
yet from the time I entered this room, you have been
conversing with me in flawless Spanish, not English.
That is not something the average cowboy picks up on
his own."

"Well, I'll be damned!" Nick exclaimed,
flabbergasted that he had been unaware that he was
speaking Spanish.

Miguel laughed. "Well, let's hope not. Although, we
men do seem to find ourselves in that predicament
from time to time. Right now, I would say that you
should consider resting awhile. Your eyes tell me that
you are in great pain."

Nick nodded his head affirmatively. "I do feel like
I've been gunshot a couple of times."

"Shall I have *Tia* Rosie bring you a mild painkiller, or—"

"No!" Nick interrupted quickly. "I mean, no, sir. I think I can handle the pain."

Miguel smiled a knowing smile. The whole *casa* had heard the rather loud debate over who was going to put his breeches on him. He knew from his own experience with his wife's aunt, who had won the debate.

"I understand completely. Perhaps you would enjoy a glass of good Kentucky bourbon, instead."

"Thank you, sir. I would, indeed, prefer a glass of bourbon."

"If you think you can manage on your own, I will give you a few minutes to make yourself comfortable before I have your drink brought to you."

Nick smiled at the man's consideration. "Thank you, sir. I think I can handle things okay."

Chapter Five

Nichole started to tremble as the significance of the paper that she held in her hand hit her. When her eyes met his, she knew that Fowler suspected the same thing that she did.

Her hand was shaking as she handed the paper back to him. Her voice was hardly more than a whisper. "Somebody found out that he's a Texas Ranger. They know who Nick is. Oh my God, Fowler, he walked into a trap!"

Fowler could tell by the rising pitch of her voice that she was verging on hysteria. He pulled her into his arms. His gut feeling told him that she was right, but he couldn't let her fall apart now. There was still a remote chance that the note had not yet reached Linc Travis.

"Honey, don't go to pieces on me now. Listen to

me. Listen to me." He gently shook her to get her attention. "There's still a possibility that this note has not reached Linc yet. This man might have been on his way to deliver it to him."

It was a small ray of hope, a very small ray. But Nichole was a fighter, and even the tiniest bit of hope was enough for her to latch onto.

She took a slow, deep breath to calm her nerves. "I hope you're right." She reached for the paper again. "Let's see if we can figure out who any of these people are."

She read the note out loud as they tried to put the pieces together.

"It's dated February 10, 1869. That's about ten days before Nick failed to meet his contact, isn't it?" She looked to Fowler for his conformation.

"Yes."

She continued reading the note. "'John, new man is not working out. I have it on good authority that he is one of *T.R.'s* men. See to it that he is removed at once.' And, it's signed with the initials, *T.S.* This note added at the bottom is in a different handwriting, it probably was written by this 'John' person. It says, '*L.*, take care of this.' And it's signed *J.N.*"

She looked at Fowler as he paced. His left arm crossed his chest and supported his right arm as he rubbed the hairs on his chin between his index finger and his thumb.

"I think we can safely assume that *T.R.* means 'Texas Rangers,' and, that the *L* means 'Linc,' and *J.N.* is 'John *N*' somebody." He stopped his pacing to look at Nichole. "The question is, John *who*, and, who is *T.S.*?"

Nichole wracked her brain, trying desperately to think of a John whose last name started with an *N*. She finally threw her hands up in despair.

"The only John I can think of whose last name starts with an *N*, is John North. But he couldn't possibly have anything to do with an outlaw like Linc Travis."

Fowler halted. "Why not? What do you know about him?"

"Not much, really. I met him and his son at the last cattle-drive party we had at our ranch before I went back East to finishing school. He owns a big spread in Falls County, and I think it extends over into Bell County. But, Fowler, he's a very rich man. What possible motive could he have for getting mixed up with someone like Linc Travis?"

"The two most common reasons in the world, greed and power. Some *very rich* men get an obsession with the power that money gives them. At this point, we're not ruling anyone out. Now, what about *T.S.?* Do those initials ring any bells?"

She shook her head slowly in deliberation. "No, I can't think of anyone around here with those initials."

Fowler squatted down on his haunches to finish going through the saddlebags. "Let's see if there is anything else in here that might give us a clue."

He dumped the remaining contents on the ground, and sifted through them. They were the usual things one would expect to find in a saddlebag. A tinderbox containing flint, steel, and a few scraps of tinder, some store-bought matches, a bag of tobacco and cigarette papers, jerky, a tin cup and plate and a half-empty whiskey bottle. The other bag contained only a change of clothes, shaving soap, mug, brush, a razor, and some spare ammunition.

"Nothing, dammit! Not a blasted thing to give a hint as to who the hell he was or where he was coming from or going to." Fowler stood up and gave the bags a kick, venting some of his disgust and frustration. "Dammit!"

Nichole was about to stand up when a slight flutter of white caught the corner of her eye.

"Fowler! Look!" She pulled a well-worn envelope out of one of the bags. "This must have been stuck to the bottom of that bag and your kick loosened it," she exclaimed excitedly as she pulled the letter out of the envelope.

She quickly scanned the letter. "It's a letter from his mother," she said incredulously.

Her look of surprise caused Fowler to chuckle. "Well, don't look so surprised. Even outlaws have mothers, I suppose. Is there anything in it that might be useful?"

"No." She shook her head as she read. "Just the usual stuff. She says she misses him. Everyone's fine and they hope to see him soon. It doesn't have a date on it." Her disappointment showed in her voice.

She folded the letter and started to put it back into the envelope. "The address! Look at the address, Fowler." She held the envelope out to him.

"Robert Baker, General Delivery, Evadne, Texas! This may be the break we need!" he exclaimed. "There are some caverns not too far from Evadne that have long been a hide-out for various gangs of Indians and outlaws. The Rangers have a hard time keeping them cleaned out because there are so many places to hide. If a person doesn't know what he's doing, he could get lost in the caverns and never find his way out again."

Nichole could hardly contain herself. "At least it's a place to start. We're about seventy miles or so from Evadne. We can be there in two days time. Come on, let's go."

Fowler grabbed her arm as she whirled around and headed toward the spot where they had left their horses to graze.

"Just hold on a minute. Before you go off half-cocked, let me remind you that you promised that you would do exactly as I told you to, remember?

"Yes, I remember. But if you're thinking that you can send me home, forget it! I told you I'm going to find my brother with or without your help, Fowler Barclay," she declared stubbornly.

"Would that I could send you home. But I know that's too much to hope for. However, I don't want a repeat of what happened in that saloon in Aerl Station. You scared ten years off my life with that stunt. Now you promise me that you won't go parading around as the Brazos Kid when we get to Evadne or else I'm going to hog-tie you to that tree and leave you here, safe and sound," he threatened.

From his tone of voice and determined look, she knew she had better reassure him that she'd comport herself according to his rules. That tree didn't look like a very comfortable place to find one's self attached to.

"I promise, cross my heart, that I will follow your orders to the letter. I will be so agreeable and amiable that you won't even know I'm here," she said in the most refined and proper manner she could manage.

He looked at her suspiciously. "Now why doesn't that ease my mind the least little bit? Your dripping-with-honey attitude doesn't fool me." He narrowed his eyes at her. "I mean it, Nichole! If I have to, I'll haul your little butt to the nearest jail and place you under protective custody," he warned.

She looked at him, wide-eyed and innocent. "I believe you. I promise I'll behave."

Nichole knew that if trouble came their way, she couldn't suddenly turn into a retiring miss, but she wasn't about to let Fowler know that.

"You're up to something. I just *know* you are. I can almost hear that little brain of yours clicking as you conjure up some new scheme. You ride right beside me where I can keep an eye on you, young lady," he admonished sternly.

Deep in the caverns northwest of Austin, a motley group of men huddled around a campfire.

Their leader, a tall, rangy man in his late thirties was listening intently as the short, half-breed Mexican relayed his story.

By the time he finished, Linc Travis's hawk-faced features were dark with anger. His beady brown eyes swept over the group of misfits lounging near the fire until they came to rest on a man known only as Red.

"You're positive it was the Brazos Kid?" he asked, never taking his eyes off the red-haired man.

"*Sí*, there was no mistake about it. It was him, all right. I came on to tell you, and Robert stayed there to make sure he was dead this time."

"Go get something to eat," he ordered tersely.

"Yes, sir, boss." The half-breed hurried away. The boss's short-fused temper was well known among the men.

Linc Travis was fit to be tied! Nothing made him madder quicker than one of the men not following his orders.

"Red, get over here!" he bellowed, his voice echoing deep into the caverns.

Red jumped to his feet. "Yes, sir, boss." He didn't know why Linc's anger was directed at him, but he figured it must have something to do with the Mexican's hasty return to camp. He shot the man a glance but the Mexican wouldn't look at him.

Linc lashed his right fist out and caught the shorter man square in the face, knocking him flat on his back before he knew what had hit him.

Red got up spitting blood and feeling for loose teeth. "What the hell!" he exclaimed, shaking his head as if to clear the ringing in his ears.

Linc drew back his fist and hit him, knocking him to the ground again.

This time Red stayed on the ground. His nose was bleeding, and he knew it was broken. He'd heard it snap with the second blow. His lip was split and beginning to swell. So was his left eye.

"You sorry son of a bitch! When I order you to kill someone, I expect you to make *sure* he's dead, you bastard!" Linc roared at the man still lying on the ground.

"He *was* dead! I swear it. Hell, I shot him three times in the back and kicked his body into a dry gulch. Ain't no way in hell he coulda survived," Red alibied.

"Oh, yeah? Then how do you explain the fact that Mex and Robert saw him, not only alive and healthy, but in a saloon in Aerl drinking beer yesterday?"

A cold chill encased Red's body. Brazos couldn't be alive! He knew he'd hit him at least twice in the back. He saw the bleeding wounds, and Brazos hadn't moaned or nothing when he'd kicked him into the gulch.

Linc's hawkish features were grotesquely twisted in anger. "What did ya do, Red? Sell us out to the Rangers? Huh?" His voice was like a deadly calm before the storm.

Red began to sweat profusely. He knew his life wasn't worth a plug nickel unless he could convince Linc that he wasn't a traitor. "No, Linc, honest. You . . . you know I'd never sell out the gang. I'm being framed. It's a setup, I swear! Ya gonna take that half-breed's word against mine? He's lying, I tell ya! Brazos is dead. Ya gotta believe me," he groveled as he inched backward from the glowering leader.

Red's eyes widened in disbelief as he saw Linc's hand move to his gun. "Nooo," he whimpered as the single gunshot rang out. His body jerked with the impact of the bullet, and his eyes glazed over as he stared sightlessly at the ceiling of the cave.

"Get the scum outta here," Linc ordered to no one in particular.

He walked over to the coffeepot sitting on the edge of the fire, poured a steaming cup of the black liquid, and casually sat down to roll a smoke.

Chapter Six

At the first glimpse of buildings in the distance, Nichole's weariness began to subside. Located on the fringe of the hill country, Evadne appeared to be a prospering town. Why this surprised her she wasn't sure. Perhaps because she knew the town was only about fourteen miles from the Outlaw Caverns, she'd been expecting a small, inconspicuous village.

Nichole eagerly looked forward to the hot bath awaiting her when they reached Evadne. After five days of washing from a canteen or in a cold stream, it would feel like pure heaven to have a steamy, hot tub to soak away all the kinks in her body resulting from sleeping on the hard ground.

Fowler looked at the expression on her face. He couldn't imagine what had put such a look of pleasure on her pretty features. He was half-afraid to ask.

But being the glutton for punishment that he was, he asked anyway.

"Dare I ask what is the reason for that exquisite expression?"

She smiled like a child thinking about Christmas. "I was just thinking how good that hot water is going to feel when I sink all the way up to my eyeballs in a deliciously fragrant bubble bath." She sighed longingly. "I must be getting old. Before I went away to finishing school, I use to think it was great to camp out on the range with my father and brothers when it was roundup time."

She was silent a few minutes, obviously in deep thought. "I guess Daddy was right when he sent me back East. I certainly didn't think so at the time. I hated the idea of being away from my family. Especially Nicky and . . . and Grandpa." She turned her head so Fowler couldn't see the tears that had sprung to her eyes.

"Did you ever have the feeling, just before you did something, that it would forever change your life? That things would never be like they were before?" she solemnly questioned.

"I guess everyone feels like that about something from time to time," Fowler admitted. "But you can count on things changing no matter what you do or don't do. Everything changes, Nichole, nothing remains the same forever. That's just part of living, I guess." He glanced over at the pensive young girl. "How long were you away at school?"

"A little over a year. And, except for Cousin Emmalee, I hated every minute of it," she said emphatically.

"Did things really change that much in a year?"

She looked at him, her green eyes sparkling with unshed tears. "It seems as if my whole life is different now. Grandpa died in January. And Nicky . . ." She swallowed the lump that had suddenly formed in her throat. "Nicky's missing. It's strange, but Nicky and I both felt that when I returned, things wouldn't be the same. I wonder now if maybe Grandpa had that same feeling."

She shrugged her shoulders. "I can't explain it now any better than I could then but Nicky understood."

"You're very close to your brother, aren't you?"

Nichole laughed. "You might say that. We're twins. He was born five minutes before me. Grandpa always said that was the reason I stayed in so much trouble, because I was trying to catch up with Nicky since he got a head start on me."

Her laugh was lighthearted, soft and very sexy. It caressed him like cool satin sheets, sending fingers of desire skittering across his skin. When she had expressed her thoughts about a hot bubble bath, his mind had conjured up a definitely different picture than the one she had mentioned.

"No wonder those men thought you were the Brazos Kid!" he exclaimed. "You never told me that he's your twin."

"You never asked," she countered.

"Tell me about the rest of your family." He was grateful for anything that would put the beautiful smile back on her lovely features—even though he was only half listening as she talked about her family—and get his mind off the aching bulge in his breeches.

Spending five days and five *very* long nights in close proximity with such a luscious female and not being able to make love to her was taking a heavy toll on his mind—and his body.

Night after night, he had lain awake long after Nichole had fallen asleep, berating himself for not taking her in his arms and making mad, passionate love to her.

Casual romances had never bothered him before. Why the hell did he have to get an adversity to them now? he asked himself repeatedly. Somehow, he wasn't sure that he wanted to delve too far into the answer to that question.

Mentally shoving the question to the back of his mind again, he concentrated on the buildings lining main street as they rode into Evadne. It boasted a fine hotel, complete with dining room, a half-dozen stores for shopping, two churches and, of course, several saloons and gambling halls.

Entering the hotel, he quickly signed the register while Nichole looked around the lobby.

Fowler knew he'd have an angry woman on his hands when she found out that he had registered them as husband and wife and taken only one suite of rooms. However, given her predilection for getting into trouble, he wasn't about to let her out of his sight!

And, if he got half a chance, he was going to hide those damned breeches of hers, at least until they were ready to ride out of town. Maybe with a skirt and petticoats to slow her down, she wouldn't get into mischief quite so fast! *Ha, fat chance!* he thought to himself.

"Please see that a tub and plenty of hot water is brought to our rooms as quickly as possible," he said to the short, chubby desk clerk.

The man looked at the register as he handed Fowler the keys. "Yes, sir, Mr. Barclay. Right away."

Out of ear shot of the desk clerk, Nichole inquired, "Aren't you afraid to use your real name?"

"Uh-uh. I haven't been in Texas long enough for anyone to recognize my name. And there's only two people in the state who know that I'm the U.S. Marshal assigned to this territory. Well, three counting you."

When he unlocked the door with the number that matched the key in his hand, Nichole preceded him into the room.

The outer room was furnished with a rose brocade couch and side chair and an ornately carved writing desk in front of the only window. Another chair and a delicate table completed the furnishings.

He eyed the couch skeptically. Well, the couch didn't look too uncomfortable. He walked into the bedroom, tossing the pair of saddlebags on the big, soft, comfortable-looking bed. *Don't even think about it,* he scolded himself.

An armoire and a free-standing mirror were the only other items in the bedroom. When he walked back into the sitting room, a plump maid with rosy cheeks was busily lighting a fire in the fireplace and giving orders to two young boys pouring hot water into the oblong brass tub in front of the fire.

When Nichole walked into the bedroom, he whispered to the cheerful maid, "Do you think you could find some of that good-smelling bubble stuff for my

82

wife's bath?" He smiled as he pressed a coin in her palm.

"Oh, yes, sir. I'm sure I can. I'll be back with it before you can blink," she assured him.

With the smile he had turned on her, she would have flown to the moon to do his bidding. She thought his wife was most surely a lucky woman to have him in her bed every night.

After the maid had poured a generous amount of bubble bath into the steaming tub, she gave Fowler a conspiratorial wink before leaving the room.

Fowler chuckled to himself as he walked to the bedroom door and tapped lightly on it.

"Your bath awaits you, my lady. Do you need any help with your buttons?" he teased hopefully.

Nichole stuck her head out the door. "Don't hold your breath. I can manage just fine, thank you. Which room are you in?"

"This one." He waited for the outburst he knew was coming.

"Oh, I'm sorry. I thought this was my room. Okay, which room is mine?"

"This one." Here it comes. He readied himself for the explosion.

She gave him a piercing look. "Fowler Barclay, you better not mean what I think you mean!" she warned.

"Hey, I was born at night but I wasn't born *last* night. So if you think for one minute that I'm about to let you out of my sight, you can just think again, sweetheart. Besides," he rationalized, "we just spent five nights camped together, alone, on the trail. So what's the difference now?"

"You damn well know what the difference is! What

are people going to think about us sleeping together in the same room when we're not married?"

"Well . . ." He looked down at the toes of his boots as he rocked back on his heels.

"You *didn't!*" The silly grin on his face told her that he had. "You . . . you . . ." she sputtered.

"You're repeating yourself, sweetheart. Now, your bubble bath is getting cold. I'll go take care of the horses while you bathe." He tweaked the end of her nose and walked toward the door before she could think of a name to call him. "And, don't worry. I'll sleep just fine on the couch," he called over his shoulder as he left the room.

He chuckled out loud when he heard the brush she had been holding hit the door he had quickly closed behind him.

After leaving the hotel, he arranged for their horses to be stabled at the blacksmith's, and asked that the horses be checked for any necessary shoe repair. Then Fowler started walking back to the hotel.

The red-and-white striped pole immediately caught his eye. He rubbed his scratchy beard as he headed toward the small shop.

When he stepped out of the building awhile later, he rubbed his smooth chin. Nothing like a fresh haircut and shave to make a man feel civilized again, he thought as he walked across the street and entered the hotel lobby.

He cautiously opened the door to their rooms. He didn't know if Nichole's anger had had time enough to cool but he wasn't taking any chances. He didn't particularly care for the idea of having his head used for target practice.

She wasn't in the sitting room. He put his ear

against the bedroom door. Not hearing any sound from the other side, he carefully turned the knob and peeked into the room.

Wrapped in the coverlet, Nichole was sound asleep across the middle of the bed.

He couldn't resist the urge to tiptoe closer. Her thick ebony hair was spread across the bed and softly curled around her face, and he couldn't refrain his errant hand from reaching out to touch the silky locks. Her long black lashes lay like feathered fans against her sun-kissed cheeks, and her cherry lips hinted at a smile even as she slept.

The thought occurred to him that she looked as sweet as an angel in repose. And, just as quickly, he remembered the way her green eyes sparked like emeralds flashing in the sun when she was angry.

Devil or angel? He didn't know. He only knew she was unlike any woman he had ever met in his twenty-eight years. And he had met a lot of them but, surprisingly, he remembered very few. Something told him that he wouldn't soon forget this little spitfire after they went their separate ways.

Nichole sighed in her sleep and turned slightly, seeking a more comfortable position. Her movement exposed one long and, oh-so-soft thigh to his hungry eyes.

It took more will power than he thought he possessed not to reach over and see if the white skin was as soft as he imagined.

He groaned inwardly as he turned and exited the room, closing the door silently behind him.

He hoped the water in the tub was cold enough to cool his ardor. He seriously doubted that it was.

When he finished his bath, he stood in front of the

fire, rubbing his hair dry with a towel. Another towel was wrapped around his waist. He was in deep thought planning how he was going to proceed to locate the Travis gang.

He felt someone staring at him a split second before he heard the startled gasp. He whirled toward the sound, instinctively reaching for the gun that he wasn't wearing.

Nichole stood rooted to the spot. At first she thought a stranger had entered her room. She almost dropped the coverlet that was wrapped around her body when she realized that the man was Fowler with his beard shaved off. She couldn't seem to tear her eyes away from his nearly naked body. He was even more handsome without the beard than she had remembered.

Her eyes took a scenic tour of his ruggedly handsome features. They traveled from the top of his still-wet and slightly curling golden blond hair, past his sapphire-blue eyes, to pause momentarily on the golden hair on his broad chest, noting the stark contrast of the white towel wrapped around his slender waist to his deeply tanned body. Her eyes continued their journey down his long, well-muscled legs to his bare feet.

When her head began to swim, she realized that she had been holding her breath as she unashamedly gawked at his resplendent virile body.

She slowly exhaled as she exclaimed, "Oh, my stars. You are gorgeous!" She didn't realize that she was still staring at his body until she caught a slight stirring behind the towel.

Her face flamed in embarrassment as her mind registered what had caused the movement. Her eyes quickly flew to his face. "I mean . . . that is . . ." One more time her tongue had outdistanced her brain.

"What the hell are you doing standing around naked!" she snapped, trying to slow her breathing and let her heart, which seemed to have plunged to a point somewhere below her navel, go back where it belonged.

Fowler simply laughed as he once more rubbed his wet hair. "I take it that you like what you are devouring with your eyes. Thank you for the compliment. And people usually take off all their clothes when they take a bath. It seems to work better that way," he teased.

She clutched the coverlet more tightly around her body. "I was not devouring you as you so ungentlemanly pointed out," she denied haughtily.

She whirled around prepared to make a grand exit only to get her feet tangled up in the trailing ends of the coverlet, and landed in a heap in the middle of the doorway, hitting her head against the door's frame.

Fowler rushed to her. "Are you all right? Have you hurt yourself?" He knelt beside her and moved her hand away from the spot where she had struck her forehead on the door.

She slapped his hand away. "Do I look like I'm all right? Of course I hurt myself, you clod!"

He ignored her outburst as embarrassment and continued to feel around the rapidly rising bump on her forehead. "Well, at least you didn't break the skin. It will probably turn black and blue, but your hair will hide it," he stated after assuring himself that no real damage had been done.

Fowler noticed that she was trembling as he helped her to her feet.

She clutched the coverlet with a death grip. His naked nearness had turned her insides to jelly. She expected her knees to buckle at any moment.

"You smell good," she said impulsively.

Fowler chuckled. "Do I smell like your bubble bath? If I smell as good as you do, I'm sure to raise some eyebrows when we go down for dinner tonight."

He shook his head disbelievingly, "Lady, you are a paradox. One minute you're calling me a clod and the next minute you're telling me how good I smell. Are you always this consistent, or am I just lucky?" he teased.

"Don't flatter yourself," she said huffily.

She took two steps toward the bedroom and suddenly felt the coverlet yanked out of her shaky grip. "What the hell!" she raged as she managed to grab one end of the cover before it fell to the floor. She tried to cover herself with the corner that she still held as she glared at Fowler's foot, which was planted firmly on one end of the spread.

"You did that on purpose, Fowler Barclay!" she accused, aware that her cotton chemise offered little protection from his hungry eyes.

He had a strange look on his face as he gave her a lopsided grin. "I'm afraid you give me too much credit for such a good idea. However, I do have some good ideas of my own." His voice was husky with desire as he caught the end of the cover that his foot was on and slowly pulled her toward him. His eyes were locked with hers, mesmerizing her to do his bidding.

When she was within his reach, he pulled her against his bare chest, and pressed his lips to hers.

With only the thin coverlet between them, their bodies seemed to ignite.

His hand moved down her back to cup gently and then caress her soft behind. He held her tight against his hardness as he kissed her deeply. His tongue slipped into the sweet recess of her mouth to mate gently with hers.

She moaned, heedless of the cover slipping to the floor, and wrapped her arms around his neck. Pressing her hot body hungrily against his, she ardently returned his kiss.

A groan of agony rose from deep within him as he tore his lips away from hers, trying desperately to retain some control while he still could. He was on fire with desire as he pushed her away only to pull her hard against him again. "God, you feel so good. Nichole, Nichole," he groaned, covering her mouth once more.

Nichole's skin prickled, and she couldn't seem to pull enough air into her lungs. She clung to Fowler, unable to get close enough to ease the feelings washing through her. She knew her heart was surely going to beat itself to death against her ribs, but she couldn't have cared less as long as he didn't stop kissing and caressing her.

The throbbing radiating from the triangle between her legs to the rest of her body was almost more than she could endure.

Pulling back, she looked pleadingly into his eyes. "Fowler, please . . . I can't . . . I don't . . ."

Fowler halted his actions, pulling Nichole to him, he rested his head on top of hers, trying to control his desire. His breathing was rapid and ragged, his heart pounded, his maleness throbbed.

When he was able, he leaned back to look deep into Nichole's eyes as if he intended to say something as he smoothed the hair away from her face. He opened then closed his mouth, suddenly uncomfortable with whatever his thoughts had been.

He moved away from contact with her body. "I think we'd better get dressed and go down to dinner before the dining room closes."

Nichole nodded her head, too embarrassed to meet his eyes. "Yes."

Had he taken her plea as rejection? Or having breached her defenses, had he decided he didn't want her? What ever the reason, she knew she should feel glad that he hadn't taken her up on her wanton behavior. She should but she didn't. There was an empty longing, an ache in the region that was her heart.

She didn't want it to be so, but she had come to care about Fowler. And she knew that could only spell disaster for her. She had never desired a man before, yet she desired Fowler. She was embarrassed and shamed by her feelings. Feelings so strong that her treacherous body acted of its own accord. Feelings that weren't suppose to be known outside of wedlock.

As she dressed, she wondered about Fowler's feelings. Did he care about her even a little? Oh, he cared *for* her, protected her, but did he care *about* her? How did a woman know?

She didn't have much experience, romantically speaking, but she sensed Fowler was a man who had to do things in his own way and at his own pace.

* * *

Carmen knew why the young man riding by her side was so quiet and withdrawn. It had been three weeks since he had regained consciousness only to discover that he hadn't regained his memory.

It made her heart ache because she deeply loved this mystery man, yet she was unable to help him.

Nick was the epitome of frustration. Dammit! It had been four long weeks since he had been shot and he still didn't know who or what he was.

Even though *Don* Miguel had assured him that he wasn't an outlaw or bandit, how could he be sure? Why had he not had any identification or papers on him? What kind of man went around anonymously? Only a man who had something to hide. That's who.

What was he hiding? Or who was he hiding from?

Only useless little bits and pieces of meaningless nothings seeped from his shut-down brain, and those usually led to more questions than answers.

The nights were the worse. Several times during the night he'd awaken from a dream but try as hard as he could, he either couldn't remember what the dream was or else it didn't make any sense at all.

The headaches had ceased almost entirely. Now he only had them when he was concentrating very hard to pull something from the depths of his malfunctioning mind. As he was now.

The dream he'd had last night was the most disturbing one yet. In his dream, he was riding alongside a beautiful young girl with long black hair blowing in the wind. Just as he was riding with Carmen now. Only he knew it wasn't Carmen in his dream.

They seemed to be happy and carefree as they rode. He could hear her laughing. It was a beautiful, sweet sound. She challenged him to a race and took off at breakneck speed across the meadow.

He called to her to stop, but she laughed and rode harder, calling over her shoulder, "Catch me if you can."

He spurred his horse, trying to catch up with the girl. Somehow, he knew that she held the key to who he was. If he could only catch her, she would tell him who he was. Where he belonged. If only he could catch up with her, but the harder he rode, the slower his horse galloped.

"I know who you are," she singsonged tauntingly as she raced farther ahead of him.

"Stop! Please. I have to know who you are. Who am I? Help me, please. Tell me who I am. Please stop," he begged.

The girl stopped and turned her mount to face him. Her image began to fade like a mirage. He rode and rode, trying desperately to reach her before she faded completely.

Suddenly, he was right beside her but he couldn't see her face. She was looking down, and her long black hair fell like a curtain across her features.

He grabbed her with both hands and shook her. "Tell me who you are!" he demanded.

The girl laughed mockingly as she turned her face toward him. "You know who I am. I'm Nolie."

He released his hold on the apparition as if he had been burned by the fires of hell.

The jeering face that stared him in the eyes was his *own* face. "Nooo," he groaned.

As her image faded into oblivion, she repeated in her singsong refrain, "I'm Nolie. I'm Nolie."

He awoke with a start, drenched in sweat, his heart pounding against his ribs. What did it mean? It had to be a part of his past. If only he could understand what the dream meant.

Damn, damn, damn! Would this nightmare never end?

"What did you say?" Carmen questioned.

He hadn't realized that he had muttered his frustrations out loud. He turned in his saddle to face her, only to see that her lovely features were now contorted with concern.

He knew he had no right to feel anything for this young girl while he was still ignorant of who or what he was. Nevertheless, that didn't stop the yearnings he felt for Carmen.

Beautiful, beautiful Carmen. What could he offer her? Him, a man with a past he couldn't remember, and a future he might not have.

To him, she was perfection personified. A gentle, chocolate-eyed angel. The only time he felt at peace was when he was with her. Her serene composure was like a soothing balm to his taut nerves. She seemed to know when he needed someone to listen to him as he tried to puzzle out his anxieties. Yet she wasn't condescending or patronizing in her concern for him.

"I was thinking about a dream I had this morning." He signed dejectedly. "As usual, it was a distorted mishmash that didn't make any sense at all. Oh, Carmen, am I destined to live the rest of my life as a man with no name?"

"Do not worry, *querido*, I pray to the Holy Mother every night to release your memory from the darkness. I feel in my heart that soon she will hear my plea and answer my prayers." Her solemn look of belief almost made him believe that some Supreme Deity might intervene on his behalf. Almost.

Carmen was such an innocent that she had not even tried to play the coy maiden with Nick. Her every look told him that she loved him, heart and soul. And, if he had been of a mind to, she would have freely given him her body, too. But for some inexplicable reason, Nick had drawn the line at plucking her innocence.

He knew he loved her every bit as much as she loved him, but what if he was not free to give his love to her? What if he already had a wife and family somewhere? What if he found out he could only bring her shame if he stayed with her when he regained his memory? He loved her far too much to take such a risk with her heart.

He, too, had said a prayer every night that he would be freed from this paralyzing bondage and that the knowledge would free him to go to her father, declare his love for Carmen, and ask for her hand in marriage.

Surely the fact that he wanted the consummation of their love to be in their marriage bed was a sign of what *Don* Miguel had called "inherent refinement and dignity."

He had clung tenaciously to that thought. He had to! His very sanity depended on that fragile thread of hope.

Chapter Seven

"That's him!" Nichole yanked Fowler's arm so hard that he almost tumbled down the remainder of the stairs.

"That's who?" he questioned as he scanned the area below them for a familiar face. He didn't see anyone he recognized.

"See that tall, burly man standing near the door, the one in the dark suit, with the silver hair?"

Fowler followed Nichole's pointing finger to a group of three men. The man with the silver hair had his back to them, but from his gesturing he was obviously issuing orders to the two younger men. "Yes, I see him. Who is he?"

"That," she said smugly, "is no other than Mr. John North, in person." She frowned as she contemplated her thoughts out loud. "Now I just wonder what would bring a man like him to a town like this, and, at this particular time? Hmmm."

Before Fowler had a chance to attempt to answer her question, Nichole grabbed him by the arm and he found himself being propelled down the stairs. Luckily for him, he was fast on his feet or else he would have reached the bottom of the steps on his nose.

"Come on. He's up to something and we're going to find out what." Nichole crossed the space between them and him, literally dragging Fowler behind her.

"You say the sweetest things," she cooed as she deliberately bumped into John North, knocking him off balance. "Oh, I'm so sorry, I should have been . . ." she innocently apologized as she grabbed his arm to steady him.

"Well, I declare. Mr. North, whatever are you doing in Evadne? I can't believe it. All this way from home and meeting someone I know. What a coincidence!" she babbled as she turned innocent green eyes on Fowler.

He didn't know what the little minx was up to, but, judging from the look on John North's face, she was the last person he wanted to see.

He struggled to regain his composure. "Uh, yes. It is a surprise, Miss Westerfield." He tugged at his shirt collar as if the tie had suddenly tightened of its own accord.

She turned adoring eyes up to Fowler and even managed to produce a slight blush. "Well, it's Mrs. now. This is my husband, Fowler Barclay. We're on our honeymoon." She looped her arm through his and gazed up at him in what she hoped was a good imitation of a blushing bride, before turning back to face the flustered Mr. North.

"Actually, we're on our way to Austin for a few days. Fowler, darling, this is Mr. John North. He's a friend of Daddy's. He owns a large spread over in Falls County." She watched with interest as the two men shook hands, trying to size up each other.

"Please to meet you, Mr. North. What brings you to this quaint little town?" Fowler watched the other man's eyes, knowing he was trying to think up a logical answer.

John tugged at his collar again. "Uh, business. Just, uh, business," he stammered nervously, his eyes glancing around to see who might be listening in on their conversation. "Well, uh, I hate to run but I have an appointment." He tipped his hat to Nichole and quickly made his escape.

"Your Mr. North seemed mighty edgy," Fowler stated as he watched the man hurry across the street.

Nichole agreed. "That weasel is up to something. Did you see how nervous he was? A long-tailed cat in a room full of rocking chairs would have been calmer than he was." She hiked up her skirts and started out the door.

Fowler grabbed her arm. "Hey, hold on. Where do you think you're going?"

"We're going to follow him, of course. See where he goes and who he meets. Don't you think it's just too 'coincidental' that John North shows up in a town that Linc Travis is known to frequent? Especially after finding a note with the name John and the initials *J.N.* on the man who tried to kill me, thinking he was killing the Brazos Kid?"

"Nichole," he said exasperated. "You can't follow someone in broad open daylight without him seeing you. Besides, people like North and Travis do things

97

under the cover of darkness. Tonight I'll keep an eye on him to see who he's meeting. And, I do mean *me, alone, by myself,* do I make myself clear, young lady?" he warned.

"But—"

"No buts about it. *You* will stay in our room tonight so that I'll know you're safe."

When it looked as if she were going to protest his order, he wagged his finger in her face and reminded her that she had promised to follow his orders to the letter.

"All right. I'll stay in my room tonight," she agreed begrudgingly.

After a leisurely dinner and then escorting Nichole back to their rooms, Fowler began to make the rounds of saloons and gambling halls in town.

By the time he had scrutinized the third one, he had decided that either Linc wasn't in town or he'd been scared off by North.

The fourth saloon proved to be more productive, however.

Fowler moseyed up to the bar and ordered a whiskey. He had spotted the Mexican sitting at one of the poker tables when he first walked in. After carefully studying him in the mirror behind the bar, Fowler was positive that he was the man who had left Aerl Station in such a hurry.

Now he had something to work on. He swallowed the last of his drink and ordered another before walking over to the table.

"Mind if I sit in?" he asked casually, keeping one eye on the Mexican to see if there was any hint of recognition. There wasn't.

The Mexican glanced up at him briefly before studying the cards he held in his hand.

"Naw. Pull up a chair," someone commented.

"Aw, hell! I ain't had a decent hand all night. Take my chair. I'm busted anyway, dammit," a pot-bellied man said as he threw his cards face down on the table, stood up and walked away.

Fowler took the vacated chair and glanced around the table before asking, "What's the game?"

The man to his right replied, "Five-card draw or five-card stud. Pot limit. Table stakes. Your deal," as he plopped the deck on the table in front of Fowler.

Fowler shuffled the cards, laid the deck on the table in front of the man to his right to be cut, picked the cards up again, and began to deal.

It soon became apparent that the man sitting beside the Mexican was a friend and probably a member of the gang, too. Sooner or later, if he bided his time, he hoped one of them would lead him to the hide-out.

Several hours later, Fowler had won several pots but he had not gained one shred of information. Poker players were tight-lipped men. Seldom was there any casual conversation at a poker table.

When the barkeep hollered, "Closing time," Fowler was more than glad. While he wasn't drunk, he was beginning to feel the whiskey coursing through his veins.

He was deliberately slow gathering up his winnings when the game broke up. He wanted to be able to follow the men when they left.

"Hey, Mex, what say you and me get us a couple of these pretty little gals to keep us warm tonight?"

The saloon girls who had been hanging all over the two men most of the night each grabbed a bottle and a man, and started up the stairs to their rooms.

One of them giggled as the man called "Mex" pinched her on the bottom as she wiggled her way up the stairs ahead of him. "Sounds like a fine idea to me, *amigo*," the Mexican agreed.

Well, so much for that idea, Fowler thought to himself as he aimed his tired body toward the door.

Before he reached his intended destination, one of the saloon girls stepped in front of him, pressing her overly perfumed body against his.

"What's the matter, handsome, all your playmates go home? I'm Flo. Why don't we go up to my room and find a few games of our own to play? Flo knows a lot of games to make a man feel real good all over," she assured him.

Fowler didn't let his pity for the aging floozy show. It was obvious that she was desperate. He had casually taken notice of the woman with the faded red hair during the card game, mostly because of how hard she worked to get one of the customers up to her room. However, he had not seen her take even one man upstairs during the whole night.

He'd always felt sorry for women like Flo, dissipated from years of too many men, too much liquor, and not enough food. They painted their faces with gobs of make-up, trying to hide the age lines so they could compete with the younger, prettier woman in the trade. Hoping to eke out enough money to survive one more day.

"Well, honey, it's like this," he said to her as he toyed with the faded black lace on her faded red dress. "You see, I got me a new bride over in the hotel across the street. And I don't think she'd take too kindly to spending tonight by herself. You know how some wives are. But I tell ya what. Why don't you get a good night's sleep, and, maybe we can get together some other night before I leave," he said as he slipped a twenty-dollar gold piece down the front of her dress.

He graced her with a wink before turning her toward the stairs and giving her a gentle nudge. "That's to hold my reservation for me."

"Any time, good-looking, you just let Flo know when you're ready and the bed will be warm and awaiting."

"Good night, ma'am." He tipped his hat to her before walking out into the cool night air.

Looks can be deceiving, he discovered later that night as he tried for what seemed like the hundredth time to find a spot on the too-short couch that didn't feel as if it were filled with boulders.

"Hell!" he muttered disgustedly. "I've slept on ground softer than this contraption!"

After twisting and turning for another five minutes, Fowler declared enough was enough! There was no good reason why he couldn't share that big bed with the soundly sleeping Nichole.

If he was very careful and very quiet, he could slip into bed, get a good night's sleep, and Nichole wouldn't even know about it until morning. By then, she'd be convinced that he could be a good boy when he wanted to.

The amount of whiskey he'd consumed went a long way toward convincing him that his thoughts were completely rational and logical.

Gathering up the pillow and blanket that she had left on the couch for him, he silently tiptoed into the bedroom.

Perfect. Nichole was sleeping like a baby. She'd never know he was there.

He carefully eased under the covers and was fast asleep before his head touched the pillow.

Nichole felt as warm and contented as a just fed kitten curled up in front of a fireplace and she snuggled closer to the source of the warmth.

That source wrapped his arms around her, pulling her closer to his hairy chest and the length of his body. They were lying on their sides, spoon fashion, her back to him. More asleep than awake, he brushed her long hair away from her neck to place a gentle kiss.

Then he kissed her shoulder as one hand cupped her full breast to knead it tenderly until it swelled with desire in his hand.

He cuddled her warm little posterior snug against his male hardness before letting his hand travel over her smooth stomach and nestle between her thighs.

She moaned as the enchantingly pleasant flutters of sexual desire began to radiate throughout her body, and moved against his hand. She felt as if she were about to burst into flames.

As his hard, throbbing manhood pressed against her buttocks, she rubbed against him, feeling him grow bigger and harder.

Moaning and writhing, she called his name. "Fowler . . . Fowler, please . . ."

At the sound of his name, Fowler came instantly

awake. Sometime during the night, he had turned on his side facing Nichole.

Now he found himself in the enviable position of holding a desirable, albeit sound asleep woman in his arms. He could tell by her movements and sleepy mumbling that she was having an erotic dream. Involuntarily, his arm tightened around her suggestively moving body. The hand was not the only part of the body that was quicker than the eye! His previously flaccid manhood leaped to erection.

He moaned in anguish as he berated himself for being ten kinds of an idiot to have believed that he could sleep in the same bed with a desirable woman and not react just as he was doing right now.

Each movement of Nichole's body sent his own body's temperature soaring. Any minute now, he knew he was going to lose control, roll her over onto her back, and bury himself deep within her.

When she called his name as if she were pleading with him to help her, he knew he was lost. There was no way on God's green earth that he could keep from making love to her.

He crooned her name in answer to her plea as he rolled her over and began to ease her prim cotton nightgown up, kissing her lips as he whispered her name.

Nichole's eyes popped open in disbelief. "What the hell are you doing in *my* bed! I thought I was dreaming."

"Well, you were dreaming until you started calling my name and begging me to make love to you. Now, what kind of a man would I be if I didn't help a woman in distress?"

He could tell by the way she sucked in her breath at his words that she was probably blushing from the soles of her feet to the top of her head. His suspicions were confirmed with her sputtering denial.

"I never . . . I didn't . . . I couldn't have!" she sputtered.

"Yes, you did, and yes, you could. And, you enjoyed every minute of it, I might add," he said smugly.

She tried to push him off her. "Why you conceited, pompous, mule-eared, numbskull, jacka—"

"Tch, tch, tch," he interrupted as he wagged his finger at her. "We're going to have to do something about your language, sweetheart. Didn't your mother teach you that ladies do not cuss?"

"You leave my mother out of this and get the hell out of my bed!" she shouted at him.

"Shhh, you're going to wake up this whole hotel, if you don't keep your voice down," he cautioned.

"You were supposed to sleep on the couch. Or was that just a ploy to make me let my guard down?" she accused.

"I couldn't sleep on that couch. I tried, but that blooming thing must be stuffed with rocks. I honestly thought I could stay on my side of the bed and get a good night's sleep, and you wouldn't even know I was here. And I would have succeeded, too, if you hadn't started moaning my name and begging me to make love to you," he accused. "After all, sweetheart, a man can only take so much tempting before he loses control."

She wasn't buying a word of his story. She pointed toward the door. "Out! Now. And stay out. So help me if I find you in my bed again, I'll—I'll whack that—

thing off and nail it to the wall with a rusty nail!" she threatened.

He covered the "thing" in question with his pillow, grabbed his blanket and stalked out the door. "Damn woman. First she seduces me and then she threatens to maim me," he muttered as he slammed the door behind him.

She punched her pillow, trying to figure out who she was more furious with. Herself, because she couldn't resist him, even when she was asleep, or Fowler, because he was so casual about the whole thing.

"Of course he's casual about making love, you ninny," she told herself out loud. "He's always been a skirt chaser, and he always will be one. After we find Nicky, he'll just go riding off to his U.S. Marshal's post like nothing's ever happened and never even give you a second thought. And you'll have to go back to the ranch and try to forget him. Forget how he made your knees turn to jelly when he looked at you with those sapphire eyes. Forget the way he made you feel like you were soaring above the stars when he took you in his arms and kissed you senseless." A tear trickled down her cheek as she whispered, "And forget that you fell in love with a man who will never return your love."

Fowler found Mex and his friend in the same saloon the next night. This time, however, they were sitting at a table near the back by themselves drinking.

Again, Fowler took a seat at one of the poker tables. He made sure he could keep one eye on Mex and the other on the swinging doors.

If Fowler's suspicions were correct, the two men were waiting for someone. He noticed that Mex repeatedly glanced at the swinging doors.

Around ten o'clock, the other man went upstairs with one of the girls, leaving Mex alone at the table. When one of the other girls approached him, he sent her away with a growl.

An hour later, Fowler had just about decided that he was going to come up empty-handed again, when a slender, slightly bowlegged cowboy ambled into the saloon.

Fowler recognized him as one of the men who John North had been giving orders to at the hotel the day before. The cowboy glanced around the room casually before stepping up to the bar and ordering a beer.

Fowler was watching the Mex who had his eye on the cowboy at the bar. The cowboy seemed only interested in his drink.

To anyone watching, Fowler appeared to be studying the cards he held in his hand. However, he was observing the bowlegged man through his lowered lashes. He saw the man turn around and face the room with his elbows resting on the bar and one boot heel hooked over the brass rail.

The man let his eyes slowly travel around the room to see if anyone was taking undue note of him. When his eyes settled on Mex, he gave an almost imperceptible nod of his head toward the back exit. Then he drained his mug, set it on the bar, and left the saloon through the swinging doors.

Fowler saw the Mexican toss back the last of his drink before he, too, left the saloon.

Fowler threw his cards in, picked up his money,

and walked toward the back of the saloon. He met Flo coming out of what appeared to be a storage room.

"Is there a back way out of here?"

Flo looked a little puzzled. "Sure, through the store room. But it don't go nowhere but to the alley behind the building. Why?"

"I'll tell ya later," he said over his shoulder as he hurried into the indicated room.

Fowler carefully eased open the back door just enough to listen for any noise outside. He heard the crunch of boots on the hard-packed ground.

From his limited view, he could see one man leaning against the side of the building. When the man raised his smoke to his lips, the glow of the cigarette butt illuminated the face of the Mexican.

He could tell by the sounds that at least one other person was there.

"What the hell do you mean Linc ain't coming! Where the hell is he? He was told to be here tonight."

The butt glowed again as Mex pulled a long drag before answering. "There's been a little trouble. Linc and the rest of the boys are on their way across the border to lay low for a while."

"Trouble? What kind of trouble?"

"That Texas Ranger who Red shot didn't stay shot. Me and Robert saw him in Aeil a few days ago. Alive and well. Robert stayed behind to finish the job and I came on ahead to tell Linc. Robert ain't showed up yet, so Linc figures that he ain't gonna and it's just a matter of days until the Rangers swoop down on us at the hide-out."

"God dammit!" the unidentified man swore. "The boss ain't gonna like this," he warned.

Mex took another long drag off his cigarette before flicking the butt away. "Can't help that. Linc said he'd contact him in the usual way."

Fowler waited until the men parted before slipping out the back door to follow the Mexican. Before the man stepped out of the alley, Fowler grabbed him around the neck, poking his gun hard in the man's back, and pulled him back into the darkness.

"Okay, *amigo*, I've got some questions and *you* better have some answers." Fowler jabbed his gun harder in the man's back. *"Comprende?"*

The man could only nod his head because of Fowler's strangle hold.

Fowler released him, shoving him up against the wall. "Now, where is Linc Travis?"

"In Mexico."

Fowler jabbed his gun in the man's stomach, knocking the wind out of him. "Where in Mexico?" he growled.

"I don't know. Just somewhere near Laredo. That's all I know," the man choked out.

"How are you to make contact with him?"

"At the cantina. I was to stay with his girlfriend, Juanita, until he made contact with me."

"Now," Fowler said as he jammed the gun still harder in the Mexican's belly, "where was the Texas Ranger when Red shot him?"

Mex began to sweat and Fowler could feel him shaking. "I . . . I don't know nothing about that. I wasn't even there. I swear, I don't know nothing," the man lied.

"Mister, you got five seconds to start giving directions before this forty-five slug scatters your guts all over this alley!"

"All right! All right! Don't shoot," the man pleaded. "I don't know exactly where, but they were somewheres near Co—"

Two shots rang out in rapid succession from behind Fowler. He whirled around, falling into a crouch, but the shadowy figure rounded the corner of the building before he could get a shot off.

He instantly turned his gun back to the Mexican, but it wasn't necessary. The man was dead.

Fowler raced to the end of the alley, hoping to get a shot at the fleeing man. He fired one shot before the mounted man was out of range. It was too dark and the rider was too far away to tell whether he'd hit him.

Suddenly pain radiated through Fowler's left shoulder. The bullet meant for him had left a gaping path where it had sliced through his upper arm.

As the sounds of shooting stopped, people rushed out into the street to see what had happened.

Fowler couldn't take the chance of drawing attention to himself and Nichole by being connected with the dead man.

As a crowd gathered in the alley, he slipped unnoticed across the street and looked into the hotel, hoping that the night clerk had left the desk to see what the commotion was about. No such luck. The man was craning his neck, trying to see out the window but he wasn't budging from behind the desk.

Damn! Fowler leaned against the wall. He had to get past the man, but, with his shirt torn and blood running down his arm, he couldn't very well go traipsing through the lobby as if he were on a Sunday stroll!

* * *

Nichole had also heard the shooting. And, being the curious soul that she was, she couldn't stand being cooped up in her room not knowing what was taking place.

Besides, if Fowler was involved he might need her help. Never did the thought cross her mind that Fowler might not *want* her help.

With this thought in mind, she came flying down the stairs and out the front door of the hotel. She headed toward the group of people milling around the alley across the street.

"Nichole."

She thought she heard someone call her name, and turned to look behind her. She immediately recognized the figure in the shadows, leaning against the wall.

"Fowler, what's happened? I heard shots." A sudden thought occurred to her. "Why are you hiding?"

"Shhh, I need your help." He was getting lightheaded from the loss of blood. He shook his head, trying to clear it.

Her attention was drawn to his torn shirt and the blood trickling down his arm. "Oh my God! You've been shot!" she exclaimed. "What happened?" She quickly tore a piece of her petticoat off and tied it around his wound.

"Shhh, keep your voice down," he cautioned again. "It's only a scratch. I'll tell you all about it when we get up to the room. Right now, you've got to help me get past that noisy desk clerk."

"Wait here, I'll be right back." With that needless admonishment, she hurried into the lobby.

"Sir," she said as she rushed breathlessly up to the desk. "Sir, I desperately need your help."

The young desk clerk looked at her in alarm. "What—what is it, ma'am?" The last thing he needed was a damsel in distress.

"I need a bottle of whiskey, quick!"

"Whiskey?" the nervous young man croaked.

"Yes, for medicinal purposes. You see, I'm prone to get the vapors." She closed her eyes and melodramatically held her hand to her forehead. "Oh, dear, I feel one coming on now." Peeking through one eye, she saw the man turn pale as a sheet.

"Vapors!" he croaked again, his voice three notches higher than before. "Oh, no, ma'am. You can't do that here in the lobby!" He grabbed his chair, ran around the corner of the desk, and shoved it under Nichole so hard he knocked her off her feet. "Don't faint! Lady, don't faint." He wrung his hands in agitation.

She had meant to alarm him but she hadn't meant to scare him witless! "Whiskey. I need whiskey. It's the only thing that will stop them," she moaned breathlessly.

He stood there, hopping from one foot to the other, wringing his hands and muttering, "Whiskey, whiskey. She needs whiskey."

Oh, for heaven's sakes! He must have the intelligence of a doorknob. She let out a loud sigh. "Oh, no! It's getting worse. I need a *bottle of whiskey from the dining room.*" Good grief! Was she going to have to take him by the hand, lead him into the dining room and point to it?

"Whiskey, a bottle of whiskey from the dining room," he repeated doltishly. Suddenly the meaning of the words seemed to sink in. "Of course! Whiskey! Dining room! Wait here!" He ran from the lobby toward the dining room as if his coattail had caught on fire.

The instant he left, Nichole ran to the door to help Fowler. She managed to get him up the stairs and into their room just in time to race back down the stairs and reach her chair before the desk clerk came bounding back into the lobby, holding the whiskey above him like a prize.

"I found it!"

She delicately fanned herself as she took the proffered bottle. "Thank you so much. You'll just never know how much you've helped me," she said sweetly as she glided up the stairs, leaving a beaming desk clerk at the bottom.

The minute she closed the door behind her, Fowler burst into a belly laugh. "That was quite a performance. I was beginning to think you were going to *give* that poor boy the 'vapors' before it was over with." He held his sides and laughed harder. "The vapors, Nichole? Really!"

"Well"—she wrinkled her nose impishly—"it was the only thing I could think of. Besides, I need the whiskey and I certainly couldn't go into a saloon to get it."

Fowler wiped the tears of laughter from his eyes with his uninjured arm. "Why do you need a bottle of whiskey?"

Nichole was already unbuttoning his shirt. "From the amount of blood trickling down your arm, I think I'm going to have to put a few stitches in this wound." She had his shirt completely off and was carefully probing it.

"Ouch! That hurts."

"I'm sure it does. Now, you tell me what took place while I practice my needlework," she said, more confidently than she felt, as she dug through her saddlebags for a needle and thread.

Fowler eyed her skeptically. "Are you sure you know how to do this?"

"Sure. I got all the way to the letter *E* on my *ABC* sampler when Mother was teaching me to embroider," she quipped.

"Uh, Nichole, I don't think it really needs any stitches. It'll be all right." He stood up, ready to make a break for the other room.

Nichole pushed him back down. "You big baby," she accused. "Lie down and be still," she ordered. "First, I'm going to clean it and then, I'm going to sew it, and, while I'm doing that, you are going to tell me what happened." She gave him a don't-you-dare-argue-with-me look.

"Yes, ma'am," he said meekly. His mother didn't raise any stupid kids. He knew when to shut up and sit, or rather to lie down.

Grabbing the bottle, he took a long swig before handing it back to her. When she poured some whiskey on the open wound to cleanse it, he sucked in his breath, paling slightly.

"It's going to feel a whole lot better when it quits hurting," she informed him.

"Very funny."

He talked while she sewed. When she finished, he was surprised at her handiwork. "I don't think a doctor could have done any better," he remarked, but she didn't seem to have heard him.

She had been very quiet while Fowler told her

about the conversation he had overheard between the Mexican and the other man just before the shooting started.

He left her alone with her thoughts for several minutes. He had known that it would be hard for her to accept the fact that Nick was really dead.

"Nichole?" he questioned softly. He had expected to see tears in her eyes when she looked up at him. Instead, he saw a look of defiant determination.

She suddenly stood up and began gathering up her things and stuffing them into her saddlebags. "Nick is not dead! I won't believe it unless I see it with my own eyes. I know you don't understand, but I *know* I'd feel it if he were dead." She continued to fill her saddlebags.

"What are you doing?"

"We're going to Mexico, of course."

"Nichole, we can't go chasing Linc Travis into Mex—" The look she gave him stopped him in midsentence. Maybe he'd been wrong about his mama and her kids after all. He slowly shook his head in consternation. "We'll leave in the morning."

Chapter Eight

Nick had been at the Villa de Cardona ranch a month. Though he had physically recovered from his wounds, as far as he was concerned, he was still a mental cripple.

The perplexing dreams continued to beleaguer him. It was almost as if his mind was giving him pieces of a jigsaw puzzle, one piece at a time, and daring him to put the puzzle together. So far, he'd been unable to put even two of the pieces together.

Today was the first day of April. Carmen was so excited that she just couldn't sit still. Her brother, Ricardo, was coming home for the Easter holidays.

She and Nick were in the garden, enjoying the pleasant spring day. To an uninformed onlooker, it was an idyllic scene. A beautiful young girl, a handsome young man, birds singing in the trees, the fragrant aroma of colorful flowers and lush green grass filling the air.

But, to Nick, it was just another day of frustration. He was deep in thought about his latest dream when Carmen came back to sit beside him on the bench beneath the towering oak tree.

She sighed a long sigh. "I still do not see him. He should be here by now." Again, she got up and walked to the end of the brick path to look down the road that led to the main house.

She was as impatient as a child at Christmas. She had been watching that road all morning, anxious to catch the first glimpse of her brother.

Nick chuckled when, once again, she plopped down on the bench beside him. "Sweetheart, you are wearing those bricks thin with your pacing. Calm down. His letter said he would be here on Friday. It's only midmorning. By the time he gets here, you'll be worn to a frazzle from walking a path in the brick to look down that road." He took her dainty hand in his, bringing it to his lips for a kiss.

"But you don't understand. I haven't seen Ricky since he went back to Austin after the holidays. He's never stayed away from the family this long before," she complained peevishly.

"Honey, as the newest lawyer on the Attorney General's staff, I'm sure he's working extra hard and long hours to make a good impression." He turned her to him to place a chaste kiss on her forehead. "Quit worrying. If he is only half the brother you claim he is, he wouldn't disappoint you even if he had to walk all the way here."

This was a side of her that he had not seen before.

She had always been so calm and serene that he was surprised by her agitated behavior.

He grabbed her hand and pulled her back on the seat beside him when she started to make another journey to look down the road.

"Will you sit still for a few minutes? You're making me tired just watching you." He shook his head in amusement. "You're as bad as Nolie is when she has to . . ." His words trailed off as they began to register on him.

"Finish the sentence," Carmen urged. "Finish the thought before you lose it, when she has to what? Concentrate, *querido*. I'm as bad as Nolie when she has to . . ." she encouraged, hoping against hope that something had begun to surface.

"When she has to . . . wait for something." He looked at Carmen. The look on her face told him that she was as disappointed as he was that nothing of significance had surfaced.

She hugged him to her. "It's all right, *querido*. It will all come back to you. Mama still thinks you are trying too hard to force your memories to return."

He seemed not to have heard her. "Why would I compare you to this Nolie person?" he pondered out loud.

He looked into Carmen's loving eyes. "That just slipped out. I'm sorry, Carmen." He sighed in resignation. "It just seems like whoever Nolie is, she holds the key to free me from this bottomless pit I seem to be in."

He knew the only thing that Carmen feared about him regaining his memory was the answer to the question of who Nolie was. She had declared her love

117

for him with unabashed candor, and he told her that he loved her, also.

He had bared his soul to her, telling her of his fears. The fear that he might not be free to marry her so they could spend the rest of their lives together. Or, that once she knew who and what he was, she wouldn't want to love him.

She had assured him that no matter what his past had been, she would always love him. And, if it turned out that he already had a wife and couldn't marry her, she would still love him until the day she died.

As he looked deep into her chocolate-brown eyes, eyes that openly declared her love for him, he knew that he, too, would love her till the day he died. "Oh, Carmen, Carmen. I love you with all my heart and soul. I'd rather die than do anything to cause you hurt or pain," he confessed.

"I know, *querido*, I know." She threw her arms around his neck and kissed him with all the yearning in her young, untried body.

He pulled her tight against him and returned her kiss with a passion that set his body on fire with the anguish of wanting and not being able to have.

He was a man drowning in passion. She was his lifeline but she was just out of his reach.

"Hey, anybody home?" the tall, handsome Spaniard called out as he hung his hat on the rack in the hallway.

"Ricky!" his mother answered as she dropped her needlework and hurried to meet him.

"Ricardo!" His father laid the ledger aside and rose to cross the room to greet his son.

Ricky hugged his mother and whirled her off her feet. "You're still the most beautiful woman in the world."

He set her back on the ground to shake his father's hand. "Hello, Father."

Miguel looked proudly at his son. *"Mi hijo*, it is good to have you home again. We have missed you." He eyed his son with a critical eye. "You seemed to have grown taller. And"—he winked slyly—"someone seems to be keeping you well fed. There's more meat on your bones than when you were here last," he teased.

Ricardo ducked his head slightly. *"Sí,"* he admitted a bit shyly.

Consuela buffeted her husband's shoulder lightly. "Miguel, do not tease the boy. Can you not see that you have embarrassed him?" she admonished.

Miguel chuckled proudly. "And do we get to meet this 'someone?'"

Ricardo smiled broadly. "Perhaps."

He looked around for his little sister. He had expected her to come running down the lane to meet him before he reached the house as was her usual greeting. Not seeing her, he asked, "Where is little Carmen?"

"She is in the garden—" Before his mother could finish telling him that she was in the garden with the young *hombre,* Ricardo took off in that direction.

"Good. I'll get to surprise her."

"But—" his mother started.

"I am thinking that Ricardo is the one who is going to be surprised," his father stated with a chuckle. "His 'little' sister is not so little anymore."

* * *

119

Ricardo entered the garden just as Nick enfolded Carmen in his arms to return her kiss hungrily.

He acted on instinct, not taking the time to question who the *gringo* might be or if the *hombre* had a right to be in the garden with his sister.

He crossed to the embracing couple in long, quick strides, anger dictating his actions. He pulled Carmen out of Nick's arms, pushing her behind him. Before Carmen or Nick had time to gather their wits about them from their passionate kiss, Ricardo slammed his fist into Nick's face, knocking him to the ground, unconscious.

Carmen screamed as she saw Nick fall to the ground. "Stop it! What are you doing!"

She started to go to Nick's side. When Ricky tried to stop her, she pummeled him until he released her. She knelt down beside Nick, carefully brushing the hair back from his forehead to see if he was bleeding. All the while crooning to him as she patted his face, trying to bring him back to consciousness. "*Querido, querido,* my beloved," she cried.

By this time, their mother and father and *Tia* Rosie had reached the garden.

"*Querido?*" He looked from one to the other for an answer.

Tia Rosie had quickly sent one of the servants to fetch a basin of cool water. "We'll explain later, Ricardo," she said brusquely as she began to bathe Nick's face.

Ricardo had never been more confused in his life. His father was issuing orders to bring a glass of bourbon. His sister was sitting on the ground with the stranger's head in her lap, crying. His mother and his aunt were kneeling on the grass as they both worked to revive this man who, from his point of view, had been taking liberties with his little sister.

And everyone was acting as if *he* had committed a grievous crime by defending his sister's honor!

Nick shook his head, trying to focus his eyes on the blurred faces that hovered above him.

"*Querido*, speak to me!" Carmen beseeched as she continued to cry. Her tears fell on Nick's face as she leaned over him to hold a cool cloth against the angry red mark where Ricardo's fist had met his face.

Miguel knelt beside him. "Here, son, take a few sips of this," he said as he lifted Nick's head and placed the glass of bourbon to his mouth.

Nick obeyed. His eyes began to clear as he looked at the anxious faces. Slowly, he raised up on one elbow, opening and closing his mouth as he felt his tender jaw with his other hand.

Miguel helped him to his feet. "Are you all right, *señor?*"

"Yes, sir. I will be in a few minutes. Just as soon as my ears quit ringing." He looked at the man who had delivered the punch. "Is it safe to assume that you are Ricardo?"

"*Sí!*" The proud Spaniard drew himself up to his full height, which was equal to Nick's. "I am Ricardo Fernando de Cardona. Who are you and why were you kissing my little sister, *gringo?*" he demanded defiantly.

Nick's eyes focused on Carmen with a look that even a blind man would have known was one of total love and adoration. He held out his hand to her and she stepped inside the circle of his embrace.

He gazed into her beautiful chocolate-brown eyes and said, "My name is Nicholas Westerfield, and I was kissing your sister because I love her."

At first, the silence was so complete you could have heard a leaf fall from the tree. Everyone seemed to be in suspended animation, stunned with disbelief. Then seeming to come back to their senses at the same time, they all began talking, the noise deafening.

Carmen threw her arms around his neck and cried, "Oh, *querido!* My beloved! The Holy Mother has answered my prayers at last!" Tears of happiness flowed freely down her face and soaked the front of Nick's shirt.

Ricardo watched in shocked silence as his mother and his aunt crossed themselves as they, too, thanked God for answering their prayers. Even the servants were jubilant. He turned to his father, trying to make some sense out of what was happening around him. "Father?" he questioned.

Miguel was beaming from ear to ear as if a great burden had been lifted from his shoulders. "Everyone! Everyone! Come, let us go into the study and have a toast. This is a time for great celebration. Our young *amigo* has finally recovered from his wounds."

As the group made its way into the house, Nick called out to Miguel. *"Don* Miguel, please, I would like a few minutes alone with Carmen first." He looked down at the happy young girl he held in his arms. "There is much I need to tell her."

The wise older man nodded his head. *"Sí.* I understand, Nicholas Westerfield. We shall wait for you in the study."

When Ricardo looked as if he were going to protest

such a request, his father put an arm around his son's shoulders and said, "Come, *mi hijo*, I will explain as much as I can."

Carmen had tears of happiness running down her cheeks as Nick wrapped her in his love and kissed her.

"Carmen, my sweet, sweet Carmen. I love you. Now that I have regained my memory, all the pieces have fallen into place and I can now speak what is in my heart. I love you and I want to spend the rest of my life with you and all the beautiful children we will have. Will you do me the honor of becoming my wife?"

Without hesitation, she hugged him to her and cried even harder, if that were possible. "Yes! Yes! A thousand times, yes! I love you, Nicholas Westerfield. I love you."

They shared a long, passionate kiss before Nick cradled her head against his chest. He knew he held a rare treasure in his arms, one he would cherish until his dying breath.

He turned her face up to him as he gently wiped away the tears that still fell from her lovely eyes. "Why do you still cry, my love?"

"I was so afraid this day would never be," she confessed. "I am so happy that I cannot help the tears. They are truly tears of happiness. Tell me, who is Nolie? I had so feared that she would be the one you held in your arms and gave your love to."

"Remember the dream I told you about? The one with the girl claiming to be Nolie, only when I caught up with her, it was my face that I saw?"

Carmen nodded her head. "Yes. Does it make sense now?"

Nick laughed a robust laugh. "Yes. *Now* it finally makes sense. Nolie is the pet name I call my twin sister, Nichole. When we were babies, I couldn't say Nichole. It always came out as Nolie and the name just stuck. That's the reason it seemed that she held the key to my past. Being twins, we were closer than most brothers and sisters. By the way, I have three brothers and two more sisters."

"And the dream you had last night, about the stars falling from the sky. Do you understand it now?"

Nick laughed. Now that he understood what the dream meant, it wasn't as frightening as it had been in the middle of the night. His latest dream had started off with the stars falling out of the sky. They were everywhere he looked, all over the ground, in the trees, on top of the house and outbuildings.

And then they all just disappeared. Except they didn't really go away. They were just hidden from him. If he opened a drawer, a star was in it. He opened a book, a star was hidden there. At the dinner table, there was a star in the mashed potatoes. Only no one but him could see these stars! Everyone at the table looked at him as if he were crazy!

And, when he was finally able to pull himself awake from the nightmare, he was almost convinced that he had surely gone around the bend. That he was, indeed, crazy.

Nick sat down on the bench and pulled off his right boot. "Let me show you what the dream was trying to tell me."

Carmen looked at him skeptically as he slipped his fingers into a slot on the side of his boot.

He pulled out a five-pointed star that had been

hidden in the design stitched on his boot. He held it out to her.

She turned the plain object over in her hand to read the inscription. "It's a badge! A Texas Ranger's badge!" She looked at him incredulously. "You're . . . a Texas Ranger!"

He nodded his head. "Yes. Let's go into the house and I'll explain everything to you and your family at the same time."

When they entered the study, Nick sought out Ricardo. He could tell from the look he received from him that, while the rest of the family had accepted him as a man of honor, Ricardo was not so easily convinced. Especially since it was *his* little sister who the man had his arm around so possessively!

However, being a gentleman, family honor dictated that Ricky make amends for jumping to conclusions. "*Señor*," he stated rather stiffly, "I believe that I owe you an apology for my hasty actions. I apologize for striking you."

Nick accepted the glass of bourbon Miguel handed him. "Actually, I believe it is I who should be thanking you for belting me. It seems to have hastened the return of my memory. For that, I am eternally grateful."

Carmen giggled as she pulled Nick down on the sofa beside her. "Ricardo should count himself lucky if you do not arrest him. I'll bet not many men get to slug a Texas Ranger and get off with only an apology."

Ricardo choked on the drink he had just swallowed.

Miguel looked at Nick. "Is this true? Have you regained your memory completely?"

"Yes, *Don* Miguel, now all the bits and pieces finally make sense. In order to explain fully, I must go back to February of this year when I received a message from Governor Pease asking me to come to Austin as soon as I could. As you know, Texas has been in an upheaval since the war. Not only from the carpetbaggers and scalawags but the Indians and outlaws have been wreaking havoc at every turn."

Don Miguel nodded his head. "Yes, we have heard horrible stories about the burning of homesteads and the killing of innocent people in the central part of the state. But I thought the United States Army was sent here to protect the people."

"Yes, well, you and I know that the Army could put all they know about fighting Indians and Commancheros in one ear and still be able to hear," Nick snorted disgustedly.

"That's for sure," Ricardo agreed. "But the federal government insists that we use the regular Army. How can the Texas Rangers have any legal authority?"

Nick smiled. "Well, we don't exactly have any 'legal authority' as such, but the governor has been communicating with President Grant about the problems in Texas and they have reached a gentleman's agreement concerning the use of the Rangers. We have the authority as 'volunteer' Rangers to use our own discretion to enforce the laws and to protect the citizens of the state.

"The president agrees that too many terrible things have been happening in the wrong places to be a coincidence. He knows there has been a flood of, shall we say, less than honorable people coming into

126

the state intent on reaping big benefits from the hardships of others.

"The war left our nation with many open and bleeding wounds. The president truly cares about the whole nation and wants those wounds mended, so that all the states can once again unite and work together to rebuild our country."

"But, Nicky, isn't that what everybody wants?"

"No, Carmen. Unfortunately, there are some who would like to see us remain splintered and vulnerable."

"I do not understand why this should be, Nicholas." Consuela was as puzzled as her daughter. "Why would anyone want such violence and unrest to continue?"

Refilling the men's glasses, Ricardo answered his mother's question as he walked back to the liquor cabinet. "For the usual reasons, Mother, greed and power. But what I don't understand, Nick, is with so much free land for the taking in West Texas, why would these people single out central Texas?"

"Now you're getting to the *real* reason behind all the problems. Texas is about to embark on the most ambitious construction of railroad transportation in its history. And the land on which the railroad builds is going to be worth much more then it is today. And whoever owns that land will gain both power and wealth almost overnight."

Don Miguel nodded his head in agreement. "But this is a big state. How does anyone know which land will be valuable and which will be bypassed by the railroad?" he queried.

"I think I am beginning to understand the situation," Ricardo said. "Whoever is behind this skullduggery is in a position to know which landowners to harass. Am I correct?"

"That's right."

Ricardo digested this bit of information for a moment. "Do you have any idea as to who this person is?"

"The governor has strong reason to believe it's a Rancher by the name of John North. He's very rich and very powerful. During the war, he started building an empire along the Brazos River in Falls County. He's been ruthless in his land grabbing. But he's also been very careful to keep his name free of scandal. So far, all of his dealings have appeared to be on the up and up legally, even if they weren't fair.

"However, about six months ago, a member of the Linc Travis gang got drunk in a bar over at Aerl Station and started mouthing off about having powerful friends in high places. Earlier in the day, he'd been seen talking to one of the men who works for John North. The next morning, he was found in an alley with his throat cut."

Don Miguel swirled the amber liquid in his glass before taking a long drink. "So you think North is paying Linc Travis to do his dirty work?"

"The governor is positive he's the one. But we didn't have any solid proof to convict him."

Ricardo interrupted him. "And that's where you come in, am I right?"

"Yes. I was to infiltrate Linc's gang and get the evidence we need to put him behind bars. The president had appointed a United States Marshal for this territory in January. He was to be my only contact once I went undercover."

Nick had an engrossed audience as he finished his story. "So, before your *vaqueros* found me shot in the back and more dead than alive, I had been riding as a member of the outlaw gang."

Nick walked over to the liquor cabinet and refilled his glass. "Besides the president and the governor, only my captain knew about my double identity." He took a swallow of his drink. "Somewhere there's a traitor, and I'd stake my life on the fact that he's not at the Ranger station."

Ricardo immediately came to his feet. "You are saying that someone on the governor's staff tried to have you killed?"

"That's exactly what I'm saying," Nick confirmed.

"I find this hard to believe. I am in the capitol all day, every day, and I had not even heard one word about a missing Ranger. Surely the Attorney General would have been notified about such a serious matter."

"Not necessarily. When I failed to meet my contact the first time, he would have assumed that I had been unable to keep our rendezvous. But, when I failed to make contact with him the second time, he would have had to assume that my real identity had been discovered. And then he'd have to wonder by whom." Nick shook his head. "No. The governor is a smart man. I'm sure it would have occurred to him, too, that there is a traitor in our midst."

"What will you do now, Nicholas?" Consuela inquired.

"The first thing I must do is get word to my family that I am alive. I'm sure they have been notified that I have probably met an untimely death." He turned to Miguel.

"I have already sent for one of my *vaqueros*. Jaime will be ready to leave as soon as you have written your letter," Miguel informed Nick without hesitation.

"Thank you, sir. You are most considerate. I'll also need him to leave a message at the Ranger post. Since Linc Travis and the traitor think I'm dead, maybe that will work to our advantage."

Miguel looked lovingly at his wife. "I am afraid I can not take credit for the idea. As a mother, Consuela insisted that your mother would be sick with worry, and we must let her know immediately that you are safe."

Nick drained the last of his drink before walking back to the sofa to stand beside Carmen. He had faced danger many times but never had he been so nervous as he was right now. Since he had never done it before, he wasn't quite sure how to go about it.

Carmen stood up and slipped her hand into his. Her hand was cold from apprehension, but she squeezed his in reassurance. He cleared his voice before addressing Miguel.

"Sir, I'm not sure how one is supposed to go about this but I . . . that is we . . ." He shifted nervously from one foot to the other, took a deep breath, and plunged in. "What I'm trying to say, sir, is that, I love your daughter and she loves me, and I'm asking your permission to marry her."

Had he looked behind him, Nick would have seen the pleasant smiles that graced Consuela's and *Tia* Rosie's faces. They knew the young couple loved each other and were not surprised at Nick's request. Miguel was not blind, either. He had known that the young man would ask for his daughter's hand in marriage if at all possible.

Miguel was watching the liquid as he swirled it in the bottom of his glass, trying to give the appearance of thinking over the request very seriously.

He knew that the young couple was on needles and pins, just as he and Consuela had been when he had faced her father to ask permission to marry.

Actually, he couldn't have been happier to have Nick for his son-in-law. While he had not met any of the Westerfields, he recognized the name and knew that they were an honorable and respected family.

But a bit of devilment made him prolong giving his immediate approval. "Hmmm, so you wish to marry my only daughter?"

"Yes, sir. I do. I come from a good and substantial family. I can guarantee you that I will be a loving and faithful husband and she will never want for anything."

Miguel looked at his daughter. "And, you, Carmencita, you love this man and wish to be his wife?"

"Yes, Father. I love him with all my heart. I loved him from the first time I saw him."

Consuela knew what her husband was up to and she could have wrung his neck for teasing the young couple so.

He felt his wife's eyes on him as he glanced her way. The look she gave him told him he had played the reluctant father long enough!

"Welll . . ." he started.

Carmen was frantic, thinking that her father was not going to give his permission and blessing. "Father, we have to get married!" she blurted out.

She heard the indrawn breath of her mother and

aunt. "Carmencita, no!" they chimed simultaneously in shocked disbelief.

Ricardo doubled his fist, ready to bash the man who had dared to dishonor his sister.

Her father choked on his drink, as he spilled the rest of it down his shirt front and onto the carpet.

Carmen's face flamed red in embarrassment as it dawned on her how her declaration must have sounded to her family. "I did not mean we *have to*, have to! I meant, we could not bear to be parted. We love each other," she explained hurriedly.

An audible sigh of relief circled the room as Consuela found her voice first. "Oh, thank heavens." She turned to her husband and scolded, "Miguel Reynaldo! You quit teasing these children and give your permission this instant. We have a wedding to plan."

Miguel beamed his pleasure as he shook Nick's hand. "Welcome to the family, Nicholas." He winked as he gave his wife a loving look. "I only hope you know what you are letting yourself in for, my friend. You see how impatient and bossy the de Cardona women can be," he teased.

Nick laughed heartily as he pulled the still-embarrassed Carmen to his chest. "You and Nolie will get along just fine, sweetheart. You are both alike in many ways. Her tongue is always outdistancing her brain, too," he declared as he kissed his blushing bride-to-be.

Chapter Nine

It had taken slightly more than a week for Fowler and Nichole to travel from Evadne through the hill country to reach San Antonio.

Two days out of Evadne, they had been forced to seek shelter in a cave from a ferocious spring storm. For the better part of a day and a night, they had been pounded by heavy rains and large chunks of hail. The violent wind had almost blown the pack mules off the slippery trail before they had found the cave.

Nichole was exhausted. They had been forced to travel in single file most of the way through the hill country because the trails were steep and narrow. Her arms felt like lead weights from the tension of holding not only her horse in check but also one of the pack mules.

She was too tired, too cold, and too wet, to complain about the loss of a day's travel when Fowler had declared that they would have to stay in the cave until the storm blew itself out.

For several days after the heavy rains, many of the creeks and rivers that meandered through the area were swollen over their banks. It had been a battle of man against nature in some cases to find a way to cross to the other side. But, working together, they had made it back to civilization.

Fowler was amazed by Nichole's perservering attitude. Not once had she whined or complained about their difficulties. She had taken each obstacle in stride and had done what needed to be done to overcome it.

Nichole felt Fowler's eyes on her as they rode into town. She glanced at him self-consciously. She knew she must look like a little tatterdemalion. She certainly *felt* like one!

When he smiled slightly and shook his head, she couldn't help but ask, "What's the matter? Do I have mud on my face again or something?" When he chuckled, she glanced down at herself to see if something was showing. She had lost most of the buttons on her shirt and she'd had to patch her breeches in a couple of places as best she could.

"No, you don't have mud on your face, and the only thing 'showing' is your beauty."

She looked at him as if he were crazy! "Beauty!" she scoffed. "I think your brain must be waterlogged. I have never, ever looked as bad as I do this minute." She brushed a piece of limp hair that had escaped from her braid back from her face.

"Well, I'll admit that a little soap and water wouldn't hurt either of us. But I was referring to your unflagging spirit. I can't think of another woman I've known, or even heard of, who would have gone through what we just did without so much as one single word of complaint." He shook his head in amazement. "You're something else, that's for sure."

"Would it have changed anything?" she inquired.

"No, I don't suppose it would have," he admitted.

"Then why waste the energy to complain? Grandpa always said, 'If words won't change things, then stick 'em in your back pocket and use the energy to take action that will change things.'" She shrugged her shoulders in agreement. "Makes sense to me."

Fowler laughed as he nodded his head in agreement. "Your grandfather sounds like a very wise man."

"Yep. I reckon he was about the smartest person I've ever known," she acknowledged.

The leaves of the cottonwood trees swayed gracefully in the slight breeze. Nichole reined her horse to a halt in front of the old Spanish mission in the center of town.

Fowler observed the building that had been the most important edifice in the history of Texas. "The mission San Antonio de Valero, the Alamo," he stated reverently.

Nichole nodded her head. "Yes. The Alamo. I've been here several times and each time I stand in awe. To think that just thirty-three years ago, a small band of Texans, only a hundred and eighty-seven men, fought to the death against an army of five thousand Mexicans to gain independence for our state."

Her eyes roamed over the remains of the lovely old building. "I imagine that hundreds of years from now, people will still be telling the story of how those brave men, William Travis, Jim Bowie, Davy Crockett, and the others, held out for *thirteen* days before they were finally overwhelmed by Santa Anna's Army."

She thought for a minute before commenting, "Actually, I guess we can't claim Davy Crockett and his band of men as Texans. They only came to Texas after hearing rumors about the impending war when Texas declared her independence from Mexico." She laughed as a thought struck her. "I guess that's why they call Tennessee, 'the volunteer' state; they'll volunteer for *anything!* But I bet if they'd had a choice, they would have been born Texans."

"Texans are a unique breed of people, that's for sure," Fowler commented.

Nichole chuckled. "We're an audacious bunch to say the least. Do you know that Texas is the only state in the union that demands and is permitted to fly our flag on the same level as the flag of the United States? All the other states have to fly their flag below the level of the American flag. How's that for audacity!" she proclaimed proudly.

Fowler turned his horse toward the livery stables as he commented, "Even the women are adventuresome and cheeky. Must be something in the water."

"Could be," Nichole laughed in agreement.

This time when they checked into the hotel, Nichole made sure that Fowler got separate rooms. She wasn't about to take a chance on another romantic encounter with that skirt-chasing rake! He might not give a second thought to his habit of climbing into a woman's bed any time he wanted to satisfy his sexual urges. But she was not going to be a party to his wanton tendencies.

Her heart had withstood as much pain as it could already. And the worst was yet to come. She refused to think about how empty her life would be when they went their separate ways after finding her brother. She knew Fowler's leaving would literally rip her heart from her body. And he would leave. To him, she'd be just another notch on his bedpost.

They had decided to spend the night at the hotel, to enjoy a hot bath and a real meal, and then continue their journey early the next morning. Besides, the irreparable state of Nichole's breeches necessitated that she buy another pair. They also needed to restock some of their supplies that had gotten soaked and ruined when one of the pack mules had lost its footing in a swollen creek.

After leaving the general store, they decided to take a stroll before having dinner. Everywhere they looked people were decorating and sprucing up in preparation for the annual April celebration. Sunday was Easter and then after that was Fiesta San Antonio.

When they stopped to watch a group of small children wielding sticks bigger than they were, Fowler was clearly puzzled.

"What are they doing? I don't see any kind of a ball around. What are they trying to hit?"

Nichole laughed merrily at the children's antics. They were so cute. Some of them couldn't have been more than three or four years old, but they were swinging as hard as their little arms would permit.

"They're practicing their *pinata* swing." She could tell by the blank look on his face that Fowler had no earthly idea what a *pinata* was.

"You don't know what a *pinata* is, do you?"

"Never heard the word before. Is it a new game?"

"No. A *pinata* is a gaily decorated piece of clay pottery, usually in the shape of an animal. They fill it full of candies, fruits, and gifts, and hang it from a tree limb just above the children's reach. Then they blindfold the children, give them a long stick and each child gets to swing at the *pinata* until one of them breaks it and all the goodies fall out. It's great fun to watch. Maybe next year w—"

There went that tongue again! Dammit! She had almost said, "Maybe next year we can come for the fiesta." She knew there would be no "we" next year! At least her mind knew it, but apparently her heart had not accepted it yet. Would it ever accept not having Fowler in her life, now that she had admitted to herself that she loved him? She doubted it very much.

Fowler seemed not to have caught her almost slip of the tongue. "What about next year?"

"I was going to say that, maybe next year, you can arrange to be here for the celebration. My family has come several times. We enjoy it more each time we come," she lied.

He turned to her with an unfathomable look in his eyes. She had sounded sad. Had she begun to accept the fact that her brother was probably dead? Maybe she was just tired. They had been through one hellish week. He certainly couldn't blame her if she was weary.

"I think it's time we went back to the hotel."

"Yes, I guess we'd better," she said in a melancholy tone as they turned to retrace their way to the hotel.

Fowler longed to take her in his arms and comfort

her. To tell her that everything was going to be all right. The problem was, even though Nichole still adamantly insisted that if Nick were dead, she would feel it, he held out very little hope of finding the young man alive.

Nichole's bleak mood followed her through dinner and up to her room. She wasn't prone to depression. Quite the opposite in fact. She had often been accused of being a hopeless optimist by both family and friends. But, right now, she felt like she wanted to crawl into a corner and bawl her eyes out.

When Fowler left her at her door, she gave him a wan smile before bidding him good night.

"Nichole? Are you all right? I mean, you aren't coming down with a cold or something, are you? Should I send for a doctor to check you?" he inquired solicitously. Her downcast behavior worried him.

"No. I'm just tired, that's all. I'll be back to normal after a good night's sleep," she said as she opened the door to her room. "Good night, Fowler."

He caught her arm and pulled her to him before she could escape into her room. He gently kissed her soft lips and stroked her back affectionately as he hugged her.

"Sleep well, my little green-eyed vixen. Remember, I'm just next door if you need me."

She nodded her head affirmatively before entering her room. She knew only too well that he was just out of reach. As soon as the door closed behind her, the tears she had fought so hard to hold back, burst to the surface and flowed silently down her face.

In the next room, Fowler eyed the soft bed. It would be good to sleep in a bed instead of on the ground tonight. However, he wasn't near ready to go to sleep yet. He paced the floor, trying to decide what he would do to kill a few hours.

Maybe he'd go sit in on a hot poker game for a while. You never knew when you might pick up a bit of helpful information, and besides that, maybe it would relieve his pent-up tension. Tension that he didn't care to examine too closely for its cause.

He didn't have to. He knew what ailed him. It was a pair of emerald-green eyes that set his blood pounding like a fever running rampant through his body. And the cure was to take the body that housed those jewels into his arms and make love to her until he was weak with exhaustion.

But that would be only a temporary treatment of the symptoms as his desire for her would only intensify. She had become like a habit-forming drug which he was quickly becoming addicted to. And he couldn't afford to let that happen.

In the first place, Nichole was from a very wealthy and prominent family. What did he, the son of a preacher, have to offer a woman like her? Nothing. That's what.

In the second place, a U.S. Marshal's job wasn't exactly a Sunday picnic. He was often the target of some young gunman looking to make a name for himself. And, when you were in the habit of chasing outlaws and Indians, you had to expect to be shot at from time to time.

What woman in her right mind wanted to live day to day not knowing if this would be the day her husband was a tat slower than the man on the other end of his gun?

Until he'd met Nichole, he'd been perfectly happy with his life. What was there to complain about? He had his choice of women. Any time he thought the grass was a little greener on the other side of the fence, he just simply climbed over it. He loved the excitement of going after the bad guys, of disencumbering the world of some of its trash.

His father made the world a better place to live in his way, and Fowler did the same. The only difference was in the method each chose. His father's way might be kinder, but his was faster and more permanent.

No. A woman like Nichole would have to have the security of a husband whom she knew was coming home all in one piece.

And kids. She'd probably want a house full of kids. He didn't even like kids! Well, that wasn't exactly true. His sister had kids and he liked them okay, now that they were older. But when they were babies, he had begun to believe that they had had an allergic reaction to him.

Every time he had held one, they either had burped on him or wet on him! And usually had done both! He'd always felt relief that he didn't have to live in the same house with his nieces and nephews. Being awakened in the middle of the night by a crying baby was definitely not his idea of fun.

He paused in his pacing to look at his reflection in the mirror. He wondered what their children would look like. Would they have dark hair and green eyes like their mother or blond hair and blue eyes like him? They would most surely be as hardheaded and ornery as their mother was. He'd bet the farm on that!

It suddenly dawned on him where his thoughts had led him. "Good God Almighty! That green-eyed witch has made me nuts!" He shook his finger at the face looking back at him. "You just forget all this utterly stupid nonsense. She wouldn't marry you even if you wanted her to. Which you *don't!*"

He grabbed his hat and slammed it on his head as he headed for the door. He'd decided to get rip-roaring drunk. That's what he'd do. "Damn fickle woman. Doesn't think I'm good enough for her, does she? Well, that's just *fine!*"

It had been hard, but Carmen finally convinced her mother and *Tia* Rosie that she was not going to have a long engagement and an elaborate wedding.

Convincing her mother had been a piece of cake compared to convincing her father. That was a whole different matter all together.

"Two days!" Miguel roared. "My only daughter wants to get married in *two days!* Consuela, can you not talk some sense into that daughter of yours? I have planned to give her the most fabulous wedding this country has ever seen, ever since the minute she was born! And now she says she is getting married the day after tomorrow? No, no, no!" His level of loudness increased with each word. "I will not have it, do you hear?" He ruffled his hands through his hair in frustration as he paced back and forth in their bedroom.

Consuela covered her ears. "Miguel, the whole county can hear you. Stop yelling. And when did she become *my* daughter? Be reasonable, *querido*. You know Nick must get back to his family in Waco. He has responsibilities as a Texas Ranger. He has to

142

finish his mission. Innocent people are being harassed, maybe even killed."

She had tried logic and that hadn't worked. Maybe she should appeal to his sense of romance. "Besides, *mi amor*, when we were their age, we could not bear the thought of being apart even two days." She smiled shyly. "Or nights. Remember, my love?" She put her arms around his neck and pulled her body close to his until she stood on her tiptoes, to plant a passionate kiss on a spot just behind his left ear, knowing full well that it was an especially erotic spot for him.

He wrapped his arms around her, pulling her off her feet, as sensual chills skittered up and down his spine.

"Consuela," he moaned as he kissed her. "That is not fair."

"Hmmm, what is not fair, my love?" she said between kisses.

"You are blackmailing me and you know it," he accused breathlessly as she worked her magic on his willing body.

"She says she will go with him when he has to leave, *querido*. It is a long way from here to Waco. Her *duenña* can not go without sleep for almost two weeks." She continued her assault on his vulnerable spot.

"Chaperone?" he mumbled in a concupiscent stupor.

"So you will send for the priest, *muy pronto?*" She could tell by his tone of voice that he was way past the realm of rational thought.

"Priest? *Si, mañana, mañana*, tomorrow," he agreed, his mind in a sensuous trance.

* * *

It was a fidgety group of four who waited with apprehension in the study, no one saying a word. Each was listening intently to the ruckus taking place on the floor above them.

At first, Miguel's voice had been as clear as if he were in the same room, but then it began to taper to a lower pitch, finally to cease completely.

They waited several minutes, each listening but not hearing any sound, save their own breathing.

Tia Rosie patted Carmen's hand in confidence. "See, I told you your mother would take care of things."

Carmen sighed in relief.

Nick nervously finished his second, or was it his third drink?

He looked at Aunt Rosie. She smiled and nodded affirmatively at him.

He looked at Carmen who smiled shyly at him and clutched his free hand tighter in hers.

He then looked at Ricardo.

Ricardo gave him a knowing smile and a sly wink. "Congratulations, Nick. By this time Sunday, you will be a blissfully wedded man."

Nick was completely befuddled. "How do you know? I don't hear anything."

Ricardo laughed robustly. "That is how I know. Mother always gets what she wants when Father quits yelling."

"Huh?"

Carmen giggled. As kids, she and her brother could always tell which of their parents had won in the battle of wits by what happened *after* their father had quit yelling. If a door slammed, Daddy had won. If no sound could be heard, Mama had won. She wasn't sure exactly what took place but she had her suspicions.

Ricardo looked fondly at his sister's happy face, and then at Nick's still-confused countenance. "Do not worry, Nick. I have an inkling that everything will become crystal clear to you in the not too distant future," he said confidently.

What he knew that Nick didn't know was that his little sister was very much like their mother in temperament. There was no doubt in his mind that she would be able to wrap Nick around her little finger without him even being aware that she was doing it. Like mother, like daughter, so the old saying went.

Besides, Ricardo thought, it couldn't be too painful. He had never once heard his father complain.

He laughed heartily before walking over to help his aunt from her chair. "*Tia* Rosie, I guess it is up to you and me to get the ball rolling if there is to be a wedding celebration the day after tomorrow."

Fowler stopped in mid-stride. He thought he heard someone crying. He listened for a minute. Not hearing anything, he decided it must have been his imagination and started to walk on. There it was again. He was positive this time that he heard someone weeping.

He walked back to Nichole's door and paused to listen. He didn't hear anything and there was no light showing from under the door. She was probably asleep by now.

He tapped gently on the door. "Nichole?" he whispered. "Are you okay?"

He pressed his ear to the door. This time he heard

her sniffle and then delicately blow her nose. But still she would not answer him.

He jiggled the doorknob only to find that the door was unlocked. Why hadn't she locked it before going to bed? Could someone have entered her room after she was asleep and hurt her? The thought sent chills through him.

He carefully made his way across the dark room to stand beside her bed. He could tell by the rhythm of her breathing that she was not asleep.

"Nichole, what's the matter?" he inquired as he lifted the globe of the kerosene lamp to light the wick.

She heard the rattle of glass against glass. "Don't light the lamp." Her voice was thick with emotion.

Fowler sat down on the edge of the bed. "You scared the hell outta me. I thought someone might have hurt you."

Someone had hurt her all right. Him. But she'd never let him know that. "Go away. Just go away and leave me alone," she said through gritted teeth.

Her attitude took him by surprise. "Nichole? What's wrong with you? This isn't like you at all." He felt her forehead to see if she had a fever. "Are you sure you're not getting sick?"

She slapped his hand away. "Don't touch me! Get out of my room and leave me alone." She gave him a shove, catching him off guard and sending him to the floor with a loud thud. "Out! Go find some . . . some floozie's bed to play in and stay out of mine! I'm not your private whore, Fowler Barclay."

More than just his pride had been injured when his tail bone hit the hard floor. "Ouch! Why you little hellcat! I ought to turn you over my knee and blister your butt good." He grabbed for her arm as if to carry out his threat.

She swung at him with her pillow, catching him square in the face, sending feathers flying in all directions. She jumped to her feet, trying to keep her balance as she moved to the far side of the bed, stopping only when she came into contact with the wall.

The bouncy springs of the mattress creaked with each movement she made as she tried to move out of Fowler's reach.

Fowler had ears like a mountain lion. He could tell even in the pitch blackness where she was.

He lunged toward her as she bounced up against the wall, losing her balance and falling back into the middle of the bed, trapping Fowler underneath her.

She had knocked the air out of his lungs and with his face buried in the mattress, he struggled to get his breath. "Get off me," he grunted breathlessly.

She was trying to, but, between his flailing arms and the springy mattress she found it impossible to get her feet under her.

"If you would quit thrashing about like a chicken with its head cut off, I might be able to!" she retorted acrimoniously. "Hold still, dammit!"

"I am holding still. You're the one rocking the bed like a ship on the high seas. How the hell can I do anything with you sitting on top of me!" he shouted.

"Don't shout at me!" she shouted at him.

"I'm not shouting, you're shouting!" he shouted back at her.

"I am not shouting . . ." Her voice trailed off as she realized that she was indeed shouting.

By this time her bout of melancholy had passed,

and the hilarity of the situation struck her funny bone. She managed to roll off Fowler as she was convulsed with rib-cracking laughter.

Fowler found the lamp and quickly lit it. The scene that met his eyes was almost unbelievable.

Nichole sat in the middle of the bed, with tears of laughter running down her cheeks. The bed linen and quilts were tangled all around her. Her hair, along with the rest of the bed, was covered with feathers from the demolished pillow.

As she was about to gain control of herself, a stray feather floated down to land lightly on the end of her nose. When she tried to blow it away, it tickled, causing her to sneeze, sending feathers floating in the air again, and dropping like falling snowflakes.

This time, Fowler joined her in her hysterical laughing, and collapsed beside her on the bed as the feathers settled all about them.

As the last feather drifted down to land on the end of Nichole's nose, the bed gave way beneath them with a loud crash, sending its occupants to the floor and the feathers flying again.

Nichole, on the verge of another laughing binge, looked at Fowler with twinkling eyes. "The feather that broke the bed's back?" she quipped.

"I know one thing for certain. I'm going to let you explain to the proprietor what happened to this room tomorrow," he said as he leaned over and planted a kiss on her upturned face.

"Me!" she squawked.

"Well, it was your fault. *You* hit *me* with the pillow, remember? Why did you hit me, by the way?"

"Never mind. It doesn't matter." She looked

around her. "What a mess! How am I ever going to get this cleaned up enough to sleep here tonight?" she wondered out loud.

Fowler surveyed the room. It looked like a tornado had hit it! "Sweetheart, ain't no way in hell you're going to be able to clean up this mess tonight."

He rocked back and forth on his heels as a mischievous grin crossed his face. "Guess you'll just have to share my room for the night. But," he hastened to add when she looked like she was about to take his head off, "you'll have to promise to behave yourself."

"Me! Behave myself! Why you . . . you . . ." she sputtered.

He grabbed her hand, pulling her out the door behind him. "That's what I like. A woman of few words."

Fowler skidded to a halt in the hallway as he came face to face with an older couple passing by.

Nichole collided with his back. She peeked out from behind him to see why they had come to such a sudden stop. She had the uneasy feeling that she really didn't want to know.

When she saw the disapproving frown on the mature woman's face, she knew her first suspicion was right. The old prude looked like she had swallowed a sour persimmon. The man with her, presumably her husband, gave Fowler an admiring grin, until the woman elbowed him in the ribs.

"Really, Herbert," she reprimanded the man, "don't encourage such decadent behavior. They are a disgrace to this hotel."

She raised her monocle to peer at the young couple closer. She gasped as she got a clear look at them.

"Good heavens! They're . . . they're covered with feathers!" she exclaimed as she dropped her monocle to fan herself rapidly.

Fowler could feel Nichole snickering behind him. He was positive that they were quite a sight to behold all right.

He tried to sound nonchalant. "Excuse us, we were just on our way to my room."

The woman apparently heard Nichole's muffled laugh. "Well, I never," she decried, shocked to the very bottom of her bony feet.

Nichole stepped around in front of Fowler. "Well, maybe you should," she stated haughtily as she regally took his arm. "Come, my dear, we must be on our way."

The woman grabbed her husband's arm and pulled him along with her. "Come, Herbert. The management shall hear about this."

"Yes, dear," he said sedately as he gave Fowler and Nichole a sly wink over his shoulder.

Nichole made a face at the ramrod back of the departing woman.

"Old prune," she accused.

Fowler burst into gales of laughter when they were safely behind the closed door of his room. "Really, Nichole, shame on you. You're outrageous. You almost shocked that poor woman out of her corset."

"Well," she said guiltily, before she grinned impishly. "I couldn't help myself. Besides, the old biddy acted as if we had committed a crime or something."

"Well, you must admit we are a pretty strange sight to be roaming the corridors of a hotel." He turned her to face the mirror. "See for yourself."

She giggled merrily. "We look like escapees from a chicken coop."

Fowler turned her around to face him. "Hmmm, I've never kissed a woman covered in feathers before." So he did. Twice.

"How was it?"

"Ticklish."

She felt so good to him, he didn't want to release her. He suddenly felt very protective of the woman he held in his arms. Remembering his earlier concern, he kissed her forehead, then tilting her face back, he placed a gentle kiss on her lips. "Are you okay?"

She nodded her head, trying to look away from his questioning gaze but his hold wouldn't let her.

"You were crying when I entered your room. Why?"

Again, she tried to twist out of his arms. Unable to free herself, she leaned her head forward against his chest. Her emotions were too tender to talk about.

How could she answer his question? How do you tell a man that slowly, minute by minute, hour by hour, you'd fallen in love with him? You hadn't wanted to. You'd fought desperately against it but it had happened anyway.

First there were the long days that you'd worked together side by side, each helping the other, and then the nights when you'd shared the duties of the camp before finally settling down to eat the meal and sip coffee as you sat around the fire talking. The two of you had worked, fought, and laughed together and it felt right. It felt good.

They had started off as reluctant partners and then slowly became friends. And then love had come. But only to one of them.

151

Nichole raised her head to meet Fowler's eyes. Eyes that were looking at her with concern and question. How could she tell him that she loved him? She was afraid to say the words out loud. But she couldn't stop the emotions, the feelings.

Without speaking a word, she kissed him, letting her kiss and her body speak all the words and feelings she couldn't say aloud.

Fowler kissed her back hungrily, running his hands up and down her slender back. "Nichole," he moaned before covering her mouth again. His heart was beating erratically. Was he misreading her actions? He didn't think so but he had to know for sure.

Raising his lips from hers, he searched her face for the answer to his question. "Nichole?"

When she opened her eyes and looked into his, he knew he had the answer he so wanted.

Sweeping her up into his arms, he carried her the six steps to the bed. Gently lying her on top of the cover, he deftly removed her clothing, never breaking contact with her body. He was driven by a desire like he had never before experienced. Primal hunger had taken his body past his endurance, beyond all thought of reason or rightness.

Nichole was so lost in her passion-clouded world that she was unaware of how or when their clothes left their bodies. When she felt the heat of his naked skin next to hers, she was too far over the threshold of pleasure to care. She only knew that if he didn't quickly extinguish the blaze that burned to the very depth of her, she would surely not survive the fire he had created within her.

When he sought entrance, he knew she was ready

for him, her creamy heat easing his way. He slid into her until he met her virgin wall. He stopped his movement to give her time to adjust to his fullness.

She didn't understand why he had suddenly stopped his probing when the heat was building so intensely. She didn't know how to tell him that she desperately needed something more. Her very soul was on fire!

Her soft cries of unfulfilled sexual desire were Fowler's undoing. Kissing her deeply, he plunged past the barrier to bury himself within her. He felt her tense momentarily with his final plunge. Her sharp intake of breath told him he had hurt her, but he knew that she must be quickly brought back to the pinnacle of desire if she was to reach her fulfillment.

Slowly, he began to stroke in and out, wanting to bring her back to her previous state of arousal without causing her more pain. Not until he felt her answering movements did he quicken his pace.

She met him thrust for thrust in the ancient-old mating rhythm, instinctively following his lead until he suddenly sent her soaring to the top and over the peak.

He felt her throbbing climax as she pulsated around him, pulling him over the edge with her. Together they soared the heights and slowly drifted back to earth on a cloud of pleasure.

He gently cradled her in his arms, bracing his weight on his elbows, as their breathing slowly returned to normal. Tenderly, he brushed her lips with a kiss as he searched her eyes for any regrets, praying she wouldn't have any.

Her lashes fluttered open and she met his gaze.

Making love with this man was more wonderful than she had ever imagined in her innocence. She smoothed his tousled hair back from his face, her hand lingering at the back of his head to pull his lips back down to hers.

He could feel her body quivering around his limp shaft. The sensation was very arousing, but he knew she would be sore and he didn't want to add further to her discomfort. He slowly eased himself out of her. Kissing her lips, he rolled over, pulling her with him. He nestled her head against his chest, tucking her securely under his arm as he kissed the top of her head.

"It won't hurt the next time, sweetheart. I promise it will only get better. It's late, we'd better try to get a little sleep before morning."

The pleasure had soothed the pain almost immediately. She felt only a contentment that had not been a part of her before this night. How could anything be better? she wondered.

Chapter Ten

Nick looked at his beautiful bride of twelve days. He still found it hard to believe that they were married, and in a very short time, would be at his home, the Rocking W Ranch. He had sent one of the *vaqueros* ahead to let his family know that they would be there within the hour.

Carmen's father, worried about the trouble in the area and the recent attempt on Nick's life, insisted that six of his best men escort his daughter and new son-in-law to Nick's home.

The de Cardona coach was a magnificent vehicle. The elaborate Concord coach had the de Cardona coat of arms in gold scrollwork on the doors and silver-encased side lamps graced the outside. The interior was done in plush burgundy velvet. The six matched black horses that pulled it were as fleet of foot as they were handsome.

He thought about their wedding day. No wedding could have been more beautiful. Word had spread like wildfire that it was to be held at two o'clock Sunday afternoon. Easter Sunday. The perfect day for new beginnings.

Nick had been flabbergasted at the number of guests who had dropped everything in order to attend. Counting the *vaqueros* and their families there must have been four hundred people there!

He had made the mistake of assuming that it would be only the family and the people who worked on the ranch. After all, given the short notice, who would have believed that half of Texas would show up!

Nick had dressed in the traditional costume of the Spanish *caballero*, borrowed from Ricardo, of course. He had looked resplendent in black trousers and the matching waist-length jacket, worn open to reveal a gray vest and white silk shirt with an attached jabot. The crimson cummerbund matched the color of the braid that ran the length of the trousers. A silver concho band encircled the black, flat topped, wide-brimmed hat.

Carmen had worn her mother's wedding gown. The full skirt with its twelve-foot train had accented the smallness of her waist. The white lace *mantilla* that covered her hair had been passed from mother to daughter for six generations.

Miguel's grandmother had brought it to the colonies as a prized possession when she and her husband had left Spain. His own mother had carefully protected it on the long journey to what was then known as New Spain, later to be known as Texas.

Each new bride had lovingly wrapped it in white

156

satin, carefully folded and stored in the hand-carved rosewood box to be saved for her own daughter's wedding day.

The wedding had been held outdoors and even the weather had obeyed Miguel's order to be perfect for the marriage of his only daughter.

Nick had been so nervous he wasn't sure if he would make it through the long ceremony. Until he had seen his beautiful Carmen being led through the rose-covered arbor on her father's arm.

She had looked so gorgeous that his breath had stuck in his throat. From that moment on, he had been dazed. As far as he had been concerned, only two people existed in the world, he and Carmen. When she had placed her hand in his at the altar, it was as if they had been enshrouded in a cloud of love, shutting out the world around them.

He remembered little of the actual ceremony. He had knelt and rose and repeated the vows as the priest bid him to, but his mind had been in a trance. Beside him had stood the most precious and cherished treasure he could ever dream of possessing in his entire life.

In the short span of a month, he had stood at death's door, found heaven in the petite package of a chocolate-eyed girl named Carmen, married this girl of his dreams, and in a few minutes, he would be reunited with his family whom he had not seen in more than two months. The only thing that could have made his homecoming perfect would be to have Nichole home from finishing school in Washington, D.C.

* * *

James and his little brother, John, were watching the horizon with eagle eyes, anxious to catch the first glimpse of their big brother.

When the carriage with its accompanying entourage came into view, the two boys stared at it in wide-eyed amazement. They had never seen anything so grand in their young lives. They had been expecting to see Nick on horseback. Since that was how he had ridden away, it never crossed their minds that he would come home any other way.

James was the first to snap out of his surprise. He ran into the house, hollering at the top of his lungs, "Mama! Daddy! Everybody! Come see! You won't believe it! Come quick!"

Cassie and Maria came running from the kitchen at the onset of James's excited shouting. Mark hurried out of the study. Amy and Kathleen almost collided as they raced down the stairs.

Having been sent for when the messenger first arrived to announce Nick's imminent arrival, Cody quickly returned and was in the back yard washing some of the grime off. When he heard James's voice, he walked around to the front of the house to see if Nick had arrived. Cody knew word had been sent to the Lazy M to let Grandpa Montclair and Lottie know that Nick was almost home, but they had not yet come.

The whole family, minus Nichole, of course, stood in the front yard with their mouths gaping open in amazement.

"What the loving hell is taking place?" Mark asked. He put his arm around Cassie as she moved closer to him.

"Who could that be? We don't know anyone with a fancy rig like that," she declared.

Little Johnny tugged at his mama's skirt. "Mommy, Mommy, is that the king of Texas?" He figured only someone very, very important could be arriving in such grand style. And a king was the most important person he had ever heard of!

Cassie patted the top of his head. "No, dear. Texas doesn't have a king. We have a governor, but that's not him either." She looked again at the impressive rig pulling into their yard. "At least, I don't think it is," she said a little uncertainly.

The group stood spellbound as Nick stepped out of the carriage and turned back to help a beautiful Spanish girl down.

Nick looked at his family standing like statues, staring at him and Carmen. He grinned a cocky, lopsided grin. "Well, isn't anyone glad to see me? I only intended to surprise you, I didn't intend to shock you speechless," he teased as he lead his bride forward to meet her new family.

Carmen had been scared to death to meet Nick's family. She was so afraid that they would not like her. And, now that they had seen her, her worse fears were confirmed. They didn't like her! They just stood there, looking from her to Nick. She was on the verge of tears when Nick placed his arm around her to nudge her forward to meet them.

"Carmen, this is probably the only time in your life, that you will ever see, or I should say *hear*, this bunch so quiet," he teased. "This is my mother and father, Cassie and Mark. Next to them are my sisters, Amy and Kathleen. The big mean-looking one there is my older brother, Cody. The two little ones looking at you like they've just seen a fairy princess are James and Johnny. And, Maria, the one who keeps up with this bunch."

He placed a kiss on Carmen's forehead before saying, "And this is Carmencita Maria Pilar de Cardona. Henceforth to be known as Carmen Westerfield, my beloved bride."

A chorus of "bride!" rang out from the eight stupefied faces before pandemonium broke loose. Everyone started talking at once as they rushed forward to greet the newest member of the family.

Cassie hugged her new daughter-in-law. "Carmen, welcome to the family. I just can't believe it. Nick never breathed a *word* about having someone special in his life. Oh, I'm so happy for you. I'm so happy for all of us." She hugged Carmen again before turning to her beaming son. "Shame on you for keeping such a secret from us!"

"Well, I didn't even know myself. It all happened kind of suddenly."

Mark shook his second son's hand. "Congratulations, son." He turned to Carmen. "And for you, my dear, I wish you all the happiness in the world." He, too, hugged Carmen. "Welcome to this crazy bunch we call a family."

"Well, I'm going to claim my right to kiss the bride," Cody stated as he stepped up and gave her a brotherly kiss. He shook his head as he looked at his brother. "How did you ever convince this little bundle of beauty to marry you? You rascal!" He grabbed his brother's hand and slapped him on the back. "Welcome home, kid. We were worried sick about you and here you were off capturing a wife."

Amy and Kathleen both hugged their new sister and immediately tripped over each other to ask questions about the wedding. "What did your dress look like? What did Nicky wear? Who all was there? How many bridesmaids did you have? Oh, just start at the beginning and don't leave anything out. Not one single detail!" they finally chimed in unison.

Carmen was a little overwhelmed by all the attention and looked at Nick for support.

Nick laughed out loud at the bewildered look on her face. "I told you the quiet wouldn't last," he warned her lovingly as he put one arm around her and the other around his mother. "If you think this is bad, wait until Nichole comes home from school. That's when you'll really get the third degree!" he proclaimed.

A sudden silence descended on the merriment like an ominous cloud.

A shiver of fear ran down Cassie's back as she looked at her husband and then back to her son. "Nichole isn't in school. She came home in March. Somehow, she knew something had happened to you. Her 'twin feeling' kept telling her you were in danger.

"When we told her what little we knew about your disappearance, she took off in the middle of the night to find you herself." She could tell by the incredulous look on Nick's face that she already knew the answer to her next question. "She didn't find you, did she?" she stated flatly as she sought the comfort of Mark's embrace.

"Son, are you saying that you haven't seen or heard from Nichole?" Mark couldn't believe this was happening. Had he gotten his son back only to discover that his daughter was now missing?

Nick slowly shook his head. "Until two weeks ago, I didn't even know who I was. I was shot in the back and left to die in a gully. A couple of my father-in-law's *vaqueros* found me when they were looking for strays. If it hadn't been for Carmen's mother and aunt's doctoring, I would be dead now." He tightened his grip around Carmen's shoulders, pulling her closer to him.

Cassie looked into her husband's eyes. "What could have happened to her? How do we start searching for her when we don't even know which direction she took off in?"

Mark kissed her forehead before taking a deep breath and exhaling slowly. "I don't know. Let's all go in the house and . . ." He shrugged his shoulders tiredly as he ran one hand through his hair in despair. "And try to figure out something."

Before the sun had peeked over the horizon the next morning, Nick and Cody had their horses saddled and were ready to ride out.

Cody had already said his good-byes to the family. He moved a short distance away from Nick and his new wife to give them a little privacy.

Carmen was trying to be brave, not wanting her tears to be the last thing Nick saw before he left. "Be careful, *querido*."

"I will. Don't you worry about anything. Mom and Dad will help you get settled in. I hate that I have to leave you so soon." He pulled her close before planting a kiss on her upturned face.

She stood on her tiptoes to receive and to return her husband's kiss. "I know, sweetheart, but it cannot be helped. You have to find your sister. Just remem-

162

ber that I love you with all my heart, darling. I will pray each night for your safe and speedy return."

As she watched him and his brother ride away, she couldn't prevent the tears from spilling over and silently trickling down her cheeks. She stood there and watched them until they were but a tiny speck on the horizon.

When she felt hands on her shoulders, she turned her face into Mark's shirt and sobbed openly.

"Don't worry, little one, everything will turn out all right," he tried to assure her. It just has to, he thought to himself.

"Come back into the house and have some breakfast," he urged. "We can't have Nick coming back to find his wife wasted away from worry, now can we?"

Carmen shook her head as she daintily blew her nose into the handkerchief he'd handed her.

When Nick had finished giving the details of his undercover assignment and his subsequent shooting, the Ranger captain rocked back in his chair and swiveled around to look out the window.

"You're positive that no one could have trailed you when you were spying on Linc when he met with John North?" he finally asked.

"Absolutely. Even the sentry posted at the entrance to the caverns was dead drunk before I slipped out the first time. And the second time I was the one who met North's man to receive instructions as to where Linc should meet him." Nick shook his head in denial. "No, I'm absolutely positive that until after we left Corpus Christi, Linc was not in the least bit suspicious of me."

The captain turned back around to look at the two

young men sitting in front of his desk. "That was after the man whom you hadn't seen before joined ya'll on the trail, wasn't it?"

"That's right," he confirmed. "And that's also when he sent me and a guy called Red on ahead, supposedly to pick up something at the San Juan Carricitos ranch. Only I never made it there."

The captain steepled his fingers as he turned over some thoughts in his mind. "You know what this implies, don't you?"

Nick nodded his head. "Yeah. Either there's a traitor here, or someone in Austin has access to the governor's private files."

"Which do you think it is?"

"Sir, there's not a Ranger among us whom I wouldn't trust with my life. I'm betting the traitor is in Austin."

He looked the captain square in the eyes. "And, if that's the case, he's got to be pretty high up the rank to get past Pease's secretary. Samuel guards the governor like a watchdog," he added grimly.

The captain left his chair to walk over and peer out the window. "You still suspect that North is fronting for someone, don't you?"

"Yes, sir, I do. I have from the beginning. North doesn't strike me as having enough brains to come up with a scheme as smoothly run as this one. I think he's a middleman for someone who can't afford even a hint of scandal to touch his name."

"You don't suppose it could be Samuel, do you?"

"Not a chance. Samuel is as loyal as they come. Besides that, he's a happy and contented man. He knows, as does everyone else in the capitol, that the governor's office would be in shambles without him.

And, believe me, everybody, including the governor, gives him his due credit.

"No." Nick shook his head. "Whoever is behind this is a cunning and ruthless person, filled with greed and lust for power. He'd have to be to have ordered the things that have happened."

"Do you have any inkling as to whom it might be then?"

Nick shook his head before looking the captain in the eyes. "No. But I *will* find the son of a bitch! And, when I get through with him, there won't be enough pieces left to stuff down a bog hole."

"I have no doubt about that. However, right now we have a more serious problem on our hands. If your theory is correct, and now I'm more inclined to believe it is than before, it would certainly explain a few things."

Nick and Cody waited patiently while the captain lit a cigar after offering one to each of them.

"When you failed to meet your contact, he hung around your rendezvous point for more than a week. When you still didn't show, he came back here to make his report. When he left my office, his intent was to nose around and see if he could pick up any information that might give him a hint as to where the Travis gang might be holed up.

"There were only three people besides myself who knew the identity of your contact. And, since neither you nor the governor have had a chance to meet him in person yet, only myself and one other person knew what he looked like."

Nick was having difficulty following the captain's train of thought.

"I don't understand what you're getting at, sir."

"Fowler Barclay is missing."

"What!" Nick jumped up out of his chair like a shot out of a cannon. "How the hell can that be?"

"I don't *know* how the hell that can be! The sentry said he rode in here by himself. He never mentioned that he was going to meet anyone or that he even knew anyone here. But, when he left here, the sentry said there was a young man riding beside him. The description doesn't fit any of our men."

The captain slammed his fist down on his desk as he rose from his chair. "A United States Marshal rides through our gates and just disappears into thin air! We haven't been able to find any trace whatsoever of him. *You* tell me how the hell that can happen!"

A prickle ran up and down Nick's spine. The hair on the back of his neck stood on end. He looked at Cody.

Cody had seen that look on his brother's face before. "You're not thinking what I think you're thinking, are you?"

"Naw!" He shook his head in disbelief. "She wouldn't have done something like that. Would she?" Nick asked skeptically.

"She always did think she could do anything you could do," Cody reminded Nick.

"It does sound like a stunt she'd pull," Nick conceded.

"How could she have pulled it off?"

"Are you kidding? You know her as well as I do."

The captain was getting dizzy looking from one brother to the other while trying to follow their disjointed conversation.

First, one of his Rangers disappears, then a U.S.

Marshal vanishes right from under his nose! His patience with mysteries had run out!

He slammed his fist down on his desk again, as he bellowed loud enough to be heard halfway to Waco. "Will you two stop talking in code and tell me what the hell you're talking about? You sound like you've been chewing on locoweed, for God's sake!"

"Uh, when did the marshal disappear, sir?" Nick hesitated to ask.

"About the middle of March. Why?" He looked at the two brothers.

"The timing is right," Cody stated.

"Sure as hell is," Nick agreed.

"Well, you're gonna have to tell him. He's your boss."

"Me! She's your sister, too."

"Yes, but, she's *your* twin sister."

"Hey, I—"

"Westerfield!" the captain roared again.

"Uh, sir . . ." Nick wasn't sure how one went about telling his superior officer that he had a sneaky suspicion that his twin sister was involved in the disappearance of a U.S. Marshal. He hedged for time, hoping for an inspiration. Unfortunately, one didn't come.

"Yes!" the captain snapped.

"What did the, uh, person who rode out with Barclay look like?"

"The sentry's report stated that he was a slender, young man. He couldn't tell his age exactly because his hat was pulled low over his eyes. He was wearing a long-sleeved, plaid shirt, a black vest, and faded denim breeches."

"Oh my God! It's her!" Nick admitted.

"Those damned breeches! It's her all right. I knew it had to be her. She's gone and got herself in trouble, again. Dammit to hell!" Cody confirmed as he ran his hands through his hair in agitation.

The brothers could tell that the captain was on the verge of exploding. He had turned red in the face, and they could almost see smoke coming out his ears.

"Uh, sir, maybe you ought to sit down while we, uh, try to explain this. I don't think you're gonna like the explanation," Nick warned.

"I can guarantee he's not gonna like it," Cody mumbled under his breath.

The captain shot Cody a silencing glare before taking his seat. "Well, go ahead," he prompted as Nick searched his brain for the right words to explain the situation.

"Do you remember my sister, my twin sister, Nichole, coming to the fort after I disappeared?"

"Do I remember!" he snorted. "Hell, yes, I remember her. She had the unmitigated gall to call me an arrogant buffoon and a bumbling jackass because I couldn't tell her any more than I had already told your parents!"

Cody tried unsuccessfully to hide his smirk. "That's our sweet-tempered little sister, all right."

Once again the captain glared at him. "Would you mind terribly much in getting to the point?" he said in a mordacious tone of voice as he turned his glare on Nick.

This time Nick also glared at his older brother. If Cody wasn't going to help him, the least he could do was keep his comments to himself and quit antagonizing the man.

"The point is, that the 'young man' who left with Marshal Barclay sounds a whole lot like it could have been my twin sister, sir. We're not positive, you understand," he hastened to add. "But it probably was Nichole," he admitted reluctantly.

"Your sister," he stated in a monotone.

"Yes, sir."

The captain's flat statement was only the calm before the storm. "Your sister!" he roared. "You're trying to tell me, that Fowler Barclay, a United States Marshal on an urgent mission, just up and took off with your sister!"

"Well, uh, not exactly." Nick wiped beads of sweat from his brow. Damn, the weather was hot today. "It's more likely that she, uh, took off with him. Or more precisely, she made him go with her."

"She *made* him go with her?" he stated incredulously.

"Let me explain, sir."

"I certainly wish you would because I don't believe a word of what I'm hearing so far."

"We're twins, you see, and there is a strong bond between us. Sometimes we can 'feel' when something is not right with the other. Nichole came home, all the way from Washington, D.C., because she 'felt' that I was in some kind of danger. And, of course, she was right. She wasn't satisfied that everything was being done to find me. So she left a note for our parents telling them that she was going to find me herself and she took off during the night.

"Knowing my sister as I do, she would have come here first, hoping to get some information about what I was working on so she'd have a place to start looking."

"She did come here and . . ." The captain wracked his brain trying to remember the events of that day. "Come to think of it, she left just before Fowler arrived." He slapped his thigh in consternation. "Dammit! Why didn't I remember? She *was* dressed in breeches. But I still don't see how she could've found out about the marshal."

"I can't explain how she could have known that Barclay might be able to help her, but I'd wager she found out somehow. Then she *persuaded* him to go with her." Nick could tell by the look on the other man's face that he didn't believe him.

"She couldn't have done that," he scoffed in disbelief.

Cody spoke up. "You don't know Nichole. She could do that," he said flatly with all the confidence in the world.

The captain steepled his fingers in thought as he swung his chair around to look out the window. Women! They were nothing but a pack of trouble. He turned back to face the brothers, resignation clearly stamped on his stern features.

"Well, what the hell are you doing still sitting in my office?" he roared in frustration. "Get the hell out there and find that . . . that . . . sister of yours, before she gets herself killed, dammit!"

Both men jumped to their feet and were halfway out the door before he'd finished speaking.

"Yes, sir!" they chimed in unison. "We're on our way."

Chapter Eleven

Fowler and Nichole had just carried the saddles to their horses and were adjusting the saddle blankets when they heard the sound of hoofbeats. They both said, almost in unison, "We've got company."

Three riders appeared on the grassy knoll about two hundred yards from them. One led a string of four horses, another, three horses and a mule, and the third man had three horses in tow. They reined up when they saw Fowler and Nichole.

"What do you make of it?" Nichole asked as she tucked her braided hair under her hat.

"I don't know yet, but, if they make a move for their rifles, grab your rifle and make a run for that fallen tree trunk over there."

After some discussion, the men started moving toward them again, their horses at a walk.

"I guess we'll have to let them come on in, since we don't know who they are or what their intentions are yet, but keep watching their rifles," he cautioned.

The men had closed just a few more yards when Fowler spoke softly, but firmly, "Start leading your horse toward the creek as though you are going to water him. When you get behind the trees, hop on him and ride straight ahead as quietly as you can. If shooting starts, ride as fast as you can away from here. When the shooting stops, if it's safe for you to come back, I'll fire three fast shots. If you don't hear three shots in a row, then keep going and don't come back. Go home."

"I'll do no such thing!"

"Dammit, woman! Do as I tell you. I'm trying to save your life!"

"No! I'm staying with you. Two against three is a hell of a lot better odds than one against three. I'm not leaving, Fowler. So you'd just better start thinking how *we* are going to handle this," she stated adamantly.

The look Fowler flung her fully expressed his anger with her for not obeying him, but he could tell by her stubborn stance that she intended to stay.

"Do you really know how to use that gun, Nichole?"

"I know how to use it."

Fowler heard the familiar click-click of a gun being cocked.

"Good girl, but leave it in your holster for now," he said as he eared the hammer back on his own Colt .45. He was sure hoping for her sake that she knew how to use it.

"I figure they are horse thieves. If you hear me say

'now,' grab your gun and take the outside man to our left first."

Since Nichole was standing to the right of Fowler that didn't make any sense to her. "Why shouldn't I take the one to my right since he is nearly in front of me?"

"Damn it, Nichole, if you want to live, do as I say! Now tell me you'll take the one to the left," he demanded.

"Okay! I'll take the one to the left."

Nichole remembered hearing her grandfather tell Cody and Nick, "When you figure trouble is brewing, take a couple of deep breaths to steady yourself." She began to breathe deeply and slowly.

"You all right?"

"I'm okay. Just following Grandpa's instructions," she replied calmly.

When the men were within thirty paces of them, Fowler spoke, "That's close enough."

The men stopped.

"You ain't feelin' none too friendly this mornin', are ya?" the one in the middle said as he spit a stream of tobacco juice on the ground.

"Don't have time for visiting, Mister. We've got a lot of traveling to do."

"Well, you won't be a doin' it on them horses," he said smugly. "Now you just move away from 'em. I don't want 'em to git hurt."

"Now!"

Nichole's hand closed around the butt of her gun, and with a smooth, unbroken sweep of her arm, she brought it up in line with the man's chest and fired. She saw him roll backwards with the impact of her bullet.

She swung her gun to the man in the center, but it wasn't necessary. Fowler had beat her to him. The force of his bullet slammed the man backwards and off his horse.

Nichole quickly swung her gun back to the man she had shot. He was still clinging to his saddle horn and trying to raise his gun. She shot him again. This time he crumpled and fell from his horse.

She was aware that Fowler's gun was roaring before she had fired her first shot, and that a plume of smoke belched out at them from the man to her right. She was even vaguely aware that something had hit the ground at her feet, spraying her boots with the caliche soil.

Fowler glanced at Nichole to be sure she was unhurt. "You all right?"

"I don't think I'm shot if that's what you mean."

He then went quickly to where the horse thieves lay, pausing briefly at each one to make sure they were dead.

Now that the danger had passed, Nichole began to feel the affects of the adrenaline surging through her body. Feeling the need to do something to conceal from Fowler how sickly and shaken she was, she reloaded her gun. But her hands were shaking so hard that she dropped one of the bullets.

When she bent down to pick it up, she saw the bullet hole between her feet. She knew in an instant that it had come from the man to her right, the one who Fowler had shot first. He was the only one of the thieves who had fired a shot.

Having assured himself that the men were dead, Fowler whirled on Nichole with the intention of giving her a tongue-lashing for not leaving as he had ordered her to. However, seeing her condition, his anger left him.

He started walking back toward her, his gun still in his hand. "Girl, you are an awesome wonderment. How in the hell did you learn to use a gun like that?"

Nichole gave up trying to reload her gun. "I told you, I watched and listened to Grandpa as he taught Cody and Nicky." She shrugged her shoulders. "Then I practiced with Nicky and sometimes just by myself. Besides, you gave us the edge, you know."

"Yeah, I know." He gave her a lopsided grin. "You're not the only one with a wise grandpa. I can still hear him telling me, 'When you're sure you're gonna have to shoot, then shoot damn it! Don't talk, shoot.'"

"Sounds like mighty good advice to me," Nichole said as she breathed a silent "thank you" to Fowler's departed grandfather for having such a smart grandson.

She looked around her at the three dead men and the nervously moving horses and mules. Counting their two horses and two pack mules, there was a total of eighteen animals. The animals could smell the scent of death that permeated the air, and they tried in vain to pull loose from the restraining ropes that tied them together.

Fowler started to saddle his horse.

Nichole looked at him in exasperation. "Fowler! What in the devil are we to do with all these animals? And what about the men? Are you just going to leave them here?"

Having tightened the cinch of his saddle to his satisfaction, Fowler walked over to the man nearest him, and squatted down on his haunches to see if he could find any identification. "We'll take them to the next town we come to and leave them with the local undertaker. The place probably isn't big enough to have a town marshal."

Not finding anything to identify the man, he tossed the body over one of the horses and then did the same with the other two men.

While Fowler was loading the rest of their belongings onto their pack mules, Nichole took the horses down to the creek to drink. Since they had taken care of their own horses before they had started breaking camp, she had only the stolen horses and the dead men's horses, probably stolen also, to water.

To say that thirteen thirsty horses and one thirsty mule was a handful was a gross understatement. Some of the horses were so thirsty that they didn't stop at the water's edge, but waded out into the creek to fill their bellies.

Fowler knew what was going to happen if she tried to take all the animals to water at one time. But was he going to warn her? Not on your life! He sat back on his heels to watch the show.

"Whoa, damn you, whoa!" It was rapidly becoming apparent to Nichole that unless she wanted to go for a swim, which she didn't, she'd better turn loose their tow ropes and fast. "Ouch! Watch out where you're putting your big foot—hoof—you four-legged clodhopper!" She pushed at the big strawberry roan with both hands and jerked her foot back just a split second before it had a chance to put its full weight on her foot.

When she had dropped the tow ropes, two of the horses and the mule had stopped in their tracks. It was obvious to her that the horses were well trained for working cattle. Why the mule stopped was anybody's guess, probably just stubbornness on his part.

As Nichole walked past the strawberry roan to gather the reins of the two horses, it swished its big tail right smack in her face, knocking her hat off her head and then proceeded to place one large hoof square in the middle of it.

"Ugh! Oh, for heaven's sakes!" she sputtered and spit as she pulled pieces of horse hair from her mouth. She bent down to retrieve her mashed hat, all the while tugging at the roan's unmoving hoof. "Get off my hat, you—you flea-bitten nag!"

The mule, having at this inopportune moment decided that it, too, needed a drink, advanced on the creek. And, not being one of God's more intelligent creatures, instead of going around Nichole, who was still bent over trying to wrest her hat from under the roan's hoof, it attempted to push her out of its way.

Nichole took a nose dive, hitting the water with a loud splash, and sending it spraying high into the air. The skittish horses side-stepped a couple of times before resuming their interrupted drinking.

The strawberry roan snorted, the mule flopped his big ears, and Fowler rolled on the ground, laughing so hard that his sides ached. Not a wise idea on his part.

Nichole came up out of the water, sputtering and spitting as she pulled her wet hair out of her face. She stomped angrily out of the water, soaked to the skin, her boots, filled with creek water, sloshed with each step she took.

She slapped the roan on the rump, grabbed her hat off the ground, and hit the mule upside the head with it. She stood there, glaring at Fowler, as he went off on another tangent of howls and guffaws.

He was so busy laughing that he didn't see her intent.

She filled her hat with water and calmly marched to where Fowler was rolling on the ground in hysterics. And, without preamble, she dumped its contents directly on his head and then whopped *him* upside the head with it!

He made a grab for her as she turned to leave him in his puddle of water. "Wait. Nichole. I'm sorry." He didn't sound sorry as he tried to control his laughter. "I shouldn't have laughed at you but . . ." Once again, his chuckles got the best of him.

He pulled her down beside him as he tried to control himself, wiping tears of laughter from his eyes. "If you could have seen yourself . . ."

"You could have come helped me, you know," she said accusingly.

"What? And miss the best show I've ever seen! Not on your life. That was better than any theatrical performance I've ever been to."

He kissed the tip of her nose and pulled a piece of moss from her hair. "But I'll make it up to you for laughing at your antics. You go change clothes and I'll gather up the animals."

"Oh, sure. After *I* do all the hard stuff, *now* you volunteer to help. Thanks a lot, Mr. Barclay. Where were you when I needed you?" It had begun to settle in on her just how funny her tug of war with the horse must have looked from a different angle.

A smile quirked at the corner of her mouth. She clamped her lips tight, trying not to giggle at the picture in her mind. Her eyes sparkled with mirth.

Finally, the hilarity of it hit her, and she broke out in chuckles.

"I guess I did look ridiculous, didn't I?" She fell back on the grass, laughing at herself. The tension from the gun fight slowly ebbed from her body.

"Well, I must admit that this is the first time I've ever seen an intelligent, hundred-and-fifteen-pound woman trying to match brains and brawn with a dumb, twelve-hundred-pound horse."

"But," she reminded him, "it wasn't a fair match. He cheated. The mule was on his side."

Fowler nodded his head, trying hard to keep a serious look on his face. "This is true."

Nichole's emerald-green eyes locked with Fowler's sapphire-blue ones. He watched the conflicting emotions chase each other across her beautiful, but wet, face.

He remembered that strange, almost sickening feeling, that followed killing for the first time. Even if it was in self-defense, it settled in the pit of your stomach like a meal gone bad.

He kissed her gently on the lips as he spoke softly, "I was proud of you awhile ago when we had to face down those men. You knew what had to be done and you did it without hesitation."

She threw her arms around his neck and pulled him close. "Oh, Fowler," she cried. "At the time, I was calm and confident because I knew it was either them or us. But, after it was over, I was shaking like a leaf."

He cuddled her close. "I know, sweetheart, I know. Try to put it out of your mind now. It isn't easy to take a man's life, but sometimes it has to be done."

He, too, had been afraid, not for himself, but for

her. He had half feared that he would find her shot and bleeding, maybe even lying dead on the ground, after the shooting was over. Even now, the thought of what could have happened chilled his very soul.

He kissed her again, this time with a passion so intense that it seared their very souls. She ardently returned his kiss and clung to him as if her life depended upon making love with this strong, protective man. They made love with a fierceness born from a need to cleanse their souls of the memory of the terrible violence they had faced together.

Afterwards, he rolled onto his back, pulling her atop him, holding her tenderly in his arms, almost as if she were a fragile piece of crystal that he was afraid he might break.

He looked into her eyes, as if trying to see into her heart. "Your eyes are the most beautiful shade of green that I've ever seen." He kissed one eyelid then the other.

"Thank you. I inherited the unusual color from my mother."

"And the most kissable lips, so soft and sweet." He kissed them again to be sure he was right. He was.

"Again, I have my mother to thank for that trait."

"Your father was a lucky man to have had such a beautiful pattern in front of him when he was making you."

He rolled to his side, propping up on his elbow so he could rest his head in one hand and gaze at her loveliness. He wrapped a lock of her hair around his finger and brought it to his face, gently rubbing its softness against his lips.

Nichole wrapped her arms around Fowler, pulling him close so she could nip at one of his earlobes.

"Well, I've never heard him complain about it. In fact, he always seems very contented." She grinned impishly. "Now I think I understand why." She rubbed her supple body suggestively against his.

"Ummm, you little minx," he groaned as he covered her naked body with his equally unclothed form.

Instantly, Fowler responded. He was hard and pulsating in eager anticipation of her unspoken promise. He cupped her breasts, bracing his weight on his forearms. Alternately, he flicked each one with his tongue while his thumb gently rubbed the unattended one.

Nichole felt herself growing hot and moist as he hungrily suckled her tender nipples with his rough tongue. Sensations of warmth spiraled through her as he sucked each bud into a hardness to match his manhood that throbbed against her thigh.

She stroked her hands down his well-muscled frame. She felt him quiver as her fingers gently kneaded the taunt mounds of his bottom.

Slowly, he moved his thick shaft into her, savoring the tight, moist heat of her closing around him. Wave after wave of intense sensation washed through her as he slowly moved inside her, then pulled almost out, only to plunge deep into her again.

She clung tightly to him, meeting his deep thrusts as he moved inside her, filling her with glorious sensations that were erupting into a wild crescendo of pleasure.

She writhed beneath him, her hips thrusting upward, frantically seeking that final stroke that would end her delicious agony. Her body stiffened as her climax consumed her, releasing a warm, enchanting feeling. Her cries of pleasure filled the morning air.

Fowler sucked in his breath as the intensity of her climax threatened to devour him. He felt her muscles close around him even tighter than before, pulling him ever deeper into her. Her pulsing and throbbing femininity sent him wildly plunging into her, again and again, then he quivered and pulsated deep within her.

He threw back his head as his body stiffened, no longer able to hold back the flood of his own release. It felt as if he had exploded into a million pieces as he spewed his seed deep within her womb. His pleasure/pain was so intense that his body shuddered from the sheer force of his climax.

They lay in each other's arms, their bodies locked intimately together, as the sounds of their ragged breathing filled the air.

Nichole could feel Fowler's heart beating wildly against his chest. She looked at him with all her love shining in her eyes as she brushed his damp hair away from his face. How she loved this man. Surely, he must feel something for her.

This had been the most intense lovemaking they had shared. Didn't that mean anything to him? Could he have made love to her so thoroughly and not care, even a little, for her? Was a man all that different than a woman?

She waited for him to say the three words that would make her heart complete. But she waited in vain.

Fowler was stunned at the intensity of the feelings that had consumed him. Never before—and there had been many, many befores—had he experienced such profound pleasure with a woman. What made this wisp of a woman so different from all the others? he wondered.

He rolled over on his back and snuggled Nichole's head against his chest, resting his chin on the top of her head as he pondered the strange, and for some reason, very disturbing feelings.

When they rode into the town of Piedras, leading three dead men, thirteen horses, and three mules behind them, they caused quite a stir. Kids playing in the street ran to tell their parents. Within minutes, the street was filled with curious onlookers watching the strange procession pass by.

Fowler asked one of the older boys, who had stopped playing ball to stare at them, who did the burying and was directed to a building on the opposite end of the short, deeply rutted dirt street.

The building was a hodgepodge of items. Pots and pans hung from the ceiling. Barrels and boxes of varied sizes lined the walls, some containing tins of food, flour, coffee, tobacco and others holding nails and various tools.

The counter top was a clutter of glass jars containing everything from pieces of candy to pickles. The dark interior was permeated with the smell of years of dust and dirt.

The little store seemed to contain everything except a proprietor. After hollering "hello" for the second time, a short, rotund man, clad only in denim pants over faded red long johns, ambled in from the back of the building. Judging from the smell of him, he hadn't been acquainted with soap and water any more recently than the store itself had!

Nichole discreetly walked to the front of the building on the pretense of looking out the window, which would have been an impossibility if she had really wanted to see anything, because of the amount of dirt covering it.

Fowler explained to the fat little man what he needed done while at the same time trying not to breathe too deeply of the malodorous air surrounding him.

The man was clearly reluctant to take care of burying the dead men until Fowler showed him his badge, assuring him that he was indeed a U.S. Marshal.

"Well, I guess that proves you're a marshal, all right. Guess I hafta do it, if'n you say so," he grumbled. It was plain to see that anything even remotely resembling work was not a high priority on his list of activities.

The man hooked his thumbs under his suspenders, looking past Fowler and Nichole to the string of animals outside his building.

"Whot about all them horses? I ain't arunnin' no free stables here, ya know. Who's gonna pay for their keep?" he grumbled again, as he scratched his overhanging belly.

"You can keep the three horses and the saddles that belonged to the dead men as payment for burying them. But, tomorrow morning, you get the county sheriff over here to sort out who the other horses belong to. He'll be able to trace them by their branding mark, if they have one.

"If he can't locate the rightful owners in a reasonable length of time, he'll most likely let you take the unclaimed ones as payment for feeding and stabling the rest of them.

"But," Fowler warned sternly, "horse stealing is a hanging offense. And I'll be checking with the sheriff on my way back through here. So you better make sure you get high behind and notify him first thing in the morning. Understand?"

The man grinned, showing a mouthful of broken and missing teeth. "Yes, indeedy!" he assured Fowler. "I'll get the sheriff over ta here right early in the mornin'. I surely will do that."

Fowler didn't believe him for a minute, of course, but he had no other choice. They couldn't take the animals with them and they couldn't just turn them loose on the range.

After giving it a little more thought, however, he was wishing he had done just that, turned them loose. He didn't know what the man would do with the saddles, but, judging from the poorness of the town's appearance, he had a pretty good idea what the fate of the horses would be.

As they rode away, Nichole was also feeling sympathy for the animals they had left behind.

"Ohhh," she shuddered. "How can anyone live in filth like that?"

Fowler shook his head. "Does make ya wonder what keeps them from dying of the crawling crud, doesn't it?"

"I feel like I need a bath just from being in that awful place."

Fowler grinned, a mischievous glint in his eyes. "I think that can be arranged. We'll find a clean spot in the creek when we camp tonight. I'll even wash your back for you," he volunteered, wiggling his eyebrows licentiously at her.

Nichole blushed becomingly. "Oh, you," she said primly as she kneed her horse into a trot. "You just find that clean spot and I can take care of the rest all by myself, thank you very much."

Fowler chuckled at her belated show of propriety. He looked toward the sun, trying to judge how long it would be before they could make camp. "Hurry up, sundown," he muttered under his breath.

As promised, Fowler found the perfect spot for bathing. And even though they could have traveled for another thirty minutes or so before stopping for the night, he could tell that Nichole needed the extra rest.

Unlike the previous nights when they had shared the task of setting up camp and bedding the animals for the night, Fowler insisted that he'd take care of things while she had her bath.

She didn't offer even a feeble protest, confirming his suspicions that she'd reached her limit for the day.

After supper, Fowler went to the creek to take a bath. When he returned to camp, he saw Nichole wrapped up in her blanket, and assumed she was already asleep.

He had just gotten comfortable in his own blanket and was on the verge of drifting off to sleep when Nichole called his name.

"Fowler?"

"Huh?"

"Are you asleep?"

"I almost was," he said exasperated. "What is it?"

"I was just wondering. If I would have tried for the

man on our right, the one you insisted on taking first, he would have beat me, wouldn't he?"

"Can't you just put that whole thing out of your mind and go to sleep?" he growled irritably, not wanting to remember it himself.

"I would really like to know," she insisted.

Fowler exhaled a sigh of resignation. "I wasn't going to tell you, but if you must know, yes, Nichole, he would have beaten you."

"How did you know that man, the one you shot first, would be the fastest?"

"Because he was wearing a tied-down, cutaway holster. That told me he was highly practiced with the use of his gun. Besides that, the expression on his face indicated that he was looking forward to the opportunity to put his skill to use," he explained patiently.

"Then the shot he fired was just a reflex to your bullet hitting him, wasn't it?"

"Yeah, I'd say so."

"Did you know his bullet hit right between my feet?"

There were several seconds of silence. Nichole could hear Fowler taking a couple of deep breaths and letting them out slowly.

"No, I didn't know that and I would probably have slept better if you hadn't told me. Now hush and go to sleep before you tell me something else that will keep me awake all night."

Nichole's heart began to beat a little faster as the thoughts flashed through her mind that on this day, this man had risked his life for her. And that they were alive now only because he was able to pick his life up again due to his own abilities and a little help from her, of course.

But she knew that at the time he had put his life on the line, he could only have been hoping that he would get some help from her.

Keeping her blanket wrapped around her, she got to her feet and crept quietly to where he lay and dropped to her knees beside him.

There was enough moonlight for her to see that his eyes were closed but she knew he was not asleep.

"What is it now?" He failed in his attempt to sound gruff.

"I just wanted to thank you. But to do it from way over there seemed too . . . too far."

"Thank me for what?"

"You know for what. You took that man first not only because you knew he would be the fastest, but also because he would be the one shooting at me. This forced you to ignore the man who would be shooting at you first. Your only hope was that I could get him. I know you risked your life for me today."

He opened his eyes. They were soft with affection as he looked up at her. He took her by the shoulders and pulled her gently and slowly toward him. "How could a man do any less for a woman he's come to . . ." His voice trailed off, thick with emotion.

Her heart skipped a beat. "Come to what, Fowler?" she asked softly, waiting breathlessly for the word she so wanted to hear.

After a moment his eyes seemed to lose some of their softness. "Well . . . what I meant to say was that I would rather have died back there than to have had to live with you dead and not being able to believe that I had done everything I could to keep you from being killed.

"Besides that, how could I face your father and mother and try to explain to them how I was still alive, but you had been killed?"

Nichole had slid down to lie beside him with her head propped up on one elbow as he talked. She tried but wasn't quite able to conceal her disappointment. She had thought that he was about to confess his love for her. But when he didn't, she felt empty and more than a little sad.

"Well, thank you anyway. I will remember what you did all the days of my life." She leaned over and kissed him lightly on the mouth.

"Now look here, young lady, you better get back over there while the getting's good."

"I don't want to get back over there. The ground is softer here," she said as she moved closer to him.

He studied her seriously for a moment. "If you are trying to tempt me, you little minx, I should warn you that a man is only up to so much in one day."

"I'm not trying to tempt you. I just really need a hug. Go to sleep, Fowler. I won't disturb you anymore."

Fowler put his arm around her, pulling her to his side. She laid her head on his shoulder, resting one hand on his chest just above his heart before shutting her eyes.

"Nichole?"

"Hmmm," she answered sleepily.

"I have a confession."

"What's that, Fowler?" she mumbled, unable to open her tired eyes.

"If you had not stuck with me today, those men would have killed me and if you had not got your man fast and with your first shot, I would be dead now. And maybe you, too. I would not have made it to him."

Nichole's eyes popped wide open. "I'm surprised that your male ego finally let you admit that I was right to stay with you. Why did it take you so long?"

Fowler shrugged his shoulders. "Partly ego, I guess. And partly because I still haven't decided whether or not I'm going to spank your backside for not obeying my orders and going home when I told you to. Now, go to sleep."

"Well, if you do decide to spank me, you will be gentle, won't you?" she purred sweetly.

Fowler sighed in exasperation. "I'm going to let you get away with poking your fun this time. But you do something like that again and I will bust your butt. Now, go to sleep!"

"Yes, sir," she murmured as she snuggled a little closer.

Cody and Nick had ridden in thoughtful silence since leaving the Ranger station. Where did one start to look for a missing little sister in a big state like Texas?

"I suppose, since you two think alike, that you have some sort of plan or direction in mind, don't you?"

Nick wasn't sure if he'd been insulted or complimented. "I'm trying to think like Nolie might. She's not stupid, you know, but she is reckless. I'm betting that since she doesn't know where to find Linc Travis she's going to find a way to let Linc Travis find her. The only problem is she wouldn't know where to start. That's why she needed Barclay to help her."

"Yeah, but how much did he know about the Travis

gang? You said you didn't have time to pass any information to him before you were shot."

"I didn't but I'm giving him credit for having enough brains to figure out a way to make contact with someone who might have pointed him in Linc's general direction.

"When things got too hot and we needed a place to hide out for a while, the gang would hole up in Outlaw Caverns down near Austin. That's where we're going to start looking and hope we can pick up a trail, unless you have a better plan." Nick looked at Cody.

He shook his head negatively. "No, that sounds as good a place to start as any. Given Nichole's propensity for mishaps, maybe we'll get lucky and find someone who might have seen her."

"Okay. Let's stop in Aerl and get a beer before we head out. That meeting with the captain left me a mite dry."

A short while later, they stopped at the only saloon in Aerl Station. After tying the horses to the hitching rail, they entered the swinging doors. The barkeep glared at Nick and Cody as they sidled up to the bar.

"Two beers," Cody said as he tossed some coins on the bar.

Nick was looking around the room to see if he knew anyone and didn't see the look that the bartender was giving him.

Cody got the distinct notion that for some reason the man was not too pleased to see them. He was just on the verge of asking Nick about it when the man spoke.

"Okay, you, out of my place. You and your other friend caused enough trouble the last time you were

191

here. I can't afford to have my saloon shot up again." He motioned toward the swinging doors. "Get going, buddy."

Cody looked at Nick and Nick stared at the man like he was crazy. "Mister, I haven't been in your saloon in months, and I certainly never had a gunfight here. You must have me confused with someone else. I'm Nick Westerfield." He motioned toward Cody. "This is my brother, Cody. I'm a Texas Ranger and we're on the trail of . . . a fugitive."

The bartender took a closer look at Nick. "Well, you do look a mite taller and heavier and, maybe a little older than the man who was here last month," he conceded reluctantly, shaking his head in puzzlement. "But I swear, man, there's a kid walking around who looks enough like you to be your twin brother."

He set two mugs on the counter and pushed the money back toward Cody. "These are on the house." He walked away still shaking his head in disbelief at his mistake.

"I think we just found our first trace of Nolie," Nick said as he took a sip of the cool beer."

Cody chuckled, "A fugitive? Really, Nick." He took a long draw of his foamy drink.

"Never mind that. I want to know more about that gun fight. Have you forgotten how much we favor each other when Nichole puts those damn pants on and sticks her hair under her hat?"

Cody choked on his beer. He had forgotten. "Good God Almighty! Surely that couldn't have been Nichole! In a gun fight?"

Nick shot him a sideways glance. "Wanna bet?"

192

Cody was thinking how nice it would be if he could lock his sister in a closet until she was a hundred and forty or married, whichever came first. He would be only too glad to turn that handful of trouble over to some unsuspecting man for a wife.

"Hey, barkeep, give us another round."

When the man put the drinks on the counter, Nick asked in a casual manner, "Tell me about this gun fight. Who shot whom?"

The barkeep scratched his graying black hair as he remembered. "Ya know, that's funny how that happened. This kid came in here and ordered a beer." He motioned toward the back end of the counter. "He was standing at the end of the bar there, minding his own business, just sipping his beer.

"Another man came in and ordered a drink. He stood around watching the poker game awhile and then he walked back and said something to the kid. A few minutes, maybe four, five minutes later, the kid started walking toward the door. That's when a man sitting over yonder"—he motioned across the room in front of him—"hollered 'Hey, Brazos' at him and was fixing to shoot him in the back. But the other man shoved the kid out the door at the same time he shot the man who did the hollering."

The bartender shook his head in admiration. "That was something to see, I tell ya. That man was faster than greased lightning. Killed him clean as a whistle with one shot."

"Who was the man who was killed?" Cody asked.

"Well, that's another funny thing. He didn't look like nobody, but the next day this little gal came into town, claiming he was her brother. She was a pretty

193

little thing. Talked and acted like a real lady. Sure hard to imagine that she had a brother who would shoot a man in the back and for no apparent reason neither."

Nick was getting his "twin feeling" again. "What was her name?"

The barkeep shook his head. "Don't rightly know, Mister. If it's important, you might go talk to the blacksmith. She made arrangements with him for the burying and claimed her brother's stuff before leaving town."

After thanking the saloonkeeper, Nick and Cody went to the blacksmith's shop.

The blacksmith told them the story that Nichole had told him. "But," he confessed, rather embarrassed, "I forgot to ask the little lady what her brother's name was, what with her being so upset and all. When I realized that I didn't have a name to put on the grave marker, I rode out to the place where she said her family was camped, but I didn't find no signs of a wagon at all. I thought that was mighty strange, let me tell you."

The description he gave of the "little lady," fit Nichole to a tee. And from the description he gave of the dead man, Nick recognized him as Robert Baker, a member of the Travis gang.

Cody waited until they were out of hearing before asking, "Why would Nichole claim to be kin to that dead man?"

"Probably to claim his belongings, hoping to find something in them to give her a clue as to what direction to start looking in. His name was Robert Baker, and he was a member of the gang."

"Do you think she found anything?"

"I don't know but I think we got our answer as to how she plans to go about making Linc come to her."

"How's that?"

"When I went undercover, I used the name, Brazos Kid. It's a game that Nolie and I use to play when we were kids," he said at Cody's questioning look. "Apparently, she's posing as the Brazos Kid, knowing that Linc will come looking for me—her—when word gets back to him that I'm not dead."

"Oh my God!" Cody blanched. "Surely the marshal wouldn't let her put herself in that kind of danger!"

"Cody, you know Nichole. How the hell could he stop her? Short of locking her up in a jail somewhere? Unfortunately, it's not a criminal offense to go looking for your missing brother. Stupid, yes, but not a crime." Nick spurred his horse to a faster pace.

Cody dug his heels into his horse to quicken its pace to keep up with Nick. "Are we still heading for the caverns?"

"No. We're going to Evadne, it's a town near the caverns. I think Baker might have had a girlfriend there because he spent a lot of time in Evadne when we'd have to lie low for a while. If they found anything that would lead them anywhere, I should think it would be to Evadne rather than to the caverns. I can't imagine Baker having anything in his saddlebags that would lead them to the caverns.

"But one thing's for certain, if we plan to see our sister alive again, we'd better hurry. Because if Linc finds her before we do, it wouldn't bother him one iota to kill a woman. He's done it before without so much as batting an eyelash."

Chapter Twelve

When they found the deserted cabin on the banks of the Rio Grande, it was almost dark. Fowler estimated that they were still twenty, maybe twenty-five miles from Laredo.

Nichole was more than glad to spend the night in the cabin and travel the rest of the way come daylight.

The fact that she had been unusually quiet and thoughtful all day had not skipped Fowler's notice. He knew she was apprehensive about what they would find once they reached their destination.

Even though the night was warm and they could have easily camped beside the river, Nichole seemed to need the comfort of having four walls around her. She had immediately set about sweeping the dirt and cobwebs from the one-room cabin with a makeshift broom fashioned from a slender, leafy branch of a nearby tree.

After watering the horses and staking them beside the cabin to munch on the abundant grass, Fowler decided to investigate the strange rock formation he'd noticed as they approached the cabin.

The cabin had been built about a hundred yards back from the banks of the river, far enough that the river could rise pretty high without flooding the cabin. Off to one side and slightly behind the cabin was a limestone outcropping, one of many they had seen as they followed the meandering river. However, what had caught his eye about this particular rock formation was what appeared to be a manmade shelter.

Taking his rifle, Fowler walked the forty or so paces to the outcropping to get a closer look at the unusual placement of boulders.

It was evident that someone, probably the person who'd built the cabin, had camped there for some length of time. He found the remains of a good-sized cook fire, more than what would have been needed for just a single night's stay. As he stood in the center and looked around, he could see that someone had even filled in the spaces between the large boulders with smaller ones. He could have easily set up a center post and thrown a tarp over the encircling rocks to make a solid shelter.

After satisfying his mind that the formation had not been used in a long time, Fowler decided to hunt for food.

Fowler shot a squirrel and two rabbits for their supper that night and for breakfast the next morning. While Nichole was making the cabin somewhat livable for the night, he cooked the game and put a pot of coffee to boil in the fireplace.

The only sounds in the bare structure were the sizzling and popping of the fire as the juice from the meat dripped on it and the swishing sound of the leafy broom.

Fowler was deep in thought. Since he was a realist, he knew that it was highly unlikely that they would find any evidence that Nick was still alive.

He figured that Nichole was trying to come to grips with the fact that she might find proof of her brother's death, if they found anything at all.

Supper had been eaten in silence. Now they sat, each holding a cup of coffee, leaning against their saddles and staring into the low-burning embers of the fire.

Fowler studied the pensive young girl. Even with the deep frown marring her forehead, to him she was still beautiful.

He had seen many different sides of her personality during their long journey to find her brother. It came as a surprise to him that he liked all the facets of this complicated woman. Complicated? Maybe complicated was too simple a description. Paradoxical was perhaps more accurate. She had an innocent look about her, yet he had seen her shoot a man without hesitation in self-defense.

Her slender, seemingly fragile appearance was another deception. He knew her to be as strong as an oak, able to bend but not break, both in body and mind. There were times when they were coming through the hill country, that a weaker person, and certainly ninety-nine out of a hundred females, would have thrown up their hands in despair, but she had uttered not one word of despondency.

And when bravery was passed out, he was certain

she must have gotten in line at least three times! Even the way they had met had taken guts. Most men, unless they were *really* stupid, and there was certainly nothing wrong with her intelligence, would have hesitated to kidnap a U.S. Marshal right out from under the noses of a company of Texas Rangers! But had that stopped her? Not in the least.

He knew her to be warm and caring, passionate and loyal, optimistic and cheerful, and tenacious as a mule.

He had laughed at her antics and he had stood nose to nose with her when her stubbornness and temper had locked horns with his.

Maybe there wasn't one single word to describe Nichole adequately. The words of a song he had heard once came to his mind. "Give me a Texas woman. A Texas woman is the only kind of woman for me." When he had first heard the song, he hadn't truly understood its meaning, but now he did. Nichole was a Texas woman. Here was a female who was strong enough to stand side by side with a man and still be a woman.

"Nichole?" The vulnerable look on her face made him want to wrap his arms around her, like one would to comfort a frightened child, and assure her that he would protect her and keep her safe forever.

No sooner had that thought crossed his mind then another, more frightening one chased after it. He could no longer deny it even to himself. As hard as he had tried not to, he had fallen in love with Nichole!

Somewhere between a gun in his back at Fort Fisher and the crackling fire in a one-room cabin on the banks of the Rio Grande, his heart had overruled his head and placed itself precariously in love.

She looked over at him almost as if she had forgotten he was in the room. "Yes?"

"You know that we might . . ." The look in her misty green eyes tore at his heart. She had such a wide-eyed, trusting look on her face. How do you tell someone so trusting, that tomorrow her world might come tumbling down like leaves from a storm-ravaged tree?

She looked away from him, having read his mind, and finished his sentence. ". . . might find proof that Nicky is dead?"

He heard her take a deep breath and slowly exhale before lowering her head to her chest. When she spoke, he had to strain to hear her words.

"Yes, I know," she whispered. "But I have to know for sure. I don't think I could live the rest of my life . . . wondering. Wondering and watching. Hoping, forever hoping, to see him riding up the road to our house."

She sat her coffee cup on the floor and cupped her face in her hands, rubbing her fingers across her eyes to message her temples gently before running her fingers down the sides of her face, along her jaw line, and finally placing her hands together in prayer fashion beneath her chin.

Fowler scooted closer to her, putting his arm around her shoulders. He tucked her against his side and kissed the top of her head.

Although her eyes held a sadness, there were no tears in them when she turned her face toward him, only a look of resignation to accept whatever they might find. "I have to know."

He kissed her forehead before cradling her head

beneath his, caressing the side of her face. "I understand."

They sat for a long time, each pondering their private thoughts and absently listening to the crackle of the fire.

Fowler was reluctant to release her but finally he said, "We'd better get some sleep. We have a long hard day ahead of us tomorrow."

Nichole nodded her agreement and silently stood up. As she began spreading their bed rolls in front of the dying fire, Fowler told her he would go check on the horses before turning in. The slight nod of her head was the only indication that she had heard him.

It worried Fowler that Nichole was so depressed. She had told him earlier, on several occasions in fact, that she would feel it if her twin were dead. She had been so adamant about it that he had to believe her. What had happened to change that? Was her "twin feeling" telling her something that she didn't want to believe?

She wasn't by nature a moody person, quite the opposite, yet he could tell that she was fighting hard to hold back the tears that threatened to spill forth from her lovely eyes. He knew she was hurting, and that made him hurt for her, but he didn't know how to ease her pain.

After spreading their bedding on the floor, Nichole curled up in hers, wrapping her blanket tightly around her. Pillowing her head on her arm, she lay on her side, facing the soft glow of the waning fire.

As she watched, images of herself and Nicky danced among the glowing embers. She and Nicky playing as children. She and Nicky trying to outdo each other as they grew older. She and Nicky confiding their secrets to each other.

And, finally, she and Nicky sitting on her bed, talking quietly just before she had left to go back East to school, the last time she had seen her brother.

She didn't realize she was crying until she felt the tears dropping on her arm and soaking through her shirt sleeve. She sniffed her runny nose, trying to find her handkerchief and to stop the flow of tears at the same time. She wasn't successful at either endeavor.

Fowler heard her soft sobbing when he entered the door. He knew she had lost the battle with her tears. Walking quietly to her, he knelt down beside her, placing his handkerchief in her hand.

With her back to the door and lost in her thoughts, she had not heard him come back into the cabin. She took the proffered cloth, trying to turn her head away so he couldn't see her face. She was embarrassed to let him see her red nose and tear-streaked face. She hated to cry and seldom did. And she didn't for the life of her understand why she was crying now! Dammit!

"Thank you," she mumbled through the cloth as she dried her runny nose and wet eyes. "I'm sorry," she apologized.

"Why?" He lay down beside her, turning her toward him and gathering her into his arms. He brushed the hair away from her forehead, placing a kiss in its place. "If anyone has a right to cry, you do."

At his show of sympathy, the tears came flooding down her cheeks again, this time to wet his shirt. He held her close, gently rubbing her back until her weeping ebbed to an occasional sniffle. "Talk to me, baby, what's with the tears?"

She shrugged her shoulders.

"Are you getting one of your twin feelings?"

She shook her head negatively.

"You still think your brother is alive?"

She nodded her head affirmatively.

Now he was confused. "Then why are you crying?" His voice clearly showed his puzzlement.

"I don't *know* why I'm crying!" she wailed as the water works started again.

Again, he held her close until this round of tears ceased. He tried to pull back from her a little so he could look at her, but she buried her face deeper into his shirt, refusing to let him see her puffy eyes and red nose.

"Don't look at me," she pleaded.

"Why not? I think you're beautiful." He tucked a tear-drenched strand of hair behind her ear.

"Humph," she muttered as she wiped her nose again. "When's the last time you had your eyes checked? I look like a . . . a wart hog when I cry. I know how ugly I look," she stated.

This time he was successful in pulling away from her. "No, you don't," he insisted as he placed his finger under her chin and tipped her face up to his. "You look beautiful to me. Yes," he inserted before she could interrupt him. "Even with your red nose and swollen eyes, I think you are lovely and beautiful." He laid a gentle kiss on each of the aforementioned objects.

She rolled to her back, taking him with her. "Liar." She wrapped her arms around his neck and pulled him down to place a kiss on his lips. "But thank you, anyway. I really don't know why I started crying. I just . . . felt like crying, I guess."

203

He kissed her back. "You don't have to apologize, sweetheart. I know you've been under a lot of strain and tension these past weeks. That's just the body's way of releasing some of the pent-up frustration."

She wiggled a little underneath him, trying to get in a more comfortable position, and he felt himself growing hard at her slight movement. *Dammit, not now, you greedy little bastard!* he silently warned his lusty manhood. Afraid he was going to embarrass himself, he started to roll off her, but she took his hand in hers and brought his fingers to her lips.

Even with her clothing and his between them, she had felt his hardness, and it had touched something deep within her. She knew he had been comforting her purely for the sake of making her feel better. Nothing in his manner or words had lead her to believe that he had had any ulterior motive. He was only sharing her sadness.

Fifteen minutes ago her body had been trembling with tears, now it was trembling with desire. Just as she had needed his comforting then, now she needed his lovemaking just as much. Having little experience in seducing a man, she didn't know how to tell him of her need. She nipped at the end of his fingers with her teeth, and felt his body shudder in response.

She looked up at him, a slight smile playing on her lips, and nipped his fingertips again. Again, she felt his body ripple and saw him close his eyes as he drew in a ragged breath. It was a heady feeling to know that such a timid gesture on her part could arouse an experienced man like Fowler.

He groaned inwardly at her innocent action. The thought of making love to her had not entered his mind. Well, that wasn't *exactly* true. Making love to this green-eyed little witch had never been very far from his mind since he had first laid eyes on her. But he had truly sought only to comfort her, nothing more. But, damn, she was going to drive him past his breaking point if he didn't put some distance between them and fast!

Once more he attempted to remove his tortured body from atop hers. This time she lightly stroked his work-roughened palm with the tips of her fingers before placing a kiss in the middle of it.

His heart skipped a beat before lurching into triple time. He opened his eyes and looked into hers. It was easy for him to read the desire written there. The little imp knew exactly what she was doing to his insides! She wanted to make love every bit as much as he did. The realization that she desired him made him grow even harder.

"Are you trying to tell me something?" he asked innocently.

"If you have to ask, I must not be doing something right." She was disappointed. She must have misinterpreted his response to her timid attempt at seduction.

"Oh, you're doing *something*, all right. But I'm not sure you understand where its leading. It's risky business taunting the tiger," he warned, his voice thick with passion. His rakish grin told her that he was teasing her.

She unbuttoned the top button of his shirt. "Oh, is that what I'm doing?" She undid the next two buttons to run her fingers through the golden hair she exposed. "Taunting the tiger?" She pulled his shirttail out of his breeches and released the remaining buttons that hid his well-muscled chest from her view. She turned hungry green eyes to his face as she drew lazy circles with her fingernails on his golden chest.

"Little girl, you're getting yourself into serious trouble," he groaned. The delicious things she was doing was making it hard for him to breath normally.

The pink tip of her tongue darted out to moisten her dry lips, sending his heated blood rushing even faster through his veins.

"What happens when one taunts the tiger?" she asked breathlessly. Her own blood pumping hotly through her body made the pulse point in her neck throb.

Fowler made a growling sound deep in his throat as he made as if to take a bite out of her neck. "Little girls who taunt the tiger usually get eaten up like this."

Nichole ducked her head to protect her throat and squealed in delight as his whisker-shadowed face found its mark on her delicate skin.

While Fowler was nipping at her throat, he had undone all her shirt buttons, baring her breasts to his hungry mouth. "And this, and this," he said as he nibbled his way down to latch his hot, moist mouth onto one of her dusky pink nipples.

His mouth seared her like a branding iron. She could feel the heat as it ricocheted inside her then radiated fingers of fire through her body.

She arched her back and held his head to her breast. She couldn't seem to get close enough to the fire that was burning her. She pushed his shirt away from his shoulders, down his arms, and tossed it aside. When she slid both hands down his back and under his waistband to rub his buttocks, Fowler arched into her.

He reached between them to unbutton both of their breeches, pushing Nichole's past her hips as he released the last button. His hand covered the dark triangle between her thighs. His mouth left her breast to travel down her soft stomach, stopping to make lazy circles around her navel, before continuing its journey to replace his hand.

He gently parted the soft covering hiding the object his tongue sought. Nichole groaned and gasped as his mouth closed over her tender bud. He held her hips firmly in his hands as he lapped at the little bud until Nichole was writhing in sensuous agony beneath him.

She alternately pushed him away only to tug him closer. His ministrations were driving her to a wild frenzy. She tossed her head from side to side as her body threatened to explode from the pressure he was building in her. She begged him to enter her and end her agony, but he denied her plea. She cried out as he finally pushed her over the edge of reality into blissful release.

Only then did he cease his assault on her delicate flesh and move back up her slender body, kissing her satiny skin on his return journey. She tasted herself on his lips when he finally covered her mouth with his.

He rolled to his back, bringing her with him without breaking their kiss. Now her hands were free to work their torture on him. She immediately rid him of his breeches, watching with unconcealed delight as his manhood sprang forth from its confinement.

What was good for the tiger must surely be good for the tigress. She straddled him as she began her leisurely exploration of his magnificent body.

She delighted as his nipples hardened into pebbles when she ran her moist tongue around each one. She followed his chest hair down to his stomach and then to his throbbing shaft. She closed her hand around him in a savage gentleness that made him suck in his breath.

When her tongue lightly touched the tip of his manhood, he jerked wildly, almost pulling out of her grasp. As the warm moistness of her mouth closed ever so gently around him, he gasped for air. He was a man drowning in erotic sensations.

When he could stand no more torture, he slid her up his body and raised her hips to settle her firmly on him. With her knees bent, sitting astride him, her hips began a rocking motion that sent him plunging to the hilt within her.

He lowered her head to his, and his tongue met hers, thrusting inside her mouth just as his manhood thrust into her body. Locked firmly together, they soared past reality into a heavenly paradise. He released her mouth and threw his head back as his body gave one final buck beneath her before spilling his sweet seed deep into her receptive body.

As the last glow of the fire's embers faded into nothingness, the soft, gentle breathing of love-sated slumber whispered around the entwined young couple in front of the now-darkened fireplace.

Sleep had beckoned to only one of them, however. As Nichole slept peacefully within his arms, Fowler's mind would not allow his body the rest it needed.

Troubled by his thoughts from earlier in the evening, Fowler carefully eased his arm out from under Nichole's head, tucking the blankets around her as he moved his body slowly away from hers.

After pulling his breeches and boots on, he picked up his shirt and silently left the cabin. Once outside, he slipped his shirt on, leaving it unbuttoned as he rolled a cigarette.

The night sounds of the river were carried in his direction by the slight wind. Overhead a full moon clearly lit his way as he walked toward the sound of water running over rocks as the river made its journey to the Gulf of Mexico.

Fowler walked along the flowing river, drawing on his smoke, as he tried to come to grips with the new revelations that had surfaced in him only a few hours before.

It had come as quite a shock to discover that he felt such strong feelings for Nichole. He had never been in love before and it frightened the hell out of him!

He had seen all kinds of love, or so-called love, and decided at an early age that he wasn't going to fall into that trap. He was too independent to be tied to one place or one woman for any length of time. Love was too demanding and too restraining. Love had too many responsibilities tied to it. Responsibilities he wasn't ready for!

Hell! At twenty-eight, he was just entering the prime of his life. He wasn't ready to be hog-tied to a wife. Women like Nichole weren't satisfied with just having a husband. Nooo, first they wanted a house, then a passel of kids in the house.

Maybe in eight or ten years, when he was too old for his job's demands, maybe then he'd think about settling down, but not now. He liked his life just as it was. He was one of the most respected lawmen in the United States, which meant that he could virtually pick and choose his assignments.

He liked the danger and adventure in his work, and having to worry about a wife and kids when he put his life on the line fighting Indians and outlaws just didn't fit in. What if he got himself killed, who'd take care of his family?

Oh, he knew his father and mother would take them in and see to their physical needs. But a wife needed a man whom she knew would return to her at the end of each day, preferably without any bullet holes decorating his body. And kids needed the firm hand of a loving father to help them grow into strong, confident adults. The last thing they needed was a part-time father, or worse yet, to become orphans!

No, he told himself, married life was not for him. Besides, Nichole was from a very wealthy family. He couldn't provide her with the way of life that she'd been used to. Not on a marshal's pay. Even though she didn't act like a spoiled little rich girl, she wouldn't be willing to live within his means for very long. And he sure as hell wouldn't live off his wife's money!

"I don't know why I'm arguing with myself," he told the frogs that had paused in their croaking as he sat down on a rock near the bank. "There's probably some rich rancher's son just waiting for Nichole to come home so he can ask her to marry him."

He didn't like that thought at all! The very idea of another man holding her in his arms, seeing her naked beauty and making sweet, tender love to her, made his blood pressure soar. "God dammit!" he swore as he tossed his cigarette butt at the frogs, sending all of them leaping into the water with a noisy splash.

He was so agitated thinking of another man experiencing the sexual delights he had unleashed in Nichole that he jammed his hands in his pockets and started walking along the river bank again.

Frustration was eating him alive. "I taught her everything she knows about making love, dammit! Now she's going to practice it with some dandified rancher's kid." He angrily kicked at a large rock.

If he had been more alert instead of drowning in his self-made anguish, he would have heard the telltale warning of impending doom. As it was, his mind belatedly registered the sharp rattling sound at the same instant he felt the snake sink its fangs into his leg.

When he kicked the rock, he had disturbed a large diamondback rattlesnake. He watched in horror as the venomous reptile slithered into the underbrush.

He looked around him, trying to get his bearings. He didn't know how far from the cabin he had wandered while mentally harassing himself. He could only hope that he would be able to get back to it before he lapsed into unconsciousness.

Removing his belt, he tied it above the two fang marks on his leg and started back in the direction from which he'd come. He was trying to keep his breathing slow and steady to prevent his heart from pumping the poison any faster through his veins than it already was.

He could feel his leg swelling, and it burned like hell as the poison began its march to end his life. He walked as fast as he dared. Already he was feeling lightheaded and a little sick to his stomach. He breathed a sigh of relief when the cabin came into his blurred vision. Stumbling into the cabin, he moved toward Nichole.

"Nichole"—he shook the sleeping girl—"wake up."

The urgent tone of his voice brought Nichole instantly awake. "What is it? What's wrong?"

"Snakebite." He slumped onto his back, sweat pouring from his face as he tried to fight off the approaching blackness.

Nichole knew what must be done to save Fowler from dying. Several times over the years, she had helped when one of the ranch hands was treated for a snakebite, but she had never had to do it by herself. A chill ran through her body even as her mind and hands worked to do what was needed.

She tossed a log on the banked embers, hoping it would catch and burn. She needed both the light it would give and the heat. She poured water from one of the canteens over her hunting knife and hurriedly wiped it on the tail of his shirt.

Fowler watched as she removed his belt from around his leg and slit the pants leg up past the puncture marks. He could feel that he was slowly slipping away. He shook his head, trying to stall it. He saw Nichole's hand tremble as she lowered the knife to his leg. He watched as she momentarily pulled it back. He heard her gulp in a breath.

"You can do it, Nichole," he encouraged. "You *have* to do it!"

She took a deep breath, then once again placed the knife against the fang marks. This time she expertly made two deep slash marks across the wound. She glanced at Fowler to see if he was still conscious. His face was contorted in pain, but he was somewhat coherent.

She bent quickly to the slash and began to suck the blood and poison from the wound. The sound of her sucking and spitting mingled with the sounds of the log catching fire. She sucked and spat for what seemed an eternity, but in fact was only a few minutes. She wasn't sure how long was enough, so she continued for what she figured was at least five minutes.

She could see the paleness of Fowler's face in the light from the burning log. She heard him mumble her name before she felt his leg go limp as he slipped into unconsciousness. When she felt that she had sucked all the poison out that she could, she quickly washed her face and mouth with water from the canteen.

After washing the blood from her knife, she thrust it into the fire. When the blade was red from the heat, she carefully removed it and before her courage left her, she quickly laid it against the gapping cut she had made on Fowler's leg. She knew she must cauterize the wound to stop the bleeding and, hopefully, keep it from becoming infected.

For Fowler's sake, she was grateful that he had lapsed into oblivion, otherwise the pain might have sent him into shock. As it was, his leg only slightly twitched at the touch of the hot blade.

She sat back on her heels, her heart pounding in her ears. Suddenly, her stomach lurched and she just made it out the door before heaving her insides on the ground until there was nothing left. She leaned weakly against the rough wall, shaking from head to toe.

When her strength returned, she entered the cabin. Only when the warmth from the fire touched her bare skin did she realize that she was still naked from their lovemaking. She dressed as her mind raced to remember the things she had to do.

After binding Fowler's wound with a strip of cloth torn from a petticoat in her saddlebags, she wrapped a blanket tightly around him. She put more wood on the fire and began cleaning the blood from the floor.

Finished, she wearily slumped to the floor beside Fowler. All she could do now was wait. Wait and pray.

"Ahhh," Fowler groaned, and grabbed at his leg. The burning was so intense he felt as if someone had stuck his foot in the fire. Already the swelling had made its way up his leg past his knee. The light from the fire showed the mottled darkness of his skin as the venom spread through his leg. The outer area was a dark red while closer to the bite it was almost blue-black in color.

Nichole grabbed his hand as he clawed at the bandage. "Fowler! Fowler!" she shouted as she tried to restrain his hand.

The sound of her voice brought him fully awake. He looked around, trying to get his bearings. He remembered the snake striking him and his slow trek back to the cabin. Things were a little fuzzy at that point. The last thing he remembered before he fainted was Nichole poised above his leg with her hunting knife in her trembling hand.

He knew from the feeling in his leg that she had cut and removed as much of the venom as she could. He now hoped it was enough to keep him from dying. If he was lucky, the snake might have already killed its supper for the night, thereby releasing some of its venom before it had struck him.

"How long was I out?"

Nichole handed the canteen of water to him. She knew he would be thirsty from losing so much blood. "About thirty minutes or so."

He took a long sip, wiping his mouth on his sleeve before handing the canteen back to her. "I need some whiskey to deaden this damn burning! It feels like my leg is on fire," he said through clenched teeth.

"You can't have any whiskey. It'll make the poison run faster through your body," she stated matter of factly.

He looked at her hunched figure as she sat close to him. "How do you know that?" He quickly held up his hand to forestall the response that he knew was coming. "Let me guess. Your grandpa taught you, right?"

She nodded her head, a slight grin tugging at her mouth. "One of the hazards of the range, especially at this time of the year, is snakebite. Almost every spring, one of the new hired hands would get careless and old Ned or Grandpa would have to treat a snakebite. However, you're the first live patient I've ever practiced on." At his alarmed look she hastened to add. "I meant, that was the first time I've ever had to do the cutting and sucking myself, not that I had practiced on dead patients."

"Whew," Fowler breathed an exaggerated sigh of relief. "I'm certainly glad to hear that." His face suddenly grew very solemn. "You know what happens now, don't you?"

She nodded gravely. "Yes. I've seen it enough times." She turned frightened eyes to his pale face. "Fowler, I'm scared. I think I should go for help. Maybe there's a doctor in Laredo. Maybe he could . . ."

Fowler took her small, cold hand in his and squeezed it. "Nichole, you know a doctor couldn't do any more than you've already done. If I make it through the next twenty-four hours, the worst will be over."

She knew that Fowler was trying to reassure her but Nichole had seen enough victims of snakebites to know that, if he did survive the next few hours, then the worst was far from being over.

On the contrary, it would be just the beginning of the hell that awaited him.

Chapter Thirteen

Cody and Nick reached Evadne as the sun made its exit for the day. They had pushed the horses and themselves to the limit, knowing that time was of the essence. Each day's delay in finding Nichole meant another day that Linc Travis might get to her before they did.

They were trail dirty from head to foot and they hadn't taken the time to shave since the day they had left the ranch. Their rough-looking appearance, however, didn't draw anyone's attention to them.

Cody looked around the town as they rode in. In general it appeared much like any other town with the exception that it seemed to have more saloons than a town of this size normally had.

Nick rode through the middle of the town, looking neither left nor right as he headed to the part of town most likely to house the answers to his questions. Cody, following his brother's lead, noticed that the appearance of this part of town was definitely less prosperous than the other side.

Cody glanced quizzically at Nick when he reined up in front of a seedy saloon and started to dismount. "Nick, are you sure it's safe to go in there?"

"Hell, no, it's not safe to go in there! It's full of outlaws and murderers, for Chrissakes!" he acknowledged. "Why do you think the Travis gang hangs out here? It sure as hell isn't to get religion."

Nick adjusted his holster before swaggering arrogantly through the swinging doors into the smoke-filled, noisy barroom.

Cody followed suit, a bit surprised at his kid brother's sudden transformation.

Nick grabbed the saloon girl closest to him and gave her a resounding kiss. "Hello, Darlin'. Did ya miss me?" he asked cockily.

She threw her arms around his neck and kissed him back, rubbing herself suggestively against him. "Where the hell you been hiding, Brazos? I ain't had no decent loving since you was here last," she stated as she brazenly caressed the front of his breeches.

With one arm looped around Nick's neck, she eyed Cody up and down. "Who's your friend here, honey?" she inquired with unabashed longing.

"Cody, meet Darlin'," Nick drawled, hugging the shapely redhead to him. "Cody's a long-time friend of mine. Got himself into a little trouble up around Waco. Thought he might like to ride with me an' Linc for a while. See how the big boys handle things," he said smugly.

Cody was going to wring his little brother's neck

the first chance he got! He could have at least clued him in on the rules of the game, he thought angrily. "Hello, Darlene," he said politely to the redhead, but his eyes spoke volumes to his brother.

The redhead laughed a hearty laugh. "It ain't 'Darlene,' it's Darlin', as in, 'oh, my darlin'!" She looked around the room as if trying to spot someone in particular. When she caught sight of her friend, she called to her. "Hey, Peggy. Look what the wind blew in."

The girl named Peggy had long, dark brown hair and from a distance, she looked a lot younger than she did up close. She made her way to the threesome, planting an eager kiss on Nick much in the same way as the redhead had.

"Where ya been keeping yourself, handsome? I've been missing ya something fierce."

Cody glanced at his brother in surprise. To him, Nick was just a kid brother, but these two women were acting as if he were some kind of a stud!

Nick smirked at him, having accurately read the surprised look on Cody's face. "Hey, friend. What can I say? When ya got it, ya got it." He kissed both women before aiming them toward a table at the back of the room.

Peggy conceded to her friend's prior claim to Nick, and immediately linked her arm through Cody's. She boldly assessed him. "You as good as your friend?"

Cody didn't have to ask what she meant. The appreciative look on her face clearly defined what she was insinuating.

"Taught him everything he knows," Cody proclaimed proudly. He didn't know what Nick was up to, but he'd play along with him. Besides, he thought to himself, this could turn out to be one hell of an interesting night.

As they made their way to a table, several of the other painted ladies fondly greeted the Brazos Kid. Cody was beginning to wonder if his brother had bedded every whore in the whole damn saloon!

When the foursome reached their table, Nick and Cody each took a chair, but the women promptly made themselves comfortable in the men's laps.

After pouring drinks all around, Nick made a toast before tossing his whiskey back. "Here's to good whiskey and bad women."

Both women laughed as they emptied their glasses with equal speed.

Nick looked lazily around the crowded saloon. "Seen Mex or Red today?"

"Guess you ain't heard the news yet," Darlin' said proud to be the one to tell him. "Mex got himself killed a few nights back."

Nick drained his glass then casually remarked, "Is that so? Who done him in? Another card-cheating poker player?"

The women shrugged their shoulders in an unconcerned manner.

"Nobody knows. We heard a ruckus in the alley, shots were fired, and Mex was dead when we got there."

Peggy leaned forward to add, almost in a whisper, "Old crazy Flo says she knows who done it, but nobody believes her. Everybody knows she's crazy as a loon."

Both women laughed unkindly, as the aging saloon whore in question weaved an unsteady path up the stairs with an equally drunk customer.

"Bet Linc was fit to be tied when he found out," Nick coached, hoping to pry some information out of one of them.

Darlin' slipped Nick's hand under her skirt as she pulled at his earlobe with her teeth. "Who cares? Let's go up to my room and have our own private party," she suggested eagerly.

Cody watched his brother's face. *Now how's little brother going to get himself out of this one?* he thought wryly.

When Nick stood up, he swayed slightly, which puzzled Cody. In the first place, he knew Nick could hold his liquor, and secondly, he knew his brother hadn't drunk enough to be slurring his words as he was now doing.

"That's an excellent idea. Don't you agree, Cody, old boy?" he drawled as he grabbed the bottle with one hand and the redhead with the other. "Let's go ta Darlin's room and have a party."

Peggy didn't give Cody time to answer. She jumped out of his lap and grabbed his hand, pulling him to his feet. "Come on, honey, don't be shy. The four of us can have a real good time."

Cody wasn't about to miss this for the world. "After you, my friend." He motioned for Nick to proceed him as he put his arm around Peggy's waist.

As they neared the stairs, Nick managed to bump into a man standing beside one of the poker tables. "Hey," Nick shouted loudly, "watch who the hell you're shoving, you bastard!"

"Who you calling a bastard? You son of a bitch!" the man growled in return, taking a swing at Nick.

Nick ducked, and the man's fist made contact with the back of another man's head.

221

The man whirled around and looked at Nick.

Nick pointed quickly at the other man. "He done it! He's the one who hit you."

The second man grabbed the first man by the shirt front and punched him in the face, knocking him back against the man behind him, who was standing with a drink in his hand, watching the poker game.

This caused the man's drink to spill on the head of one of the poker players. The poker player immediately jumped to his feet, shouting, "What the hell did ya do that for?" while at the same time plowing his fist into the man's stomach.

Someone yelled "Fight!", and within seconds, tables and chairs were falling and fists were flying. No one seemed to care who they were hitting just as long as they were hitting someone.

Nick pushed the girls up the stairs, hollering after them, "Wait for us, Darlin'. We'll be up after we crack a few heads."

The girls didn't hesitate as they quickly sought the safety of their rooms.

"Come on, let's get the hell out of here," Nick told Cody, heading for the back door.

Cody was fast on his heels as Nick lead the way through the storeroom.

Once outside, Nick stopped and looked around to be sure they hadn't been followed.

"I wondered how you were going to get us out of that mess. But," Cody admonished, "we don't know any more now than we did before, except that a Mexican got killed. Any more bright ideas, little brother?"

"Yes. Shut up and help me get this barrel under that window. I've got to talk to Flo. She may be a drunk, aging whore but she's not crazy. If she knows who killed Mex, she might know why he was killed."

After positioning the barrel under the upstairs window and getting a boost from Cody, Nick cautiously peeked into the room, before raising the window and easing himself over the windowsill.

Fortunately for him, Flo's customer was passed out dead drunk and snoring loud enough to bring the rafters down. Unfortunately, so was Flo.

He gently shook the sleeping whore's arm. "Flo," he whispered. "Flo, wake up. I hafta talk to you. Flo!"

"Huh? Yeah, jest a minute, hon . . ." Her words trailed off as she fell back asleep.

Nick pulled her to a sitting position and tried again, this time a little firmer. "Flo! Dammit, wake up! It's me, Brazos." He gently slapped the side of her face.

She managed to get one eye open to squint at the face peering into hers. "Brazos?" Recognition seemed to dawn slowly on her liquor-soaked brain. She gave him a lopsided, inebriated grin. "Hi, Braz . . (hiccup) Brazos. (Hiccup) Buy me a drink?" She looked around her in confusion. "Saaay, where the (hiccup) hell am I?"

"Shhh, we're in your room. Tell me what I want to know and I'll buy you a whole bottle of whiskey. Who killed Mex? And why was he killed?" He thought Flo was dozing off again, so he shook her once more.

Her face immediately brightened at the word "bottle." "Bottle?"

"Yes, a bottle. Now, who killed Mex?"

"Mex?" she murmured hazily, trying hard to comprehend who Nick was talking about.

"Yes, dammit! *Think*, Flo. Mex, the Mexican who rode with Linc Travis. Who killed him?"

"Oh, hi . . . (hiccup) him. Don't know. He was arguing with someone in the alley, then that good-looking blond fella . . ." She paused as she suddenly remembered the man's promise. "Ya know, he told me ta wait fer him, gave me a twenty-dollar gold piece, too, but he never did come back. Wonder what happened ta him. He sure was . . ."

Nick ground his teeth together as Flo's mind began to wander. He shook her to get her attention. "Never mind that. What about a blond man?"

"Oh, him. He was talking to that Mexican fella when he got shot. The Mexican got shot." She bobbed her head as she tried to clarify her words. "Not the good-looking one."

Nick placed both hands on Flo's bone-thin shoulders, turning her to look him straight in the face. "Now, think real hard, Flo. What did the Mexican say to the blond man? It's very important that you get it right. Tell me *exactly* what was said and I'll give you another twenty-dollar gold piece."

Her rheumy eyes lit up at the thought of another gold piece. She tried as hard as she could but she turned tear-filled eyes to him, disappointed that she couldn't remember because she badly wanted that gold piece. "I can't 'member *exactly* what was said," she sniffed. "I only 'member some of it," she wailed.

"Shhh, okay, okay! Just tell me what you can remember and I'll still give you the money."

She immediately brightened. "Ya will? Really?" At the nod of Nick's head, she again tried to recall the conversation that she had eavesdropped on. "He said Linc had gone to Mexico and . . . something about killing a Texas Ranger. And that other man said his boss was gonna be mad. Then he said he had to go 'cause he was suppose to meet Linc at the . . . at the . . ." She seemed to be struggling to recall a word, when suddenly the word came to her. "Container," she said proudly. "He was gonna meet Linc at the container."

"Container?"

"Yeah. His girlfriend was at the container in Mexico." Flo was proud of herself for remembering enough to get her gold piece.

Container in Mexico? Cantina! "Flo! You mean 'cantina.' The Mex was meeting Linc at a cantina in Mexico."

"Yeah, that's right."

"Good girl. Now think real, real hard. Where in Mexico is the cantina?"

She screwed up her face in deep concentration.

Nick knew the woman was trying as hard as she could. "Okay, Flo. I'll name some towns and you tell me if any of them sound like the word he used. Okay?"

Flo apologetically nodded her head. "I ain't never been no place 'cept here."

Nick assured her that that was all right, then he began to name off the towns that bordered Texas. When he hit the word "Laredo," Flo bounced up and down on the bed.

"That's it. That's the word. Laredo!"

Nick grabbed Flo to still her excitement. Her bouncing had shaken her customer slightly awake. He let out a loud snort and rolled over to his other side. Nick held his finger to his lips to shush Flo, waiting until he heard the man resume his loud snoring before he continued.

"Now, are you sure that's all that you remember?"

Flo thought for a minute, then nodded her head. "That's when that Mexican fella was shot and that blond fella ran across the street to . . ." She suddenly drew in her breath. "I *do* 'member something else!" she said excitedly. "He said he couldn't come upstairs with me 'cause he had him a new bride over at the hotel. That's where he ran to after the Mexican got kilt."

"Good girl!" He pulled a gold piece from his pocket and handed it to the aging woman.

She clutched it to her bosom and smiled proudly.

Nick patted her hand, cautioning her, "Now, one more thing, Flo. Don't tell anyone else what you've told me. Okay?"

She solemnly nodded her head.

"And don't tell anyone, not even one of the girls, that I was here. Okay? Promise me."

"I promise, Brazos. I won't say a word to anyone," she said earnestly.

"Good girl."

Cody paused once more to look up nervously at the window. What in hell's name was taking Nick so long? He resumed his pacing between the back door to the saloon and the entrance to the alley, keeping a close watch to make sure no one saw them.

He released a sigh of relief when he saw Nick lower himself over the windowsill and down the wall to the ground. "What in the hell took you so long?" he whispered angrily as loud as he dared.

Nick had pressed his luck as much as he intended. "Come on. I'll tell you when we get out of here."

After getting their horses from in front of the saloon, Nick headed up the street toward the largest hotel. Since he had only stayed at the cheaper ones on the other end of town when he had been with the gang, he didn't figure anyone would recognize him in the better one.

Nick eyed the young man behind the desk as he walked up to it. Turning the register around, he began to flip backwards through the pages.

The young desk clerk quickly grabbed the book. "Sir! What do you think you are doing? This is hotel property. You can't go prying through hotel property. It's against the rules."

Nick gave him a stern-eyed look before showing him his Ranger badge. "I'm here on official business, young man. Am I going to have to arrest you for interfering with the law?"

The young clerk's Adam's apple bobbed up and down as he swallowed nervously. "No . . . no sir. I'm sorry, sir. I . . . I didn't know who you were." He handed the book back to Nick. "Here, sir, just . . . just read all you want to."

Nick quickly scanned the signatures until he found the one he was looking for. He turned the book around and pointed to the name. "This man is the one I'm looking for. How long did he stay? Was there anyone with him?"

The clerk read the name. "Fowler Barclay? Barclay? Yes, yes, I remember him. They stayed two days, I believe. Yes, yes, I do believe that's correct."

"They? Who was with him?"

The man looked at the book again, then turned it back around to show Nick and Cody. "Why, his wife, of course. See, right here, 'Mr. and Mrs. Fowler Barclay.' They were newlyweds I believe I heard him say. Right pretty little thing, she was. Long black hair

227

and pretty green eyes. I remember her because she didn't look sickly, but the poor thing had the vapors. Right here in the lobby! I told her that was against the rules, but she did it anyway. I had to fetch her a bottle of whiskey. That seemed to make everything better."

Cody and Nick looked at each other, each wondering what in the hell their little sister was up to now.

Nick's face took on a thunderous appearance as a thought crossed his mind. "How many rooms did Barclay take?"

Surprise registered on the desk clerk's face. "Why, just one, sir." As Nick's face darkened, the clerk quickly added, "Most married couples only take one room, sir."

Cody knew exactly what was going on in his brother's mind because the same thought had entered his own. However, he was in better control of his temper as he turned back to the clerk. "One more thing, has anybody else asked about this man?"

"I don't think so. I'm here most of the time but I could ask my relief help if anyone's inquired about him."

Cody shook his head. "Never mind." He flipped the man a coin. "If anyone should ask, you don't know nothing and you've never seen us or them, understand?" His steely sapphire eyes told the nervous man that he had better understand.

"Yes, sir. I mean, no, sir. I mean, I don't know nothing and ain't seen nobody."

Once they were out the door, Nick's temper exploded. "That son of a bitch! I'll kill him when I get my hands on him!"

Cody, being older and a little more levelheaded, tried to talk some sense into his brother. "Nick, don't go off half-cocked. I know what you're thinking, but, until we talk to Nichole, we won't know anything for sure. Hell, knowing Nichole, *she* might have forced *him* to stay in the same room with her for fear he'd leave without her, or something. You know how impulsive she is. If she had her mind set on something, she'd not give one whit about propriety or what anybody else thought. You know that," he chided.

What Cody said did make some sense, but Nick still couldn't get the thought out of his head that this Barclay fellow might have taken advantage of his sister. And, if he found out that his feeling was correct, heaven help the man because Nick intended to pound him into the ground!

Nick looked at his brother. "We'll see."

Hoping to get Nick's mind off his murderous thoughts, Cody inquired, "Did you learn anything from Flo?"

Nick told him what Flo had said, adding, "It's my thinking that they're on their way to Laredo."

Cody shook his head. "Yeah. That's my thinking, too. Okay, let's head for Laredo and hope we can overtake them before they get there."

Nichole suddenly jerked awake. She didn't remember falling asleep but she must have dozed off for a few minutes from sheer exhaustion. She placed her hand against Fowler's forehead. It felt a little warmer than it should, but she was hoping it was from the heat of the fireplace and not the beginnings of a fever.

Judging from the color of the sky, it would be hours until daybreak. She was wishing she had a timepiece when she remembered the pocket watch that Fowler carried.

Without disturbing him, she quickly retrieved it from the pocket in his breeches, and moved it closer to the fire's light. She was disheartened to see that it was only three o'clock in the morning.

It seemed like it had been hours since Fowler had lapsed into unconsciousness. She held the timepiece to her ear, thinking maybe it had run down. But it hadn't; she could plainly hear the consistent ticking away of the minutes.

She had done all she could to make Fowler as comfortable as possible. She felt his forehead again. Was it her imagination or did it feel hotter? *Lord*, she prayed, *please don't let him get a fever.*

When she checked his wound to see if it was bleeding, she was shocked at how much the swelling had increased and how fast it was spreading up his leg. She decided that she'd have to remove his breeches before the swelling got so bad that it completely cut off the circulation to his leg.

After tugging his pants off, she could see that his leg had taken on a darker, almost black color around the wound, radiating into a dark red as the poison worked its way up his leg and through his body. The swollen area felt hot to the touch, and she knew there was a burning fever in his leg. After covering his naked torso, she placed her hand on his forehead again.

This time there was no denying the fact. Fowler definitely had a fever and it was rapidly growing worse.

She hurriedly went through both of their saddlebags. Leaving them each only one change of clothes, she tore the remaining clothes into strips to use as bandages.

Pulling on her boots, she gathered up both canteens and the largest cooking pot they had, and made her way to the river to fill them with the cool water.

For the rest of the night, she alternately bathed his fevered body with the cool water and trickled a few drops down his throat.

As the darkness fought its final battle against the sun, Fowler began to moan and move about restlessly.

Even in his weakened, delirious condition, she was no match for his strength. All she could do was try to keep him from clawing at his leg while at the same time dodging his flinging arms.

She knew from past experience that he must be in excruciating pain. She had heard men who had recovered from rattlesnake bites tell how it felt like someone was moving a hot branding iron over their body as the poison worked through their veins.

Nichole was thinking about all the horror stories she had heard instead of watching out for Fowler's arm. She suddenly felt his hand make contact with the side of her head, sending her sprawling across the floor.

Tears of hurt and frustration burst forth as she crawled back to where he lie. "Dammit, Fowler Barclay!" she bawled as she wrung out another cool rag to wet his fevered body. "Don't you dare go and die on me! Do you hear me?" she shouted at him, knowing full well that he couldn't understand a word she was saying.

"I don't care if you don't love me back. I don't care if you make love to every damn woman in the whole damn state!" she raved in frustrated exhaustion. "But you better not die on me! So help me, if you do,

I'll . . . I'll just kill you, dammit! Do you hear me?" she shouted vehemently, tears running down her face.

She wet another cloth, but this time laid it against her face. She knew she was on the verge of hysteria. She sobbed hopelessly into the wet cloth until she had no more tears left.

Her crying released some of her tension, and she dried her eyes and went back to bathing Fowler's body.

Around the middle of the afternoon, Nichole noticed that Fowler didn't seem to be thrashing about as much. Dare she hope that his fever was going to break?

She had made two trips to the river for fresh water, but other than that, she had not left his side, not even to eat. The lack of food was beginning to make her feel lightheaded and slightly sick to her stomach. She decided that she'd better eat something. She certainly wouldn't be any help to Fowler if she became ill. She reheated the coffee and ate two biscuits and some beans, leftovers from supper.

By late afternoon, there was a definite change in his condition. He still had a fever, but it wasn't as high as before. He seemed to be resting a bit easier, too. In fact, his breathing was so quiet that Nichole placed her hand against his mouth several times to be sure he *was* still breathing.

From time to time, he weakly tried to claw at his leg, which was still very badly swollen, almost to the point of bursting, but she had reason to hope that the worst might be over. Still, she was afraid to relax her guard. All that night and well into the wee hours of the next morning, she continued to bath his feverish body and to dribble some water through his parched lips.

It was nearing four o'clock when she last looked at his watch. Her body was numb from exhaustion. She bathed him with a cool rag and leaned her head against his, just for an instant of rest.

"Wa . . . ter."

His voice was so weak and cracked, she felt rather than heard his plea. She came awake instantly. Good Lord! She had fallen asleep. It was almost sunrise. She must have dreamed that she heard Fowler's voice because she didn't see any sign that he was awake.

"Thir . . . sty."

She grabbed the canteen, positive this time that she had heard him. She raised his head and placed the canteen against his mouth.

He took several sips before she eased his head back down. "Not too fast," she cautioned.

He tried to open his eyes, but that seemed to cause him pain. He moved his mouth as if to talk, but she placed her finger against his lips.

"Don't try to talk, darling. Just rest." Tears of joy were falling unchecked down her cheeks. He wasn't going to die! He was going to get well, her heart sang. She lifted his head again and let him take a few more sips of water.

"Sleep," he whispered weakly.

"Yes, darling, you go back to sleep. I'm right here. A team of mules couldn't drag me away from your side," she assured him.

He shook his head and tried to pull her hand to his side. "You . . . sleep . . . here," he managed to whisper before sleep claimed him again.

She lay down beside him and holding his hand in hers, she fell into a deep sleep.

She awoke later in the morning to the feel of his hand caressing her face. She winced when his hand touched the spot where he had struck her in his delirium.

He brushed the hair away from her face and peered through hazy eyes at the bruise there. "Did I do that?"

She took his hand in hers and kissed it. "You didn't mean to, you were out of your head with fever. I just didn't duck fast enough." She chuckled, trying to make light of it.

"I'm sorry."

"Don't worry about it, Fowler. It wasn't your fault," she again tried to assure him. "Here, drink a little water, then I want you to go back to sleep while I fix something for you to eat." She helped him raise his head to take a couple of sips of liquid.

After settling the blanket around him and making sure he was asleep, Nichole took her gun and went in search of meat to make a broth for Fowler's supper.

When Fowler woke up again, it was late afternoon and the smell of something delicious was tickling his nose.

"Nichole?" He looked around the one-room cabin; not seeing her anywhere, he laid his head back down.

His leg still pained him horribly. He rubbed as much of it as he could reach from his prone position. He had seldom been ill in his life, and now to find himself in such a condition that just lifting his arm made him tremble from weakness was both frustrating and embarrassing.

He was wondering how the hell he was going to get outside to relieve himself when Nichole soundlessly opened the door and slipped quietly inside.

Seeing he was awake, she bent down to feel his forehead. Finding it still warm to the touch, she frowned. "You still have a fever. How else do you feel?" she inquired.

"Hungry and like my leg is in that fire over there."

Being careful not to expose any more of his nakedness than was absolutely necessary, she laid one corner of the blanket back to examine his wound. She frowned when she removed the bandage and saw that it had begun to ooze a bit of bloody liquid.

He watched her face as she carefully laid the cloth back. She looked exhausted and worn to a frazzle.

Her hair, usually neatly braided, was twisted in a knot at the back of her head and several pieces had escaped the pins, giving her a slightly wild appearance. The dark circles under her eyes made her face look pale even in the shadowed glow of light from the fireplace.

When he saw her frown, he tried to raise his head to see what it was that she was frowning about. The effort was more than his weakened body could handle. Moaning in dizziness, he shut his eyes and dropped his head down.

"From the feel of it, it's a gory mess, isn't it?"

"Hmmm," she murmured as she gently pressed around the wound, noticing that he winced from her gentle touch. "It's beginning to drain some, but I don't think it's infected." She carefully placed a clean bandage on it before turning her gaze back to his pained expression.

"I've got some broth ready. I killed a couple of rabbits this morning and found some wild onions in the woods to give it a little flavor."

"I hate broth. I need some solid food to get my strength back, not some water that a rabbit ran through," he grumbled.

She gave him a look that brooked no argument. "Be that as it may, you will sip a little broth until we're sure you can keep it down. Understand?"

"If you insist, *Doctor* Westerfield," he grumbled again, this time making a face at her.

She had been outside relieving herself when Fowler had awakened, and while doing so, she had thought that they were going to have a slight problem along that line. She knew that he would need to empty his bladder sooner or later, but he was too weak to make it outside on his own and she wasn't strong enough to support him.

She had figured out a solution, but she didn't know how to broach the subject without embarrassing the both of them.

"Ah, Nichole I, ah . . ."

"Fowler, if you need . . ."

They had both started talking at the same time. He looked very uncomfortable and her face had turned beet-red. They both laughed uncomfortably, bidding the other to speak first.

"Oh, horse feathers!" Nichole exclaimed as she stepped over to retrieve the tin can that she had rinsed out at the river. Setting it beside him with a plunk, she declared, "I can't get you to the bushes and I can't get the bushes to you, so you'll just have to make do with that." Her face was scarlet as she quickly stepped out the door to give him a measure of privacy.

Fowler chuckled and shook his head in bemusement, while at the same time greatly relieved that she had found a solution for his predicament.

Would she never cease to amaze him? Here was yet another side of her that he had not seen before. She was practical and ingenious as well as smart and courageous.

He knew that he would have died without her help. And it had taken a hell of a lot of guts for her to get the poison out of his system as efficiently as she had apparently done.

Nichole had been right about his stomach rebelling against food. Almost from the instant that the warm broth hit his stomach, he had had to fight to keep it down.

And he had fought hard. For her to see him heaving his guts out would have been the final indignity! He won the battle, but it had left him weaker than before, if that was possible.

Nichole could tell by the bilious look on Fowler's face and the beads of perspiration on his forehead that the broth was about to turn him inside out.

On the pretense of trying to bring his fever down, she bathed his face in cool water, hoping it would relieve the nausea and help him preserve his dignity.

She breathed a sigh of relief when he was finally able to drift off into a deep, healing sleep.

Within minutes, she joined him in the first peaceful sleep she'd had in more than two days.

Chapter Fourteen

There were few towns between Evadne and Laredo and, except for San Antonio, most of them didn't amount to much. Usually what was designated as the "town," consisted of a general store, a blacksmith's shop, and a saloon or two. But for the most part deep south Texas was sparsely populated except for cacti and coyotes.

Cody and Nick walked out of what might loosely be called a general store in Piedras, drawing a deep breath of clean air into their lungs.

"Damn!" Nick swore. "I've smelled outhouses that smelled better than that place."

"Whew!" Cody concurred. "Well, at least we found out that they passed through here about a week ago."

"If you can put any store by what that fat little man said. It could have just as easily been closer to two weeks as one." Nick gave a disgusted look up and down the wind-blown dirt street, wondering why anybody would stay in a place as poor as this. He always felt sorry for the children who had to live under such desperate conditions. He shook his head sadly. The skinny, barefoot little urchins managed to survive somehow though.

"Well, at least it seems like this marshal Nichole abducted is a capable man with a gun. I'd hardly think our little sister is leaving this trail of dead bodies all by herself," Cody stated as they mounted their horses.

"I guess that's some small consolation," Nick begrudgingly conceded.

Cody knew that his brother was still stewing about the relationship between the marshal and their sister. What he couldn't understand was why? As hardheaded as Nichole was, they both knew that nobody, other than their parents, could make her do anything that she didn't want to do.

He had given up days ago, trying to reason with Nick. One thing he knew for sure, Nichole was not the *only* hardheaded twin in the family! To make matters worse, Nick couldn't even put into words what was really bothering him about the situation.

They had known from the start or at least strongly suspected that Nichole had somehow hoodwinked the marshal into helping her find Nick, but that had not seemed to bother Nick then. It was only after they found out that one of them, and it could have been Nichole just as well as the marshal, had registered them as man and wife, that Nick had suddenly gotten a burr under his saddle.

Cody shrugged his shoulders, knowing that whatever was really bothering Nick, he'd have to work out for himself. Right now, the imperative thing was to catch up with Nichole.

Nichole slipped quietly through the door, trying not to wake Fowler. She had been down to the river to bathe and wash her hair. Now she sat cross-legged in front of the fire, brushing the tangles from her wet tresses.

It had been more than a week since Fowler had been bitten by the rattlesnake. The nausea and headaches had passed, and his leg was healing nicely. However, Fowler was still feeling the effects of the venom. The first day he had insisted that he was going to move around some, he had hardly done more than sit up before his weakened body trembled from the exertion and his face had taken on a stark white color. But with each passing day he grew stronger.

The previous day he had been able to sit up almost all morning and he had even been able to put a little weight on the injured leg.

Nichole knew he was trying too hard, too fast, but she also knew she'd have about as much luck trying to spit in the wind as she would trying to get Fowler to rest more.

"What are you doing?"

She had been in such deep thought while brushing her hair to dry it that the sound of Fowler's voice startled her, causing her to drop the brush. It made a loud thumping noise as it bounced across the floor.

"Good heaven's, Fowler. You just scared ten years off my life." She crawled on her hands and knees to retrieve the brush and resume her slow movements. "How long have you been awake?"

"Since you sneaked out from under the blankets." He caught a lock of her silky hair and lifted it to his nose to smell its clean fragrance.

She giggled softly. "I wasn't 'sneaking,' as you put it. I was trying to keep from waking you. You need your sleep to get your strength back."

He gave her a disgruntled look.

"Don't say it," she quickly stated, holding up one hand to ward off his protest. "When you can move about without turning pasty white from weakness or pain, *then* I'll believe that you're well enough to travel and not a minute before."

He dropped the lock of hair and stared up at the ceiling. "You're still going into Laredo, aren't you?"

She didn't have to answer. The defiant tilt of her chin told the story plain enough.

They had argued late into the night about Nichole's announcement that she was going to ride into Laredo this morning to get supplies. She had been hoping that after sleeping on the idea, he wouldn't still be as angry as he had been when she had first mentioned it.

Obviously, from the tone of his voice, the passing hours had not improved his temperament one whit.

Frowning her displeasure at him, she inquired, "Fowler, why are you being so—so damned pig-headed about this? We're out of flour, cornmeal, beans." She emphasized each item as she counted them off on her fingers. "I opened the last of the canned food two days ago and I used the last of the coffee this morning. Now someone has to go get some supplies, because I, for one, don't intend to starve to death in this cabin!"

He knew she was right, of course, but he didn't like

the idea of her riding into a rough town like Laredo by herself. And it really chafed him that he was still too weak to go himself. He slammed his fist on the floor in frustration.

"Hell's bells, Fowler Barclay! You're acting as if I'm some kind of a nincompoop who can't even ride into town without getting lost or something!" Her voice rose almost to a shout.

"That's not the reason, and you damn well know it!" he fairly shouted at her as he tried to rise to his feet.

"You are absolutely the most infuriating man I've ever met in my entire life!"

"What you really mean is that I'm the only man you've ever met who has the audacity to stand up to you."

Each taking a defiant stance, they glared at each other, snapping emerald-green eyes clashing with smoldering sapphire-blue eyes that would neither concede nor compromise.

Suddenly Fowler reached out and grabbed her. Wrapping his arms around her slim body, he hugged her close, burying his head in her sweet-scented hair. "Sweetheart, I know you can take care of yourself. I've seen you handle a gun. It's just that I—I can't stand the idea that something might happen to you and I wouldn't be there to protect you," he confessed.

Nichole was taken aback. That was the closest that he had ever come to saying that he cared for her. Did she dare hope that he might love her? Just a little? She held her breath, silently praying that he'd confess his love for her.

When Nichole didn't respond to his words, he drew

back and looked deeply into her eyes. "I know your family is going to hold me responsible for your well-being. How would I ever be able to face them with the news that I had let something happen to you?" That wasn't what he had meant to say, but from the look on her face, he knew she would probably laugh if he expressed his deeper feelings for her. His pride could not withstand that humiliation.

She had saved his life, she had nursed him when he was ill, but nothing had really changed. He was still only a preacher's son and a marshal. And she was still a wealthy rancher's daughter, who needed all the things he would never be able to give her.

Responsible! All she was to him was a responsibility? *You fool! You stupid, stupid idiot!* she ranted at herself. *He's grateful that you saved his life and he feels indebted to you. He thinks he has to repay you by getting you back to your family unharmed. He doesn't love you. His kind doesn't know the meaning of real true, lasting love. All he wants, has ever wanted, was a quick toss of a skirt. And, fool that you are, you played right into his hands.*

Her hurt pride made her words sharp and cutting. "Don't worry about it, Fowler. My family would never hold anyone other than myself responsible for my actions. Besides, they don't even know you're with me, remember? So don't be concerned about your 'responsibility.'"

She pulled out of his arms and turned her back to him so that he wouldn't see the tears that threatened to add humiliation to her hurt feelings.

Fowler stood for a minute, staring at her rigid back, wondering what he had said to cause her to lash out at him like that. "Nichole?"

"Get washed up for breakfast. I want to get an early start."

She moved away from him to kneel on the floor in front of the fire, busying herself with stirring the last of the corn meal into a pan of boiling water to make porridge for their breakfast.

All through their silently eaten breakfast, Fowler continued to wonder why Nichole had seemed so upset when he had expressed his concern for her.

Nichole stared unseeing into her bowl of bear mush. Bear mush. She hadn't called it that since she was a little girl. She could remember Grandpa Westerfield sitting on the side of her bed, trying to convince her to eat a little bit more.

She must have been six or seven years old at the time. She'd been in bed with a real bad cold and sore throat. Her throat was so swollen that all she could swallow was liquids and very soft foods for two days.

Grandpa Westerfield had been trying to cheer her up by telling her outrageous stories about the years he and her grandpa Montclair had been fur trappers in Canada. When her mother brought her supper to her and she saw that it was porridge again, Nichole had refused to eat.

That was when her grandpa had told her the story about his run in with the bear that ate his breakfast. She had laughed and accused him of reading too many fairy tales, but he had solemnly insisted that mush was a bear's favorite food, especially if it had honey on it like hers did.

She wasn't sure at the time whether to believe him but, if it was going to attract bears, then perhaps she'd better eat it before one came to her bedroom.

A lonely tear slipped down her face at the thought of her beloved grandfather. She dashed it away with the back of her hand and quickly rose to her feet, strapping on her gun belt and grabbing up her saddlebags.

Her abrupt action had taken Fowler by surprise. He was still wondering why she seemed so . . . touchy lately. He could only blame it on tension caused by his snakebite and her missing brother.

Forgetting about his leg, he quickly stood up, too. Nichole saw his face blanch as pain shot through his body. Grabbing the branch that she had cut for him to use as a crutch, she helped him balance on his good leg until the pain subsided.

"Agghh," he cried out in agony.

"Good Lord, Fowler! What in the world made you do a damn stupid thing like that?" she chastised him. "Sometimes I think you don't have the sense God gave a pissant!"

Taking a deep breath to ease the pain, he tried to sound as stern as he could with his leg shooting sparks of fire up his torso. "Nichole, hasn't anyone ever told you that ladies don't cuss. Dammit! Sometimes you sound like a damn drunk sailor!"

"Well, since I've never heard a 'damn drunk sailor,' I wouldn't know what one sounded like, so it must be the company I'm keeping," she retorted sassily.

"I'll bet your mother used a lot of soap on that cheeky mouth of yours," he quipped. "Too bad your father didn't use his belt on your bottom once in a while. Maybe between the two of them, they might have made a proper lady out of you!"

"A proper lady!" she sputtered in outrageous indignation. She shook her finger in his face. "Fowler Barclay, *you* wouldn't know a proper lady if one hit you over the head with her parasol!"

"See what I mean."

Nichole gave him a blank look.

"You just proved what I said," he stated smugly. "If she was a proper lady, she wouldn't be hitting me over the head with her parasol. Now would she?" he rocked back on his good leg, proud that he had gotten the last word in.

But, just as pride goes before a fall, so do smart-aleck marshals. When Fowler shifted back on his heel, his makeshift crutch skittered out from under him, sending him sprawling on his backside as he wildly grabbed the air in an attempt to avoid the inevitable.

Nichole couldn't restrain her laughter at his comical efforts to keep from losing his balance. Her mirth turned to sudden fear, however, when he grabbed his injured leg and howled in pain.

"My leg! My leg!" he moaned as he rolled to his side with his back to her.

Nichole rushed to kneel beside him. "Are you hurt? Did you break the wound open?" She tried to pull him onto his back to make sure he had not further injured his leg.

Fowler suddenly turned over, wrapping both arms around her. "No. But it was a good way to get you in my arms."

"Oh, you . . . you . . . faker! How dare you scare me like that, you cad!" She buffeted his shoulder in an attempt to free herself. "You outrageous, incons—"

Fowler effectively stopped her tirade when he covered her mouth with his.

She ceased struggling as the warmth of his kiss pervaded the very essence of her soul. Against her will, she melted into his embrace and returned his kiss with an ardent passion that threatened to kindle the flame that simmered relentlessly just below the surface of her consciousness.

Fowler looked longingly into her passion-softened features. He laid his hand against the side of her face, almost in a reverent manner, brushing her kiss-swollen lips with his thumb. "When you look at me like that, I feel as if I might drown in the crystal green pools of your eyes. You make me feel things I've never felt before, never *wanted* to feel before, with a woman."

As he lowered his lips toward hers once more, he murmured in a barely discernible whisper, "What have you done to me? How did you manage to steal my very soul without me even being aware you were doing it?"

Nichole knew she should stop his lovemaking while she still had the presence of mind to do so. She had promised herself that she would never fall under his concupiscent spell again. She knew that he did not love her, and would never be able to return the love she felt for him. But her resolve was a lot easier to make than it was to keep. Especially when he held her so tenderly, touched her so sensuously, and kissed her so passionately.

When his lips touched hers, all of her well thought out reasons for stopping him were dissolved just like water dissolves a lump of sugar. How was it that this man had the power to elevate her to a fever pitch that she was unable to control? She didn't know and she didn't care just as long as he didn't stop the sweet, torturous havoc he was wreaking on her body.

All that mattered was here and now. She would have many years after they parted to figure out the whys. But for now, all she could do was lose herself in the wondrous feelings that were overwhelming her sensitive body.

When their heated lovemaking came to an end, they lay in each other's arms, thoroughly seated and contented. Fowler looked at Nichole with an expression that she could only guess at. It seemed as if he was about to say something, but decided not to.

Once again, she silently begged him to utter the words that would release the pain from her heart. But once again, she waited in vain.

Instead, he said in a voice still husky from desire, "Please be careful. I'll be as edgy as a cornered animal until I see your beautiful face smiling at me. Promise me that you won't tarry any longer than absolutely necessary." He gently shook her when she didn't immediately give him her promise.

"I promise that I won't dillydally, Fowler. I'll return just as quickly as I can." She turned away from him and slowly began to pull her hastily discarded breeches and shirt back on.

He lay where he was and watched her as she dressed, wondering at the note of sadness in her voice. Was it really sadness? Maybe it was just his imagination hoping that she might feel sad about being apart from him for the better part of the day.

He watched as she pulled her vest on, stuck her hair under her hat, and strapped her gun belt on, after checking to be sure each chamber was loaded. A sudden thought occurred to him.

"You're not afraid to go into Laredo by yourself, are you?" He raised up on one elbow, his voice heavy with concern.

"Of course not! Why should I be? I can take care of myself, remember?" she snapped.

As he rose to his feet, she turned away from his unclothed body. Already recriminations were rearing inside her. If she didn't get out of the cabin immediately, she was going to burst into tears. Every time they made love, she hated herself a little more for not being strong enough to resist his magnetic pull.

"I have to go," she said hurriedly as she stepped toward the door. "If I want to get back before nightfall, I've got to leave now."

"Nichole?" Again, he thought he detected a different tone in her voice. Puzzled at what was bothering her, he decided that when she got back, he was going to force her to tell him what was troubling her. Even if he had to hog-tie her to do it!

"What?" she answered, but she wouldn't turn around to face him.

He reached her side with two hastily maneuvered hobbles and turned her around to face him. "Nichole, I . . . I'll miss you." God, how his heart ached to tell her how much he loved her! He pulled her to him, giving her one last hug.

She moved out of his arms. "I have to go."

He watched her until she was out of sight before hobbling back to lie down on the rumpled blankets, his thoughts troubling him almost as much as his weakness.

* * *

Nichole's first impression upon seeing the town of Laredo was to wonder if it ever rained in this part of the state. The hot, dry wind blew the dirt about incessantly. Dust devils romped across the open countryside at their leisure, spraying everything and everyone in their path liberally with their stinging particles.

By the time she reached the business district, both she and her horse were covered with a layer of grime. She patted Cocoa's neck after looping the reins around the hitching post in front of the first store she stopped at.

"When we get back to the cabin, the first thing we'll both do is go for a cooling swim in the river."

Cocoa flicked her ears and swished her long tail as if in complete understanding and agreement with her mistress's promise.

After purchasing the needed supplies from the friendly man behind the counter, she inquired if there was a store in town where she might purchase some ready-made clothing. Since she had torn her only gown and petticoat into strips to use as bandages when Fowler was ill, she needed to replace them. On the off-chance that they decided to stay at one of the hotels for a few days, she didn't want to look like a hoyden.

He directed her to a store across the street and three buildings down from his, assuring her that she'd be able to find exactly what she needed there.

After securing the full saddlebags behind her saddle, she reined Cocoa in the direction of the store with the faded red lettering on the plate glass window that stated simply "Clothing."

When she entered the store, a jolly little woman

bounced out of her chair, which was positioned to catch the midday light, to greet her.

"Hello, come in, come in. How can I help you today?" she inquired as she laid aside the material she had been working on.

Nichole smiled at the tiny woman with the ageless face. She could have been fifty just as easily as seventy. But, from the sound of her voice, Nichole guessed her age to be closer to the former than the latter.

"I'd like to see some of your ready-made clothing, please."

The woman eyed the young girl's slender figure with an expert eye for size. "Is this for everyday wear or a party? Maybe for a special young man, eh?" she asked with a twinkle in her eyes.

Nichole shook her head and laughed. "No. No special occasion. Just a simple cotton gown will do. And I'll need a chemise and a petticoat, too." She followed the woman to a rack of clothes near the front window.

The woman quickly reached for two gowns. "Either of these should fit you perfectly with just a few stitches to nip in the waist," she assured Nichole before clasping her hands together in wistful admiration. "Oh, to be so tall and slender as you. You would make any of my gowns look beautiful."

Standing a full head and shoulders above the petite woman, Nichole felt like a giant. "Well, I don't know about that, but thank you anyway," she said laughingly as she looked at the gowns.

One was a soft lilac color with tiny puffed sleeves and a heart-shaped neckline. A velvet ribbon in a darker shade of lilac encircled the waist before it flared into a full skirt. The other one also had a fitted bodice that flared into a full skirt. It was of gray cotton with tiny pink flowers. It had a scooped neckline and elbow-length sleeves that were edged with ruffles made from the same material. Pink velvet was sewn on the sleeves just above the ruffle.

Both gowns were so beautiful that Nichole couldn't make up her mind which one she liked better. So she did the only sensible thing to do under such circumstances. She bought both of them.

The seamstress insisted that Nichole have a cup of tea and some fresh-baked cookies with her while she made the necessary alterations.

The next hour and a half were spent in cheerful chatter as the modiste's nimble fingers almost seemed to fly as she made tiny little stitches down the sides of both gowns to fit Nichole's slim waist.

When she left the shop, Nichole felt more relaxed than she had in weeks. The gowns and undergarments had been carefully folded and wrapped in brown paper. Securing this package on top of her saddlebags, Nichole prepared to head back to the cabin.

She had not intended to be in town as long as she had. If she didn't hurry, she'd find herself on the road after dark, which did not appeal to her at all.

Already the town was beginning to come alive with activity now that the afternoon *siesta*, nap time, had ended. And, from the loud sounds floating through the swinging doors of the many saloons in town, it was shaping up to be a rowdy night.

As she walked Cocoa back through town, she passed a street vendor pushing his two-wheel cart. The aroma of hot tamales made her mouth water and her stomach growl in a most unladylike fashion. She reined up beside him to see what he had to sell.

She purchased two hot tamales, a dozen eggs, and a squawking chicken. She hungrily devoured the tamales while he wrung the chicken's neck, wrapped it and the eggs for her to add to the growing bundles tied behind her saddle, and once again she headed back the way she had come.

"God Almighty!" exclaimed the paunchy, middle-aged man as he grabbed his breeches and hopped on one foot trying to get them on without falling down in his haste to dress.

He had walked over to peer idly out the open window while he relieved himself in the chamber pot just in time to see the rider pass beneath him.

He couldn't believe his eyes. "Wait till I tell Linc who I jest seen!"

Dixie, the pretty whore whose bed he had spent the morning in, rose on one elbow to look blearily at the excited man. "Who did ya see, honey?" she yawned sleepily, before falling back on the rumbled sheets. She patted the bed beside her. "Hank, honey, come on back ta bed. It's too early ta git up. I ain't gotta be downstairs fer hours yet."

He rushed back to her side. "Dixie! I jest seen the Brazos Kid. The Brazos Kid, right here in Laredo, I tell ya!"

Dixie yawned again. "So? Who's the Brazos Kid, anyhow?"

Hank wasn't paying any attention to her as his mind began to clear from his hangover. Linc had sent him to Laredo to wait for Mex three days ago. But Mex hadn't shown up yet. After seeing Brazos riding so boldly through town, Hank had a notion that Mex hadn't shown up because Mex was dead.

Why would Brazos be in Laredo? he asked himself. Only one reason he could think of. To find Linc and kill him. He better get his ass to Linc, pronto! No. On second thought, what if he followed Brazos to wherever he was staying? Then he could lead Linc and the boys right to him. That ought to impress Linc for sure. Might impress him enough that Linc would make him his right-hand man now that Mex was dead.

"Yeah. That's what I'll do. I'll follow him an' then go tell Linc." Hank was talking out loud as he pulled his boots on and grabbed his gun belt.

"Hey!" Dixie shouted as Hank headed for the door. "Where the hell do ya think yer goin'? Where's my money?" she demanded petulantly.

Hank hurriedly tossed a couple of coins on the bed, and ran out the door.

The sun hung low on the horizon. Fowler had hobbled from the cabin to the door so many times in the past two hours that he had almost worn a rut in the floor. He let out a string of expletives when he realized that all his unsteady walking had produced was a throbbing ache in his leg. The direction that she would come from was still as empty as it had been the last time he had managed his step-thump, step-thump gait to look for Nichole.

"Dammit to hell! It shouldn't have taken her this long to get to town and back," he muttered out loud to the four walls around him. He turned and stepped away from the door. After putting a few small logs on the fire, he eased himself onto the blankets to rest his aching leg. "I knew I shouldn't have let that woman go off by herself, dammit. One more hour," he promised himself. "If she isn't back in one more hour, I'm going after her, sore leg or no sore leg."

The sounds of a rider reached his ears at the same time he heard his horse whinny a greeting to the approaching horse. From the answering whinny, he knew Nichole had finally returned.

By the time he got to his feet and positioned the crutch under his arm to make his way to the door, Nichole came charging through it with an armload of packages.

Fowler's relief that she was back, unharmed, turned to anger when he saw the packages she toted. "What the hell did you do! Go on a damned shopping expedition?" His voice sounded angrier than he had intended. "You go into town for a few supplies and come back loaded down like a damn pack horse! No wonder it took you so long. Did it ever occur to you that I just might be worried about you?" he demanded sharply.

Nichole had felt a little guilty at taking so long in town, especially since she had promised him that she would hurry. However, at his verbal attack, she forgot her guilt and launched a counterattack. "Just who the hell do you think you are, yelling at me like that? You're not my keeper, Fowler Barclay. And for your information, you have no right to try to tell me what I can or cannot do about anything."

Dumping the packages on the floor by the door, she glared at him before turning on her heel and exiting the cabin. When she returned, she had the bulging saddlebags over one shoulder and was lugging her saddle. The look that she gave Fowler just dared him to make another nasty remark about her purchases.

Without a word or a look in Fowler's direction, she took the package containing the chicken and the black iron kettle down to the river. When she returned, she hung the kettle filled with water and the cleaned, cut up chicken over the flames to boil.

Still ignoring the man intently watching her, she mixed flour and water to make dumplings. She was so tired of rabbits and beans that it was almost worth the chewing out she'd received just to have something different to eat.

If Fowler could have reached his backside, he would have kicked himself. Dammit! He hadn't meant to be so harsh with her, but to think that while he was half sick with worry, she'd been shopping, seemingly without a care in the world.

Well, what the hell did he expect? She didn't love him. He was just a means to help her locate her missing brother and that's all. And he should have known that by now. Of course, she wouldn't be concerned that he might be worried about her because she didn't give a damn about his feelings. Why should she? Just because he loved her, didn't make her return that love. He had nothing to offer her. He was just a poorly paid U.S. Marshal and she could have her pick of all the rich ranchers' sons in the whole damn state! Why didn't he quit torturing himself with thoughts of things that could never be? *Fowler, you're a glutton for punishment*, he silently berated himself.

* * *

Hank easily trailed the rider to the cabin. If he had given any thought to the matter, he might have wondered at the ease with which the Brazos Kid led him to where he was staying. But instead, he patted himself on the back and basked in the praise he imagined he'd receive from Linc Travis.

He stayed hidden from the cabin so he wouldn't be seen and waited just long enough to note that there was only one other horse staked out beside the cabin. Satisfied, he hightailed it back toward Laredo, anxious to get to Linc with his information.

If he rode hard, he could be at the hide-out in Mexico in three days.

The silence in the cabin was broken only by the sounds of the bubbling chicken and dumplings and the crackling logs in the fireplace.

Nichole was at odds with herself. How could she have been so relieved to see the cabin ahead of her, and anxious to be with the man inside one minute, and the next minute find herself yelling and fighting with Fowler?

She had always had a bit of a temper, but her mercurial moods the past few days were something even she was having a hard time understanding. If this was something that went hand in hand with loving someone, then she wasn't sure she wanted that honor.

The more she thought about it, the guiltier she felt. After all, she had been on the verge of apologizing to Fowler for taking so long in town, when he had launched his verbal attack on her. She had ridden Cocoa harder than she normally would have because she was worried that Fowler might be concerned over her being gone so long.

She glanced over at the man leaning against one of the saddles. He didn't look any happier than she felt.

Face it, Nichole. What really has your hackles up is that he wasn't as glad to see you as you were glad to be back. You lashed out at him because your damned pride was bruised that he didn't grab you in his arms and tell you how glad he was that you were back, she admonished herself.

She thought that she had come to grips with the fact that just because she loved him, didn't make him love her in return, and that she couldn't force him to love her, just because she wished it with all her heart.

She sighed out loud as she walked over to Fowler, and sat down in front of him, forcing him to meet her eyes.

"Fowler, I was wrong to be angry just because you were. When I walked in the door, I was about to apologize for losing track of time and causing you to worry about me." She shrugged her shoulders, not prepared to admit the truth to him. "I just have a bad temper sometimes, I guess."

Her eyes dropped to her hands coiled together in her lap as she waited for his reply.

Her apology made him feel more like a heel than the brow beating he had been giving himself.

He took her hands in his and brought them to his lips, placing a kiss on them before tilting her chin up so she could see his face.

"I was wrong to yell at you like that. I guess I was just tense from my forced inactivity. And lying here listening for the sound of your return and worrying about all the things that might have happened to you just pushed me past my tolerance level. Patience is not one of my virtues, if I have any," he reluctantly admitted. "I'm sorry I yelled at you without giving you a chance to explain why you were so late."

A slightly sheepish smile touched the corner of her mouth. "Well, you would have yelled at me anyway, even after I had explained, because I didn't have a good excuse for making you worry. So, I guess, maybe it was better for you to yell at me then and get it over with. At least this way we can enjoy our supper without getting indigestion from being mad at each other."

He flashed a lopsided grin. "I was wondering how long you were going to punish me with those delicious smells. My stomach is growling like a hungry bear. Another minute and I might have crawled on my hands and knees and pleaded for your forgiveness just for a taste of that chicken and dumplings," he joked.

The heavy blanket of tension that had enveloped the cabin had lifted just like a morning fog. Both of them were glad that they were once again relaxed with each other. Now they could return to the comfortable camaraderie they had shared from the beginning.

Chapter Fifteen

In his haste to reach Linc with his news and receive his expected praise, Hank had pushed his horse to its limit, arriving at the entrance to the canyon about midmorning on the third day.

"Hey!" he hollered to the lookout he knew was hidden in the rocks above him. "It's me, Hank! I'm coming in!"

The man recognizing Hank's voice stepped into the open and waved Hank in, then he walked over to the ledge facing the canyon and hollered to the next man, "Hank's coming in! Nobody's with him!" before resuming his spot hidden in the rocks.

The canyon Hank rode through was so well hidden in the mountain range known as the Sierra Madre Oriental, that few white men had ever been there and even fewer had left there alive.

Originally inhabited by an ancient tribe of Indians,

it was now a refuge for murderers, bandits, and various other outlaws, including Linc Travis and his gang. Though Hank didn't have a woman, many of the outlaws had girlfriends or wives and families who lived permanently in the self-contained village.

The women and children seldom left the safety of the canyon, depending instead on their men to bring them news and sometimes presents of cloth and trinket jewelry from the outside world. They seemed to be perfectly content to tend their gardens, clean their small huts, raise their babies, and gossip with the other women in the village, much like the women whose husbands made their living on the right side of the law.

Surprisingly, there was very little trouble between the different bands of outlaws who congregated there. And usually any dispute was quickly solved with a well-placed knife or bullet. There was an unspoken code adhered to in the mountain valley: If you started a fight, you were on your own. No one from your gang was permitted to help you. That was the only way that the outlaw retreat had been able to survive and Hank was relieved it had for it was his home.

As he dismounted, he looked for Linc. As soon as he saw him, Hank ambled toward him.

Linc's face contorted in anger as Hank imparted his information about the Brazos Kid. His eyes narrowed as Hank told how he had followed Brazos to the cabin outside Laredo. Grabbing Hank's shirt front, he pulled him closer and snarled, "Are you *sure* you saw Brazos?"

A dumbfounded Hank nodded his head. He had

expected to receive praise, not angry suspicion. "Boss, I tell ya he rode right under my window. I got a good look at him. I'm positive without a doubt that it was him. I swear."

Linc loosened his grip on Hank's shirt, pushing him backwards as he did so. "You'd better be right. If I cross that border into a trap, I'll slit you from ear to ear," he promised menacingly. "Tell the men that we ride for Texas in thirty minutes."

"Thirty minutes! Boss, we can't—" After seeing the glower on Linc's face, he decided against finishing his protest. "Yes, sir. Thirty minutes."

Precisely thirty minutes later, Linc and eight hastily readied men rode up the winding path out of the canyon and past the two men standing guard.

Nick scanned the horizon with his field glasses as he had done several times during the past three days. Cody could tell without asking that Nick had not seen what he was hoping to see.

Scowling blackly, he jammed the glasses back in his saddlebags. "Damn that stinking man! We should have caught up with them by now if he'd known what he was talking about."

Cody agreed but he knew it wouldn't change anything. "Well, they couldn't be too many days ahead of us. We've been traveling nearly twice as fast as they would have been able to because of their pack mules slowing them down. We ought to overtake them in a day or two. Surely that man couldn't have been off by more than a week."

"Humph, I wouldn't bet on it," Nick snorted contemptuously.

* * *

Nichole looked around the one-room cabin that had been her temporary home for almost two weeks. She couldn't help but wonder what had happened to its previous owners as she gathered up everything that they wouldn't need the next morning.

Fowler had declared that his leg was sufficiently healed for them to leave at first light tomorrow. He had taken the animals to water and then staked them closer to the river where there was better grass to graze for the night. Then he had come in and prepared for bed.

Now tired, Nichole settled in her blankets, and immediately fell asleep.

But Fowler lay as wide awake as the owl hooting in a tree down by the river. He had taken a short ride after supper to give Bandit and himself some much needed exercise, hoping that he'd sleep better tonight than he had been. It hadn't helped.

Although his leg still pained him some, he couldn't stand the thought of even one more day of forced inactivity.

As he let his mind drift idly, waiting for sleep to claim him, he began to have that prickly feeling that comes just before trouble strikes.

He rose from his blankets and slipped quietly to open the door. Standing in the doorway, he cocked his head and listened intently for any sound as his eyes scanned the area. The moon was at its fullest, illuminating the night with its brilliance. He didn't see or hear anything.

He didn't hear anything! No frogs croaking, no owl hooting, no crickets or other insects making their usual night noises. Nothing. Not a sound. That was what had alerted him, it was too quiet!

Again, he scanned the horizon for any movement. Almost at the same instant that he saw a reflection of moonlight bounce off something metallic, his horse whined nervously.

"Nichole! Grab your gun belt and clothes. We've got to get out of here!" By the time he had spoken the words, he had pulled his breeches and boots on, and grabbed his gun belt and both rifles.

The sound of urgency in his voice brought Nichole instantly awake. She jerked her boots on, grabbed her clothes and gun belt, and headed after Fowler out the door. Some instinct warned her to be as quiet as possible.

Remembering the protected area he had found in the limestone outcropping, Fowler aimed Nichole in that direction. Running the forty yards or so, they hurriedly climbed over the boulders and crouched low in its center.

"What's wrong? Why did we have to leave the cabin?" she whispered as she hurriedly pulled her clothes on.

Fowler motioned her attention toward the river. The group of men could easily be seen through the trees lining the banks as they rode toward the cabin. "Just a hunch. But that doesn't look like the welcome wagon to me. And we couldn't afford to be trapped in that cabin with no way to escape."

Linc and his men had been riding the shallow river bed for the last half mile, using the trees along the banks as cover.

Hank thought he had pushed hard to get to the canyon, but Linc had pushed even harder to get there, cutting almost a half day off Hank's time.

The men and horses were near exhaustion from the grueling pace Link had set, when he motioned them to a halt.

Hank was riding just behind Linc. He pulled up beside him.

"This the place?" Linc questioned.

"Yeah. That's it," Hank replied as he frantically searched the area until he spotted their horses. For a minute, he'd been afraid that Brazos and his partner had already left. The fear of what Linc might have done to him for leading them on a wild goose chase made him shiver. He motioned toward the horses. "That's the same horse I saw when I followed Brazos here."

Linc silently watched the cabin to see if their arrival had alerted the sleeping occupants. Satisfied that it hadn't, Linc motioned for Hank and another man to slip around to the back of the cabin to make sure they didn't escape that way.

As they moved toward the back of the cabin, Hank spotted the boulders off to the side of the cabin and motioned for the other man to follow him as he began to make his way toward the rocks, thinking to use them for cover. Should Brazos and his partner try to flee in that direction, they could easily get the drop on them.

Fowler and Nichole watched as the group of men stopped at the river bank. They saw the man in front motion to two of the men behind him. All of the men dismounted and two of them, gun in hand, crouched down and made a wide circle as they ran toward the back of the cabin.

Nichole looked at Fowler with admiration. "Thank

heavens for your hunches," she whispered. "I get the very distinct notion that they didn't come to have breakfast with us. I count nine of them."

Fowler saw that the two men sent to cover the back were heading directly toward them. "I'm fixing to even the odds a little and make it seven," he whispered back as he took careful aim and squeezed off two shots in rapid succession.

The two men headed for the rocky outcropping hit the ground—dead.

Linc and the other men were about halfway between the cabin and the place where they had left their horses when the two shots rang out. They turned tail and took cover behind the trees, shooting in the direction of the outcropping as they ran.

"Son of a bitch!" a surprised Linc swore as he hid behind a tree. "That has gotta be the luckiest sonofabitching Texas Ranger ever! But his luck jest run out. Don't waste bullets, men. They're hid in them rocks. We'll wait till daylight then smoke 'em out. Brazos won't leave here alive!"

Nichole had her rifle ready as she tensely waited for the men to make a rush on them.

Fowler's eyes rapidly scanned the area where the men had taken cover.

After waiting anxiously for what seemed much longer than just a few minutes, Nichole asked, "What are they doing? Why haven't they tried to rush us?"

"I figure they'll probably wait till daylight before they make their move. We have the advantage because we know where they are and can pick them off with ease if they try to cross that open space, but all they know is that we're somewhere in these rocks."

"It's Linc Travis and his bunch, isn't it?" Nichole knew the answer to her question.

"Uh-huh." Fowler glanced at the moon then pulled Nichole against him, placing a kiss on the top of her head. "You try to get some rest. I'll wake you if they start moving, but I don't think they'll try anything until morning."

Nichole nestled against Fowler's side, suddenly chilled from the night air. She knew she wouldn't be able to sleep but she felt the need to be as close to him as possible. She was scared. More scared than she'd ever been in her life. One way or the other, assuming that she and Fowler weren't killed in the melee, in a few hours she'd know if her brother was still alive.

Fowler felt her shiver. He wrapped one arm around her and moved her closer to the warmth of his body. However, since it was a comfortable May night, he doubted that she was chilled from the night air. "Scared?"

She nodded her head. "A little," she admitted softly.

Fowler longed to tell her not to worry, that everything would be all right, but they both knew the odds they faced. Instead of voicing false promises, he hugged her still closer.

The first hint of a new day was still chasing the shadows of the night away when Linc made his move. He had spread his men out, hoping to get one of them closer to the rock formation by drawing Brazos and his partner's attention away from that side of the outcropping.

Linc opened fire on the two people hidden in the rocks as soon as his men were in position.

Fowler knew immediately what Linc had in mind when he saw how far apart the men were spaced when they started their barrage of bullets.

"They're going to try to get our attention focused on one end of the firing so they can slip around the other way and catch us by surprise," he stated matter of factly. "You keep the left side covered and I'll take the right side."

Fowler had killed two men and Nichole had killed one when she had to turn away to reload her rifle. Using the rocks as protection, she hunkered down and quickly reloaded and was just swinging her rifle back over the top of the rock when she caught sight of two riders in the distance.

The riders were heading in a full gallop in their direction. Nichole squinted her eyes against the sun that was just making its appearance on the horizon.

Something about one of the horses caught her attention. Another few seconds brought it close enough for her to see it better. That was Cody's horse! She'd know that big Appaloosa anywhere. Cody! That was Cody!

Nick and Cody had made camp not more than a mile from the cabin the night before. They had hardly taken more than a few sips of coffee when they heard the first gunshots in the still morning air.

Cody started saddling the horses while Nick doused the fire and gathered their belongings. Within five minutes they were in the saddle and headed in the direction of the gunfire.

Nick pulled his field glasses from his saddlebags and focused them on the cabin. Moving them slowly across the tree line, he could see men crouched behind the trees but he couldn't get a clear, unobstructed view of any of them to recognize them as Linc's men.

He saw one man fall to the ground, followed quickly by two more. He continued to move the glasses until they suddenly brought two horses into sight.

"That's Nichole! I see her horse!" He quickly swung the glasses to the rock outcropping, scanning it for a glimpse of his sister. His heart plunged to the pit of his stomach when all he could see was a man's profile.

"Do you see her?" Cody asked impatiently. "Is she all right? Dammit, Nick! Say something!"

Then just as suddenly he saw his sister raise up to swing her rifle to rest on top of the rocks. She was looking in their direction, but he didn't think she would be able to recognize them from that far away.

"Yes! Yes!" he shouted, relief engulfing him. "I see both of them. The men at the river have them pinned down in the rocks on the other side of that cabin."

Nick's words were carried on the wind to his brother as he started at a full gallop to help his sister. Cody's horse was matching his, stride for stride.

"Fowler! It's Cody! That's Cody's horse!" she shouted.

Fowler was too busy shooting to take his eyes off the men returning his shots to look for himself, but he fervently hoped she was right.

269

It suddenly occurred to Nichole that the other rider . . . Was it? Could it possibly be Nick? She watched as the man took off his hat and waved it at her. It had to be Nick! For an instant she was so astounded that she couldn't move. He waved his hat again. "Nick! That's Nick with Cody!" she shouted excitedly as she waved her hand in the air in answer.

By this time Fowler could clearly see the two men approaching. When they turned off toward the river, he knew their intent. "Pour on the fire. We'll keep them pinned down till your brothers can get behind them."

When Nick and Cody started shooting at Linc from behind, Linc decided he'd better make a run for it. The three men still alive saw Linc running away and knew that they were going to be left behind to fight Linc's battle alone. They, too, tried to make a break for their horses.

Fowler and Cody each shot one man and Nichole wounded the third one. The wounded man, desperate in his attempt to escape, wildly charged in Cody's direction. Unknowingly, Cody had blocked the path between him and the closest horse, his only means of escape.

But Cody was also unaware of the man behind him until Fowler's carefully aimed shot brought him down before the man had a chance to shoot Cody in the back.

Nick saw Linc run for his horse and quickly overtook him. He didn't slow his horse's speed, and the big gelding hit Linc full force, knocking him sprawling in the dirt, and sending his gun skittering across the hard-packed ground.

Linc frantically crawled on his hands and knees, trying to retrieve his gun. By the time he was able to grab it and regain his footing, Nick had turned his horse around and was aiming his own gun at Linc's head. "Drop your gun, Linc, or you die where you stand."

Linc hesitated only an instant before deciding that he couldn't possibly raise his gun and shoot Nick before being killed by the menacing Ranger. He dropped his gun, and, raising his hands above his head, he cut loose with a string of profanity.

Nick reined his horse alongside the cussing man, keeping his gun leveled at him. "I heard you were looking for the Brazos Kid, Linc. Well, here I am," he stated acrimoniously. He motioned toward the opening near the cabin. "Get moving."

Cody saw that Nick had captured Linc. "Nichole! Marshal! Hold your fire!" he shouted. "We've got Linc and we're coming through!"

Nichole climbed over the rocks and raced across the space separating her from her beloved brothers. She flew into Cody's arms, nearly knocking him off his feet.

Fowler had caught up with her and was tying Linc's hands behind his back by the time she turned Cody loose and grabbed Nick.

She was laughing and crying at the same time in her exuberance to see her twin alive and safe. "I knew you were alive! I knew it! That idiot captain of yours tried to convince me that they had done everything possible to find you and were convinced that you were dead. Oh, Nicky," she wailed as she hugged him tightly to her. "I knew it couldn't be. I

271

knew I'd feel it if it were so, but I couldn't convince anyone to believe me."

Nick held his crying sister to his chest as he looked across the top of her head to watch Fowler as he secured the outlaw to a nearby tree, feeling a strange animosity toward the man. "You didn't seem to have any trouble convincing the marshal to believe you," he said, his tone not quite concealing his hostility.

Fowler approached the strikingly identical brother and sister. He had heard Nick's remark, but after the violent battle they had just fought, he paid it little mind, thinking it was just a lingering tenseness from the situation.

Nichole blushed. "Well, I did have to use a small bit of persuasion to get his cooperation," she admitted sheepishly.

Nick glared at the approaching man. "I'll just bet you did."

Nichole looked up at her brother's rigid face, puzzled at his tone.

Fowler extended his hand in greeting to Nick. "Now I can see why it was so easy for Nichole to trick people into believing she was the Brazos Kid. Hello, Nicholas. I'm Fowler Barclay."

Nick reluctantly shook hands with the man who had spent the past six weeks with his sister.

"Fowler, this is my older brother, Cody," Nichole said proudly.

Cody and Fowler had quickly taken the other's measure as the introductions were made. Being a good judge of character, Cody assessed the big man who stood eye level with him as being forthright and competent.

"Pleased to meet you, Marshal." Cody shook his

hand. "Thank you for protecting our little sister so well."

Fowler laughed good-naturedly as he wagged his head in amusement. "It wasn't an easy assignment at times, I can assure you. I don't believe that I've ever met another woman quite so . . . determined as Nichole. I hope all your sisters aren't as headstrong."

Cody laughed as Nichole playfully punched Fowler in the stomach.

"Headstrong! Humph. You're a fine one to talk, Fowler Barclay. You're just miffed that I can hold my own, unlike some of the other females you've met."

"I must admit, you can hold your own," Fowler said with a mischievous glint in his eyes.

Cody got the distinct notion that there was a double meaning behind the words the marshal and his sister were bantering back and forth.

Nick scowled at the marshal, apparently sensing something between them, too. Turning to Cody, he stated caustically, "Are we going to stand here all day jawing? I don't know about the rest of you but I'm ready to get back to Waco. I do have a new bride whom I hurriedly left behind to chase after this little termagant, remember?"

Nichole's mouth dropped open in shock. "Bride? What the hell do you mean, bride? Nicholas Westerfield, do you mean to tell me that while we've been chasing outlaws from one end of Texas to the other, that you were off courting a woman?" she shrieked in shocked outrage.

Nicholas winced at his slip of the tongue. He had forgotten that Nichole didn't know anything about his shooting and subsequent marriage to Carmen.

Putting his arm around his sister, he turned her in

the direction of the cabin. "Now, Nolie, don't get your dander up. That's not the way it happened . . . exactly. Let's make some coffee and I'll tell you all about it."

Fowler watched Nichole as she walked back to the cabin with Nick. He felt an emptiness edge into his heart. He was glad that they had found her brother, but, now as he watched her walk away from him, he was already feeling the pain that he'd been unwilling to admit, even to himself, would enter when she left.

Fowler glanced self-consciously at Cody. "Reckon we could horn in on their reunion long enough to get a cup of coffee, too?"

Cody had been observing the interaction between the marshal, his sister, and her twin with an amused attitude. He was thinking that it was going to be an interesting journey back to Waco.

"We can probably sneak a cup without them noticing," he said, leading the way back to the cabin.

Fowler silently drank his coffee and watched Nichole as her brother told about his shooting, the amnesia that followed, and the part she had played in his dreams.

When Nick began telling her about his bride and his new in-laws, his face glowed. It was obvious that he was very happy and very much in love with his Carmen.

"Oh, Nicky, I can hardly wait to meet Carmen." Nichole threw her arms around his neck and hugged him. "I'm so happy for you. She sounds like a beautiful person. I know I'm going to like her."

Nick hugged his enthusiastic sister back. "Thank you, Nolie. I know you'll like each other."

Fowler felt a peculiar twinge of envy as he listened to Nick, who was verifying what he already knew to be true. The daughters of rich ranchers married the sons of rich ranchers, not the son of a preacher, even if he was a U.S. Marshal.

Fowler dejectedly slung the dregs of his coffee into the fire before rising to his feet and smothering the remaining flames with ashes.

Nichole looked from Fowler to her brothers. "What happens now that you've captured Linc Travis?"

"He's Fowler's prisoner," Nick volunteered.

"I'll take him back to Austin to stand trial. With Nick's testimony, we won't have any trouble getting a conviction. Hopefully he'll decide not to swing alone and will tell us who he's working for so we can get the man really responsible for all the killings and dirty dealings that have plagued central Texas," Fowler stated blandly, not quite meeting Nichole's questioning look.

She couldn't read the closed expression on his face. She had been afraid that they would have to go their separate ways without getting to talk now that her brothers were here.

She was relieved that she'd get to spend a few more days with Fowler. Surely between here and Austin, they would find a way to spend a few minutes alone. There were too many things left unsaid between them.

And Nichole still held out hope that Fowler would declare his love for her and ask her to marry him. She knew there would never be anyone else in her life now that she had fallen in love with him.

The thought that she might spend the rest of her life alone, without the only man she could ever love, was a depressing one. And, even though she knew that her family could, and her brothers probably would, force Fowler to marry her if they knew what had taken place between them, she didn't want him on those terms.

If he didn't love her enough to marry her willingly, then she'd rather spend the rest of her life with her memories of their wonderful lovemaking than live with a man who would soon grow to hate her for taking away his much-loved freedom.

No, the decision had to be his. She wouldn't accept anything less than his love.

Chapter Sixteen

"How's my little sister holding up?" Cody asked as he stopped beside Nichole and leaned into the swiftly running river to wash some of the grime off his face and hands before scooping up a handful of the refreshing water to drink.

Nichole was on her knees at the edge of the water, splashing it over her hot face and arms. She sat back on her heels, glancing in the direction of Fowler and Nicholas as one tied his prisoner to a tree while the other staked the horses out for the night.

"What is it with those two?" she said irritably, having lost her usual good temperament several days ago. She was hot, hungry, dirty, and exhausted. "If it's not Fowler pushing us, then it's Nicky cracking the whip! What the hell is their all-fired hurry to get Linc Travis to Austin? Do they think that someone is going to try to rescue him before we get there? All the men who were with him were killed back at the cabin. How would anyone know he's been taken prisoner?" She shook her head in puzzlement. "I just don't understand why they're pushing us so hard."

Cody looked in the direction of his brother and the marshal. He, too, was wondering why they both seemed hell bent to set some kind of record getting from Laredo to Austin, but more puzzling than that was their attitude toward each other.

Or, more precisely, his brother's attitude toward the marshal. Nick seemed bound and determined to keep Fowler and Nichole from so much as even talking to each other without him between them. For some reason, which Cody wasn't quite sure of, Nick had developed an intense dislike for Fowler.

It started the day that Nick found out that they had shared the same hotel room back in Evadne, and had greatly intensified when he'd found out that Nichole had nursed Fowler when he'd been bitten by a rattlesnake.

Cody had seen Fowler looking at his sister when he thought no one else was watching. He looked at her like a man who had lost his heart and she had found it. But his actions and manner didn't match the message his eyes were sending.

Fowler had stayed as far away from Nichole as he possibly could without seeming to be rude. He only spoke to her if she spoke to him first and then his answers had been almost abrupt and to the point.

Cody shared his sister's puzzlement. But he had a feeling that whatever was eating at Nick and Fowler had absolutely nothing to do with the prisoner.

"I don't know, Nichole. Sometimes prideful men do strange things," he commented absently.

Nichole was too tired to play word games. "What does that mean?"

"Huh? Oh, nothing. I was just muttering." Cody sensed that Nichole had some hurt pride herself. "Why don't you take a quick bath? It'll ease your saddle sores and help you sleep better. Those bushes will give you some privacy, and I'll see that Nick and Fowler don't disturb you for a while."

The idea was too appealing to turn down. Nichole quickly fetched a bar of soap and some clean clothes from her saddlebags.

"Nolic!" Nick halted her before she'd made her escape back to the river. "What do you think you're doing? We don't have time for you to lollygag in the water."

"Nick, leave her alone," Cody interceded. "I told her I would stand guard so she could take a bath. You and Fowler have been pushing us almost to the point of exhaustion. Enough is enough already, dammit! Leave her alone."

Nick glared at his brother.

"Go on, Nichole, and take your bath. I think we can make coffee and open a can of beans without your help tonight," Cody stated, giving Nick a look that clearly stated that he had reached his boiling point, too.

Nichole looked from brother to brother as they stood glaring at each other. When she glanced in Fowler's direction, he quickly turned away, busying himself with his bedroll.

As Nichole lathered her body and hair with the

sweet-smelling lilac soap, she pondered the past four days. She had hoped that she and Fowler would have some time together to talk, but so far it had been impossible to say more than a couple of words to him.

Every time she tried to talk to him, either he tersely answered her or Nick barged in between them. Fowler seemed to be deliberately avoiding her. And Nick seemed to think that she needed a chaperone and had appointed himself to the job!

Her time was fast running out. At the pace they were traveling, they'd be in Austin within two days. As the cooling water washed away the grime from her body, it seemed to clear her mind as well.

A plan began to form in her mind. For the past four nights, Nick, Cody, and Fowler had taken turns guarding Linc. Tonight would be Fowler's turn to take the first watch. Come hell, high water, or twin brother, tonight she was going to spend some time with Fowler, alone.

Fowler leaned casually against a boulder along the river's edge as he smoked a cigarette and let his mind wonder over the earlier rift between Nichole's brothers and his relationship with them.

He and Cody had hit it off well from the start, but Nicholas was a different matter all together. Nicholas seemed to have taken an instant dislike to him and he could only wonder why.

Maybe Nicholas was usually surly and curt. But that didn't fit the impression that Nichole had given of her twin brother. And, since they were twins, how could they be so different in personality? No. It had to be something else.

He took another pull on his smoke before flipping the butt into the river. His mind's eye slid to the bushes that had concealed Nichole when she had bathed earlier in the evening.

He knew from memory how beautiful she would have looked as she lathered the fragrant soap across her full breasts, down her slender sides, across her flat stomach. He could picture her hands rubbing the bubbly lather over her gently rounded hips and firm buttocks before gliding down her long slender legs.

He groaned in silent agony as he felt himself growing hard just fantasizing how sleek and beautiful her young body must have looked covered in soap bubbles. His hands itched to feel her softness. His heart pounded against his rib cage as his blood pumped faster through his veins.

He closed his eyes and shook his head, trying to clear the scene from his mind. He took several deep breaths in an effort to stop the fierce pounding in his manhood. Now his nose was playing tricks with his mind! He imagined that he could smell the lilac scent that clung ever so delicately to Nichole when she had walked past him on her way back from her bath in the river.

When he opened his eyes, he had to blink twice to be sure that his eyes weren't playing tricks on him as well. Had he longed so hard for Nichole that he had conjured up her image?

Nichole tilted her head slightly as she bedazzled him with her smile. "I didn't mean to startle you. I couldn't sleep and I thought maybe you might like some company." Damn, that sounded contrived even to her ears. She just wasn't any good at playing coy.

"Nichole?" He hadn't imagined her. She was

standing in front of him in all her loveliness. He held out his hand to her and she stepped into his arms without hesitation. He breathed deeply of her sweet scent, storing it away in his deepest memory as he wrapped his arms around her and held her close.

He knew he was only torturing himself, but he couldn't seem to refrain from his self-punishment. He kissed her hungrily. He was like a man dying of thirst and she was his oasis. He held her tightly against his yearning body.

She eagerly pressed her body against his, feeling his obvious need of her. It felt like it had been four years rather than four days since he had held her so close and so tenderly. She returned his kiss with unashamed passion, parting her lips for his tongue's gentle invasion.

They seemed to meld together as his tongue mated with hers. The moonlight cloaked them in a lover's web as they eagerly and hungrily embraced.

"You shouldn't be here," Fowler groaned huskily. "You know I can't resist you." He buried his face in her thick black hair, trying desperately to slow his racing heart.

"I know. But I had to share a few minutes with you before we reach Austin," she whispered breathlessly. "Fowler, there's so much that needs to be said and so little time to say it."

"Nichole, Nichole," he groaned in agony. "You have no idea what you're doing to me." He ran his hands along the sides of her face and into her hair, devouring her lips once more. He leaned her head back to look into her beautiful emerald eyes glistening in the soft moonlight. "If only . . ."

Nichole held her breath in anticipation of Fowler's

words of love. *Now! Now, Fowler, please say the words I've longed to hear for so long. Please, please tell me you love me*, her heart cried out in expectation.

A look of pure pain crossed Fowler's face as he looked into her upturned face. He wanted to tell her of his love, to beg her to love him in return, to be his wife, to bear his children, to grow old together.

But the words wouldn't come. His mind wouldn't let his tongue betray his pride. He knew it would be a mistake. Even if she did agree to marry him in the heat of passion, he knew she'd soon regret her weakness.

They came from two different worlds. He didn't fit in her world and he could offer her little in his. He'd already given her his heart and that was the only thing of value that he owned. He would have given his right arm if it could have been different, but it wasn't and he knew it could never be otherwise.

An anguished groan escaped from deep within him an instant before he claimed her lips for what he knew would have to be the last time. He knew he could never kiss her or hold her in his arms again. He didn't trust himself not to shatter his pride and pour out his undying love to her.

And if he did, he knew his mind and soul would not be able to survive the pain of seeing her eyes mirror her pity for him.

"Nichole," he moaned as he ground his lips into hers for the final time.

"Nichole!"

Nichole whirled guiltily around at the sound of Nick's venomous voice. "Nicky, I—"

"Go back to bed," he ordered.

"But, Nick—"

"I said go back to bed!"

Nichole looked from her brother's glowering face to Fowler's equally stern one, hoping, praying, that he'd ask her to stay. When he didn't, she turned and hurried back toward her bed roll before either man could see the tears that cascaded down her face.

She had her answer. Fowler didn't love her. If he did, he would have taken a stand against her brother and declared his love openly for her. His silence spoke louder than any words ever could have.

Misery consumed her body and soul as she silently sobbed herself to sleep.

Fowler stood his ground as Nicholas took the few steps separating them.

"I'm going to tell you this only once, Barclay. You better hear me and you better hear me good. You leave my sister alone. I don't want you coming anywhere near her after we leave Austin," Nick threatened in a voice as cold as steel. "You may think that because you're a United States Marshal that makes you special. But you ain't nothing but a gunslinger with a badge in my book.

"Nichole doesn't need the likes of you sniffing around her skirts. You don't have a thing in the world to offer her but the prospect of becoming a widow at an early age and leaving her with a houseful of kids to raise by herself when some outlaw fills your body full of bullet holes. My sister doesn't need that. Do I make myself clear?"

Fowler couldn't deny Nick's accusations but he didn't take threats from any man. His eyes narrowed in anger as he looked Nicholas up and down. "Nichole is a full-grown woman and, in case you haven't noticed, she has a mind of her own. I think she's perfectly capable of speaking for herself. It's none of your business, Nicholas," he warned sternly. "Stay out of it. This is strictly between me and her."

"Why you sonofa—"

Cody had seen Nichole slip away from camp when she thought everyone else was asleep. He smiled, thinking that maybe now she and Fowler could work out their problems without having Nick hovering over them like a hawk. His smile quickly turned to a worried frown, however, when he saw Nick immediately rise from his blankets and follow his sister.

Knowing Nick's growing dislike for Fowler, Cody decided that he'd better follow the both of them, just in case things got out of hand.

Cody had been listening to the two men taunt each other long enough. He decided he'd better intervene before they started in with fisticuffs. "Nick! I think we'd all do well to get some sleep. You two can finish your altercation *after* we get Linc Travis safely behind bars. This is neither the time nor the place for you two to be exchanging blows."

Nick gave Fowler one last glare before turning his back and stalking angrily away.

Cody shook his head in consternation as he watched his brother walk back to camp. "I don't understand why he's become so overprotective of Nichole all of a sudden. I've never seen him act like this."

Fowler laughed derisively. "You mean I bring out his good side?"

Cody turned to face Fowler. "I like you, Fowler, and given the chance, I think we could become good friends. I'm not going to issue any threats or warnings like Nick did but I am going to say this. I love my sister very much and I don't want to see her hurt. I've seen the way you look at each other when neither of you thinks anyone else is watching. It is clearly obvious that there is some kind of attraction between the two of you.

"I don't know what took place between you during the long search for Nick and I don't want to know. I don't consider that any of my business. Nichole is a woman and she's always had a mind of her own. But I will ask this of you, unless your intentions are honorable, leave her alone. She's too trusting and honest. She doesn't know how to flirt and play coy little games like most women. And she probably wouldn't recognize a man who was toying with her affections —until it was too late."

Fowler jammed both his hands in his pockets as he met Cody's eyes. "I do care for your sister, Cody. A hell of a lot more than I want to," he admitted dejectedly, kicking at a clump of dirt. "But Nick's right. I don't have anything to offer a woman like Nichole. I'm not some rich rancher's son. I make enough money to support a wife and kids but nothing to brag about. And certainly not enough to give a woman all the things that Nichole has had all her life.

"Besides, you know the kind of life I lead. When I finish this assignment, I have no idea where I'll be sent next or how long I'll be there. That's no fitting life for a wife and family." Fowler let out a long sigh of resignation as he looked off into the dark night. "I know the best thing I could ever hope to do for Nichole is just to disappear from her life forever." He looked sadly back to Cody. "Which is exactly what I have to do—for her sake."

Cody could almost feel Fowler's pain. "I think you don't know my sister very well. If you love her, and she loves you, then all the gold in the world or lack of it wouldn't make one whit of difference to her."

"Maybe so. But I care too much for her to take that chance," Fowler admitted honestly.

As Nichole dressed for dinner, her stomach was doing flip-flaps. After tonight, she knew she'd never see Fowler again. Tomorrow she, Cody and Nick would leave for home. Home. It seemed like forever since she'd been home.

She tried to replace her sad thoughts of losing Fowler with happy thoughts of seeing her mother and father and all her little brothers and sisters.

Losing Fowler? How could she lose something she'd never had in the first place? she berated herself.

As she donned the beautiful lilac gown that she'd bought in Laredo, she thought back to that day, or more specifically, to that night.

After she and Fowler had made up, each accepting his or her own part in the argument, Fowler had insisted that she model the gowns for him.

It had been like playing dress-up. She had tried the gray-and-pink one on first, watching his face to see if he liked it. He had complimented her, telling how lovely she was in it. But when she'd worn the lilac gown, his eyes had danced and glittered like a little boy looking at big jars of candy in a store!

Seeing his look, she had deliberately pranced and preened in front of him. When he tried to grab her, she had swished the full skirts in his face and whirled just out of his reach. She knew she was teasing him and she had enjoyed every minute of it!

Oh, but when he'd finally caught her! The teasing had been worth it. They made glorious, sensuous, beautiful love until the wee hours of the morning.

Nichole sighed as she finished her toilette. Was she forever destined to remember all the times she and Fowler had made love? Would there always be something that jabbed her memory? Probably. Her time with Fowler had been a very special part of her life. Possibly more special then anything else that would happen to her for the rest of her life.

But, she lifted her chin as she scrutinized her image in the mirror, *I will not become embittered because it didn't mean as much to Fowler as it did to me. He never led me on or deceived me with pretty words of love. I made my own choices and I will learn to live with them. I'll tuck them deep within me, to cherish forever. No one will ever know that I'm not the cheerful, serene person they see on the outside.*

With that final heart-to-heart talk with herself, she left her hotel room to meet her brothers and Fowler in the hotel's dining room for a courtesy farewell dinner before they went their separate ways the following morning.

"I don't know why the hell you had to invite that marshal to join us for dinner," Nick grumbled as he and Cody entered the dining room.

"Just because you and Fowler have your differences doesn't mean I have to be rude to him. In case it hasn't occurred to you, little brother, if it hadn't been for him, our sister might very well be at the mercy of Linc Travis and his gang or even dead. We owe him a lot. Besides, I happen to like and respect him. And you better at least act civil to him for a few more hours for your sister's sake," Cody warned sternly.

"Don't worry. I'll be the perfect gentleman, but I don't have to like it," Nick stated acrimoniously.

Fowler had seated himself where he could see the staircase from their table in the dining room. He covertly kept an eye on it for the first glimpse of Nichole as he chatted amiably with Cody, ignoring the undercurrents of hostility in Nick's curt answers.

When he saw her descend the stairs, he almost lost his breath. He thought she had never looked lovelier. With her dark hair softly caressing her shoulders and the glow from the gaslights reflecting in her eyes, she was breathtakingly beautiful.

And that dress! Oh, how he remembered that dress. His heart pounded in his chest as he thought about their night of lovemaking after she had teased and taunted him when she had modeled it for him.

If he lived to be a hundred, he'd never be able to see the color lilac without thinking about that night of ecstasy!

He stood as she approached their table. "Hello, Nichole." *She's the most beautiful woman I've ever seen in my life!*

"I hope I didn't keep you waiting too long." She smiled at the three men. *My God. He's even more handsome in a suit!*

She settled her skirts as Cody helped her into her

chair which, whether by design or happenstance, was between her brothers. Fowler faced her directly across the table.

Cody smiled a secretive smile. Nichole and Fowler might think they were successfully hiding their love. But a person would have to be blind not to see that if there were ever two people more in love, he couldn't imagine who it would be. He figured it'd be two, three months at the outside before they decided they couldn't live without each other.

Nichole glanced at Cody. "What are you smiling about?"

"Who, me?" He shrugged his shoulders carelessly. "Oh, just thinking how good it's going to be to get back home, I guess. How about a toast?" He poured a glass of champagne for Nichole and refilled the men's glasses before lifting his glass in the air. "Here's to home and happiness." *Welcome to the family, Fowler,* he silently added.

Four glasses clinked together. "To home and happiness."

Fowler's sapphire-blue eyes met Nichole's emerald-green ones across the top of the glasses.

May you find happiness, my handsome marshal. I will always love you.

I pray that the man who wins your hand will be able to give you everything you ever want, my green-eyed witch. I will love you until the day I die.

Chapter Seventeen

The past two and a half days had seemed like the longest days in Nichole's life. Each step her horse took had taken her just that much further from the man she loved. Each night she had lain awake until the wee hours of the morning, unable to put her troubled thoughts to rest.

And, when she finally fell into an exhausted sleep, it was to dream of the man she had bid farewell to in Austin. She must have asked herself at least a thousand times when the hurting would stop. Was her life to be ruled forever by memories of a handsome blue-eyed marshal?

When the trio first rode away from Austin, her brothers had tried to recapture the easy-going camaraderie of their youth. But they soon gave up when it became apparent that Nichole was with them only in body. Her thoughts were many miles behind them.

They had said their good-byes to Fowler after dinner the night before, but there was still some little part of Nichole that held out hope that Fowler would show up at the last minute before they rode away from the capitol city. But it was not to be.

The hardest thing she had ever had to do in her life was to mount her horse and ride away without looking back. But she had done it. Even though her heart was crumbling into tiny little pieces, she had squared her shoulders and ridden away determined to put the past behind her.

An old adage came to her mind, "Today is the first day of the rest of your life." *What a rotten way to start the rest of my life*, she thought forlornly.

Cody could tell that his sister was hurting. Even though she tried to hide her feelings, he knew her too well. He hoped that the star-crossed lovers would find a way, and soon, to iron out their differences and be together. He missed his happy, bubbly, mischievous imp of a sister, and he wanted her back.

Maybe their mother would have the answer to solve Nichole's problem. He certainly hoped so.

Nick felt like a heavy weight had been lifted from his shoulders. He knew Nolie was unhappy now, but she'd get over it once she got back home around family and friends. Several of her male admirers had inquired about her while she was away at school. There were two or three of them whom he felt would make an excellent choice of husband for his sister. From his point of view, marriage was the greatest invention ever!

He could hardly keep his horse to a comfortable trot. He wanted to race the wind to reach the loving arms of his new bride. If he had his way, he'd find a deserted island somewhere far away for just the two of them to spend a long, long time alone. Wasn't love the grandest thing!

There was no doubt in his mind that his Carmen would be sitting on the veranda, watching the road for him. Running to meet him when she first caught sight of him.

As her home came into view, Nichole felt that the past was truly behind her. She was home. Home. Somehow the word didn't seem the same. Or maybe, it was because *she* wasn't the same. When she had made her hasty exit in the middle of the night to find her brother, she had been an invincible, daring young girl, convinced that if she put her mind to it, there wasn't anything she couldn't do. She was returning as a woman. A woman with a broken heart. A woman unsure of what her future held, of what she wanted out of life.

Carmen was indeed sitting on the veranda, eagerly awaiting the return of her handsome husband.

There had been a violent spring storm that had left most of the telegraph wires down for several days. Cody's telegram had been delivered late the night before telling the family to look for them about noon Wednesday.

When Carmen saw three specks appear in the distance, she jumped to her feet, afraid to breathe until she could be sure it was them.

She knew for certain it was Nick when she saw one of the riders waving his hat in the air and galloping ahead of the other two riders. Nick! Nick was home!

In her excitement to reach her husband, she almost forgot to tell the others that they were in sight. She hurriedly ran back into the house and shouted, "They're here! I can see them coming down the road," before running back down the steps and racing toward the galloping rider.

Nick had to laugh at the sight that Carmen made with her skirts hiked above her ankles and her tiny feet running as fast as possible. When he reached her, he leaned from his horse, swooped her up in his arms, and sat her before him on the saddle.

When Cody and Nichole passed the embracing couple, they both laughed at the sight. Oblivious to the rest of the world, their arms wrapped around each other, they were hungrily kissing and trying to talk at the same time.

"Oh, *querido*, how I have missed you." Carmen was so happy to be back in the arms of her love that she was both laughing and crying at the same time. "I love you. I love you."

"My sweet, sweet Carmen. I missed you." Nick buried his face against his wife's neck, inhaling her sweet scent as he crushed her body to his. "It seems like I've been gone forever. I love you, my darling."

If Nick's horse had not begun snorting and tossing his head to protest his extra load, the much-in-love couple might have continued their happy reunion longer.

Nick leaned back to brush the tears of happiness from Carmen's big, brown eyes. "This is ah . . . slightly . . . ah . . . uncomfortable. Maybe we should continue our homecoming somewhere more comfortable. Like the privacy of our bedroom."

Carmen's eyes twinkled. She could feel his manhood pressing against her stomach. Brazenly, she patted it as she laughed. "I agree, my love. A man in your condition should not be sitting on a horse." She giggled impishly when Nick grabbed her hand to still it.

"Carmen . . ." he groaned. When he glanced toward his family standing in the front yard waiting to greet him, he wondered how the hell he'd be able to get off his horse in his "condition."

Nick didn't have to worry about anyone noticing him. As he dismounted and helped Carmen from the horse, he could hear his siblings squealing and laughing in excitement as they hugged Nichole.

Cassie eyed her daughter critically as Nichole embraced her younger brothers and sisters. Something about her eldest daughter was different, but she couldn't quite put her finger on it.

When Nichole rushed into her mother's arms, hugging her tightly, Cassie had her answer. Her eyes. There was a sadness about Nichole's eyes that had not been there before. Even though her mouth was smiling and her words were words of happiness, the joy didn't reach her eyes.

When Nichole turned to her father, she wasn't sure what to expect. She had felt his stern look boring into her as she greeted the rest of the family. "Hello, Daddy."

She waited with bated breath as her father hesitated, searching her face intently. He, too, sensed something changed about his daughter, but it didn't lessen his anger at her precipitous behavior.

"Daughter, you do sorely try my patience. Do you have any idea how worried we've been? Or how many nights that your mother and I have lain awake wondering if you were safe or lying dead somewhere? How could you . . ."

Cassie gently laid her hand upon Mark's arm. Although she didn't say a word, Mark seemed to read her mind. He stopped his upbraiding in midsentence and opened his arms to his errant daughter.

Nichole rushed into her father's arms. "Oh, Daddy, I'm sorry. I'm so sorry," she sobbed as she buried her face in his firm chest.

A silent message passed between Mark and Cassie. "We'll talk about it later, Nichole," he said in a milder tone as he patted her trembling back.

Nichole stepped away from her father. Whatever punishment he meted out, she felt that it was well deserved. She truly hadn't given any thought to the worry she might be causing her parents. Her only thoughts were to find her brother when it seemed that everyone else had given up any hope that Nick might still be alive. "Yes, sir," she replied meekly.

Nick pulled Carmen with him as he approached his twin. "Nolie, this is Carmen, my wife," he stated proudly as he looked at her with love shining boldly in his eyes.

Carmen looked at her new sister with apprehension, not sure what Nichole's reaction would be. She had heard so much about Nichole that she felt a little intimidated now that they were finally meeting. She smiled shyly at the girl who favored her husband so much.

Carmen looked from brother to sister, thinking that the features that made her husband so handsome were the same features that made her sister-in-law a very beautiful woman. "I am glad that we finally meet. Nick has told me so much about you."

Nichole looked at the pretty girl who stood by her brother's side. She could tell that Carmen was very much in love with Nick. "Well, don't believe everything that he told you. He got us into as much trouble as I did." Nichole laughed as she hugged Carmen. "Welcome to the family, Carmen. Although I'm not sure if I should give you my congratulations or my condolences," she teased.

Although she was happy for her twin and his bride, it only made her heart ache all the more for what she had lost. She desperately wanted to be alone. She was afraid that she would embarrass herself at any moment. She could feel the tears welling behind her eyes as the pain stabbed her broken heart.

Carmen could sense a great sadness about her new sister. "I'm sure that you are tired after your long journey. Maybe tomorrow we can get together to compare notes about your mischievous brother." Carmen smiled lovingly at her husband. "I suspected all along that he was not the innocent bystander in some of the escapades he told me about." There was a hint of mischievousness in her own eyes.

Nick was quick to protest. "Hey! Two against one. That's not fair."

Mark laughed heartily at the dismayed look on Nick's face. "Son," he said, putting his arm around Nick's shoulder, and turning him toward the house. "I guess it's time we had a father-and-son talk about women in general and wives in particular."

Nick looked skeptically at his father, who was trying very hard but losing the battle to keep a straight face. "Dad, why do I get the idea that it's too late for this talk?"

Mark just laughed as the family trooped back into the house.

Pleading tiredness and a headache, Nichole quickly escaped to the solitude of her bedchamber. Alone for the first time in several days, she gave in to the tears that had lingered just below the surface, crying until exhaustion finally claimed her.

When she awoke the next morning, she felt worse than she had the night before. Still wearing her riding clothes, she lay on top of the quilt covering her bed. Someone had removed her boots and covered her with another quilt, but had left her undisturbed.

Her head ached and her stomach churned as she opened her eyes to the morning sun streaming through her window. She turned onto her back and listened to the familiar sounds that had greeted her each day of her life until she had gone away to school. They were a soothing balm to her bruised soul.

She heard a tapping at her door, and Maria entered with a tray.

"Since you missed dinner last night and breakfast this morning, I thought you might like a strong cup of tea before you dress to come downstairs for dinner."

"Thank you, Maria." She looked out the window as her attention again returned to the morning sounds of the ranch. "You don't know how good it is to wake up and hear the sounds that you've known since you were a child. I had almost forgotten how . . . comforting they were," she said lackadaisically.

Maria looked at her questioningly. "Are you all right, little one?"

Nichole sighed as she thought to herself. *Am I all*

right? No. But I will survive. No one ever died from a broken heart. Out loud, she replied, "I'm still a little tired I guess. Would you have one of the boys bring up some bath water? I feel like I'm wearing half of south Texas."

"I've got the water heating right now. By the time you finish eating, it'll be ready." Maria eyed her closely. "Are you sure you're feeling well? You look a little peaked."

Nichole nodded her head. "I'll be all right in a few days. We didn't eat very well on the trail and we pushed hard to get home. I'm sure all I need is your good cooking and some rest and I'll be fit as a fiddle in a day or so."

The next morning Nichole barely had her eyes open before she had to run for the chamber pot. Even after emptying her stomach, she still felt sick. She weakly climbed back under the covers, chills consuming her body. Two days later, her stomach was still rebelling. Even the word "food" made her ill.

Cassie bathed her daughter's pale face with cool water. "I still think we should send for Doctor Gregory, Nichole. This is the third day that you've been sick."

Nichole weakly shook her head. "I'm sure it's just exhaustion, Mother." She evaded her mother's face as she added, "I've been under a lot of . . . tension lately. I just need to rest, that's all. I'm sure I'll be fine in a day or two."

Later that day Cody told his mother and father about Fowler. How he'd seen them look at each other when they didn't think anyone else was watching, and Nick's strange animosity toward him. "I think the man really loves her, but he's too damn proud to admit it."

Mark looked at his wife. "Sounds like they are both too proud or stubborn to admit it. Your mother and I suspected that something had changed about Nichole." He laughed dismally. "Your sister has never been as meek as she has been since she returned. As I'm sure you know."

That evening Cassie implored Mark, "Is there nothing we can do? Nichole is miserable. She's making herself sick over this."

Mark sadly shook his head. "I'm afraid not, sweetheart. If Fowler truly loves her, he won't be able to stay away from her. If he doesn't . . . Well, there's nothing we can do to change that either. They are both adults. They'll have to work this out by themselves, I'm afraid."

Cassie knew her husband was right, but it still hurt her to see her daughter suffer so. Cassie suspected that Nichole was deeply in love with Fowler, even though she had said very little about him. But, until Nichole wanted to talk about him, Cassie wouldn't pry.

The next morning found Nichole again hugging the chamber pot, but unlike the three previous mornings, she began to feel better by mid-afternoon. She even joined the family for dinner that night.

She didn't know what had made her so sick but she was glad it had passed. She was surprised at how hungry she was.

When Nichole awoke the next morning, she felt

very lethargic. Normally early morning was her favorite time of the day. She usually woke up refreshed and ready to meet the world head on. But for the past few days she'd felt like she'd have a hard time just making her limbs move, never mind meeting the world head on!

"Oh, well," she muttered as she dragged herself from the covers and dressed. "At least my stomach ailment is gone. Be grateful for small favors, Nichole."

As she passed Nick and Carmen's room, she thought she heard a noise. Since she had slept so late, she figured the rest of the family were busy with the day's work. She paused to listen. There it was again. She tapped gently on the door and entered at Carmen's call.

Carmen was still in her nightclothes and was wiping her ashen face with a cold cloth. The room reeked of sickness. Nichole hurried to Carmen's side and helped her back into bed.

"Carmen, why didn't you tell someone you were ill? Where's Nicky?"

"It is nothing, Nichole. It will soon pass. Nicky left early with the rest of the men to move a herd of cattle to the back pasture. I did not want to worry him," she said weakly. "It is nothing to worry about. The sickness won't last long."

Nichole tucked the covers around Carmen's petite form. "Oh, I feel just terrible. You must have caught whatever it was that I had."

Carmen chuckled and replied skeptically, "No, I don't think so. But do not worry. Already I am feeling better. Go have your breakfast. I will dress and be down shortly. Please do not say anything about my illness. I am so looking forward to going into Waco to shop tomorrow and Nicky might not let me go if he thinks I am unwell."

Nichole had forgotten about the shopping trip planned for the next day. All the women were going to spend the day in town, shopping and even having lunch at the new hotel that had opened while she was back East.

She used to enjoy spending the day shopping and visiting with her friends, but lately it was hard for her to get enthusiastic about anything. Maybe tomorrow she'd have more energy.

"I don't know about you, but I, for one, am starving," Nichole said as she and Carmen made their way, arms loaded with bundles, toward the newly opened hotel.

Carmen laughed. "Spending money takes a lot of energy. I had forgotten how hungry all that work makes one."

"I still think you should have bought the bolt of silk. That coral color would look lovely on you."

"Hmmm," Carmen paused. "Maybe I should have. You go on ahead. I need to go back to the mercantile anyway. I just remembered that I forgot to get something Maria wanted. I'll look at it again and meet you in the dining room."

"Take your time, I'll stop by the parsonage and see if Mother is ready to eat."

Fifteen minutes later, Carmen sat in Doctor Stewart Gregory's office anxiously awaiting what she was almost positive he would tell her.

She felt a bit guilty about fibbing to Nichole, but she wanted visit the doctor without any of the family knowing. If she was right, she wanted Nick to be the first to know.

When the doctor entered, she could tell by the look on his face that she was right. His broad smile confirmed what she had hoped would be his diagnosis.

"Congratulations, Carmen. I'd say that around the middle of January, you and Nick should be having a late Christmas present. You are definitely pregnant and at this point, everything looks good. You should have a fine, healthy baby."

Carmen couldn't stop the tears of joy. "I am sorry I cry, Doc Stu, but . . . I am so happy that I cannot help it," she apologized.

Doc Stu, as he had been called almost from the first day he'd arrived in town, patted her hand tenderly. "That's quite all right, Carmen. And perfectly normal for a mother-to-be. Wide swings in emotions is only one of the side effects you have to look forward to," he joked. "Morning sickness, tiredness, backaches, weight gain, are all part of the birth process. But, in the end, it will all be worth it when you hold that tiny warm bundle in your arms."

Carmen dabbed at her tears as she smiled. "I can hardly wait. January seems so far away."

"It'll be here before you know it. In the meantime, you must take care of yourself. You can continue with your usual activities, but try to rest some each afternoon. And, if you're worried about anything or you feel something might not be just right, send for me. I'll be stopping by from time to time when I make my daily rounds to check on you." He winked conspiratorially at her. "Now, I'll have a legitimate excuse to stop by for some of Maria's good cooking."

Nick had hardly been able to constrain himself. He was so proud, one would have thought the entire idea had been his!

He and Carmen had decided to tell the family the happy news as soon as dinner was over and dessert and coffee were served.

If he knew his father, Mark would break out a bottle of champagne to celebrate the announcement of the birth of his first grandchild.

Nick might have *thought* that he was being very calm and secretive, but Cassie and Mark could tell that something was going on. The way that their next to the oldest son had strutted into the dining room would have put any peacock to shame!

As Maria set the last piece of pie on the table and turned to go back to the kitchen, Nick stood up and pulled Carmen to her feet beside him.

"Maria, I'd like for you to stay for a moment. Carmen and I have an announcement to make to the family."

All eyes turned in their direction.

"Come January, we will be adding a new name to the family Bible." Nick cleared his throat, suddenly overcome with emotion. He hugged Carmen to him, looking down into her chocolate-brown eyes with love. "We're . . . I mean, Carmen is going to have a baby."

A chorus of excitement rang out as the happy couple was congratulated.

"A baby! How wonderful! I've missed having a baby in the house," Cassie exclaimed with joy as she hugged her daughter-in-law.

"I thought you were awfully smug about something tonight. Congratulations, son. This calls for something special. Maria, bring up a bottle of champagne from the root cellar. This calls for a celebration!" Mark declared proudly. "I'm going to be a grandfather!"

Carmen looked apologetically at Nichole. "I'm sorry I fibbed to you today. But I wanted to be positive before I told Nicky. That's why I slipped off to see Doc Stu."

Nichole rounded the table to hug Carmen and her brother. "So that's where you disappeared to. I did think it odd when you remembered that you needed something else from the mercantile and then came back empty-handed. I'm so happy for you, both of you," she said sincerely.

"I was afraid you might give away my secret when you found me with the morning sickness yesterday." She turned loving eyes on her husband. "I had a hard time concealing it from Nicky until I was sure. I didn't want to get his hopes up only to find out that I was mistaken."

Everyone was so excited and talking all at the same time that no one noticed when Nichole suddenly blanched and started to tremble.

She slowly lowered herself into a chair as her ears began to ring and blackness threatened to claim her as the impact of Carmen's words washed over her.

Morning sickness! Oh, my God! Is it possible? Could I be. . . .

Frantically, Nichole tried to remember when she had last had her monthly flow. She had been so consumed with finding Nick that it had never even crossed her mind! How long had it been? Think! Dammit, think! When was the last time?

Not since she'd returned to Texas, she realized sickly. She had not bled for two months!

More than three weeks had passed since the announcement of Carmen's pregnancy and Nichole's realization that she, too, was with child. Three agonizingly long weeks of worry and indecision on Nichole's part as to what she should do. Time was running out and still she had not reached a decision.

She had first considered telling Fowler and just as quickly decided against the idea.

Yes, he had a right to know that he had fathered a child. Yes, he would probably agree to marry her. He was a proud man, and she didn't figure that he would knowingly let a child of his be labeled a bastard.

But he didn't love her, and she couldn't bring herself to put him in a position of feeling trapped into a loveless marriage. Which he would surely feel if she told him about the baby.

No, that was not an option that she felt was open to her. A marriage without love would be hell for both of them.

Once having decided that, then she could see only one way in which she could keep from embarrassing her family with her disgrace and leaving a mark of stigma on an innocent child.

She'd have to go away. Leave her family, her home, everything she loved and cherished because she couldn't let her family pay the price for her indiscretion.

The decision of where to go was easy. Since she had left Cousin Emmalee and Washington, D.C. before she had completed finishing school, she would tell the family that she wanted to return there and complete her studies.

They'd probably fall over in a dead faint! But, on the other hand, maybe they'd think she was finally showing some responsibility. Whatever the case, they wouldn't try to stop her from going.

After she'd been there a few months, she'd write them with the news of her "marriage." Given her past impetuous behavior, they'd probably just shake their heads and declare, "Here she goes *again*". She'd worry later about what to do about her nonexistent husband.

With that decision made, all she needed now was enough courage and strength to tell her family. The long days and sleepless nights of worry had taken a great toll on her already. Between worrying, not sleeping, and not eating very much, she had lost so much weight that her gowns were beginning to hang loose on her.

Beginning today, that would change, she decided as she dressed for the day. After all, she had a precious little life growing in her that she had to consider.

She placed her hand lovingly over her still-flat stomach and whispered, "Don't worry, little one, I'll love you enough for both a mommy and a daddy."

"Nichole! Hurry up! Everybody's ready but you." Amy burst into her sister's room.

Connie Harwell

"Now just why are you so excited about going to church today, may I ask?" Nichole knew the answer without asking. "It wouldn't have anything to do with seeing the new parson's son again, would it?" she teased.

Amy blushed becomingly. At fifteen, she was blooming into a real beauty. "Oh, Nolie. Isn't he just . . . just so *handsome*," she said breathlessly before she caught herself and turned two shades redder. "I mean . . . he's nice. I mean he's . . ."

Nichole laughed, shaking her head in amusement. "Amy, you and he never spoke one word to each other last Sunday. He seems to be as shy and timid as you."

"That's not so," she protested. "We said . . . hello. And he smiled at me. And I smiled back! So there," she said triumphantly. "Oh, do hurry, please. If we get there early, maybe Mama can invite the parson and his family to have Sunday dinner with us before someone else does."

"Aha, little sister has already found the way to a man's heart. Maria's cooking will get 'em every time. Okay, I'm ready."

Nichole couldn't help teasing her sister one last time. "Let's go catch us a preacher's son." She winked as she linked her arm through Amy's.

"Nolie!" Amy groaned, and blushed furiously.

He had deliberately held back until his anxious eyes caught sight of the slender girl with the long black hair and laughing green eyes. Green eyes that had tormented his days and tortured his nights.

He hungrily devoured the sight of her. It seemed

more like a century than a month since he'd last seen her. He frowned slightly. She seemed to be different somehow. She looked pale and tired, and her clothes fit her too loosely, like she'd lost weight. Why? Had she been ill? Or . . . did he dare hope that she had missed him as much as he had missed her?

No. That couldn't have been. He'd been standing in front of the marshal's office the day she and her brothers had left Austin, hoping to see her before she left. She had ridden away from him without even looking back.

Idiot! You were only a means for her to find her brother, nothing more. How long is it going to take you to accept that fact? he silently upbraided himself.

As he started to turn away from the church, he heard someone call his name. He turned to see the preacher rapidly advancing on him.

"Marshal! There you are. I've been looking all over for you. I thought you might have decided to leave before my sermon." Reverend Dixon smiled kindly. "I must admit I've lost a few parishioners *during* my sermons, but I don't believe I've ever lost one before I even started preaching." He laughed good-naturedly.

"Come with me. I want to introduce you to the townsfolk before the service. I'm sure everyone will be glad that we have a United States Marshal assigned here. Maybe we can live down our infamous nickname. Six-shooter junction, indeed!" he snorted in disgust.

Nichole sat next to Carmen in their family's pew and went through the motions of paying attention. She stood when they stood. She sang when they sang and she bowed her head in prayer at the proper cue. But her mind was not on the day's services. She listened absent-mindedly as the preacher made the usual announcements for the upcoming week.

Suddenly, a word penetrated her haze. What had the preacher said? She quickly looked to the front of the church.

"Marshal Barclay will be assigned to this territory permanently, and I'm sure you will all make him feel welcome and at home."

All the air seemed to be suddenly sucked out of her lungs. Out of the whole building! Her eyes met the eyes of the man she'd never expected to see again.

Fowler Barclay stood at the front of her church. She must be losing her mind! No. What had the reverend said? Assigned here? Fowler Barclay would be living here? In Waco! Oh, God, what cruel trick was fate playing on her?

"What?" Nichole started as her mother shook her arm.

"I said, are you all right? I thought I heard you moan or something."

"Ye–yes. I'm . . . okay," she stuttered as she opened her Bible to the page indicated by the preacher. "I'm fine."

Amy leaned over and whispered, "Isn't that the marshal you kidnapped?"

"Shush. Yes, it is."

After the sermon, Nichole headed straight to the wagon, hoping to avoid seeing Fowler. It was not to be.

Suddenly he was there, standing in front of her.

"Hello, Nichole." His deep voice ricocheted around her heart.

She squared her shoulders and looked him directly in the eyes. "Hello, Marshal Barclay," she said with more bravado than she felt. "When did you get into town?"

"A week or so ago."

So, he'd been here more than a week and hadn't even tried to see her. If she had any lingering doubts, that alone told her where she stood with him.

"Well, Waco's a nice place to live. I hope you like it here. Now, if you'll excuse me, I see someone I need to speak to. Good day." She wasn't sure if her trembling legs would support her as she turned and walked away.

Fowler stood watching her walk away from him, again. He wondered at her cold attitude. She wasn't the same lighthearted woman he'd known such a short time ago. Or was it perhaps that she didn't want to claim a friendship with a lowly working man?

"Fowler! Good to see you." Cody had witnessed his sister's reaction to the marshal, and was puzzled by it.

Fowler accepted Cody's handshake. "Hello, Cody. It's good to see you, too."

Nichole watched out of the corner of her eye as her brother and the man she loved, the man who was the father of the child she now carried, talked animatedly.

Her heart was beating in triple time just from their brief exchange. The fragrance of his cologne mingled with the smell of tobacco and the manly scent that was uniquely his clung to her mind. How often she'd lain awake at night, remembering the scent of him.

How she longed to be standing there, laughing and talking with him now.

She knew what she had to do. She had to leave as soon as possible. She couldn't stand the torture of seeing Fowler every time she came into town. She wasn't strong enough to survive that kind of pain.

She'd tell the family tonight that she was returning to finishing school and Cousin Emmalee's. She'd leave the day after the fourth of July celebration.

In less than a month she'd be gone. Could she survive that long? To know that he was so close to her, yet she couldn't reach out to him? Was she strong enough to do it?

For her sake, for her family's sake, and, more important, for her unborn baby's sake, somehow, she'd have to find the strength.

Her heart was tearing apart inside her as she thought about closing the door on this part of her life. Leaving her family and friends behind would be hard. But. . . .

She turned and looked at Fowler. Unconsciously, her hand moved to her stomach protectively.

His eyes met hers across the space separating them. He couldn't fathom the message he saw there. Was it pain?

Leaving the man she loved would be a pure living hell!

Chapter Eighteen

Once having reached her decision, Nichole was anxious to set the wheels in motion to carry out her plan.

She decided that the best way to tell her family of her decision was during the evening meal that night.

She had hoped to do it earlier and get it over with, but Amy had gotten her wish. Reverend Dixon, his wife, Jennifer, and their son, Jonathan, joined the Westerfields that afternoon for Sunday dinner.

"I wrote a letter to Cousin Emmalee this afternoon," Nichole said casually. "I've decided to return to Washington, D.C. and finish school. Would you get one of the hands to post it for me tomorrow?"

Mark and Cassie quickly exchanged looks of surprise. "Isn't this a rather sudden decision?" Mark queried.

"Are you sure this is what you want to do, Nichole?" Her mother was puzzled. She and Mark had talked about making their headstrong daughter return to complete her schooling and decided, considering all that had happened in the past few months, that she would probably view it as punishment for taking off on her own to find Nick.

Both had taken notice that since Nichole had returned from her adventure, she seemed to have matured some. Maybe too much. She was often pensive and uncommunicative. Gone was the energetic, impulsive, and ofttimes helter-skelter girl who always had to match her brothers step for step. Nichole had definitely changed. And, if the truth be known, her parents missed the vibrant, always happy and laughing girl she had been.

Nichole laid her fork aside and looked at her parents. "Yes. I've given it careful thought and decided that it is the right thing to do." She smiled, but the smile didn't quite reach her eyes. "Besides, Daddy spent a lot of money to send me back East to make a proper lady out of me. The least I can do is complete the schooling. Who knows, maybe it'll work?" she jested.

"When do you plan to leave?" her mother asked hesitantly.

"I don't want to miss the fourth of July festivities, so I'll leave on the fifth." She was anxious to change the topic lest her family perceived her resignation rather than desire to go back East.

Turning to Carmen, she enthusiastically talked about the upcoming event. "The whole town turns out to celebrate. It's like one gigantic picnic. There are horse races, and sack races, and tug-of-war contests and apple dunkin'. And after the sun goes down, there'll be fireworks and a big dance. Everybody has a good time and goes home exhausted, looking forward to the next year's celebration."

"Maybe your basket will bring the highest bid again this year. Since you weren't here last year, Cindy Lou had the highest bid but it was barely half the price that yours always brings," Amy declared.

Carmen looked confused. "You sell baskets?"

Nick laughed as he explained. "It's a fund-raising event for the church. All the single girls fix a picnic basket and then the single men bid on them. The highest bidder on a basket gets to share the lunch with that girl. It's all supposed to be secretive so the man doesn't know who his lunch partner will be, but if a girl is sweet on a certain man, she has her way of letting him know which basket is hers."

"Nichole's basket always gets the highest bid," beamed her little brother proudly.

"I don't know. Nichole might have some stiff competition this year," Cody observed with a teasing grin. "Amy seems to have an admirer, too."

Amy blushed becomingly. "I just hope he bids *something*," she admitted.

Nick was quick to volunteer. "Maybe I ought to have a 'brotherly' talk with him. He is awfully shy when he gets around you," he teased.

Amy was mortified. "Nicholas Westerfield! Don't you dare! Mother!" she beseeched.

"Nick, behave yourself. Amy, he's only teasing you," Cassie soothed.

Kathleen, who was still too young to participate, eagerly asked, "Can I help Amy and Nichole decorate their baskets?"

Before her mother could answer, Nichole announced, "I'm not going to fix a basket this year."

"Why ever not?" Amy couldn't believe that her sister wasn't going to take part in the fun.

"It wouldn't be right," Nichole said sadly. All eyes were on her, waiting for her to explain her statement. "I mean, it wouldn't be fair to whomever might buy my basket. Since I plan to leave the next day, I don't consider myself an eligible female this year," she hurriedly explained.

"But, Nolie . . ." Amy wailed.

Cassie had a feeling there was more to it than just her leaving for a few months, so she interceded quickly. "Maybe Nichole is right, Amy. If there's not someone special whom she wants to influence, it would be unfair to let a young man think so."

Amy still didn't believe that Nichole would pass up all the fun. "Well, it's still weeks away. You'll change your mind by then."

Nick watched Nichole as she gave her lame excuse. He didn't believe a word of it. Something was troubling his twin and he intended to find out what it was. He had been so caught up in his love for Carmen and the child, his child, that she was carrying, that he hadn't noticed until tonight, how unhappy Nolie seemed to be.

Carmen looked at her husband as he sat on the side of the bed later that night. She knew something was bothering him because he had been so pensive after dinner. He had been so preoccupied when they retired to their room, it was almost as if he had forgotten she was there.

He had removed his shirt and absently laid it across a chair before sitting down to remove his boots. He had paused, one boot on and one boot off, deep in thought.

"Do you want to talk about what is troubling you so, my love?"

Her soft inquiry brought him back to the present. "Huh? Oh, I'm sorry, Carmen. I didn't mean to ignore you. I was just pondering Nolie's strange behavior. She's just not her old self anymore," he explained. "I would have bet anything that a team of wild horses couldn't drag her back to finishing school. She *hated* it there! It was in every letter she wrote to me. Now she's willingly going back?" He shook his head in disbelief. "No. I don't believe that for a moment. She's my twin. I know her too well. There's something wrong here and I intend to find out what it is."

Carmen suspected what the "something wrong" was, but she couldn't tell Nick her suspicions. She knew how he felt about Fowler Barclay, even if she didn't understand why.

"Could it have something to do with Marshal Barclay, maybe?" she hinted.

"Barclay?" That thought hadn't crossed his mind.

"Maybe your sister . . . cares about him more than you know. She seems like a woman with a broken heart. As I would have been had you not loved me as much as I loved you, *querido*."

Nick looked at his wife with disbelief. "How could she love Barclay?"

"Why not?"

"Well, because . . . because he's a lawman. That's why. His kind doesn't stay put anywhere very long. Nichole wants a home, kids, and stability. Like we do."

"Are you so sure, my love? I don't think fate takes things like that into consideration when two people are destined to love each other. And, if their love is meant to be, nothing will stand in its way," she cautioned.

Nick looked at Carmen quizzically. He had not considered that Nichole might have strong feelings for Fowler. Had he been too quick to jump to conclusions and blame Fowler for the passionate embrace he had caught them in? If Carmen was right, why would Nichole be so anxious to get away from Fowler?

Three days later, when she found Nichole sitting alone on the porch swing, Carmen decided to see if she could give fate a helping hand.

"Are you still mad at Nicky?"

Nichole didn't try to pretend that she didn't know what Carmen was talking about. Of course Nicky would have told her about the angry words they had flung at each other when Nick had tried to talk her out of returning to school. She shook her head. "No. I know he doesn't understand why I ha . . . want to go back to Cousin Emmalee's."

"Do you think he would love you less if you told him the reason?"

Nichole looked at Carmen incredulously. "You know, don't you?"

Carmen silently nodded her head.

"How did you know? I haven't told anyone. Not anyone!" she whispered in alarm.

Carmen shrugged her shoulders. "I could sense a great sadness about you and because you have the same symptoms as I. But, do not worry, I don't think anyone else suspects anything."

Tears filled Nichole's eyes as she looked off in the direction of Waco. She was not even aware of the invisible pull that existed. "Oh, Carmen, what am I to do? I don't want to leave my home and my family, but I can't stay here and cause them shame for my stupidity." She sniffled as the pent-up tears of frustration and strain flooded her eyes and ran down her cheeks unabated.

"Do you love your Marshal Barclay?"

Nichole nodded her head. "With all my heart. I know I can never love another man," she said with conviction.

"Does he know about the baby?"

"No."

"And you're going to leave without telling him." It was a statement of fact rather than a question. "Why, Nichole? Is it not possible that he feels the same way about you?"

"Oh, Carmen, if that were only true, I'd be the happiest woman in the world. But it's not. He doesn't love me. He loves his job, the danger and excitement of it all. He doesn't have time for a wife and family. He's used to doing and going as the notion strikes him. To force him to give that up would only make us both miserable."

"Maybe there is a reason that he has not declared his love for you, yet. Surely he must feel something for you. All those weeks that he helped you search for Nicky and protected you from harm. At least talk to him, even if you do not tell him about the baby."

"I can't do that, Carmen. He has to want to make a

commitment to me because he loves *me*, not because of a sense of duty. I won't settle for less than his love. I can't." Once more her eyes drifted in the direction of that invisible tug at her heart.

Carmen was as frustrated as Nichole. What a tangled mess this was. But her intuition told her that if she could just get the two lovers together and talking honestly, they would find a way to work out their problems. But who could she turn to for help? Nick was out of the question because of his unreasonable dislike of Fowler. Her mother-in-law was, also, out of the question. She'd probably guess in an instant that Nichole was *enceinte*.

That left only Cody who was very perceptive and a good judge of character. Being a man, he might have sensed Fowler's true feelings for Nichole. She had to find Cody and feel him out on this matter.

"I think I'll walk around for a while. Doc Stu told me to get some exercise every day. Would you like to come with me?" Carmen inquired.

Nichole shook her head. "I think I'll just sit here. You go ahead. Carmen . . ." Her voice broke slightly. "Thank you for caring. I needed someone I could talk to."

"Don't worry, Nichole. Things have a way of working out the way they're supposed to."

Nichole was already lost in her thoughts and didn't seem to hear Carmen's parting statement.

Carmen found Cody in the stables, checking a gash on one of the horse's hind legs.

"Hello, Carmen. You're looking radiant this morning," he noted.

"Thank you." She motioned toward the large, brown-eyed mare. "Is she going to be all right?"

"Yeah. It's a deep cut, but so far it's not infected and is healing good." He didn't think that she had come to the stables to check on the well-being of the horses, but he continued doctoring the leg and wrapping it with bandages, giving her time to voice her feelings.

This was harder than she'd thought it would be. She couldn't find a way to open the conversation about Nichole that sounded casual. And she certainly didn't want to reveal her new sister's secret.

When he'd finished his task, he eyed the petite young woman curiously. "Do you want to tell me what's on your mind, little sister or am I supposed to guess?"

Carmen let out a sigh. "I don't know how to ask this without seeming to be interfering in things that are none of my business."

"Why don't you just say it plain out and let me decide if you're interfering?"

She looked him straight in the eyes. "Okay. What do you think about Fowler Barclay?"

"Hmmm, well, let's see. I think he's a very competent lawman. He's good with his gun. He seems to be a decent, likable sort of fella." He could tell by her restless shifting from one foot to the other that she wasn't getting the answer she wanted to her question.

"What you really want to know is how does he feel toward Nichole, isn't it?"

"Yes. That's why she's going back East. Cody, she's miserable. She loves him. Really loves him, but she's convinced that he doesn't feel the same about her.

And I just don't believe that for a minute. I think he does feel something for her. I saw the way his eyes followed her every movement Sunday. And, from bits and pieces of things that you and Nicky have said, whether he knows it or not, I think he cares a great deal for her."

Cody thoughtfully considered Carmen's words. "I figured that had something to do with Nichole's leaving. I've never known her to run away from a problem before. I'm still hoping she'll change her mind and stay."

"She can't," Carmen said absently, not realizing her slip of the tongue.

"Can't? Why not? Why can't she change her mind?"

"I meant won't. She *won't* change her mind. Don't you see how hard it would be for her to see Fowler every time she goes into town?" Carmen hoped she had covered her slip. She wasn't sure how Cody would react to his sister's secret, but she was positive about Nick's feelings. She only wanted to help fate a little bit. Not start a feud!

Cody studied her for a minute. He knew she was trying to hide something. But why? What could possibly make Nichole feel that she *couldn't* change her mind? She had been acting strangely lately. In fact, if his suspicions were correct, it would explain a lot of her actions since she'd been back.

"Yes, I can see where that might cause Nichole some distress. With Fowler assigned here, she'd be bound to run into him frequently." Cody could almost see Carmen breathe a sigh of relief thinking that he believed her explanation for her slip. "We might just have to let nature take its course. But, if it

322

will ease your mind any, Fowler does care about Nichole. Very much so. That's why he thinks he can't declare himself and ask her to marry him. But that could change," he declared judiciously.

Carmen smiled gratefully at Cody. "Thank you for telling me that. Nicky is so touchy when Fowler's name is mentioned. And I truly don't understand why."

"Don't worry about it, Carmen. I have a notion his opinion of Fowler will soon change," he said prophetically. "He's always been very protective of his twin."

When Carmen left the stables after talking to Cody, she did feel better about her plans to give fate a little assistance. Now all she had to do was figure out how to pull it off.

Cody, on the other hand, was in a real quandary as to how to solve this delicate matter. He didn't realize he was scowling at the same time he was absent-mindedly pulling pieces of hay out of the bale he was leaning against.

"Hey, big brother. These animals will starve to death if they have to wait for you to feed them one straw at a time," Nick chided when he entered the stables.

Cody looked at his brother. "Do you know why Nichole is going back to Cousin Emmalee's?"

"Not really. I guess you heard that we had a big argument about it. But I don't believe her story about wanting to finish school. Do you know the real reason?"

"I think so. She's running away from Fowler Barclay."

Nick smiled broadly. "Well, if that's the reason,

then I will gladly help her pack. The further she gets away from him, the better off she'll be."

"You better not be too quick to help her leave," Cody cautioned. "Not unless you want our niece or nephew to grow up without a father."

"What?" Nick couldn't believe he'd heard correctly. "You mean Nolie is . . . is . . . No." He shook his head in denial. "Not Nolie! She wouldn't . . . she couldn't . . . but she can't be, she's not even married!" he finally declared emphatically.

Cody shook his head at his brother's lapse of logic. "Really, Nicholas. Besides, I don't know anything for sure. I'm just guessing. Right now what we have to decide is what to do about it."

"I know what I'd like to do about it," Nick said angrily.

"Violence is not the answer. Besides, I feel certain that Nichole loves Fowler. And I know for a fact that Fowler feels the same about her. He as much as admitted it to me when we were on the trail. What we have to do is to get them talking to each other honestly."

"Cody, I don't understand. If Nichole loves Fowler, why would she want to get away from him? And, if Fowler loves her, why wouldn't he *want* to marry her?"

"Because they both think the other one doesn't feel the same. They are both proud and stubborn people." Cody chuckled. "Actually, they're a matched set. They deserve each other. Also, Fowler has this stupid notion that since he isn't wealthy, he can't give our sister all the things *he* thinks *she* wants."

"Uh-oh," Nick grimaced. "I guess my angry tirade

only reinforced his thinking that he wasn't worthy of her, huh?"

Cody nodded his head. "I 'spect it did. Well, I think tomorrow you and I need to have a little chat with our future brother-in-law."

"I'm certainly glad that you were here when this happened."

Fowler sat in the governor's office going over all the details available to him. "No one saw anyone near the place who shouldn't have been there?"

The governor shook his head. "We've had very strict security around Linc Travis. No one could get near him without the proper authorization. In fact, we managed to keep his capture out of the newspapers to be sure he lived long enough to testify. There were only a few people who even knew where he was being held prisoner." He shook his head in consternation. "I don't like the sound of this at all, Fowler."

Fowler carefully read the guard's report again. "I think it's time we looked at our own house, Governor. None of Linc's men escaped the shoot-out near Laredo. So I know he couldn't have gotten any help that way. I've had my deputies keeping an eye on John North. I know for a fact that he hasn't been anywhere near Austin. So we can rule him out. That only leaves someone here in the capitol."

"I'm afraid so," the governor reluctantly concurred. "But who the hell is it?"

"You can bet that whoever broke Linc out, did so not because he wanted him free, but to kill him before he could implicate the leader." Fowler rose to his feet. "I want to talk to this guard before I try to pick up Linc's trail. I need to get going before it gets too cold."

The governor shook his hand. "I don't have to tell you what a bitter pill this is to swallow. To know that someone I've trusted has turned traitor . . . Well, you just find that bastard. I want to see him dangling from the end of a rope right in front of the capitol!" he said vehemently.

"I'll do my best to accommodate you, Governor. Oh, one other thing. It might be a wise idea to let Nick Westerfield know that Linc Travis has escaped. If Linc should get that far, he might try to kill Nick again."

"I'll send a message right now to warn him."

Linc had no way of knowing that Marshal Barclay had passed within a few miles of him earlier that same day as the marshal made his way into Austin and Linc made his escape.

After his brief spell in jail, he decided that he wasn't going to be captured alive. Something had snapped inside him, being caged like an animal. His only thought was to get to John North.

He'd kept his mouth shut so far, but if North didn't get him out of the state, North would have no need for all the land that Linc and his gang had made it possible for him to purchase for pennies on the dollar.

"He'll get me to safety or I'll kill him with my bare hands," the half-crazed man muttered.

It never occurred to Linc that maybe John North wasn't responsible for his escape.

* * *

Nick frowned as he read the governor's message. "Damn!" he swore as he wadded the paper into a ball in his fist.

When he and Cody had ridden into Waco to talk to Fowler, his deputy had informed them that the marshal was in Austin, getting ready for Linc Travis's trial that was scheduled to begin the day after tomorrow. The deputy didn't expect him back for at least another week, maybe longer.

"Is something wrong, son?"

Nick let out a disgusted breath. "Linc Travis escaped from jail yesterday and may be headed in this direction." He looked his father in the eyes. "Linc is a murderous maniac, Dad. If he's headed after me for revenge, he'd just as soon kill everyone here and burn the house to the ground to get to me. In fact, it gives him some kind of diabolical pleasure to torture and kill innocent people."

"I'll have some of the men stay close to the house and post guards around the area in case he does try something. I suppose you're going to try to find him."

"Yeah. I'll leave as soon as I fetch Mother and the girls from Grandpa Montclair's. I want to talk to Carmen before I leave. I don't think Grandpa and Lottie will be in any danger, but I'll tell Eddie what's going on so he can keep an eye out, just in case."

Nick rode to the Ranger post first to see if they had any information. They didn't know anything more than he did.

Playing a hunch, he decided to nose around John North's ranch. Even though they hadn't been able to arrest him yet because of lack of evidence, Nick still had a gut feeling that North was fronting for someone. If that was true, then Linc would most likely try to make his way there for protection.

Fowler was surprised at how easy it had been to pick up Linc's trail at the secluded cabin that had been turned into a security jail. He couldn't imagine the man being so careless. Even though he was taking an overland route instead of the public roads, his tracks were easy to follow.

Too easy, in fact. It almost appeared that Linc wasn't even trying to cover his tracks. This worried Fowler. Could he be walking into a trap? Or had Linc gone over the deep end? Was he so desperate to reach his destination that he wasn't taking the time to hide his tracks?

Another thing worried Fowler. The direction that Linc was taking could mean that he was headed after Nick. Fear gripped him as he considered the possibility that Linc might try to vent revenge against Nichole and her brother for their part in his capture.

Fowler spotted vultures circling overhead. He feared what he would find. Just the day before, he'd found the badly injured horse which Linc had ridden to escape from Austin. It had a broken front leg and looked as if it had been ridden long and hard. Fowler had shot it to end its misery.

Expecting that Linc would try to steal another horse since he was now on foot, Fowler had planned to stop at the next farmhouse he came to.

He recognized Linc's murderous signature as he rode into the yard. One man was lying near the well, dead from a gunshot in the back. Another man in his early teens, probably his son, had been shot in the face apparently as he tried to keep Linc from entering the house.

Fowler estimated that they had been killed around midday yesterday. Gun in hand, he cautiously entered the house, keenly alert in case Linc might have decided to hole up there for a while.

Once inside, Fowler found that the first two rooms had been totally ransacked and plundered. Furniture overturned, chair cushions and bedding torn apart. It was obvious that Linc had been looking for anything of value he could steal.

The kitchen was just as bad. Dishes and crockery were strewn about the floor. A large and once beautiful china cabinet lay on its side, the glass front smashed and the side stomped in. Fowler shook his head at such wanton destruction. The absence of any food made Fowler surmise that Linc had apparently taken as much food as he could carry.

Leaving the house, Fowler continued his search, afraid of what he might find when he reached the barn. He didn't find any more victims there, however, only a lazy milk cow munching on some hay. He had feared that he would find the mutilated body of the man's wife somewhere in the area.

He could only hope that she had either not been at home at the time of the killings, or she had somehow managed to escape.

He holstered his gun as he walked around to the front of the house.

A sound caught his attention. He stopped and listened intently to determine in what direction it had come from and what could have made the noise.

Straining his ears, he could barely hear what sounded like the muffled cry of a baby! Slowly, he walked back around the corner of the house and listened again. But he didn't hear anything.

He knew his mind wasn't playing tricks on him. He had definitely heard a baby's cry, but where the hell was it coming from?

"Hello," he shouted. "I'm a United States Marshal. I won't hurt you. It's safe for you to come out from where you're hiding."

This time the baby's crying was louder and at least two other voices could be heard. The sound led him back into the kitchen. But he still didn't see any place, a pantry or closet, where someone could hide.

He heard a thumping or bumping noise and followed its sound. It came from under the area where the china cabinet lay smashed and broken.

After shoving the heavy piece of furniture out of the way, he saw a concealed door leading down into a root cellar.

He hurriedly opened it to find a woman, a baby, and two older children huddled, frightened, and pitiful-looking, in the dark area.

"Thank you, Mister, thank you," the woman cried. "I thought we were going to die down here. Me and the children hid in the root cellar when the shooting started. After the shooting and noise stopped and I heard a horse leaving, I tried to push the door open, but I couldn't. Something was blocking it."

She handed the baby up to him and then helped the other children, a towheaded young boy and a little girl, up the wooden steps. When Fowler helped the woman out of the cellar, she stood in what was left of her kitchen, dazed.

She had heard the destruction taking place while she hid below, but nothing could have prepared her for what her disbelieving eyes saw.

Fowler picked up a chair and helped the sobbing woman to sit. The boy protectively reached up and took the crying baby from Fowler before joining his little sister at their mother's side.

"Ma'am, you've got to pull yourself together."

The little girl tugged on her mother's skirt. "Mommy, I'm thirsty and hungry. Mommy, Mommy?"

"Me, too," the young boy added.

The woman wiped her dirt-streaked and tear-stained face with the bottom of her apron as she tried to calm herself.

"Yes. Yes. We need water and food." She looked at Fowler. "We've been trapped in there since yesterday morning," she explained.

"I'm sorry, ma'am, but you'd better keep the children away from the front of the house. I'll fetch some water from the well for you."

Her eyes met his and she understood what he meant. She mutely nodded her head.

As they ate some jerky and canned beans that Fowler had in his saddlebags, he inquired, "Do you have any kin nearby? Or maybe a neighbor who I can take you and the children to?"

"Yes, that would be very kind of you. My . . ." Her voice choked with emotion. "My husband's brother has the farm adjoining ours. If you'll take us there, I'd be grateful."

* * *

After leaving the woman and her three fatherless children in the care of her brother-in-law, Fowler again headed after Linc Travis.

He breathed an audible sigh of relief when the trail he was following began to veer off to the east, away from Nichole's home.

As darkness closed in, Nick carefully scouted the area surrounding the headquarters of North's ranch. He found the body of one of Fowler's deputies. His throat had been cut and, from the condition of the body, he'd only been dead a few hours.

His hunch had been right. Linc Travis was probably inside the main house with John North now.

Nick had not seen any guards or unusual activity around the house and outbuildings. He wanted to get closer to the house, but he'd have to wait until it was completely dark and the ranch hands had settled in the bunkhouse for the night.

He ate some hardtack and jerky while he waited for darkness. Fortunately, there was little moon tonight. He had just started to make his move toward the house when he heard the sounds of a horse approaching. Nick pulled back into the woods to watch.

The rider stopped not more than a hundred yards to Nick's left as he carefully surveyed the area before him. Then he cautiously nudged his horse forward, aiming it toward the side of the house opposite the bunkhouse.

Nick observed the mysterious rider, but from that distance and with little light, he could only make out the dim outline of horse and man. He watched as the man silently disappeared around the back of the house.

The hairs on the back of Nick's neck stood on end only a fraction of a second before he felt the cold jab of a gun in his back.

"Don't make a sound or you're dead."

Nick froze in his crouched position. He'd been so intently watching the rider that he had let his guard down. He silently cursed himself for such a stupid mistake!

He heard the crack of metal against bone, rather than felt the blow on the back of his head before falling into the black abyss of unconsciousness.

Fowler had spotted another set of tracks, fresher tracks, not more than a few hours old about three miles from John North's ranch.

Whoever the new rider was, he had left the main road and taken to the cover of the woods, following almost on top of the trail that Linc Travis had made.

Fowler ground-tied his horse about a half mile before reaching the ranch house. He silently stalked the second rider until the darkness made it impossible for him to see the tracks.

He knew his deputy was concealed somewhere in the encompassing trees and underbrush. He stealthily made his way toward the area where he expected to find him.

When he found his deputy's body, his eyes scanned the area for any movement before he furtively moved closer to the clearing around the house and outbuildings. He had seen movement ahead and slightly to his right.

When Nick came to, he was lying on his back, looking up as thousands of stars danced above him.

Slowly, some of the stars began to disappear and the rest settled down to their proper place in the sky.

He blinked, trying to focus and to remember what had happened. When he tried to sit up, a hand covered his mouth, muffling his groan.

"It's a good thing you have such a hard head, Nick," the man on the other end of the hand whispered as he helped Nick to a sitting position.

"Fowler?"

Chapter Nineteen

"Yeah. What the hell are you doing here?"

Nick tenderly rubbed the rapidly rising lump on the back of his head. "What the hell did you hit me for?"

"Sorry about that, but I didn't know it was you until after I'd slugged you. When I found my deputy's dead body, I figured Linc Travis had killed him. When I saw some movement in the dark, I thought it might be him."

"It probably was Linc who killed him. I found your deputy earlier when I got here. He'd only been dead a few hours then. I figured that Linc was already in the house. I was waiting for darkness so I could get closer to the house to see if I could hear anything."

"I picked up another set of tracks, fresher tracks, leading here about three miles back. Did you get a look at the man?"

Nick shook his throbbing head and wished he hadn't. "I saw him, but it was too dark to make out who it was. That's why you were able to slip up on me without my hearing you. I was watching to see where he went. He wasn't one of the ranch hands, that's for sure. He was being too cautious and he went around to the back of the house."

"Hmmm, maybe we'll find out who's really behind the land-grabbing scheme." Fowler peered through the darkness at Nick. "How's the head? Are your eyes uncrossed yet?"

"Sore. Come on, let's get closer. This time we're going to get enough evidence to put North in jail along with Linc," he said with conviction.

The two men soundlessly made their way across the clearing to the house.

They could hear voices, but were unable to make out the words. One man seemed more agitated than the other, his voice rising in anger.

Fowler carefully tried the window in the room next to where the voices seemed to be coming from. It slid silently upward. Nick followed him over the window-sill.

Now they could hear loudly and clearly what the two men were saying.

Nick recognized John North's voice as he tried to calm an agitated Linc Travis.

"All right. All right! Calm down. I'll find a way to get you safely across the border. Just let me think a minute," North reasoned as he paced the room.

He had to find a way to divert Linc's attention so he could get to the gun that he kept hidden in his center desk drawer.

Linc had outlived his usefulness. North had thought that his partner was going to silence Linc before he could implicate either of them at the trial. Apparently something had gone wrong. He certainly hadn't expected Linc to escape and come to his home!

Suppose the posse had followed Linc to his ranch? He had to kill the man and make it look like. . . .

"Quit your stalling, North. And don't you go thinking to try anything funny. 'Cause none of your hirelings knows I'm here and you ain't armed." Linc walked over to the liquor cabinet and poured himself a drink. "Ah, good whiskey, 'boss man,'" he said snidely as he turned around and leaned his elbows against the bar.

"But I guess you can afford the best of everything, can't ya? How much you made so far? Couple of million, maybe? And that's just the beginning, ain't it? Once the railroad starts moving through here and all them new towns start springing up, you gonna be one rich son of a bitch, ain't ya?" he sneered as he smashed his empty glass against the wall and began advancing on North.

North started backing up. "Now, Linc, stay calm. I'll take care of you. Haven't I always been fair with you?" he bargained. "You and your men have been paid very well for helping me. You can't deny that. And . . . and I'll help you now." North walked around the desk and sat in his chair.

"I just have to figure out the best and safest way to get you across the border."

"Well, you better make it fast. Because I ain't gonna swing from no hangman's noose without you

337

right beside me. *Comprende, amigo?*" Linc's face was contorted with anger.

"Ye–yes, I comprehend. And you're right, of course," he hurriedly added. "Friends should take care of friends."

A plan suddenly formed in North's mind. "I'll, ah, I'll use one of my closed carriages to get you across the border. Yes! That's perfect. No one will be able to see you and the lawmen won't suspect a private carriage." He opened the drawer that held a cash box—and his gun. "But you'll need some money."

As he opened the lid of the cash box, he glanced up at Linc, hoping to draw his attention away from his hand. "Are you sure no one followed you here?"

Linc's anger again twisted his face in an ugly sneer. "What do you take me for? Couldn't nobody follow me, I tell you."

"Good. Good." North praised as he closed his hand around his gun and raised it to point directly at Linc Travis's chest.

Looking through a crack in the door, Fowler decided that he and Nick had heard enough. He could tell from North's movement that he was reaching for a weapon and Fowler didn't want Linc killed. They needed him alive so he could testify against North.

He was just about to open the door and step into the room when Nick's hand stayed him. Nick motioned to a tall man who had just entered the room from the hallway.

Fowler didn't recognize him, but Nick did.

The man had his gun drawn and aimed at Linc Travis. "That's not exactly correct, is it? You left a trail any blundering, one-eyed fool could follow."

North breathed a sigh of relief. "Thank heavens, it's you. I thought you were going to take care of this idiot before he could testify," he accused.

Linc looked from North to the stranger in surprise. "What the hell are you trying to pull?"

"I think it would look better if you killed this . . . intruder, with your gun, John. The authorities will think you were trying to defend yourself against a robber," the stranger stated calmly, never taking his eyes off Linc.

Without hesitation, John North drew his gun from his desk drawer, aimed and fired.

Linc's eyes widened in disbelief as his blood spread across his shirt front before they glazed over in death. He fell face forward with a thud.

North was sweating profusely. He laid his gun aside and wiped the sweat from his forehead with the back of his hand. "God, I'm glad that's over." He repeated his earlier question. "I thought you said you were going to take care of him in Austin?"

The stranger calmly walked over to where John was standing, and casually picked up his gun. "I decided to take care of *two* idiots at the same time."

North blanched at the man's words. "Thad, you . . . you can't mean it!" he protested. "What about all our plans? All of our hard work?" he asked disbelievingly.

"With the paper trail of dummy corporations you've so kindly set up for me, I won't have any trouble keeping my identity a secret now," he boasted.

North's fear turned to anger. "You'll never get away with this! Never!" he raged in desperation.

"Of course, I will," the man said calmly and smoothly. "It's very obvious what took place here. You were confronted by a robber. You shot him, but, before he died, he managed to get off a lucky shot that killed you. Simple." The man took Linc's gun from his holster and now aimed at North. "It's a perfect plan, if I do say so myself," he bragged cunningly.

Fowler and Nick stepped into the room, with their guns trained on the two adversaries.

"I don't think so, *Senator* Sheffield," Nick stated urbanely.

At the sound of Nick's voice, the senator whirled around and fired a wild shot in his direction. Nick, taking care not to kill him, smoothly shot the senator in the shoulder. His gun clattered uselessly to the floor as he grabbed his bleeding shoulder.

North tried to make a run for the doorway, but Fowler's voice drew him up short. "Stay where you are, North, unless you're ready to die right now."

North decided to stand still.

"Senator?" Fowler glanced incredulously at Nick.

"That's right, Fowler. Oh, I guess the two of you haven't been properly introduced. Senator Thadd Sheffield, I'd like you to meet United States Marshal Fowler Barclay."

The day had come. Nichole bid a tearful farewell to her family as the stage that would carry her to the train depot in Calvert was being loaded.

Her brothers and sisters hugged her one last time before stepping back to let her say good-bye to her mother and father.

Cassie cried as she hugged her daughter. "You write me every week, do you hear me?"

"Yes, Mama, I will. I promise I'll write often."

Mark's voice was husky with emotion as he kissed her forehead and hugged her to him. "If you change your mind, Nichole, and decide to come home, send us a wire and we'll meet you at the train depot. Promise me you won't start home without letting us know."

"Yes, Daddy," she said tearfully as she hugged him and her mother again. "I love you both very, very much."

She turned to Nick as he stood to the side with his arm around Carmen. "Nicky, you take good care of her." He nodded his head. "And send me a wire as soon as the baby gets here. I want to know when I have a little niece or nephew."

"Don't worry, Nichole, you'll know which it is, as soon as we do," Carmen said as she again hugged Nichole. She whispered for Nichole's ears only, "There's still time to change your mind and stay."

Nichole shook her head. She took one last look at the family she loved so much before stepping up into the stagecoach.

The driver, seeing that everything was loaded and all the passengers were on board, flicked the reins and headed the horses in the direction of his next stop.

Mark put his arm around his wife as they stood watching until the vehicle was out of sight.

The family had come in on the buckboard, but Cody, Nick, and Carmen had ridden their horses to town. Carmen had to see the doctor and then she and Nick were going to have dinner in town and return to the ranch the next day. Cody had something he needed to do, so he wouldn't be returning to the Rocking W until the next day either.

Fowler Barclay left his office and looked at the few remaining people on the street. He was glad the last three and a half weeks were behind him.

In order to save his own neck, North had been more than eager to cooperate with the governor's office. He had supplied them with names, dates, and property deeds, some that went back for more than a year, of all the people who had been scared away or killed in order to get control of their land.

It would take several months to locate all the rightful owners or their heirs and see that their farms and ranches were returned to them.

All monies and property belonging to John North and Thadd Sheffield had been confiscated. The property would be auctioned and the proceeds would be distributed as fairly as possible to help compensate the victims for their losses.

Hopefully, most of the families would want to return to their land, to rebuild and prosper, now that they could live there in peace.

When the trial was over, Fowler, along with an escort from the Army, had personally delivered John North and Thad Sheffield to the federal prison.

Now, he was free to think about his own life for a while.

Usually, when he finished an assignment, he felt a sense of accomplishment and pride. But this time all he felt was a sense of letdown and exhaustion.

Could it be that the life of a lawman, always on the move, and never having a sense of permanency had lost its appeal? Had he, at last, purged his restless soul? Sowed all his wild oats, as his father had often prayed he would, before a bullet with his name on it found its mark?

He didn't know. Maybe it was just that the last few months had taken a heavy physical toll on him and once he was rested, he would again itch to right a few wrongs in the world but then, maybe not.

Over the years, he had managed to save some money. A little from his pay as marshal, but most of it had come from his winnings at the poker table. The thought was always in the back of his mind that, assuming he didn't meet an untimely death, he'd like to buy a small spread somewhere and raise fine race horses.

But he'd pictured that time as being when he was too old to keep up with the bad guys. Not in the prime of his life!

So why had that plan been in his thoughts more often lately?

He knew the answer to that, even if he did try to fool himself into believing otherwise. Nichole.

She had invaded his soul and captured his heart. And he hadn't even realized that he was under siege until long after the battle had been waged.

He remembered the day when he'd suddenly realized that the all-consuming feelings he felt for the high-spirited, green-eyed woman was that illusive emotion called love.

He'd tried to fight it. Mercy, how he'd tried to fight those feelings! They made him feel vulnerable and inadequate, as if he'd lost control over a portion of his life, a vital part of himself.

At first, he'd tried to justify all the reasons why he couldn't, or shouldn't, love Nichole. Logic knocked a hole in that bucket. He could change any of those feeble excuses if he truly wanted to.

Then he'd tried to convince himself of all the reasons why Nichole couldn't, or wouldn't, want his love. But none of those held water, either. Nichole had been a virgin when she had willingly come to him. She had felt the undeniable magnetism that constantly drew them together. She must have felt the same passion as he.

In the end, he'd been forced to admit the truth. He was a coward.

Him! The man who had looked down more gun barrels than he could remember! The same man who had flaunted good sense and laughed in the face of danger too many times to count! The fearless Fowler Barclay, like the mighty Samson, had been brought to his knees by a beautiful woman armed only with a four-letter word—love.

He had had many long, tedious days and even longer, lonely nights to think about his predicament.

Finally, he had come to the only conclusion he could. He loved Nichole and he wanted to marry her. Now, all he had to do was garner enough courage to face her, admit his love, and ask her to be his wife. Ask her to share the rest of his life with him. And he was determined to do just that. Right after he'd had a couple of stiff drinks to bolster his courage.

He tossed the cigarette butt on the ground and snuffed it with his boot heel, with the intention of crossing the street to the saloon before riding out to the Rocking W Ranch.

He had made his decision but little did he know that fate was about to change his plans.

"Don't make any sudden moves, Mister. Don't even think about going for your gun unless you want a window in your back."

He felt the cold end of the gun in his back at the same instant he heard the low, muffled voice behind him.

Oh, no! Not again! Déjà vu rippled through his body.

"What is it with you Texans? Don't you have *any* respect for the law? You can't go around kidnapping U.S. Marshals just any time you feel like it! Damn it!"

"Shut up and do as I say! Now, turn around real slow and walk back into the jail," the muffled voice said at the same time that Fowler felt his gun being lifted out of his holster.

Once inside the building, the man warned, "Don't turn around. Where's the keys to the cells?"

Fowler nodded his head toward a hook on the wall. "Hanging over there." He heard the jingle of the keys as the man took them from the hook.

"Okay. Now, you're going to walk into the cell in front of you, all the way to the back wall. Get going."

Fowler was puzzled, but he did as he was instructed. He heard the cell door close and lock behind him. Before he could turn around to see who his captor was, the lamp was blown out, plunging him into total darkness.

Fowler held his breath as he waited for the bullet that he was sure would end his life.

But he waited in vain. Instead of the earsplitting report of a gun, he heard the sound of the jail door open and close as the dark figure of a man slipped out of the building, locking it behind him!

What the hell was going on!

The stage had stopped at a way station for supper and to get a fresh team of horses before continuing on to Calvert.

Nichole tried in vain to find a comfortable position in which to rest as the stage bounced along the road. She could tell that the driver hadn't forgotten where any of the ruts were since the last time she had ridden the stage. He was still managing to fall into every one of them!

She had been plagued with sleepiness the past few weeks because of her pregnancy, but, every time she dozed off, one of the wheels would hit a hole and she'd bang her head against the side of the coach.

She looked at the little boy across from her. She envied him. He had laid his head in his mother's lap and was fast asleep. How she wished she could lay her head in somebody's lap and sleep.

Once again, she squirmed, this time to lean her back against the side of the coach. Maybe that would brace her enough to keep her from being knocked senseless before the stage reached its destination.

She had just dozed off again, when she was suddenly thrown off the bench onto the floor as the stagecoach was abruptly pulled to a halt.

"Are you hurt, ma'am?" the man who was traveling with the woman and child asked as he helped her back on the seat.

"No, I don't think so," she answered as she tried to smooth her gown back into place. "What in the world happened?"

346

"I don't know. Maybe something is blocking the road. I'll step outside to see if I can be of assistance to the driver," the gentleman replied as he exited the coach.

Three hooded riders, each dressed completely in black, blocked the road and each had a gun aimed at the driver.

"I ain't got no money on this stage," the nervous driver said. "You can plain see I ain't even got nobody riding shotgun. All I got is passengers and mail. I ain't got no money, I swear."

One of the hooded riders reined in beside the driver. "We aren't here to rob you, so don't go trying to be a hero. All we want is one of your passengers."

The man from inside the coach had walked up on the opposite side of the driver and was even with the front of the stage before he realized why they were stopped.

"Sir, there is only myself, my wife and son, and a young lady on this stage. Surely you don't mean to . . . to kidnap one of us. Do you?" he asked incredulously.

"You're smarter than you look, Mister. But I wouldn't call it kidnapping. We're only 'borrowing' her for a short time."

"Sir, this is despicable! Absolutely reprehensible behavior! I must sternly protest your actions. I shan't permit you to harm that innocent young lady."

The rider moved around the stage to point his gun at the man. "Oh, you 'shan't,' shan't you?" he mimicked. "I'd say from that quaint accent that you must be from jolly old England."

The man drew himself up to his full height. "That is quite correct, sir."

"Well, 'sir,' if you and your missus intend to return to England, I'd advise you to do as I say and don't give me any more guff," the rider warned ominously. "Now, you take this rope and these rags," he tossed the items to the man on the ground.

"Wh–what am I do with them?"

"You are to get back in the stage and tie the young lady's hands together, then blindfold and gag her. You can tell her that neither she, nor your family will be harmed if she cooperates with us. I give you my word on this. Next, you are to help her out of the stage and onto the horse that my partner is holding. Ya got that?" he sneered.

"Ye–yes. I understand."

The man who had been giving the orders turned back to the driver when the man had entered the coach. "When you get to Calvert, leave Miss Westerfield's baggage there. Someone will pick it up later. Do you understand?"

The driver nodded.

"When she is mounted and the man gets back in the stage, you can continue your journey."

"I reckon that's all I can do fer now. But I'll sure be a joinin' Mark Westerfield and his boys to see that ya git yore comeuppance. Ya can bet they'll be down on ya'll quicker 'en the wrath of God."

Loud voices could be heard coming from inside the stagecoach as the man explained to Nichole what he was suppose to do.

"That's the most preposterous thing I've ever heard! I refuse to let some . . . some hoodlum take

348

me from this stage," she stormed angrily. "How dare he even try!"

The hooded rider would have been disappointed if the young lady had not put up a fight. He pulled his horse even with the open door. Without uttering a sound, he pointed his gun directly at the peacefully sleeping young boy.

The Englishman looked at her pleadingly. "He gave his word that none of us would be harmed if you cooperated."

Nichole looked at the gunman with the black hood covering his features. "What good is the word of a highwayman?" she snapped acrimoniously. But she knew she was defeated. She didn't doubt for a minute that he would shoot an innocent child if she didn't go with him.

She sighed in defeat and held out her arms. Her only hope was to find a way to escape the kidnapper after the stage had safely carried this family away from harm.

Nichole felt her first real sensation of danger when she stepped out of the coach and saw that there were three hooded men instead of one as she had assumed.

She stiffened with terror and turned anxious eyes to the Englishman.

He shook his head, sympathetic to her plight. "I'm sorry, miss, but I have my little boy to think about," he apologized as he secured the blindfold around her head.

The hooded rider with the horse she was to ride didn't say a word as he unceremoniously hoisted her up and plopped her into the saddle when she tried to struggle away from the Englishman's help.

The man who appeared to be the leader of the gang motioned to the driver to get on his way almost before the Englishman had time to close the door of the stagecoach.

Thoughts were running fast and furious through her mind. Who could these men be and what could they possibly want with her? Could they be some of John North's men out to avenge their boss? Or maybe someone connected with the senator, thinking he could hold her hostage in exchange for the senator's release?

Her mind was full of questions, doubts, and fears but no answers, as the night riders took to the back trails and away from the public roads where someone might have been able to come to her aid.

With her eyes covered, she had absolutely no sense of direction. She strained her ears, trying to hear something, anything, that might give her a clue as to where they were taking her, but all she could hear was the normal night sounds.

They traveled at a fairly fast clip for several hours. From the smell that reached her nose and the slight, almost imperceptible, noise that sounded like gently running water, she thought they must be near a stream or a river.

Her horse's forward movement was slowed and then pulled up close to the man who was leading it. She was certain now that they were at a source of water.

One of her captors hands suddenly circled her waist and lifted her off her horse. He seemed to comprehend that she might be a little dizzy from riding with her eyes covered, which she was, as well as being nauseous.

His hands remained at her waist until she was steady on her feet before he released her. She heard her horse being led away and wondered if they had reached their destination.

If so, what would happen to her now? For some reason, which she couldn't explain, she didn't think that her kidnappers meant her any immediate harm. Common sense told her that if they did, they would have already done it.

Except for the fact that she could hear footsteps and horses moving around her, she would have been afraid that they had left her alone wherever it was that they had stopped. Since they had taken her from the stage, they had not spoken one word aloud. At least, not that she had heard and they were still silent.

It was not knowing who her captors were, or what they planned to do with her or to her, that had her nerves frayed. And, with the gag still in place, she couldn't ask any questions.

One of the men took her by the arm and indicated by his downward pull that she was to sit down, but still, no one spoke to her.

After she was seated on the ground, and the man walked away, she could faintly hear the three night riders whispering, but still she was unable to distinguish any words that might give a hint as to her fate.

Suddenly, she was gripped with panic. She heard the creaking sound that a saddle makes when someone puts his foot in the stirrup to mount a horse!

Was she to be left here, gagged, blindfolded, and with her hands bound together?

She listened intently as one rider galloped away, followed closely by the sounds of a second rider leaving the area. She breathed a sigh of relief when it seemed that at least one person had been left to guard her.

Reverend Dixon was sitting at his desk in the small office at the back of the church, reading over the sermon he had just finished writing for Sunday morning's worship.

Pleased with his efforts, he was just about to rise from his chair and go home, when a shadow fell across his desk.

He turned to see who had entered his office. He'd been so deep in thought that he had not heard anyone come into the church.

He found himself facing a hooded figure dressed in black, holding a gun on him. "Oh, my goodness!" he gasped in alarm. "This is a house of worship, how dare you blasphemy God's house by coming in here with your gun drawn!" he protested.

"Sorry, Preacher, but your services are needed elsewhere right now, and at this late hour, I figured I needed a little persuasion to get you to come with me."

"Oh, for heaven's sakes," he scoffed. "If someone needs me, of course I'll come with you. Now, put that thing away before it goes off and hurts someone, son," the preacher admonished sternly. He could tell from the slight build, and the obvious effort to make his voice sound more manly, that he was facing a rather young and nervous lad.

The black-clad man took a step backward and motioned for the preacher to proceed him out the door. "Just get your Bible and come with me, Preacher."

"Oh, all right. But that gun is not necessary, I

assure you. Where are you taking me? Has someone died?" the preacher inquired as he complied with the man's orders.

"You'll find out soon enough. Just start walking. I'll tell you when we're there."

Fowler paced agitatedly back and forth across the small space in the cell. It had been hours since he'd been locked up and in his own jail at that!

What was the purpose? Was it just to humiliate him? Over and over his mind went through various reasons, but he couldn't come up with anything that made the least bit of sense.

He knew it would still be several hours before any of his deputies showed up for duty. All the men had been putting in long hours while he'd been finishing up with the Travis/North/Sheffield mess so he had let all the deputies off for the whole night.

Since they didn't have any prisoners (unless he counted himself, and he sure as hell wasn't, not if he could find a way to get out without anyone finding out about it), he'd figured that if anyone needed him, they'd come to his room at the hotel.

The sound of a key unlocking the front door caught his attention. A shaft of moonlight split the darkness as a figure entered the jail.

Fowler tensed, not knowing what to expect next. He recognized the sounds of the chimney being raised on the lamp. He saw the wick catch fire, and soon the jail was flooded with light.

The man settled the lamp's shade back in place before turning around to face Fowler.

"Nick! Thank God, it's you. I thought I was going to have to stay locked in here until morning!" Fowler exclaimed as he recognized his friend. "Bring the keys and get me the hell out of here!"

Keys? How did Nick get the keys?

Fowler suddenly became very cautious. Something wasn't right here. "Where did you get the keys? And how did you know I was locked in the jail?" His eyes narrowed as he watched Nick casually sit down in *his* chair, at *his* desk!

Nick leaned back in Fowler's chair and propped his booted feet on one corner of the desk, swiveling the chair to get a better look at the man in the cell.

"I got the keys from that hook over there. And I knew you were locked in the cell because I'm the one who locked you in there. Now, any other questions?" he said with a smirk.

"You!" Fowler exclaimed. "Why the hell did you do that!" His fists were balled and he was ready for a fight.

Nick casually rolled a smoke. "Yes, me. As for why, because I want my nephew or niece to have a father when he or she arrives. Care for a smoke while we wait?" he calmly offered.

"What do you mean, 'wait!'" he demanded. "Nick, have you lost your—" Nick's words suddenly penetrated Fowler's brain.

"Nephew? Niece?" Fowler's voice seemed to have jumped several octaves higher. "You mean Nichole . . . There's a ba–ba—" He was shocked. That thought had never crossed his mind. Idiot! He felt like banging his head against the bars of the cell that still imprisoned him.

"Now, you're catching on, *brother*. The word is 'b,a,b,y' as in wet diapers, crying all night. *Baby*,

Fowler, the word is baby. Nichole is going to have a baby. Your baby. And, since a mother needs a father, I aim to see that she has one. That's you. Now. Do you want this cigarette?"

Fowler mutely nodded his head. His spinning head. He was going to be a father. Him. Why hadn't Nichole told him herself?

"Why didn't Nichole tell me herself?" he voiced his question aloud.

Nick had resumed his seat at the desk after lighting and handing the cigarette to a badly shaken Fowler. "Well, funny thing about us Westerfields. We're awfully proud people. We try to handle all our problems by ourselves. Sometimes we don't even tell our family that we have a problem. Westerfields are awfully stubborn, as well as proud people." Nick paused to take a pull of the cigarette he'd rolled for himself.

"And that seems to be the case here. You see, Fowler, Nichole doesn't think you love her. I think you do or else you wouldn't have . . . Well, you get the picture, I think. Anyway, Nichole decided to handle this little 'problem' all by herself. So, she left on the afternoon stage to go back East—."

"Left!" Fowler interrupted with a shout. "She can't do that! She's got *my* baby!"

"Oh, don't worry, Fowler. She's on her way back right now as we speak," Nick assured him confidently.

"How can you be so sure? What changed her mind?" he asked anxiously.

"Because we kidnapped her off the stage," Nick said smugly.

"Kidnapped her! Who did?"

"Cody, Carmen, and me."

"How the hell did you do that?"

"Well, Nolie doesn't *know* that it was us. Not yet, anyway. We wore hoods and we were careful not to say anything within her hearing. That way she couldn't recognize our voices."

"But, when you started back toward Waco, didn't she become suspicious?"

Nick shook his head. "Uh-uh. We blindfolded her."

"You blindfolded her?"

"Yep."

Fowler looked at his soon-to-be brother-in-law skeptically. "Let me see if I've got this straight. The three of you, dressed as night riders, kidnapped Nichole from the stagecoach, tied her up, blindfolded her, and now, you're bringing her back to Waco to marry a man she doesn't think loves her?"

"Yeah." Nick nodded, grinning sheepishly. "That's about the way it went."

As the hilarity of the situation hit Fowler, he started to snicker. Then he began to chuckle. Finally, he threw his head back and laughed so hard he had to sit down as tears rolled down his cheeks. "I don't believe this. This is outrageous."

When Fowler had decided that he was going to ask Nichole to marry him, he had pondered what he could do or say to change her mind if she turned him down. Now he had his answer.

Nick waited until Fowler had controlled his laughter. "Can I take this to mean that you will willingly marry my sister?"

Fowler nodded his head as he dried his tears. "Yes! Unequivocally, yes! I love Nichole. I've loved her for a long time, Nick," he said seriously. "I was afraid that she didn't love me. And, being proud and stubborn is, unfortunately, not a trait limited to the Westerfields. We Barclays have more than our share of it, I'm sorry to admit. Anyway, I was afraid she would reject my love because I wasn't born to riches, and because she could have her pick of anyone she wanted and a hundred other excuses I kept coming up with.

"Truthfully, I had just decided that I was going to ride out to your place and tell her how I feel and ask her to marry me when you decided to lock me in here."

"I'm glad to hear that, Fowler. I, ah, guess I owe you an apology for the things I said when we were taking Linc Travis to Austin. Nolie and I have always been close. And I guess I was just being overly protective of my sister. I apologize and welcome you to the family," Nick said sincerely. "You'll be good for Nolie. She needs a strong hand to rule her. Grandpa and Dad spoiled her rotten. She thinks she can do anything a man can do."

"Apology accepted, Nick. And you're right. Nichole is a very headstrong woman. Which brings up a good question."

"What's that?"

"Nichole obviously didn't intend for me to know about the baby or she wouldn't have left town without even telling me. So what makes you think she's going to agree to marry me now just because I know?"

"Hmmm, I see what you mean." Nick rose to his feet and started pacing back and forth across the room as he thought out loud. "She's going to be furious when she finds out who kidnapped her. And, that we told you about the baby."

Nick stopped his pacing and looked at Fowler. "We'll just have to work out a plan to convince her that she has no choice but to go through with the marriage tonight. Then, before she can have it annulled, it's going to be up to you to convince her that you love her and wanted to marry her even before you knew about the baby."

Fowler nodded his head in agreement. "I have a plan, but it's going to require a little more help from Cody and Carmen."

Fowler explained his plan, and Nick agreed that it was the only way to handle the situation.

Chapter Twenty

As Fowler and Nick waited for the rest of the "wedding party" to arrive, they talked about their future plans.

Nick had released Fowler from his cell and the two now sat with their feet propped up on Fowler's desk, sipping whiskey from a bottle Fowler kept stashed in the bottom desk drawer.

"What are your plans, after you convince Nichole not to annul the marriage? Will you keep your post as a marshal?"

Fowler swished the amber liquid around the sides of his glass thoughtfully. "No. I'll resign my post as soon as the president can send a replacement." He looked up at Nick. "What you said on the trail was correct. Nichole deserves to have a man she can count on to be around to help raise all the children I hope we'll have."

He took another sip of the smooth liquid. "What I'd really like to do is find a piece of land that I can afford and start a horse ranch. I've always wanted to raise and train race horses. Even as a small boy, I'd sneak away from my father to watch the races whenever I could."

Fowler chuckled as he remembered his father's consternation. "My father's a preacher," he explained. "And a horse race is not the place that a preacher's son is suppose to be. But I'd do it anyway, and Dad would catch me every time. And every time he'd make me memorize Bible verses as my punishment. I'd wager that I could recite the entire Bible from front to back by the time I was fourteen years old!"

Nick looked at Fowler in surprise. "How in the world did a preacher's son come to be a lawman? Somehow that's not exactly the background I'd have expected to be conducive to gaining your unmistakable skills with a gun."

Fowler shrugged his shoulders. "It just happened. Don't get me wrong, Dad's never been a coward. He firmly believes that God helps those who help themselves, so he wouldn't hesitate to kill someone who was a danger to him or his family, but he's probably one of the kindest, gentlest men you'd ever meet. He understood that his way wasn't right for everyone, even for the son of a preacher man. So, he helps people his way. I do it my way."

Nick threw back the rest of his drank and poured another. "Are you planning to go back to Tennessee to start your horse ranch?"

"No, there's too many people back home. I like this

part of Texas. There's room to breathe and grow here. And I guess it is still untamed enough to appeal to the wild streak in me."

Fowler finished his drink and tipped his chair back on two legs. "I hope to find a piece of land around this area that I can afford and still have some money left to buy a couple of good stallions and a few good brood mares. Even then, it'll be four or five years before I could turn a good profit."

Nick smiled. He was pleased that his sister wouldn't have to move away from the family.

"Well, I know where you can get a fairly large chunk of prime grazing land complete with a river running through it. And I'll guarantee that the price is right."

Fowler's chair hit the floor with a thud as he sat up to hear more about Nick's find. "Where is this land? How much is it? Who owns it?"

"Next to mine. A dollar a year. And Nichole owns it. Or at least she will after ya'll say your 'I do's.'" Nick grinned from ear to ear at the confused look on Fowler's face.

"Huh?" Fowler decided that Nick had had more whiskey than his brain could handle. He stuck the cork back in the bottle and dropped it into the desk drawer, shutting it firmly. "Maybe we'd better have some coffee to sober you up."

Nick laughed. "I'm not drunk, Fowler. Let me explain."

"I wish you would because you haven't said anything that makes sense yet."

"Last year Grandpa Montclair turned eighty years old. He has more money than he and Lottie could spend if they live to be a hundred and eighty, plus his ranch, the Lazy M, is as big as Dad's. He's always planned to divide his estate equally between his seven great-grandchildren. He's actually Mother's grandfather but we've always called him Grandpa," he explained.

"Anyway, last year at his birthday party, he announced that instead of having to wait until his death to receive our inheritance, he had decided that as each of us married, we would receive our share of the land as a wedding present from him and Lottie.

"That way the newlyweds would have a place to start building their future together. Each couple is to pay one dollar a year to lease the land until Grandpa's death, at which time we get full title. In the mean time, the land is ours to do with as we want. Carmen and I staked out the spot where we'll build our house as soon as fall roundup is over."

Fowler's mouth was hanging open. He couldn't believe his ears! "That's . . . that's incredible. I can't believe—"

"Wait," Nick interrupted. "There's more."

"More?"

Nick nodded his head. "Since Dad intends to divide his ranch, the Rocking W, among all of us kids upon his death, and with the two ranches adjoining, Dad and Grandpa combined the acreage of *both* ranches and mapped out the entire area, designating the boundaries for seven equal parcels of land.

"Since all of the land is prime land, and the Brazos River meanders through both ranches, all they had to do was divide it in such a manner that each parcel has a part of the river running through it."

Fowler was so stunned, he sat for a full minute before he could even begin to utter a coherent thought. "I'm—I'm flabbergasted to say the least." He shook his head as if to clear his brain. "At your grandfather's age, I can kind of understand his thinking on the matter, but, Nick, your father is still a youthful man. How could he even consider giving away parts of his ranch at his age?"

Nick understood Fowler's astonishment. "They had that all figured out, too. You're right, of course. Dad's not ready to start giving away his land now. But it didn't make much sense for each kid to have two separate pieces of land. So this is the way they set it up. The first parcel starts on the back side of Grandpa's land, and the last parcel ends on the front side of Dad's land.

"Since Cody is the oldest son, Dad's homestead should rightfully go to him. So that section is Cody's. Then, starting at the back of Grandpa's and swinging around, by the time the younger boys get married, Dad figures he'll be too old to work the ranch and will be glad to turn it over to them."

Fowler shook his head. He was dumbfounded. "I still can't believe it."

Nick agreed. "Neither could Cody, Nichole, or I when Grandpa first came up with the idea. I doubt that the younger kids even understand it yet."

Fowler suddenly jumped to his feet and started pacing as thoughts began to rush through his mind. "Do you know what this means?" He didn't wait for Nick's answer. "It means that we can use all the money I've saved to buy more brood mares instead of having to buy land. That way we can get our horse ranch going a lot faster and we still won't have to cut corners too closely in the meantime."

Just as suddenly, he stopped his pacing and looked at Nick. "You have no idea how it galled me to think that I would have to ask Nichole to do without things until our ranch could start making money. Every time I thought about it, it almost made me sick to my stomach," he admitted honestly.

Nick understood Fowler's feelings, even if they were misguided. "Fowler, I know my sister. There's not a doubt in my mind that Nolie would live in a one-room shanty and wear rags as long as she knew that you loved her. Don't underestimate her. She's stronger than she looks. She'll work side by side with you to help build a future."

"I know that, Nick. But no real man wants to feel that he isn't doing right by the woman he loves."

Just then, they heard a knock on the jail door. Nick's eyes met Fowler's.

"Well, Fowler, it's time to start laying the ground work for that future."

Fowler walked into the cell he had previously been locked in and heard Nick lock it behind him again.

Nick replaced his black hood, then opened the jail door and stepped outside.

After whispering something to the slim figure who held a gun on the preacher, Nick opened the door and motioned for them to enter. "Sorry to drag you out so late at night, Reverend, but as they say, there's a time and a place for everything. Well, now's the time and this is the place."

Reverend Dixon quickly looked around the room. He felt his first sense of alarm when he saw Marshal

Barclay on the wrong side of the bars. He clutched his Bible tightly to his chest as he approached the cell.

"Marshal, what is going on here?"

Before the marshal could answer, another knock sounded on the door.

Nichole estimated that it had been close to an hour since she had heard two of her kidnappers ride away. The one left behind to guard her had not been unkind to her, only uncommunicative.

Shortly after the others had ridden away, he had briefly removed her gag and pressed a canteen of water to her lips, indicating that she should drink.

After drinking all she wanted, she tried to ask what he planned to do with her, but he quickly replaced the gag.

Since that time, she had not heard any movement from the man until he had tugged in an upward motion on her arm, indicating that she should stand up.

He helped her to mount her horse, then set a leisurely pace when they started moving again.

It couldn't have been more than fifteen or twenty minutes before Nichole began to hear sounds that clearly attested to the fact that they were nearing a town. But which town was the question.

Another five minutes passed before her horse was again halted and she was helped down. She was led a few steps away from her horse and then stopped. She could definitely hear the sounds of a saloon.

The thought crossed her mind that all saloons must be alike, because the music coming from that twangy piano was as offkey as the piano in the saloon in Waco.

They paused only a few seconds before they turned a corner, walked a few more steps, and stopped.

Nichole heard her captor knock on a door. She heard the door open and heard some whispering take place before she was led into a building. The door was closed and locked behind her.

She heard a man's voice gasp. "Now see here! Enough is enough!

The voice sounded vaguely familiar to her.

"Marshal, isn't there anything you can do to stop this?" the voice pleaded.

Marshal? What the hell was going on here? she wondered as she felt hands untying the blindfold and gag. She squinted against the light as her eyes tried to focus.

"Miss Westerfield!" the familiar voice exclaimed.

"Reverend Dixon?" Her vision was beginning to clear as she looked around the room. When she saw Fowler, she took a couple of steps in his direction before one of the hooded men stopped her with his gun.

"Fowler! Oh my God!" It suddenly dawned on her that Fowler was *behind* the bars of the jail cell.

Both Fowler and Reverend Dixon were being held at gun point. They were prisoners just as she was!

"Can't you see that the lady is upset? What harm would it cause to let her come over here by me?" Fowler shook the locked cell door. "It's plainly obvious that I am not in a position to help her."

The man holding the gun on her hesitated before motioning her toward the cell.

Nichole ran to Fowler. With her hands tied, she

couldn't reach through the bars, but Fowler pulled her to him as best he could.

"Shush," he crooned as Nichole suddenly burst into tears. "It's going to be all right. They're not going to hurt us if we do as they wish."

Nichole's fear and frustration at being in a situation that she had no control over finally got the best of her. She had been brave and not shown any fear up to this point in the ordeal, but now, she was fresh out of being brave.

"Now, now. Nichole, calm down before you make yourself sick. It's going to be okay," Fowler assured her as he patted her back.

One of the kidnappers pressed a handkerchief into her hand as she sobbed.

Reverend Dixon saw the three hooded people look at each other before the smaller one, the one who had brought him to the jail, offered the handkerchief to Nichole. What a strange thing for a kidnapper to do, he thought.

When Nichole regained her composure, she whispered to Fowler, "Who are these people? What do they want with us?"

Since the reverend had not been told anything either, he was wondering the same thing.

"Well, considering the fact that we have a preacher, a man, and a woman, that indicates to me that there's going to be a wedding," he stated.

Nichole wiped her eyes with the dainty handkerchief. "Wedding?" she repeated.

The word didn't seem to register with her. So Fowler tried again. "Nichole, love, I think you and I are about to become man and wife." He looked at Nichole to see if that registered with her.

Nichole was looking at the handkerchief in her hand as if she'd never seen one before. She held it to her nose and sniffed.

Perfume? She sniffed again to be sure. The dainty cloth smelled like—perfume! Fowler's words seemed to have clicked in her mind at the same instant that she recognized the fragrance on the handkerchief.

She suddenly pulled free from Fowler. He could tell from the look in her eyes that all hell was fixing to break loose. For the first time that night, he was glad he was on the *other* side of the bars.

Holding her hands up, her calm voice belied the rage beginning to boil within her. "Untie my hands, please."

Fowler complied with her request, wondering what she was about to do. He didn't have long to wait.

Nichole whirled so fast that it startled Reverend Dixon. He took a step back from her as she looked from one to the other of the three hooded people.

"Married, is it?" Before anyone could react, she reached over and grabbed the hood from the person nearest her.

Carmen's long dark brown hair came tumbling down about her shoulders.

Reverend Dixon gasped. A woman! He had been taken at gun point from his church by a woman! And not just any woman at that but Nichole's sister-in-law.

As Cody and Nick both removed their hoods and the reverend recognized them, he was more confused than ever. "Would someone please tell me what is going on?" he implored.

Nichole whirled on the reverend. "I'll tell you what is going on. These three . . . traitors think they are going to force me to wed the marshal!" She turned and advanced on Nick.

"Now, Nolie." Nick tried to calm his sister.

"Don't you 'now, Nolie' me! You—you rat!" She whirled on Carmen. "And, you! You of all people to betray me. How could you? I thought you were my friend. I thought you understood more than anyone else, how I felt about this."

Cody decided that he'd better take control of the situation. Bad decision on his part. He hadn't taken more than two steps in her direction before he was backing up again.

"And you, Cody Steven Westerfield!" Nichole had spun on her heel and was advancing on Cody, shaking her finger at him as she advanced. "How dare you let them do such a thing to me! Do you have any idea how frightened I was? And what about that poor family on the stage? How could you do this to me? And to them? And to Reverend Dixon? Damn you, Cody!" Nichole was so mad, she was almost yelling by the time she had finished raking the three of them over the coals.

"Don't cuss, Nichole, it's not ladylike. Sorry, Reverend," Cody apologized to the preacher. "She's just a little . . . distraught. You know how it is with nervous brides."

"Not ladylike! Now's a hell of a time to be worrying about my reputation! After what you three have pulled, I won't be able to show my face in this town for the rest of my life! Does everybody in town know about this little charade or just half the county?" she raged.

Fowler had watched and listened to Nichole's ranting and raving with amusement. She certainly was a little spitfire, that was for sure. But he was afraid that she was getting herself so worked up that it might be harmful to her and their baby.

"Nick, unlock this door and let me out," he stated. "Nichole, calm down. Nobody but the people in this room know that anything is going on."

Something in his tone told her that Fowler had played a part in this fiasco.

"Nick! Don't you dare unlock that door. And just what part did you play in this little charade, Fowler?" she snapped as she walked toward him.

He decided to plead innocent until she calmed down. "Me? I'm an innocent bystander."

"Ha! Innocent my a—"

"Nichole!"

"Hind leg," she amended in deference to Reverend Dixon's presence.

Fowler's temper was beginning to simmer. Enough was enough already! "Nick, the keys," he demanded.

"Nick! Don't you dare!" she countered.

Nick looked from Nichole to Fowler. Of the two, he decided he'd rather face his sister's wrath than Fowler's. Besides, he was anxious to finish what they'd come there for. Then his sister would be Fowler's problem.

Nichole glared at Nick as he approached the cell door with the keys before she spun around on her heel and headed for the front door. Cody blocked her way.

"Where do you think you're going?" Cody asked.

Nichole took a deep breath and exhaled slowly trying to calm herself. "I am going to spend the night at the hotel. And tomorrow I am going to get on the stage and continue my journey away from this place."

Fowler, freed from the cell, advanced on Nichole and taking her arm pulled her over to stand in front of the preacher. "No, you're not." He slowly emphasized each word. "You are going to stop acting like a spoiled brat and marry me. Now."

"I am not acting like a spoiled brat and I am not going to marry you!" She tried in vain to pull free from Fowler's hold.

"Yes, you are," he stated autocratically.

"No, I'm not. Let go of me!" she insisted as she tried harder to pull free from his hold.

"I am not going to let go of you. Not now, not ever." Fowler looked at the preacher. "Okay, Reverend Dixon. You can start the ceremony now."

"No, you can't!" Nichole shouted at the preacher. "Aren't you listening to me, Fowler? I'll say it slow so you can understand. I will not marry you." She turned to the preacher. "You can go, Reverend Dixon. There is *not* going to be a wedding. Not now, not ever."

"Stay where you are, Preacher," Fowler commanded.

Reverend Dixon didn't know whether to stay or to leave. He had performed a couple of what were commonly known as "shotgun" weddings, where a father had to convince a reluctant groom of the merits of marriage to his daughter.

But this was the first time he'd ever been asked to perform a wedding where the bride was the one being held by shotgun and in jail to boot!

He pulled at his shirt collar as if it were too tight

and cleared his throat. "Ahem, this is most irregular. If the lady does not wish to wed, I think—"

"Shut up!" Fowler and Nichole shouted at the same time before returning to their face off.

"Now you listen to me, my little spitfire," Fowler warned in a strong, steady voice. "You are going to stop this nonsense and marry me right now. Because if you don't"—Fowler lowered his voice to whisper for Nichole's ears only—"I am going to tell the whole town about that cute little birthmark on the left cheek of your pretty little behind."

Nichole's face flamed scarlet. "You—you wouldn't dare! You des–despicable—" she sputtered.

"Yes, I would dare. I will not permit you to deny me my fatherly rights. I swear I'll follow you wherever you go and hound you until you do what is right," he whispered again.

If looks could kill, Nichole would have been a widow before she was a bride. She glared at Fowler as her mind debated whether he really would do what he had threatened.

Fowler turned around to address the preacher, who was still pulling at his tight collar. "By the way, Reverend Dixon, did you know that—"

Nichole sucked in her breath. He would! "Stop!" she shouted. "You win."

"My father is a preacher, too?" Fowler continued smoothly.

The reverend looked from Fowler back to Nichole clearly puzzled at the turn of conversation. "Ah . . . no, I . . . ah . . . didn't know that."

Fowler smiled as he put his arm around Nichole and drew her closer to him. "I believe you can start the ceremony now, Reverend."

The reverend was not the only one puzzled at what Fowler had said to cause Nichole's sudden change of mind. Nick and Carmen looked at each other, then at Cody who shrugged his shoulders in an I-don't-know manner.

"Smile, darling, or the good preacher here might not think you're sincere."

Nichole glared at Fowler. "Don't press your luck, Barclay. Just because I'm marrying you doesn't mean I have to like it!" she snapped testily.

"Miss Westerfield, if you don't, ah, what I mean is . . ." Reverend Dixon saw Fowler raise his eyebrow at him and decided real quick that it might be a good idea for him to just get on with the business at hand. "Ah, yes, well. Dearly beloved, we are gathered here today to join this man and this woman in holy matrimony. Do you, Fowler Barclay, take this woman to be your lawfully wedded wife, to have and to hold, in sickness and in health, until death do you part?"

Fowler looked at the woman standing beside him and answered in a firm voice, "I do."

"Do you, Nichole Westerfield, take this man to be your lawfully wedded husband, to love, honor and obey him, in sickness and in health, until death do you part?"

"No!"

"What?" the preacher croaked.

"Say I do, Nichole," Fowler warned ominously.

Nichole's chin jutted out as she looked defiantly down her nose at Fowler. "I refuse to promise to obey you. Take that out," she demanded of the preacher.

"But . . ." the preacher started to protest.

Fowler waved his objection away. "Take the word

'obey' out, she wouldn't do it anyway," Fowler acknowledged, his eyes twinkling with amusement. Of one thing he was absolutely positive: Life with Nichole would never be boring.

Reverend Dixon repeated his question, leaving out 'obey' and held his breath as he waited for her answer.

Nichole looked at the five pairs of eyes trained on her. She had chilly-dipped and stalled as long as she could. Sighing in defeat, she gave a less than enthusiastic reply. "I guess I do, since I don't seem to have any choice in the matter."

"Then I pronounce you man and wife," the preacher hurriedly proclaimed before she had a chance to change her mind. "You may kiss the bride." *If you're brave enough*, he thought.

Fowler was brave enough, all right. He pulled Nichole into his arms and laid a kiss on her that made her tingle all the way down to her toes and back again!

When he finally released her to come up for air, she pushed away from him and snapped, "I hate it when you do that!"

Fowler smiled his knowing, lopsided smile. "Liar. You love it when I do that. You just hate to admit it."

"Humph!" she snorted as she tried to push past him. She knew that if she was to resist his male magnetism, she'd have to put as much distance between them as possible. Things had certainly not gone as she had planned, so now she needed to be by herself to do some serious thinking.

If Fowler loved her, she'd be the happiest person in the world. But that was not the case. She knew the only reason he'd married her was because he'd either been forced to by her brothers, or from his sense of responsibility to the baby she carried. Either way, he'd married her because of the baby, not because he felt anything for her.

Tears of depression and disappointment lingered just below the surface. She desperately wanted to remove herself from the presence of the people surrounding her before she disgraced herself by crying and lost what little pride she had left.

"Where do you think you're going?" Fowler demanded.

"I am going to the hotel. It is late and I am tired. Good-bye," she stated primly as she again tried to side-step him and leave.

Fowler's jaw tensed with his barely controlled anger. "You are not going anywhere until we get a few things straight between us, *Mrs.* Barclay."

Snapping green eyes did battle with steel-blue eyes, neither giving an inch. "I think we have said all that needs to be said, *Mr.* Barclay!" Nichole, with her hands planted firmly on her hips, stood her ground. "I do not have anything more to say to you."

"Good! Because I have a lot of things to say to you. And you are going to hear me out."

"Get out of my way," she insisted again.

"Nope." He shook his head. "Not until we have a heart-to-heart talk."

Too late, Nichole saw his intent. Fowler stooped down and, catching her behind the back of her knees, hoisted her up and slung her over his shoulder like a sack of flour. He turned around to thank the minister for his services.

"Thank you, Reverend Dixon, for coming here on such short notice. Nick, if you'll take care of the preacher, I'd like a word in private with my wife."

"No!" Nichole shrieked. "Reverend, don't leave," she entreated. "Fowler, you put me down this instant!" She kicked her feet and pummeled his broad back to no avail.

Fowler whacked Nichole's backside as he admonished, "Behave yourself, wife, or you're going to make the good preacher think we're not a happily married couple."

"Nicky! Cody! Somebody make this . . . brute put me down!" she wailed as Fowler turned and walked toward the cell at the farthest end of the jail where they would have the most privacy should anyone enter the front door.

Seeing the preacher's worried frown, Nick hastened to assure the man that everything would work out. "Don't worry, Reverend. Those two love each other like a pig loves his mud hole. They just forgot to tell each other. I'm sure they'll work things out before the night is over."

The reverend was still uneasy about the whole thing. "Well, if you say so."

After paying the preacher and ushering him out the door, Cody turned to face Nick and Carmen. All three could hear the loud shouting match taking place at the back of the jail. "Do you think one of us needs to go referee those two?"

Picking up the keys to the cell, Nick shook his head. "No. I think Fowler can handle things without any more help from us."

Carmen, as well as Cody, could tell by the mischievous grin on Nick's face that he was up to something. When he put his finger to his lips and then tiptoed quietly to the back cell, they were positive he was up to something.

"Nicky," Carmen whispered when he returned, "what did you do?"

Nick grinned roguishly before blowing out the lamp. "Just making sure that neither one of them can leave until they work out their problems. Come on, let's leave the lovebirds to their squawking and go to the hotel."

Carmen drew her breath in sharply. "You locked them in the cell?"

"Yep."

Cody threw back his head and laughed. "You two have been pulling pranks on each other since you were little tykes, but this is the best one yet."

Nick laughed. "Well, one thing's for sure. By the time morning comes, Nolie will either be ready to string me up by my toenails or love me to pieces for my interfering."

Nichole stood in the middle of the cell with her hands over her ears, determined not to listen to the man she had just married. "I don't want to hear anything you have to say. Just leave me alone."

Fowler, just as determined that she was going to listen to him, grabbed her hands away from her ears and held them to his chest. "Nichole Barclay, you are going to hear me out if I have to tie you down and sit on you!"

Nichole had used up every ounce of strength she possessed. The weeks of worrying had taken their toll on her. The emotional strain of saying good-bye to her family, whom she didn't expect to see for several years, the fright of being kidnapped and the stress of her shotgun wedding were more than she could handle in one day.

Fowler saw the silent tears flood her eyes and spill down her cheeks at the same time he felt her body go limp.

Scooping her up in his arms, he walked over to the cot and sat down. Holding her in his lap, he rocked her back and forth like a baby.

"Oh, honey," he crooned, clutching her head to his shoulder. "Everything's going to be all right. Shush, don't cry, sweetheart, you'll make yourself sick."

Nichole couldn't have stopped crying if her life depended upon it. She buried her head against Fowler's warm neck and sobbed.

Listening as heart-rending sobs wracked her body, Fowler felt as helpless as a newborn babe. It tore his heart out that she hated him so much that she had gone to pieces at the thought of spending the rest of her life with him.

He held her and rocked her until the tears subsided into sniffles. His thoughts were tearing him apart. He loved this woman whom he held in his arms more than life itself.

He wanted the baby she carried—their baby—to grow up knowing its father's love. He wanted to be there each day of its life, to share in the happiness of watching him or her grow up. To be there to hear his child's laughter as he discovered the world. To watch as he took his first steps and to catch him if he fell.

But most of all, he loved Nichole and wanted her

love in return. He and Nick had been so smug in thinking that once they were married, everything else would fall into place.

They had been wrong. You can't force someone to love you. And Fowler wanted Nichole's love most of all. It was obvious that he would never have it, and he loved her too much to hold her against her will.

He knew what he had to do.

"Oh, sweetheart, what have we done? What have we done?" he murmured as he continued to rock her until she was completely quiet in his arms.

He kissed her forehead before leaning her back to peer into her tear-swollen eyes. "It's going to be all right, Nichole. I promise. After . . ." He swallowed past the lump in his throat. "After the baby comes, we'll . . . get a divorce. I'll set you free. We don't have to live together in the meantime. All I ask is that . . . that . . ." God, this was even harder to do than he'd thought. "I . . . I don't want a child of mine to grow up without a name. I couldn't stand the thought of him or her being looked down on as a bastard. Will you grant me this?"

As he looked at her anxiously, he was appalled to see the tears come flooding out of her beautiful emerald-green eyes again. His heart sunk as he realized that she wouldn't even give him that much.

She knew he'd only married her because of the baby. She didn't want his pity, she wanted his love! But he didn't have any love for her, only a sense of honor for the baby they had made. She had never been more miserable in her life. He didn't even want the pretense of a marriage. They would not even share a house together until the baby's arrival. How he must hate her. She couldn't stop crying so she ducked her head and nodded her consent to his request.

Fowler let out the breath he'd been unaware he was holding. At least his child would have his name. There was little else he could do. He had to set her free. He loved her too much to do otherwise.

"Will you tell our child about me?" he asked, his voice shaking with emotion.

"Yes." She dried her eyes, trying to pull herself together. She knew that she'd have to accept what fate handed her and do the best she could. "I'll tell him about his daddy." Her voice cracked as she said "daddy" and the tears started again. She cleared her throat and took a deep breath. "And . . . and I'll not try to turn him against you. I promise."

Fowler was hurting like he'd never hurt before. It felt like a hand had reached inside him and was tearing his guts out. "Will you promise me one more thing?"

She nodded her head.

"Will you promise not to hate me?"

She raised her head and looked into the midnight-blue eyes that she loved so very much. "I could never hate you, Fowler," she declared honestly. "I'm just sorry my brothers dragged you into this and humiliated you. I never meant for that to happen. That's why I wasn't going to tell you about the baby. I knew you'd feel obligated to . . . to marry me."

"Obligated!" He couldn't believe his ears. "You think the only reason I married you was because I felt *obligated*?" He stood up so fast he almost dumped her on the floor before she could get her feet under her. He walked to the cell door, then whirled around and stalked back toward Nichole. He was seething with anger. He had never felt such intense rage before in his entire life!

"Is that what you think? That I married you out of a sense of obligation!" By the time he reached her, he was shouting. "Damn it, woman! Answer me!"

"You don't have to shout. Yes. Yes, I know that's the reason you let them coerce you into marrying me!" She didn't know why, but her temper began to flare at his highhanded tone of voice. "Isn't it?" she demanded, daring him to deny it.

"No!" he shouted so loud the bars rattled. "Good God Almighty! I can't believe what I'm hearing. In case you didn't notice, I was not the one being forced to marry. *You* were. Dammit it, woman! Don't you even know when a man loves you?"

"Wha—what did you say?" Her voice was barely a whisper. She was shaking from head to toe. She couldn't have heard him right.

He placed his hands on each of her arms and held her facing him. "I said, I love you. I . . . love . . . you." He watched her eyes for her reaction to his words.

She pulled out of his grip, turned away, and walked to the back of the cell before spinning around to face him. Her eyes were flashing green sparks when she marched back toward him. "Why the hell didn't you say so!" she demanded angrily as she smacked him in the stomach with her fist.

"Ugh!" he grunted. Her punch had caught him completely off guard. "Why did you do that? And what the hell are you so mad about?"

Shaking her finger in his face, she backed him up until he was against the bars and couldn't go any further. "Do you know how many nights I lay awake agonizing and crying because I didn't think you loved me?" she stormed. "Have you any idea of the torture you've put me through? Knowing how much I love you and thinking you didn't care one whit about me? Can you even begin to imagine how I felt thinking that our child would grow up without knowing his father's love?" Her voice grew calmer as her anger began to subside. "Why didn't you tell me you loved me?" she asked in bewilderment.

Fowler took her into his arms, pressing her head against his chest. "For the same reason you didn't tell me. I was afraid. Afraid, hell! I was terrified that you didn't love me. I had made up my mind that I was going to ask you to marry me and if you said no, then I'd just have to find a way to convince you to say yes."

Nichole snuggled against Fowler's chest. She could feel his heart beating against the side of her face. It was a comforting sound. "Why didn't you ask me, if you had already made up your mind to?"

Fowler laughed. "I had just gotten up my courage to ride out to your place and pop the question. But a funny thing happened on the way to the altar." He paused, waiting for her to ask what happened. She didn't disappoint him.

"What happened?"

"I had a gun stuck in my back and I got kidnapped, *again*." He laughed from deep within his chest. The sound was like a soothing balm to Nichole's frayed nerves.

Nichole nestled closer. "What happened then?"

"After Nick told me why I was being held hostage, I knew I had the solution to my problem of what to do if you said no. That's why I decided to go along with their plans for our wedding. I just didn't realize how it would look to you."

He held her away from him so he could look at her. "I really do love you, sweetheart. I think I must have loved you from the very beginning. I just didn't know it at the time. I'm not a poet, darling. I don't know how to say all the flowery words women like to hear. But believe me when I tell you that I love you with all my heart."

She stood on her tiptoes and kissed him with all her love shining in her eyes. "I don't need pretty words, darling. You've said the only three words that really count." Looking deep into his eyes, she declared. "I love you and I will love you through all eternity."

They kissed with a hunger born from the knowledge that they had come so close to losing something very, very precious and special.

"Well, now that we've got all that cleared up, I have a suggestion, Mrs. Barclay." His voice was husky with desire.

"Oh, what have you got in mind, Mr. Barclay?" She could feel his elongated hardness pressing against her stomach, throbbing with each beat of his heart.

"Why don't we go to my room at the hotel and make wild, passionate love all night long? After all, it is our wedding night." His hands moved up and down her spine, making her body quiver with each caress.

She giggled with delight. "I'll race you to the bed."

"I'll carry you. I can run faster," he teased as he pushed the cell door to open it.

Nothing happened. He pushed harder, not believing what his hand was telling him. "What the hell! The door's locked."

"No." Nichole tugged at the door with the same result. "Nicky? Cody? Come let us out." No one answered. She hollered again but still no answer. "They've locked us in jail!" she declared disbelievingly. "So help me, I'll wring their necks when I get my hands on them. I'll . . . I'll . . ."

Fowler walked over and sat on the cot, laughing at the absurdity of it all.

"It's not funny, Barclay," she insisted as she pushed and pulled fruitlessly at the cell door before finally giving it an angry kick—which still didn't budge the door and only hurt her foot.

Fowler tried to control his mirth. "Yes, it is, sweetheart. Just think what a story this will be to tell our grandchildren. We spent our wedding night locked in jail!"

Nichole sat beside him, disappointment clearly evident on her face. "It's not fair! I didn't get to have a proper wedding and now I don't even get to have a wedding night."

Fowler leaned over and nuzzled the sensitive spot on her neck just below her ear. "Why not? I doubt that anyone's going to disturb us for the rest of the night. I don't think your brothers will be brave enough to face either one of us until morning."

"Hmmm." His kissing and nuzzling were doing delicious things to her insides. She turned to him, curling her arms around his neck, and lay back on the cot, pulling him down on top of her. "Do you think so?"

She could feel his eager male hardness pulsing as he settled himself between her legs.

"Uh-huh." He slowly unbuttoned each button as

his lips brushed along her neck and down her cleavage. He gently sucked and lapped at her full breasts, circling each tender rosette with his tongue. His mind told him to go slow but his body was impatient for the love he had so badly yearned for in the weeks they were apart.

The roughness of his tongue on her sensitive breasts sent sparks of fire shooting to the very core of her womanhood. She moaned and arched against him, wanting him to fill her with his love and assuage the burning desire that had gone unchecked for so long. She felt as if her body would surely burst into flames from the heat building inside her. She tugged at his belt buckle, anxious to free his hard, hot manhood.

Fowler raised himself and quickly stripped away the clothes that were hindering the urgent melding that their bodies cried out for. When he entered her creamy warmth, he sucked in his breath at the sensation that spread from their joining bodies and flooded his very being. It was nothing short of sheer will power that kept him from spilling his seed at the very instant of his entry.

Nichole could feel the restraint that her lover was fighting so hard to keep, but she too was fighting for control. The instant he impaled her with his hot, swollen manhood, she began to quiver. His hardness made her writhe and arch against him, trying to get even closer as wave after wave of intense sensations flooded her but yet kept her just out of reach of the ultimate serenity of fulfillment.

She twisted her head from side to side in her sweet agony as she felt the flames burn hotter. "Now," she moaned. "Please, now." Her urgent plea sent him plunging deeper into her before he pulled slowly back and then began to thrust faster and even deeper into her welcoming body.

She arched one final time against him and was rewarded with the breath-stealing climax that had been lingering just below the surface. He lost control when he felt her tightening around him as she reached fulfillment. The tiny gripping spasms triggered his own release, sending his seed spewing deep into her womb, and flooding his body with a peacefulness he had never experienced before.

Nichole was awaken by the feel of Fowler gently placing kisses along her neck as he worked his way up to her mouth. She languidly stretched and wrapped her arms around the man she loved.

Sometime in the wee hours of the morning, after they were happily exhausted from their hours of lovemaking, Fowler suggested that perhaps they should get dressed. He didn't know how early or who would come to let them out of the jail, but he didn't want them to be found naked. He figured he'd have a difficult enough time explaining the circumstances without adding nudity to the list!

"Wake up, my sleepy-headed wife," Fowler whispered as he kissed her again.

Nichole shook her head. "Uh-uh. I want to stay just like this. I'm too comfortable to move," she whispered back, her voice thick with sleep.

"I think we're about to be set free from our cage. If I'm not mistaken, I think I hear your father's voice in the outer office."

"Daddy!" Nichole was instantly awake and looking fearfully at Fowler, praying he was teasing her.

"That's right. Daddy." His voice had a ring of finality about it. "Quick. Kiss me before your father makes you a widow."

Fowler's mouth covered hers before she could reply. Her eyes grew wide in alarm when her father appeared in front of their cell. Fowler felt her stiffen in his arms and knew the time of reckoning had come.

"Daddy!" Nichole squeaked.

"Good morning, sir," Fowler said nonchalantly.

Mark didn't say a word to the couple sitting in the middle of the rumpled cot. He simply unlocked the door and motioned them into the outer office.

Nichole walked ahead of Fowler until she reached the intended destination. She stopped dead in her tracks when she came face to face with her entire family. Every single one of them was there! Even Grandpa, Lottie, and Maria.

Nichole groaned and turned to bury her flaming face in Fowler's chest.

This was worse than Fowler had expected. "Sir, I can explain—"

"Never mind. Nick and Cody have already explained the, ah, circumstances of your *elopement*," Mark emphasized the word, looking Fowler directly in the eyes to make sure the young man understood his meaning.

Fowler understood his intentions but he still didn't know what his father-in-law had planned. He eyed him skeptically. "Then you're not angry that we, ah, eloped?"

"Angry!" Mark roared. "Hell, yes, I'm angry! I didn't get to attend my son's wedding and I'll be dammed if I'll be cheated out of giving my daughter away." He looked Fowler square in the eyes. "Young man, you have one hour to get shaved, to change clothes, and to meet my daughter at the front of the church. Is that clear?"

"Yes, sir." Fowler wasn't about to press his luck. He gave Nichole a quick smack on the lips, and headed for his room at the hotel.

"Cassie, you and Maria help Nichole get ready. The rest of you, come with me," he ordered briskly. "One hour, not a minute more," he reiterated.

"Yes, dear." Cassie smiled sweetly at her husband.

For the first time, Nichole noticed that her mother was holding the dress that she had worn when she had married Nichole's father. Tears sprang quickly to her eyes. She had always dreamed of being married in her mother's wedding dress and now it seemed that her dream was going to come true.

Reverend Dixon looked up from his papers as the commotion started at the back of the church. When he saw Mark Westerfield striding purposefully toward him with Cody and Nick close behind, he turned his eyes toward heaven and groaned, "Oh, no, not again. Lord, you are sorely testing this poor servant of yours." He wasn't sure whether he was to be kidnapped again or hung. He breathed a great sigh of relief when Mark explained his plans to him.

Exactly one hour later, dressed in her mother's wedding gown, Nichole walked down the aisle of the church on her father's arm.

Texas Woman

Fowler stood proudly at the end of the aisle, waiting to receive his beautiful bride.

News of the wedding traveled fast. The church was nearly filled, but neither Nichole nor Fowler was aware of anyone but each other.

If anyone noticed that Reverend Dixon stumbled over the word 'obey' and then glanced quickly at Nichole, who giggled and at Fowler, who smiled knowingly, they never said a word.

Epilogue

January, 1870

"Where the hell is he? What's taking him so long?" Nick paced from one window to the other to peer out into the frozen darkness. "He should have been back by now."

Mark shook his head, thinking back to the seven times, no make that eight times, that the varnish had been worn off the floor between the two front windows as an anxious father-to-be moved from one to the other, looking for the doctor.

His father had been the first to mark the original path on the day of Mark's birth, and Mark had added to it with the impending birth of each of his children. After the doctor arrived, the path would extend to the doorway as the nervous father would repeatedly walk to the door and look up the stairway as if he expected to see his newborn slide down the banister at any moment!

Now it was Nick's turn to make the journey, while Mark remained calm and issued the time-honored sage advice just as his father had.

He sat back in his chair and steepled his fingers, watching as the harried father made yet another trip to the windows.

"Calm down, Nick. Everything is going to be fine. Cody and Doc Stu should be here soon. The heavy snowfall during the night is probably slowing them down a bit. They'll make it, don't worry."

Fear etched Nick's face. "You don't suppose . . ." Nick whirled and walked to the door as footsteps sounded on the stairway.

Nichole walked or rather waddled into the library. For weeks the family had been watching every move she and Carmen made. Everyone including Maria—and she was rarely wrong—expected Nichole to deliver before Carmen did because she had grown almost twice as large as Carmen in her last few weeks.

But it appeared that Carmen and Nick would have the honor of presenting the first grandchild.

"What's happening? Is Carmen all right? Is the baby here? What are you doing down here? Where's Mother?" Nick plied his sister with questions, not stopping to give her time to answer.

Her brother's nervousness made her smile. She wondered if Fowler would turn into a mass of quivering jelly when her time came. She placed her hand to the small of her back to ease the ache that had been plaguing her since shortly after Carmen had gone into labor.

She shook her head at her brother. "For heaven's sake, Nicky. Will you calm down? Carmen is doing fine. No, the baby's not here. Mother is with Carmen, and I came down to see if Fowler was back from checking on our horses yet."

The two young couples had joined the family for dinner at their parents' house the evening before, and had been caught by surprise when a blustery blue norther blew in, bringing a heavy snowfall with it.

Mark and Cassie had convinced the young people to stay the night and make the return trip to their own ranches in the daylight. With both women in the last days of their pregnancies, Fowler and Nick agreed that it would be safer to wait until morning. But during the wee hours of the morning, Carmen had gone into labor.

Nichole walked over and parted the curtains to look out, shaking her head in disgust. "Can you believe this? We hardly ever have this much snow. Naturally it'd wait until *this* winter to dump six inches on us," she bemoaned.

"Don't take it personally, sweetheart," Fowler said as he entered the hallway, shaking the snow off his hat and removing his overcoat before walking over to wrap his arms around his rotund wife. "I doubt that old man winter takes any notice of soon-to-be mothers when he decides to decorate the land." He kissed her upturned lips as he patted her protruding abdomen. "How's my kid?"

"Your kid is giving me a backache. How are our brood mares?" she countered.

"The mares are fine. Are you in pain?"

"Unfortunately, no." She rubbed her back again.

"I've been bending over bathing Carmen's face. My back's just sore. Nothing to worry about," she assured him.

Mark glanced at his daughter and smiled a knowing smile. He had heard that same remark from his wife shortly before she had gone into labor with Cody. He smiled to himself, thinking that by this time tomorrow, he'd have two grandchildren.

"How is Carmen?" Fowler inquired.

"She's doing fine." She glanced at her brother who was again making his rounds between the windows. "Why don't you see if you can calm Nicky down? He's going to be a basket case by the time his baby arrives."

Nick suddenly lunged for the door. "He's here!" He jerked the door open and nearly dragged the doctor off his horse and into the house. "You took your sweet loving time getting here, Doc!" he castigated.

"Good heavens, Nick. At least let me shake some of this snow off me. Maria will take the broom to my backside if I track up her clean floor," Doctor Gregory chided good-naturedly. Being well experienced with anxious first-time fathers-to-be, he wasn't the least bit offended by Nick's abrupt attitude. "Hello, Mark, Fowler." He nodded to each man as he removed his wet coat.

Nick grabbed the coat out of his hand, and thrust it at Fowler. "You don't have time for pleasantries. My wife's having a baby," Nick tensely asserted. "Do something."

Doctor Stewart Gregory rolled his eyes skyward and shook his head before turning to Nichole. "When did the pains start and how far apart are they now?"

Nichole started up the stairs as she answered, "They started about four hours ago, but they are still about ten minutes apart, her—" Nichole stopped talking when she noticed that Doc Stu had turned around to face Nick, who was following them up the stairs.

Doc Stu gave Nick his sternest look. "Nick, wait for me in the library. I'll come back down and talk to you in a few minutes."

Carmen looked expectantly at the doctor after his examination. "Well, is everything okay?" she asked anxiously.

Doc Stu patted her hand and smiled understandingly. "You're doing just fine, Carmen. The baby's doing its part, but I'm afraid it is still going to be awhile yet," he said apologetically as he saw her grimace as another contraction overcame her. "This part isn't much fun, is it?" She shook her head in agreement with him. "Well, if it's any consolation to you . . ." He chuckled as he turned toward Nichole. He knew that the family had been taking bets on which woman would have her baby first. "You're ahead of Nichole."

The words had hardly left his mouth when Nichole reached out to clutch the bedpost as her skirts and the floor were suddenly drenched with water.

Her face twisted in pain as she tried to smile. "I'm not too sure about that, Doctor."

Cassie and Maria helped Nichole to the closest chair. "Nolie, are you all right?" her mother inquired.

Nichole looked at her sister-in-law in sympathy.

"Sorry, Carmen. I don't mean to infringe on your special day, however . . ." She had to pause as another, even harder pain consumed her. "I don't think I'm going to have much choice in the matter," she acknowledged humorously.

"Maria, we may have our hands full," the doctor commented. "I'll go talk to Fowler and Nick, while you help Nichole change into a nightgown and get settled in bed. Then I'll take a look at her."

Nick was looking up the stairs as Doc Stu left Carmen's room. When he saw the doctor, he took the steps two at a time to meet him. "How's Carmen? Is the baby okay?" he asked anxiously.

"Carmen is fine and the baby is fine, but it's still going to be awhile yet, Nick." He looked at the worried young man. "Actually, Carmen is in better shape than you are."

By this time they had entered the library where Mark and Fowler were in deep conversation. They both looked up at him expectantly.

"Nick, there is one thing you can do to help," the doctor suggested.

"What?" Nick jumped at the chance to do something, anything. He had only briefly talked to his wife before the women had hustled him out of the bedroom with orders to stay out. "What can I do?"

"Get two glasses and pour them about half full of your dad's best bourbon."

Nick hurried to the liquor cabinet to do the doctor's bidding.

Mark and Fowler smiled knowingly at each other. They both knew what the good doctor was up to.

Nick fixed the two glasses and handed them to Doc

Stu. "Are you sure it's all right for Carmen to drink this now?" he asked, a frown making deep creases in his brow.

"Oh, these aren't for Carmen." He took one of the glasses and handed it to Fowler. "They are for you and Fowler. It's going to be a close race to see which one is the daddy and which is the uncle first," he explained.

This statement brought Fowler and Mark to their feet. "What?"

Fowler looked momentarily alarmed. "You mean Nichole is . . . is . . ."

Doctor Gregory nodded his head, grinning as Fowler's smug, confident look rapidly changed to the look of an anxious father.

Mark shook with laughter. "That sounds like something Nichole would do. Even when it comes to having babies, she's not about to let Nick get ahead of her."

Fowler tossed back his drink, his hand not quite steady as he placed the empty glass on Mark's desk. "Can I go up and see my wife?"

"Yes, but only for a few minutes." He turned to face Mark as Fowler vaulted up the stairs. "Seems like you and I both are going to have our hands full."

Fowler sat on the side of the bed and enfolded Nichole's small cold hand in his large warm one as he searched her face worriedly. She squeezed it and smiled lovingly at him. "Don't look so worried, darling. We'll be"—she bit her lip as she waited for the painful contraction to subside—"fine. Before long you'll get to hold your son in your arms," she assured him.

He smiled. "It might be a girl, you know. If so, I know she'll be as beautiful as her mother." He felt her grip tighten on his hand again as another pain wracked her body. He lifted her head and held her against his chest until she could catch her breath. "Oh, sweetheart, I wish I could take the pain for you," he whispered into her hair as he felt her tense with yet another pain.

This time when she was able to catch her breath, she smiled wanly at him and joked, "I wish you could, too. This is not fun." Another pain, the strongest one yet, hit her. "I think you better get Doc Stu up here," she gasped.

Fowler looked at her in alarm. "What's wrong! Has something gone wrong?"

Nichole could only shake her head as the pains were coming so fast she hardly had time to catch her breath between them.

Fowler rushed to the door, yanking it open to shout for Doc Stu just as the doctor stepped into the room. He took one look at Nichole and ordered Fowler to send Maria in and then wait in the library with Mark and Nick.

"Well, young lady, you don't waste any time once you decide to do something, do you?" Doc Stu observed as he washed his hands with the hot water Maria had just left there for him.

Three anxious men paced the library as the minutes ticked by.

Luckily for the doctor, Nichole was in the room next to Carmen's. Nick's baby seemed to have decided that it was time for its entrance into the world, too. For the next thirty minutes, which seemed like hours to the three pacing men, Doc Stu alternated from one room to the other.

Each time a door opened and closed, the men stopped in their tracks to listen. When they heard the other door open and close, they continued their pacing.

Suddenly, a quietness settled over the house. All three men sensed it at the same time. It was like the lull before a storm. They halted in their tracks and listened intently.

A small, angry little cry severed the silence. Before the men could reach the doorway, Cassie hollered down, "It's a boy!" and then a door slammed shut.

Nick and Fowler looked at each other and repeated the joyous words simultaneously. "A boy! It's a boy!"

As it dawned on them that they didn't know which one of them had a boy, another little cry rent the air.

They stood in suspended animation, waiting for the verdict.

This time Cassie and Maria called out at the same time, "It's a girl! It's a boy!" and two doors slammed shut.

Mark looked at his son and son-in-law. "A grandson and a granddaughter." He beamed proudly.

Fowler and Nick, clearly puzzled, looked at each other then at Mark. "But which is which?" they asked almost simultaneously.

When they heard soft footsteps descending the stairway, they charged the door.

Cassie looked at the two anxious faces.

"Well?" they asked in unison.

Cassie looked from one face to the other then said, "You both have a son, and, Fowler, you have a daughter."

Fowler was having a little trouble comprehending what his mother-in-law was saying. "Well, what do I have, a boy or a girl?" he demanded.

"Both. And they are beautiful. All three of them are beautiful." Tears ran down Cassie's face as Mark hugged her to him. "We have three gorgeous little grandbabies."

Fowler, in a state of shock, sat down on the stairway with a thud. "Twins? I . . . we . . . have twins?" He couldn't believe what he had heard. He had a boy *and* a girl!

Mark hugged his wife as he laughed at the irony. After all the years that Nicholas and Nichole had spent trying to one up the other one, Nichole had finally managed to outdo her twin.